THE UNFORGIVING MINUTES

MARY MONICA PULVER

DIAMOND BOOKS, NEW YORK

THE UNFORGIVING MINUTES

A Diamond Book / published by arrangement with
the author

PRINTING HISTORY
St. Martin's Press edition published 1988
Diamond edition / April 1992

ISBN: 1-55773-686-3

Diamond Books are published by The Berkley Publishing Group,
200 Madison Avenue, New York, New York 10016.
The name "DIAMOND" and its logo are trademarks
belonging to Charter Communications, Inc.

PRINTED IN THE UNITED STATES OF AMERICA

10 9 8 7 6 5 4 3 2 1

Diamond Books by Mary Monica Pulver

KNIGHT FALL
THE UNFORGIVING MINUTES

To Gary, who told me what,
and Scott, who showed me how

If you can fill the unforgiving minute
With sixty seconds' worth of distance run,
Yours is the earth and everything that's in it,
And, which is more, you'll be a man, my son!

—*Rudyard Kipling*

THE
UNFORGIVING
MINUTES

Chapter
1 †

The door to the squad room slammed open and Tonk entered, bringing with him a knight in armor. Not shining armor, but functional-looking armor, with dings and traces of rust about it, and a sweaty look to the man himself, as if he'd been arrested coming off the field of battle. The knight's hands were fastened behind his back.

Captain Frank Ryder had been filling his mug with coffee at the urn. He turned, blinked, and demanded, somewhere between anger and amazement, "Where did you find him?"

"Nice, huh?" said Tonk, grinning, then saw Ryder was not amused and said, "He's dusted, I think. He was on the steps in front of Tintagel, that restaurant looks like a castle? Had his tin hat on and was trying to get people to fight with him. Right, Sir Geoffrey? Or have you decided to tell me your real name?"

"On my honor as a true knight I am Geoffrey of Brixham," said the knight. Dwarfed by Tonk, he was nevertheless a respectable six feet tall, about twenty-five, with a well-trimmed beard and dark-auburn hair.

"Booking's down the hall, Tonk," said Ryder. His tone was tired; Tonk was a new detective and new to the Organized Crime Unit, but he had already worn out his welcome.

Tonk went behind his prisoner to unhandcuff him. "They're doing a great big domestic, must be twenty people in there, all drunk. So I said I'd get a statement while I waited."

The knight, neither frightened nor embarrassed, rubbed his freed wrists and looked around the small basement room. Like the rest of the Safety Building, it was new and mercilessly lit, but the furniture consisted of four shabby wooden desks and eight chipped, green metal filing cabinets. "Is this your dungeon?" he asked.

Tonk laughed. He was both tall and broad, a genus *Footballus*

1

collegium, fair to the point of pinkness, with a heavy sheaf of straight blond hair cut at an angle across his wide, low forehead. He leaned close to the knight's face to say slowly and clearly, "No, this is not a dungeon, this is a police station. You are under arrest. Do you understand?"

"Yes, m'lord," replied the knight, but not in that way that indicates understanding. He frowned, swallowed thickly, and touched a place just above his right ear.

"You gonna get sick again?" asked Tonk, his ominous tone indicating the answer wanted.

"No, m'lord," said the knight obediently.

"Good." Tonk explained to Ryder, "I almost had him in my car when he puked his guts out." Tonk turned back to his prisoner, poked him with a massive forefinger and said, "Some of your stuff is in my trunk. I'm gonna go get it." He glanced at Ryder and said, "Watch him for me?" and went out without waiting for a reply, yanking at the door so it slammed shut behind him.

"So," said Ryder to the knight, "what's this all about?"

The knight made a small bow in Ryder's direction. "My lord, I was taking part in a tourney when I somehow became lost." He again touched the place over his ear. "And I have a terrible headache. Do you have any aspirin?"

Ryder, ready to be amused, replied, "Sorry, I'm fresh out." He thought, This man doesn't live entirely in the Middle Ages if he knows about aspirin. Nevertheless, he approached with caution. Ryder was short for a cop, and no longer young, stocky, with a rumpled face under a dense crop of white hair.

"Perhaps a chirurgeon at the tourney . . ." mused the knight. He asked, "Do you know where the Dragon's Day Tournament is taking place?"

Ryder smiled despite himself, and said, "Tonk's wrong, isn't he? You haven't been using angel dust; your problem is you've only got one oar in the water."

Sir Geoffrey twisted his head in puzzlement. "I have no boat."

"That's just as well," said Ryder. "Follow me." He walked to the desk nearest the door; the knight obediently followed, clanking as he moved. He was wearing leg and arm armor, a breastplate with jointed shoulder protection, and a brief skirt of densely woven mail. Ryder caught glimpses of a red quilted coat under the metal. "Sit down," he said, indicating an old wooden chair beside Tonk's desk.

"Thank you, m'lord." The armor was so nicely made that the

knight could not only sit in it, but no gaps showed at the armadillo joints of his knees when he did. The armor was plain and obviously heavy; the chair creaked but held.

For once, Ryder wished Brichter were present. Brichter had once been a paramedic. Right now Ryder would like an intelligent, if condescending, medical opinion. But Brichter was up at the jail, questioning a dope pusher he had taken out of Chauncey's last night—or so Ryder had been reliably informed.

The Organized Crime Unit Ryder headed was a semi-autonomous section of the Charter Police Department. Plagued by a serious infestation of organized crime and political corruption, each fed by the other, the citizens of Charter had at last roused themselves to demand action. The city government, impoverished by its problems and afraid of losing power in a real reform, authorized the Organized Crime Unit but failed to fund it sufficiently. It ended up in a converted stockroom in the basement of the Safety Building and managed to garner enough condemned furniture that its three investigators and one supervisor could all sit down at the same time. But even with federal aid, OCU was understaffed, overworked, and inadequately equipped to accomplish its mission. So it didn't help when one of the investigators took a giddy delight in arresting people who didn't even know there was such a thing as organized crime.

Around Sir Geoffrey's neck was a chain of heavy gold links and about his waist was a white web belt whose long end was knotted once around the buckle so it hung straight down. Despite these decorative touches, the functional look of the outfit struck Ryder once again. This wasn't stage armor; this was a serious attempt at the real thing.

"You always dress like that?"

"No, m'lord," replied Sir Geoffrey, pale and lightly perspiring. Again he touched the side of his head. "Only for tourneys, like Dragon's Day today." His voice was even and pleasant, though his expression was a little vacant. "I was doing all right until Sir Humphrey the Vigilant killed me." He frowned, not at Ryder.

Ryder, also frowning, said, "He *killed* you?"

A wry smile appeared. "I'm not as tough as I look."

"So you think you're dead."

The smile almost became a laugh. "Nay, that was in chivalrous combat! I died twice at the last Pennsic War."

"Pennsic War?" Ryder was wishing they hadn't begun this conversation.

"You've never heard of it? You must be a mundane." Sir Geoffrey's grin broadened, and his bright brown eyes turned sharp as a hawk's. "It's a friendly little war; loser keeps Pittsburgh."

Ryder laughed uncertainly, and the squad-room door slammed open again; Tonk was back.

The big detective came around the open door and kicked it shut. He was carrying a curved shield flat on one arm, balancing a very battered helm on it. In his other hand was a big wooden sword whose tubular blade was wrapped in silver duct tape. The tape was notched and split. I bet that's how the armor got beat up, thought Ryder.

Tonk waved the sword. Ryder stepped back and the knight stood. "Boy, is this thing balanced!" crowed Tonk. He took a big sideways swipe—the ceiling was far too low for an overhead swing—which came close enough to Ryder's face to make him flinch.

"Whoa!" said Ryder.

"Wouldn't this be great for riots and—" began Tonk, starting a second swing. But the knight was in front of him, the blade smacking hard into his palm. Ryder had not seen him move.

"I beg your pardon, m'lord," said Sir Geoffrey courteously, "but you could hurt someone with that."

"Put the damn thing down, Tonk!" ordered Ryder.

"Sure," said Tonk, "but I wasn't gonna hurt anyone with it." He went to his desk, dropped the sword, shield, and helm on it and said, "C'mere, you," to Sir Geoffrey, indicating with a gesture that he was to sit down.

Ryder said, "I thought it was made clear that prisoners are to be questioned in the field and brought in only for booking; any subsequent questioning can be done upstairs at the jail."

"Well, yeah, but like I told you—"

"I don't recall making any exceptions," interrupted his boss. Tonk looked about to embark on one of his earnest, rambling explanations, and Ryder raised a forestalling hand. "All right, all right, try to get some kind of statement, if you can, or at least his real name and address; then take him out to County. Where you were headed in the first place. Where I told you to go, to talk to the administrator about the theft of drugs from their pharmacy."

Tonk yanked open a drawer, pulled a yellow form from it and began inserting it in his typewriter. "You're saying I should just skip booking."

"Booking won't mean a thing to this man until he's had a few gallons of Thorazine, and maybe not even then."

Ryder went to finish filling his mug. Of his three men, he considered only one to be a solid, all-around talent, the one with the odd front name, Crispin McHugh. He was currently talking with County Attorney Jimmy Bartholomew about an upcoming trial. Unlike Tonk or Brichter, McHugh was also a personal friend; he and Ryder went back a long time together. Ryder glanced at Tonk, who was laughing at some improbable reply from his prisoner. He wished Brichter and Tonk would rub off on each other a little. Then Tonk might arrest someone who mattered for a change and Brichter might turn into a human being. He sighed and went into his little office.

The office showed signs of having been a walk-in safe, which explained its size—Ryder could just about touch all four walls from a single spot in the center of it. He went behind his miniature desk and sat down to begin shuffling papers. He was currently filling out a federal report seven pages long, not counting attachments. All federal reports were bad, he considered, but this one was a bitch. It was three days overdue, and unless he cheated, it wouldn't get into the mail until Monday: The Post Office closed on Saturdays at noon and it was eleven now. Ryder looked at the work beyond the report waiting to be done and surrendered to the exigencies; he lied on the last three attachments. He made sure the lies agreed with the honest figures he'd already compiled, and gathered up the finished report. He'd make copies now, come back and get the envelope ready to mail, and hope the mail lady remembered this backwater location on her pickup list. Then he wanted at least to sort and stack the maze of papers on his desk before going home.

He went through the squad room—Tonk was still amusing himself with his prisoner—climbed the stairs to the second floor, and got in line at the photocopier. Ten minutes later he came through the door back into the basement corridor, and almost knocked over Sergeant Brichter.

"Sorry, Obie," said Ryder.

"Any landing you can walk away from," said Brichter and continued up the passageway.

"Wait a minute; where have you been?" asked Ryder. Because that door led in from the parking ramp, not from the upstairs jail.

"Looking for that new pimp I hear is in town," said Brichter without stopping.

"Hold it, dammit," said Ryder, and Brichter stopped without

turning around. He was about five ten or eleven, narrow, with thinning no-color hair and a shabby brown suit. At the angle he was standing to Ryder, a slight stoop was apparent.

Ryder wanted to go on with a sharp question, but bit his tongue. Brichter was a troublesome man, and Ryder liked a peaceable squad room. His inclination was to find a way to pass this one along, as numerous other heads of units had. But Brichter, unlike Tonk, was as bright as he was ill-tempered, and with the warnings not to pair him with anyone—Brichter was death on partners—came his reputation for building airtight cases. Ryder needed that kind of expertise, and so was holding off on acting on his inclinations until he was sure he had no other recourse. He unclenched his teeth and asked in a tone kept carefully neutral, "Did you finish your arrest report on Woodruff?"

"I didn't arrest him."

"McHugh saw you take him out of Chauncey's last night."

"And if, instead of testifying to a conclusion, he'd hoisted his leaden ass off the bar stool and followed me, he might have seen me take the man home."

"I thought you walked in on Woodruff as he was tooting up in the john."

"That's right."

Ryder was too surprised at this cool retort to respond at once, so Brichter began walking up the passageway again.

"Look," said Ryder, hurrying to catch up, "I know I'm only your boss, so consider it mere nosiness when I ask you why you didn't bust Woodruff. He's connected, isn't he?"

"Yes, he is, but he claims he can tell me a lot about the drug business in Charter in return for special handling, including not having to go to jail. He was so messed up last night I didn't think questioning him would produce anything useful, so I took him home."

"And you think he'll stay there until you get ready to question him."

Brichter turned pale gray eyes on Ryder. "He wouldn't let me take him to the hospital, and he knows our jail is no place to get away from drugs. I call to check on him every couple of hours and he's always there, maybe because I heard first thing this morning that Houseman wants particularly to speak with him, which message, when I passed it along to him, about scared the pee out of him. I'm not sure what's behind that, but so long as it makes him wish to stay at home, I'm content. He should be starting withdrawal in a few hours, and when he's finished with that, we'll talk some more."

"What's he been using?"

"Coke, mostly. A little heroin once in a while, too." They were nearly at the door.

"Well, all right," Ryder said grudgingly, "Look, Obie, I don't see why I had to pry this information out of you. You're forthcoming enough when it suits you, so I think you understand that I—"

But Brichter had opened the door to the squad room and gone in. Ryder again bit his tongue and followed. He would not continue the lecture in front of witnesses.

Brichter, as usual, made a straight line for the coffee urn. If he had a fault—and he had several—it was drinking too much coffee. He lifted his orange mug from the metal tree. *Illegitimi non Carborundum* bristled around it in Gothic lettering. He nodded at the sentiment, filled the mug and turned, tasting. And over the top of it caught sight of the knight in armor beside Tonk's desk.

The knight, in turn, looked back. Then, "Lord Stefan!" he said, starting to his feet.

"Sit down, you ass; that isn't Lord Stefan!" said Tonk.

"Fat lot you know, Tonk," remarked Brichter, putting his mug on the table and starting for them. "Geoff, what are you doing here?"

"You *know* this turkey?" asked Tonk.

The knight replied, "My lord, I was in a tourney and—and I got lost. I am—" He touched the side of his head with his fingertips once again. "I have a terrible headache. Have you got any aspirin?" He repeated the gesture.

"In a while, maybe," said Brichter, still frowning, but for a different reason. He reached for Sir Geoffrey's arm. "Come over to my desk, okay?"

"What the hell!" said Tonk. "He's my prisoner; you leave him alone!"

"Shut up, snot-brain," said Brichter.

"Lord Stefan, that was discourteous," said the knight.

"Leave him alone, Obie," said Ryder.

"That goes for you, too," said Brichter over his shoulder, lifting Sir Geoffrey to his feet.

"God*dammit*—!" began Ryder.

"One minute," interrupted Brichter, beginning to walk off, Sir Geoffrey in tow. "Just give me one minute. And pray I'm wrong, because if I'm not, I'll kill Tonk and maybe you, too."

In the startled silence that followed, Brichter led the knight across the room. Sir Geoffrey's earlier athletic grace had somehow become a shamble. He half-sat, when pushed, on the edge of Brichter's desk. Brichter put the heel of his hand on the man's forehead, tilting it back toward the glowing ceiling. His voice became gentle, a tone Ryder had never heard from him before. "Did someone hit you on the head today, Geoff?" he asked, bending close. For a shocking instant it looked as if Brichter were going to kiss him, but he was only comparing one eye to the other. Ryder made a noise of sudden comprehension.

"I believe it was Sir Humphrey the Vigilant," said the knight.

Brichter released the man's head to pick up the receiver of his phone. He punched a fast seven numbers and said, "This is Sergeant Brichter, Charter Police. We need a rescue squad in the basement of the Safety Building, Room B-32, stat. We have an adult male, age twenty-five, with concussion and possible intracranial bleeding." He repeated the location and hung up.

When he turned to look at the two, his face was white with fury. "Who brought him in here?" he asked.

"I did," said Tonk. "So what? Is he a friend of yours?"

"That's not the point. How long has he been here?"

Tonk shrugged and looked away. "Not long."

"About an hour," said Ryder.

"An *hour*? You let a man with a head injury sit here for an *hour*?"

"What do you mean, head injury?" demanded Tonk. "You think maybe I hit him when I arrested him? I never—"

"My lords," said Sir Geoffrey to no one in particular, touching the side of his head, "I have a terrible headache. Does anyone have any aspirin?" He repeated the gesture.

"Have either of you given him any?"

"No," said Ryder, half-ashamed, "I got busy and forgot."

"And I must've told him a hundred times I never use the stuff," said Tonk.

"Well, thank God! It's stupid to give aspirin to people who may be bleeding inside their skulls. Of course, stupidity is what we've come to expect of you, Tonk; but you, Captain, you've been around awhile! Don't you know a head injury when you see one?"

Ryder's color deepened. "You think I've been sitting out here laughing along with Tonk? I told him to get a statement if he could, then take your friend out to County for an evaluation."

"And that's what I was trying to do," complained Tonk. "Only he'd say things like he was born in 1342 and today was Dragon's Day. How does that add up to a head injury?"

"Look at him!" Brichter was shouting now. "How long a list do you need? He stinks of vomit, he's cold and pale, he's got a severe headache, he walks like a drunk, he can't remember you already told him you're out of aspirin, he's got an automatic gesture and, that most classic of symptoms, the pupils of his eyes are two different sizes!"

"He walked fine when I brought him in!" said Tonk, raising his own voice. "And go ahead, look at him! The way he's dressed, anyone would think he was crazy! You don't get close enough to look at the pupils of a crazy man's eyes!"

"Why is he dressed like that, Obie?" asked Ryder, more to stop the argument than because he wanted to know.

"He's a member of the Society for Creative Anachronism."

"Who the hell are they?" asked Tonk.

"It's an organization that researches the Middle Ages. Like Civil War buffs, only further back. It has about twelve thousand members nationwide. The local group is holding a tourney in Riverside Park this weekend." There came, faintly, the sound of a siren, and Brichter broke off to harken to it.

"Then he's not crazy?" asked Ryder.

"No," said Brichter. "He took a real blow in a real fight with a man called Sir Humphrey the Vigilant, who has a notoriously strong arm."

"Has he got a real name?" asked Tonk.

"Geoffrey Collins." Was the siren growing louder?

"That's right!" said the knight, surprised to have forgotten. "I'm Geoff Collins."

"He asked me to call Lady Anne of the Snows on my 'farspeaker,' " said Tonk. "What's that mean?"

"Lady Anne is the Society name of Anne Collins, his wife. I should think 'farspeaker' an obvious enough term even for you."

" 'To love one only,' " said Sir Geoffrey, his hand drifting to a blue cloth embroidered with snowflakes tied around his arm, " 'cleave to her, and worship her by years of noble deeds; for indeed I know of no more subtle master under heaven than is the maiden passion for a maid, to teach high thoughts and amiable words, and courtliness, the desire of fame, and love of truth, and all that makes a man.' " He released the cloth to touch the side of his head with his fingertips. "I have a terrible headache. Does anyone have any aspirin?"

"Jesus!" whispered Brichter.

"I don't understand why he couldn't explain all this to us," said Ryder.

"Because another symptom of concussion can be a form of amnesia. The victim will remember things about his surroundings at the time of the accident, but little else. So Geoff knows that he is Sir Geoffrey of Brixham, tournament fighter, but—" He turned and asked, "Do you live near here, Geoff?"

The siren became very loud, then cut off. Sir Geoffrey looked around the room for clues, then asked humbly, "Could you tell me the name of this town?"

"Charter, Geoff. Charter, Illinois, a pleasant little city of 150,000 unindicted co-conspirators. Sometimes called the cocaine capital of the state. The false motto of its *stinking* police department is 'To Protect and to Serve.'"

The phone on Brichter's desk began to ring, and, listening for the hustle of paramedics, he picked it up. "Organized Crime Unit, Detective Sergeant Brichter."

For a moment he thought no one was there, then a voice harshened by nerves said, "One of these days, Sergeant Brichter, you ought to take a look at that old man out at Tretower Ranch. You might find that broker you're so hot after."

"Yeah?" he said, listening half to whoever it was and half to the sound of running footsteps coming up the hall. "Who is this?"

"You want proof I know what I'm talking about?"

"That would be nice." His tone was ironic and Ryder wondered whom he was insulting now.

"You think Woodruff's your new informant, don't you? Well, you're wrong!"

That got Brichter's attention. "Hey!" he said. "Who did—" But whoever it was hung up.

The door opened and three firemen/paramedics came in with a wire stretcher. Brichter dropped the receiver into its cradle and involved himself in a discussion of symptoms, and when they took Sir Geoffrey away, he went with them.

Chapter

2 ✝

Sunday morning, Ryder entered the squad room and stopped to shake raindrops from his hat. The lights were on, and he saw a figure in brown cords and sweater crouched by the coffee urn. When Ryder closed the door firmly, the figure stood and revealed itself to be Brichter, rumpled and badly in need of a shave.

"You look like hell," said Ryder.

"No. I look like I haven't been to bed since yesterday morning." Ryder walked into the room and stood dripping. "How is he?"

"Geoff? He's fine. They drilled a hole in his skull to take out some clots. Instant cure for the amnesia and the aphasia he'd developed. They're watching him closely, but if all goes as expected, they'll release him this afternoon."

"So soon?"

"The only people who go home well from the hospital nowadays are the doctors."

Ryder chuckled as he shucked off his raincoat. "I'm glad he's all right. But what are you doing here on a Sunday when you could be home catching up on your sleep?"

"Woodruff was shot last night."

"Your new informant? The hell you say! What happened?"

"He opened his door to someone who shot him twice in the face. That's where I've been till now; I got home from the hospital just in time to get the call." The coffee urn began to grumble, and Brichter, satisfied it would produce the needed beverage shortly, moved away from it.

Ryder hung his coat on a rack near the door and said, "Obie, I want to talk to you."

Brichter gave a wary glance over his shoulder; he'd heard that tone of voice before. "What about?"

"It hurts me that we missed seeing your friend was in trouble

11

yesterday. I tore strips of hide off Tonk about it, but if you'd care to give me my reaming out, here's your chance."

Brichter was silent awhile, then said, "Styles differ. Remember the Miller case? He was stabbed with a very thin, sharp blade and walked two blocks before he collapsed, never realizing he was hurt."

"Have I missed something you've already said?"

"Not so far this morning."

Ryder rubbed his upper lip noisily. "Seriously now, is there anything I can do?"

Again the silence, though its texture this time seemed different. Brichter said quietly, "Don't transfer me."

"Why should I want to transfer you?"

Brichter shrugged. "If I knew the answer to that, maybe I wouldn't be transferred so often."

"You honestly don't know?"

"I have a number of theories. Maybe I'm too smart for this job. Maybe I get depressed too easily, or maybe my mother didn't love me enough. Take your choice. Or make up your own. My so-called personality problem is everyone's hobby."

"You don't think you have a problem?"

"Sure I do. My problem is I'd like to work with some honest cops on a decent force, for a change."

"Hey, now, I know we're going through a bad patch right now, but we're by and large—"

"A puddle of vomit," interrupted Brichter. He turned to the file cabinet he was standing beside and pulled open a drawer. "We're up to our armpits in corruption; there isn't a division in the department untainted. We get a rumor of a cleanup, and there's a dozen cops with ads in the paper selling condos or lakeshore land in Wisconsin. There are attractive women and expensive tailors looking for new men to support them—and some cops trying to pretend they've always been this poor. If the graft is cut out, half of us will have to declare bankruptcy."

"Obie—"

"Oh, not that it will happen; the Chicago outfit operates a major branch in this town, and their grip is strong. They're into business as well as government. This town is so corrupt, when our mayor has lunch with our local boss of organized crime, it gets reported on the society page. This rumored crackdown is a response to some noise from a few citizens—one of whom is the new owner of our *Daily Clarion*—who are sick of the smell. When they get tired, or compromised, they'll quiet down and it will be business as usual. To make reform in a police department stick, it has to come from the chief. And our chief of police has his hand so deep in the till no one's seen his elbow since he bent it to take his oath of office."

"Obie—"

"You think I'm exaggerating? How about this: Whoever killed Woodruff stuck a dime in his mouth, to pay the snitch's passage to hell."

"How does that prove anything?"

"It was night before last that Woodruff offered to turn informant, and you can bet he told no one about it. I told only the head of patrol, asking him to have an eye kept on Woodruff's place. A few hours later Houseman was looking for Woodruff, and less than twenty-four hours after that he was dead. You may believe in crystal balls, Captain; I believe the word went from this building straight to Houseman."

"Any idea who?" asked Ryder.

Brichter made an upward spiraling gesture meant to include all the floors above their heads. "How many suspects do you want? What do you know about Nick Tellios?"

Ryder blinked at this sudden change in subject. "He's the little old fart who took a splinter out of my grandson's finger at the police-fireman's softball game last summer without making him cry. Why?"

Brichter found a folder and pulled it out. "Remember that phone call I got, just before the paramedics came to take Geoff to the hospital?"

"Yeah?"

"It was from a woman who said that if we want to know who the drug broker in town is, we should look at that little old fart."

"Bullshit! Who was this woman?"

"I don't know, but she offered as proof the fact that I only thought Woodruff was going to be my new snitch. And she was right about that." Brichter opened the folder. "I see we've got a file on him."

"That's because he was in the Chicago outfit, years back."

Brichter started for his desk. "He come down to start up the branch office?"

"No, his sister-in-law and her husband were killed by a burglar they interrupted—don't you remember that case? Hell, no, you were away, in the Navy or at the university about then. I wasn't assigned to it, but like everyone else I wanted a piece of solving it, because the Price couple were a nice pair, well off, decent. Bred show ponies. But we never did find out who did it. Tellios came down to the ranch to arrange for their kid Katherine, who was about six, I guess, to be taken care of. Their will had named him her guardian, which was stupid, him being what he was; but he was fond of the kid, and them living a peaceful life in the country never figured they'd die before him. And maybe it didn't work out so bad after all. She turned out to have some mental problems, and he gave up his connections in Chicago to stay here and take care of her permanently."

"You're sure he retired?"

"There hasn't been a peep from his direction since he came down. I happen to know he was having a big fight with his boss in Chicago, I think he just said the hell with it, sold his Laundromats and retired. He wasn't like most wise guys; he'd put money aside so he could retire in comfort. Katherine being what she was, he had her as an excuse not to go back to Chicago. They said she should have been put away, but she started doing better, though she never got really well. I've seen her in town a time or two; it's not like he has to keep her locked in the attic. She must be about twenty now. Tellios has always taken good care of her; he even hired a tutor for her when she couldn't go to school."

"The tutor's still out there; he's a friend of mine." Brichter misinterpreted the look on Ryder's face. "Oh, I've got a number of friends. Just none of them cops." He looked into the folder. "I see no one's turned over Tellios' rock lately."

"What rock? He's not hiding out there; he comes to concerts, hospital fund-raisers, baseball games. He bought the hot dogs for St. Gabriel's Handicap Fair, and half of the city's new fire truck was paid for out of his pocket. He's Charter's official nice old man."

"Uh-huh."

"Look, we can't go rousting a man just because he was a crook fourteen years ago! If for no other reason, we haven't got the manpower!"

"So you assume he's not a crook because you haven't got the manpower to check." Brichter sat down at his desk and began reading the bottom page of the file.

"Is that mouth reflex or something you study up on at night?"

"I've got a book on the theory of insults. Speaking of that, did I tell you Joe Januschka tried to buy me a drink a couple of weeks ago?" Januschka was Charter's crime boss, the one who lunched with the mayor.

"I trust you were insulted enough to send it back."

"No, I took it to his table. And I stuck its little straw in his mouth and told him that next time he wanted to suck up, to use that."

Ryder laughed, then said, "It's too bad in a way; if you had McHugh's talent for acting, there might have been a chance for you to go undercover and get a look at his organization."

"Yeah," Brichter said flatly, turning down a page in the file folder.

Ryder asked, "Why don't you and Cris get along? He's clean; the last man who tried to bribe him got thrown down a flight of stairs."

"Call it a difference in styles," said Brichter, who had never thrown anyone down a flight of stairs.

Ryder, baffled but unwilling to terminate this conversation just yet, said, "Maybe I should also tell you that on my list of things to do this morning, I've added writing a memo reminding everyone that strange behavior may indicate a medical emergency. No names given, but I'll admit we had a close call recently."

Brichter turned in his chair, his grim expression thawed by surprise. "I appreciate that, Captain."

Ryder said, "You see? I do listen when I'm spoken to sharply."

A smile tweaked the thin mouth. "I'll remember that." He leaned sideways but couldn't see the coffee urn from where he was. "Is the coffee ready yet?"

Ryder looked over; the red light gleamed. "Yeah," he said, and they went to take their mugs off the tree. Ryder's had a drawing of a cat knitting a mouse, and was the first gift his grandson had given him that he hadn't had to pretend he liked. "What's that mean?" he asked, filling his mug and nodding at Brichter's orange one.

" 'Don't let the bastards wear you down,' or so I'm told."

Ryder made a sound that was halfway to a chuckle, and sipped his brew. "Was it really a close call with your friend Sir Geoffrey?"

Brichter shrugged. "He could have gone another few minutes before lapsing into a coma. Maybe Tonk would have noticed that."

"He will from now on."

"I wish to hell we weren't always playing catch-up. Tonk shouldn't need a course in basic first aid. I should have paid more attention to Woodruff's panic when I told him Houseman was looking for him. Things happen and we react. We need to be the ones doing, making them react. And reaction time in this game is so short, a fast decision can make or break a case. If not someone's life."

"Another book on your shelf?"

Brichter smiled. "No, it's a personal theory. It's not our big decisions—career choice, mate, which college—that make us who we are, it's our little ones, the ones made minute-to-minute. Cumulatively, or even individually, they're the unforgiving ones."

"So what one-minute decision have you come to about Tellios?"

Brichter said, "With your permission, I'd like to look into the tip."

Ryder thought. "You know, I had a friend on the Chicago cops. He told me about that chain of laundromats Tellios owned. He said you could get anything you wanted at a Tellios Laundromat. Tellios was careful and clever, so nothing was ever proved, but my friend said you could get dope, a gun, a passport, a corpse that could pass for accidental, anything, if he trusted you and you could meet his price. If he didn't have it on hand, he'd arrange for someone else to get it for you."

"Which comes curiously close to what my lady tipster said he's doing now as drug broker: arranging for buyer and seller to meet in safety for a share of the money that changes hands."

"Yes, all right. But look carefully, hear? He's got a lot of important friends in this town."

"Yes, sir."

Ryder went into his office, but didn't immediately settle down to work. This was the first real conversation he'd had with Brichter, something more than giving orders or having an exchange of information. His estimate of Brichter's intelligence had been confirmed, but Ryder was of the school that thought it was possible to be too damn bright. The man had no manners, no tact, no social skills worth mentioning, but he did have an IQ that would knock the socks off anyone. So he played that one note for all it was worth, and it aggravated the hell out of everyone else.

Maybe there was a way to get him to lighten up, stop counting every unforgiving minute. He needed to do something foolish or impulsive. Fall in love. Ryder smiled at the notion. He assumed Brichter had at some time done the moral equivalent of running hand-in-hand through a field of daisies, but Ryder meant the wrong kind of love, with the wrong woman, for the wrong reasons; the crazy kind, where the poor dope sits under a window at night bawling love songs, playing a lute—badly—between choruses, and not caring a lick that the whole world was laughing at him.

People enjoy finding out that other people are the same kind of asses they are; it makes them like one another. And being liked would work magic on that unforgiving sap out there in the squad room.

Brichter slouched in the front seat of his elderly purple car. He was very tired now—and angry, the latter a condition he'd taken care to hide from Ryder. Because, by right, he should have become aware of the Tretower situation a long time ago. He glanced at his watch and shifted position restlessly. Three kids went by, chattering and laughing in the frail spring sunlight, winter coats open, hats stuffed in pockets. One had a kite. Brichter glanced up into his rearview mirror to see a dark green antique MG pull up behind him.

A stocky man with graying fair hair got out. He was wearing a tweed sports coat with leather patches on the elbows and a yellow wool neckscarf. Brichter rolled down his window as the man approached. When he spoke, his accent gave away his British origins.

"I know parking's difficult round the Civic Center, but are you sure it's all right to leave my car here? Sorry I'm late, by the way; I had a bit of trouble breaking loose."

"I bet. Get in."

Gordon Ramsey studied the stiff, tired face of his friend. "Look, if you've had a hard night or something, we could skip the concert, go another time."

"Do I have to goddamn arrest you? Get in!"

Ramsey hesitated, then obeyed. Brichter started the engine and made a U-turn. Ramsey asked, "Where are we going?"

"My place."

"The performance begins at two, Peter. It's nearly that now."

"Shut up, okay?"

Ramsey sighed and looked out the window.

Brichter drove in silence the few blocks to a run-down three-story wood frame building and parked in a small lot made from the back half of the backyard. They climbed sagging wooden steps to the two-room apartment Brichter called home. "A little paint might cheer this place up, hmmm?" noted Ramsey. Brichter did not reply. They walked into the middle of the little bed–sitting room.

"Are you mad at *me*?" asked Ramsey.

"Yes, dammit, I'm mad at you!"

"What did I do?"

Brichter turned on him. "It's something you didn't do; something you haven't done for nine years!"

Ramsey forced a smile. "I've only lived here for eight years, Peter."

"And for how long before that did you know Nick Tellios?"

A sudden wariness on Ramsey's face betrayed him, and he saw Brichter's face change, too, in response to that betrayal. "What have you found out?" he asked.

"I hear that Tellios is the man who brokers the really big drug deals around here, the ones that have made Charter the place to go when you buy your cocaine in kilos rather than ounces."

Ramsey was surprised—and, curiously, relieved. "Rot!"

"And, you, Dr. Ramsey, are this close"—Brichter held up thumb and forefinger a scant quarter inch apart—"to being arrested!"

"*Me?* For what?"

"You cretin, you work for Tellios! You've lived in his house for eight years! Don't tell me you know nothing about what goes on out there! At the least, you're a material witness! For all I know, you, not Tellios, are the brains behind the Tretower operation!" Brichter turned away from the horrified look on Ramsey's face. "My God, how often have you listened to me complain that all I can arrest is the small-time pusher—and then gone home to help your boss arrange a steady diet of coke for users in the whole upper Midwest! And you have the temerity to ask why I want to arrest you!"

Ramsey groped for the daybed and sat down. "That's what you think, is it?" He wiped his mouth and chin with a pudgy hand.

"Can you convince me otherwise?"

"I have to, don't I? But how?"

"Not by lying. Be very careful what you tell me, Gordie. You don't know how much I already know, and if I catch you in a lie, you're on your way to jail. You can decide not to tell me anything; that's your right, and it may be the wisest thing for you to do right now. You can say you want to consult a lawyer before answering my questions, or that you want a lawyer to hold your hand while we talk, and that's okay. I'll even arrange to rent you a lawyer if you can't afford one. Understand?"

Despite this gentled-down restatement of the Miranda warning, Ramsey looked thoroughly alarmed. "I thought we were friends!"

"So did I, Gordie; so did I. Now, start at the beginning: Why did you come to work for Tellios in the first place?"

Ramsey studied the faded leaf pattern on the old rug under his feet. "I needed to get away from the campus for a little while, to think and write." This was the explanation he had offered a few years before, when he'd run across Brichter at a concert of medieval music, but now it sounded as threadbare as the rug looked. "He offered me a cottage separate from the big house he lives in, a salary, and a single pupil to keep my teaching skills sharp."

"Eight years is a long 'little while,' Gordie," said Brichter.

"Yes, I know. I probably couldn't go back to the university now if I wanted to." He looked up at Brichter. "And as long as Kori needs me, I don't want to."

"Kori?" Ramsey had pronounced it Koh-REE, and Brichter echoed the pronunciation.

"Katherine, if you prefer. Everyone out there calls her Kori."

"She's the niece, the lunatic, right?"

"She is not a lunatic, and she is precious as a daughter to me."

"Oh, yeah?" This was not said sarcastically, but in the tone of one making an interesting discovery. Brichter pulled a wooden armchair away from a desk-table and sat down in front of Ramsey. "Go on," he ordered.

"First, you must agree that this is utterly off the record."

"No way. Go on."

"No. I will do or say nothing that might harm her."

"The hell with her; I'm not after her! I'm interested in Tellios! Give, Gordie!"

"You'll harm her if you go crashing in out there, tossing her uncle into jail."

"Maybe spending a night in jail would be good for him. Maybe a prison sentence would be even better. If she's guilty, she goes with him. If she's innocent, she needs to be taken away from him. Talk, Gordie."

Ramsey sighed. "What do you want to know?"

"What does Tellios do out there?"

Ramsey glanced out the window. The sky was bright blue. "He gardens; he has a fine collection of roses and a large vegetable garden. He cooks. He has me up to the house for dinner now and then and some intellectual conversation, hmmm? He entertains guests." Ramsey looked out the window again. Brichter, remembering a trick he'd seen Ryder use, said nothing, and Ramsey sighed. "He has a surprising number of guests from out of town."

"Tell me about them."

"They're young, mostly, and some are foreign. Central American slinks and home-grown toughs in expensive suits. They fly in—that's why Tellios worked so hard to improve our airport, hmmm? So his friends, landing after long flights, would find a long runway and modern control tower to assist them."

"They travel a long way just to pay their respects?"

"I've seen nothing of money, or drugs. I've overheard only fragments of conversations, as they go to and from their cars. The foreign ones speak Spanish or, once, French. Tellios has made it clear I am to keep my distance."

"What else?"

"That's all."

"You've got to know more about it than that! Eight years, Gordie!"

Ramsey studied the way his pudgy hands were clasped. "You don't know how incurious you can come to be around someone like him." Again Brichter waited, and Ramsey said, "Do you know, I've been trying to think of a way to ask for your help without having the conversation we're having. Because he's been— difficult lately. Which is an understatement on the order of the antelope saying the lion is feeling peckish. We're all walking on eggs out there."

"Why? What's happened?"

"I don't know; and I daren't ask, of course. I've heard you speaking of drug arrests you've made. You complain your section is hamstrung, but it's doing something right, because there have been fewer visitors, and I believe business is falling off."

"I'd love to believe that! So okay, if you're so alarmed, then don't go back. I can protect you."

"There's more to it than that. And, anyhow, I can't abandon Kori. Peter, I've done everything in my power to keep her clean in that cesspool; if I stay away, God knows what may happen to her!"

"What could happen? Are you saying he abuses her?"

Ramsey made a gesture of frustration. "What do you know about her?"

Brichter got out his fat notebook and found the right page. "Her real name is Katherine McLeod Price. Her parents were shot by a burglar, possibly in her presence, fourteen years ago, when she was six. Nick Tellios is her uncle by marriage and her legal guardian. She was diagnosed by a psychiatrist who examined her at the ranch as schizophrenic and paranoid schizophrenic. There was a considerable estate left to her by her parents, but she has never been considered capable of managing it. There are seven purebred Arabian horses at Tretower, all registered in her name, but others handle the business end of the ranch. She'll be twenty-one in September."

"Very impressive. And only two errors. She is not insane. And she is the one running the ranch."

"How do you know this?"

"Because she uses my personal computer to keep track of her breeding and sales business, which last year made a profit of four thousand dollars over all expenses. Mr. Tellios tells people that she's running things, but says it with just the right kind of smirk and no one believes him."

"And you're equally sure she's not insane?"

"Tellios had a psychiatrist, who, when his chain was pulled, produced the necessary jargon."

"How do you know this?"

"It's a logical deduction. The psychiatric diagnosis is false, therefore he was either paid to make it or was forced to, hmmm? The latter fits a pattern; he would not be the only one Tellios controls."

"Blackmail?"

"Yes."

"What's he got on you?"

Ramsey twitched at this accurate leap to a conclusion. "That I will not tell you, as it involves a number of innocent people who could be irreparably harmed by my disclosure. And I have no idea what he holds over the others."

"Who are they?"

"At the ranch there's Guy Riscatto, who is officially the trainer of her horses, and the one who shows them; Paul Shiffler, foreman, chauffeur and general dogsbody to Tellios; and Mel Downey, the barnyard equivalent of a charlady. Pirates to a man, but terrified of Tellios and by his order obedient to Kori. And there are some others in town. Someone in the county prosecutor's office, I believe, and a member, or members, of our city council. I couldn't name them."

"Who's the psychiatrist?"

"I don't know his name, either."

"You must have some idea who these people are; don't they visit the ranch?"

"He has visitors, but to separate those who come because he summons them from those who come on business or merely because he is their friend is a task beyond me."

"Could one of the others separate them for me? Could Kori?"

"Kori might, but I don't know if she would even consent to speak with you."

"Why not? Doesn't she know what he is?"

"I'm not sure. She displays great respect and a certain amount of affection for him, along with instant obedience. He claims that he loves her, and perhaps he does in a filthy sort of way. But it's a love based on his power over her. Like a cat that grows fond of a mouse it has caught. You know how the mouse learns to lie still and not provoke the cat. That's Kori."

"Are you saying she's in danger?"

Ramsey lifted his hands in a gesture of frustrated ignorance. "I don't know that he'd harm her—but I can't say that he wouldn't. There's a depth to that relationship I've never plumbed. But it's changing, too. Kori is, after all, quite grown. I think she's aware of this recent shift in his balance, and I think it has triggered a series of dreams."

"What have dreams—"

"Bear with me, hmmm? She's been having a persistent dream about a laughing man who lifts her over his head and calls her Vin-gallon, as if that were her name. It appears Vin-gallon is a Welsh endearment, which took me considerable research to establish, as I have very little notion of the vagaries of Welsh spelling. It is, in fact, spelled *f-y*-apostrophe-*n*-space-*g-a-l-o-n*, which translates 'my heart.' "

Brichter started to say something dismissive when his omnivore mind caught a snag. "Who out there is Welsh?"

"That, my dear divisional sleuth, is the point. No one. Well, except her. 'Ap Rhys' is a very common Welsh surname, frequently anglicized to 'Price.' And 'Tretower' is a Welsh place-name. I think it's her father she's dreaming of."

"Does she remember her parents?"

"She has no waking memory of them, not even of the night they were murdered—a murder which, by the way, was never solved."

"I know."

"But now she's also had a nightmare, this time of that dreadful night. She sees them dead, or dying, and says the man—I haven't told her I think she's dreaming of her parents—tells her to run away. But she is pursued around the house by a policeman, who at the end finds her in a kitchen cabinet full of large bowls and shakes her and shouts at her."

"What do you make of it?"

"Repressed memories will often surface in dreams. I don't know if she realizes it's a memory surfacing, but she has decided she's afraid of policemen."

"Does Tellios know of the nightmare?"

"He woke her from it two nights ago and insisted she describe it, saying telling the dream would take away the terror of it."

"Which is true, of course. Hmmm. If she does know anything, would she testify against him in a court of law?"

"I—don't know. Last year I would have said not. I've been feeding her massive doses of C. S. Lewis as an antidote to the filth she's exposed to from the unspeakable trio of hirelings, and if she errs, it's on the side of righteousness. She's been odd since the nightmare, perhaps because it has triggered other memories, perhaps because her uncle reacted peculiarly to it—she hinted as much. If she's come to understand her uncle's basic nature, then yes, she is ready to respond to an offer of help. But it must be real help, on the order of taking her away and hiding her from him. I'm afraid for her."

"I want to talk to her before I take any action of that sort."

Ramsey blinked up at him. "That's impossible. Only the rare person can claim to have had a real conversation with her. He normally arranges for her to be elsewhere when there are visitors at the ranch."

"Then the hell with it. I've got you, I'll keep you. I bet a long, careful interview would produce enough information from you to justify a warrant."

"And what if it didn't? I've told you all I know already, I swear. And you can't think to make me abandon her."

Brichter turned away and pulled an earlobe, his gesture of frustration. Then he turned back. "So all right, go back. Snoop around, find things out for me. Find out enough so I can get that warrant."

"How can I go from eight years of trying hard not to see anything to suddenly developing an interest? He'll suspect at once what's happened, and he won't waste time asking me to deny it, he'll just kill me. No, that won't do at all!"

Again the ear was pulled. "Then what the hell do you want me to do?"

"Find the others; the alderman, the psychiatrist. Perhaps they can tell you what you need to know."

"That could take weeks. You say things are coming apart out there; can you hold on for weeks? With no promise of success, even if I do manage to connect with one of them?"

Ramsey wanted badly to say yes, but couldn't.

Brichter said, "All right. So arrange for me to visit out there. Tell him it's just a quiet supper for the two of us."

Ramsey protested, "He'll never agree to that!"

Brichter said, "Tell him whatever you have to. Then tell Kori and/or whichever of the unspeakables you think most likely to co-operate to slip by the cottage. If I like what I'm told, I can get the warrant in an hour and pull a big, old-fashioned raid."

"You're insane, Peter. No one will speak to you at the ranch with him there—not that it will get that far. Tellios would never agree to a policeman coming to the ranch, and he'll be furious that I dared ask."

But Brichter had made a decision. "Try," he said, itching for a chance to walk on Tellios' turf. "Call me with his answer."

Ramsey drove back to the ranch and went up to the big house, hoping Tellios was not at home. But he was, and he invited Ramsey into the old front parlor, which he also used as an office. It was big and high-ceilinged, with an outsize bay at the front. Tellios had decorated it with sham Victorian furniture, all plum velvet and oak. Several real-looking ferns stood in the bay. He and Ramsey sat on oval-backed chairs under a tall, velvet-draped window. Late-afternoon sun poured over them.

"I crave a boon of you," said Ramsey, because Tellios liked ornate language.

Tellios, a little old man with a patrician head spoiled by a severe overbite, nodded. His eyes steadied on Ramsey's middle. "What can I do for you?"

"I want a friend to visit the ranch."

The eyes, a dusty brown, shifted to Ramsey's ear. "I thought we had agreed you were not to entertain guests out here. Who is this friend?"

"Peter Brichter."

"Brichter?" Tellios' eyebrows rose. "Do you mean the police-man? I thought his name was Obie."

"Obie is a nickname. His friends call him Peter."

"Professor Ramsey, you surprise me. You are . . . audacious."

"I'm sorry you think me audacious. Peter was a student of mine at university, and has been my friend a very long time, since before I met you. Since before he became a policeman."

"You rarely ask favors of me, which is too bad." Tellios was looking beyond Ramsey at a silken rope holding back a curtain. "But this—I am surprised at you."

Frightened, Ramsey lied boldly. "I have no intention of betraying you or your interests to Peter. It is simply that he asked why I never invite him over, and my usual excuses sounded feeble."

For the first time, Ramsey felt the impact of that dusty-brown stare. "Tell me why I should allow a policeman to visit my home."

"He would be visiting me," amended Ramsey, "in the comfortable house you have provided for my use. It would be a quiet dinner at home, with conversation for an hour or two after, nothing more."

"No?" Tellios appeared about to erupt into one of his rare fits of anger, then he relaxed and, surprisingly, laughed. "No, I have a better idea. Invite him to dinner up here, at the big house. I'll be the host. After all, I enjoy a quiet evening of conversation too. What day did you have in mind?"

Ramsey found his mouth hanging open. He pulled it shut to say, "I was thinking of tomorrow, Monday, if that's not too soon."

"Certainly, if he's free. He may come early to visit the cottage if you like, but I want you both here at six-thirty for a drink. Dinner will be at seven. Contact him, and let me know his reply."

Chapter

3 †

Monday morning Brichter spent an hour updating the file on Tellios, then, Ryder being still tied up in a meeting, went upstairs to Personal Crime. He dug into the cabinet holding unsolved homicides to pull the file on Price, Helen and David. He looked at photographs of the scene, which was in a formal living room. Two bodies were on the carpet. A woman with a swollen horror for a face had apparently suffocated after being shot in the throat. She was lying partly behind a long couch. A man was near an overturned occasional table, a phone and small flower vase on the floor near him. He'd been shot at least twice, in the side and in the face. The expensive, barely disturbed beauty of the room only added to the shock of the bodies. For a six-year-old to walk into this, to find Mommy and Daddy like this— Brichter said something rude under his breath and turned to the paperwork on the case. The rest of the house was even less disturbed, according to the report, than the living room. Apparently the Prices had walked in on the burglar before he'd begun his work.

There was no sign of forced entry, but country people rarely locked their doors.

The call for help had come from David Price, who had said only that he and his wife had been shot and could someone come at once, before being interrupted by his killer finishing the job.

Brichter found the occurrence report filed by the first cop on the scene, one Patrolman Michael Nelsen, who described in a flat-footed way what he found.

Nelsen never went anywhere, he "proceeded." He proceeded out to the ranch at 21:10 hours, proceeded into the house, proceeded into the living room, and proceeded hastily back out again to report the bloody horror on the carpet. A two-year-old midnight-blue Lincoln sedan had arrived, and a man had proceeded from the car to the house and verbalized, according to Nelsen, "My god, it's Helen!" The man had identified himself as Nicholas Tellios and further stated he was a brother-in-law of the dead woman. He expressed concern for the welfare of the "deceased's," a "female daughter" named Katherine. The two proceeded separately on a search of the house and Nelsen "disclosed" the child in a kitchen cabinet. The child tried to be hysterical, but Nelsen could not spell that and so he decided that she had merely "screamed and bit." Tellios came and took her away, "quited" her and put her to bed. Detectives then arrived and Nelsen returned to patrol.

Brichter replaced the file and went down to ask what sector Nelsen patrolled nowadays, only to find it was his day off. A call to his house was answered by his wife, who said he was out of town. Brichter sighed and went back to the squad room.

He knocked on the door to Ryder's tiny office.

"Come in," called Ryder.

Brichter opened the door. "Good morning, Captain. If you have a few minutes, I'd like to talk with you." Brichter began his friendships by becoming formal.

"Sure, come on in. What's up?"

"I have some more information on the Tellios case."

"Is it a case?"

"Yes, sir, I think at this point it is." Brichter gave a brief account of his conversation with Ramsey, concluding, "And he called me yesterday evening to say Tellios had asked me to dinner."

"Was Ramsey sure about what he told you?"

"Yes, sir."

Ryder frowned up at Brichter. "Sit down," he said, gesturing at the single hard chair in front of his desk. "Then how come Tellios invites a cop from the Organized Crime Unit to dinner?"

Brichter worked himself in between the single chair and Ryder's desk. The back of the chair was a scant inch from the wall and his knees when he bent them were equally close to the desk. "What better way to damage us than by getting one of us on his chain?"

"You seriously think Dr. Ramsey is describing the actual setup out there?"

"He's describing the situation as he sees it, and he's had a long time to hone his observations."

Ryder leaned back in his chair until it touched the wall behind him. "All right, good work, Obie. Now, is there any way we can cut McHugh into the deal, send him out there instead of you?"

Brichter felt his jaws tighten. "Why?"

"Because you are probably one of the best investigators I've ever worked with, but there are subtleties of human behavior that escape you. This situation calls for an oily-tongued con artist, and fortunately we have one right in the squad room."

Brichter tried to speak calmly. "With due respect, Captain, I disagree. This is my case, I found out about the situation, I think I should be the one to go ahead on it."

Ryder's chair snapped forward. "Listen to me. If Tellios plays tough guy at you, you'll come right back at him with one of those smart-ass cracks, pure reflex. He'll kick you out and any attempt we make to try to get in out there again will be seen for what it is."

Brichter stood, kicking the chair aside. He dropped forward on the small desk, well into Ryder's space. "I am goddamn sick and tired of your perception of me as some kind of idiot savant, good at investigating and bad at everything else! You don't know what I am or am not capable of blowing, since anything I start up that calls for special skills you take away from me and hand to McHugh. Now hear this: For eight years my good friend Gordon Ramsey has been stuck in a hole he describes in his own words as a cesspool, one dug by a certain carp-faced bastard who has no business walking around free. I'm the one he asked for help, so I get to be the one who helps. There is no way I'm going to politely step aside and let someone else do the job. Tellios is my meat!" And Brichter looked like a wolf standing over it.

Ryder lost his temper. "All right, go on, go out there! But if you blow it as bad as I think you will, don't expect more than the cheapest funeral the department can buy!"

Brichter came out of Ryder's office with a look of vindication he felt no need to hide.

"I couldn't hear the words," said a voice, and he turned to see Tonk grinning at him from across the room, "but the tune came through nice and clear. That door is awful thin; if you listen hard, I bet you can hear his pen scratching as he writes up your transfer. You've never learned how to get along, have you? And you think you're so smart."

Brichter said mildly, as he started for his own desk, "I tried thinking you were smart once, but that didn't work."

Tonk made a noise like "Bshhhhh!" and tore a manila folder in half. His desk was covered with stacks of file folders. Ryder, trying to find a task Tonk was good at, had set him to sorting out old cases, removing anything of current interest and tossing the rest.

Tonk tore again, yawning a huge, complacent yawn, indicative of a man replete, and Brichter wondered where the lady with a similar yawn was this morning. Tonk, notorious and unrepentant, bought condoms by the case and took any reproach on the subject as a sign of envy.

"Where's McHugh?" asked Brichter.

"He's got court this morning, remember?" Tonk yawned again. "That loan shark, what's 'is name, Whitlock, his trial starts today."

Whitlock was the meanest loan shark in Charter, a redheaded, bandy-legged bully with a quick grin that seldom faded, even when he was breaking the kneecap of a debtor behind in his payments. Brichter had begun the case some months back, building a slow, solid file of circumstantial evidence, but Ryder had turned it over to McHugh, who had run a fast, brilliant undercover operation that resulted in Whitlock's arrest. Brichter's file and McHugh's recordings had gone to the county prosecutor, resulting in the trial beginning this morning. With luck, thought Brichter, Whitlock was bound for Joliet, where he'd stay for a nice long time.

The squad-room door opened and McHugh entered in a rage. It was barely ten, early for an adjournment. Tonk and Brichter watched him stomp to his desk and slam his briefcase down on it.

"Something wrong, McHugh?" Brichter asked mildly.

"THAT GODDAMNED JUDGE EVERETT!" roared McHugh.

Ryder appeared in his doorway, looking startled. "What's happened?"

"My Whitlock case has been dismissed!"

"Jeez, how'd that happen?" asked Tonk.

McHugh yanked his tie loose. "Actually, it wasn't the judge's fault. It's our goddamned county prosecutor! Jimmy Bartholomew told me he thought the trial was next week, for Christ's sake! I talked to that bastard Saturday and he sounded all ready to go. Today he comes in and he hasn't got diddly in his briefcase. He waives an opening statement, his first witness gets up there and Jimmy can't remember the right questions, he lets the defense offer a couple of motions and bang! next thing you know we're out on our ears and Whitlock is free as a frickin' bird."

"I'm sorry, Cris; that really stinks," said Ryder, angrily sympathetic.

"Yeah, thanks." McHugh picked up his briefcase and dropped it symbolically into his wastebasket. He glanced over at Brichter. "Aren't you going to make one of your cute remarks?" he asked.

"Probably. But not right now. Tell me, is it possible someone got to Bartholomew?"

McHugh frowned. "Who? He's the big man, so it would have to be Januschka. And Bartholomew hates Januschka's guts, everyone knows that."

Brichter said, "Assume there's someone else who could. Did Bartholomew act like he'd been gotten to?"

McHugh looked thoughtful. "Okay, it did seem that way. He looked like he'd been up sick all night, and I couldn't catch him afterwards to ask what the hell happened. But if not Januschka, who?"

"Nick Tellios." Brichter floated the name out like a fly fisherman and let it lie in the air between them.

"Nuts!" snapped McHugh. "Tellios has been retired for years! Lunch with the mayor, donations to the chamber orchestra—he's gotten respectable since he moved down here."

Brichter said, "Someone who presumably knows says Tellios is the broker we've been looking for."

Ryder said, "Obie thinks we should take a closer look at Tellios and his string of influential friends."

"And you *agreed*?"

"Bartholomew and Tellios were on speaking terms a year or so back. I remember wondering what the hell a retired mafioso and a hard-nosed prosecutor had in common."

McHugh sat down. "Yeah, I remember wondering too. But this morning Jimmy acted more like he was running scared than doing someone a favor."

Brichter said, "I know someone who claims he's being blackmailed by Tellios. And according to this file, Tellios did two years for blackmailing a politician's wife."

McHugh looked toward Brichter without seeing him, turning over those interesting facts in his mind, comparing it to the county prosecutor's behavior that morning. "Well, I'll be damned," he murmured, and bent to fish his briefcase out of the wastebasket.

"I gave Obie the go-ahead to look into it," said Ryder. "But until we know more, this is to be kept very securely under our hats."

Tellios, never in a hurry, was holding a leisurely conversation about how to corrupt a city with Joe Januschka.

They were opposites in many ways, Tellios and Januschka, including both ends of the physical spectrum. Tellios was small and bird-boned, big-headed, soft-spoken, an elder statesman of crime, proud of his subtle mind. Januschka was not yet fifty, a massive structure of bone, muscle, and fat, ill-tempered and aggressive. Yet it was Januschka who was the boss in Charter, and Tellios was careful to offer only advice, never instructions. He ran his operation independent of Januschka, which was fine, but recently he had begun interfering in Januschka's running of the city, and Januschka resented it.

"It's friends, Joseph," said Tellios, "the whole thing rests on friends. How do you make a friend? You find out what he needs or wants, and you get it for him. Political functions are a nice place to start. Having paid a hundred bucks for a plate of creamed chicken over a stale biscuit, they feel cheated unless something exciting happens. They drink too much and become . . . subject to impulse. So you arrange something, and if he takes you up on it, then he owes you. When the time is right, ask for something little, something unimportant. If he gets it for you, he's your friend. After that you can do whatever you want with him. See? Easy."

"Yeah," said Januschka. The pair sat at one end of a dining-room table in Januschka's house, toying with melon balls and fresh strawberries.

"I retired to Charter fourteen years ago," Tellios continued in his thin rasp. "And I was really retired. Chicago sucks, Joseph, don't fool yourself it doesn't; you were smart to come down here. But life in the country gets boring without a little action. There's always people looking for a safe place to meet, to do a little business, and they're willing to give a share of the transaction for such a place. But in a small place like this you've got to watch out for nosy people. So I made a friend here, a friend there, and now I can operate in safety. You have to take care of your basics first. You should get yourself a banker, Joseph; set up a regular checking account."

"Huh," said Januschka; "people I deal with prefer cash."

"Yes, but politicians don't like big wads of cash; it makes them nervous. And charities don't like contributions in cash, either."

"I don't believe in charity."

"It can cover a multitude of actions. I wanted our airport improved, so I had a friend start up a committee and I gave them a check just like I gave to public radio and the firemen. But if you move ten grand or more through a bank, they send the feds a form. I don't need the feds coming by asking where I got the money to give to charity, so I got myself a banker, one who files those CTR forms in his wastebasket."

"Yeah," said Januschka. "But this town is already set up for me, so why're you telling me all this?"

"Because these things go in waves. Something will set off a cry for reform and things will get tight for a while, then you have to start all over again. I'm seventy-four, Joseph; it may be that I won't be here to prepare things for your successor."

"Huh," said Januschka. He poked a melon ball with his fork and ate it, staring at Tellios until it was swallowed. Tellios returned the look, surface-calm, but aware he had again underestimated Januschka's intelligence. But instead of a display of temper, Januschka only asked, "You got any advice about that Organized Crime Unit they let the cops set up?"

"I think I have a way to fix that too," said Tellios. "There's a cop named Brichter who works in the Organized Crime Unit. Do you know him?"

"Are you kidding?"

"What's he like?"

"I can't say it's ever been a pleasure to have him around. Your plan involve him?"

Tellios selected a strawberry. "Yes, why?"

"You may have to change your plan. He's a twenty-four-carat pain in the ass. More to the point, he ain't for sale and you can't scare him. When he decides you're next, he goes out and builds a case so airtight it'd give Murray Slovik the green squirts."

"Where's the handle on him?"

"What handle? I've tried everything and I can't grab him any way that don't make me quick let go."

"Are you saying he's some kind of hero?"

Januschka laughed, waving his fork. "Not to the cops. To them he's a hot potato; they transfer him from Homicide to Narcotics to Organized Crime as fast as they can push the paper through. He's too clean. He won't go along. Hasn't got one friend in the whole department. And he's weird. He's good, so they can't fire him, but the chief will probably give a medal to the man who shoots him."

"What do you mean, 'weird'?"

"You know, weird. He knows stuff like how many degrees it is on the sun—he's on a list to buy a plane ticket to the moon—but he also belongs to a club that pretends it's still the Middle Ages. Maybe it's because he's not getting laid. I can't find any sign of a girlfriend, and he's never been married."

"Is he gay?"

"Naw, I told the Undertaker to try him out on that, and he sent

Dickie to him, but Brichter put poor little Dickie down so hard he
cried for a week. He don't drink, he don't get high, he's gonna be
canonized a saint one day after he's dead. Which I wish he was,
he gives me a lot of grief. Why do you need to get to him?"

"Not him, the Organized Crime Unit. You forget, I'm also doing
business with people they might be interested in. I want to make a
friend in the unit if I can."

Januschka grinned and waved a laden fork. "No need to mess
with Brichter. He was about as nice to Jilly as he was to Dickie, but
Tonk thinks she's the greatest thing since sliced bread."

"Jilly?"

"One of the Undertaker's ladies. Built like it won't ever quit, but
smart."

"Can he control her?"

"Undertaker clears his throat, she checks to see if she's got a run
in her stockings. She's his, eyebrows to toenails."

"Tonk . . . he's the new detective, isn't he? I seem to recall him
being called for unnecessary roughness while arresting whores
while he was still riding around in a squad car."

"So maybe that's why I told her not to bill him for her services."

"How long has this been going on?"

"Only about a week. But she's already got Tonk to agree to
move in with her. And she phones me every day with a report. Says
he's got the IQ of an ashtray, but he loves getting laid. And she can
get him to talk about his job before, during, and after."

"Very well done, Joseph."

Januschka speared a roundel of honeydew. "I'm glad to hear you
approve for once."

"Now, another topic: Do you know where Norman Whitlock
is?"

"He's in court; his trial started today."

The little old man began to slice a melon ball in half. "No, his
case has been dismissed. Hasn't he called you?"

"No— Why the hell did he call you and not me?"

"Why should he call me? No, someone else called with the
news." Tellios ate the bit of melon, and there was such smug satisfaction in the act that Januschka gripped his fork tight enough for it
to hurt.

"You fixed it, didn't you?" he accused. "Why the hell didn't you
ask me before you did that?"

"Why should I ask your permission to do a favor for one of your people? I'm sorry if that displeases you." Tellios did not sound the least sorry.

"How did you manage it? Jimmy Bartholomew was trying that case himself; it's the biggest case of the year!"

"I believe we've already discussed my method of collecting friends."

"You mean to say *Bartholomew*—? When did this happen? Goddammit, why didn't you let me know you got to him?"

"I didn't think it was relevant. You so seldom ask me for favors, Joseph."

"Yeah, and why should I? I'm running things, remember? I don't need any of your favors!" He pointed his fork at Tellios. "But this is different! When you start messing with my people, that's my business! Whitlock's connected, he works in my town, that makes anything you do with him my business!"

"Of course, and that's why I asked to see you. May I borrow Whitlock to do some work for me?"

Januschka swelled as if he were about to burst. Then he had an idea. It was so good his rage vanished and he almost smiled. "I don't think so. I hate to spoil any plan you might have, especially after you went to all that trouble, but I've had so many problems with Whitlock I was hoping he'd get sent away for a nice long time. You don't want him, believe me."

"What kind of problems have you had?"

The truth would do. "He's a bug, Nick. He almost ran himself out of business because he's so rough. He thinks the sounds hurt people make is funny."

"I see."

"Yeah, so unless you got somebody you want dead, you shouldn't rely on him too much."

Tellios moved his melon balls around with his fork as if looking for one in particular. "So where would I get in touch with him?"

Rage began again to mottle Januschka's dark cheeks, then he re-alized what Tellios was saying. "Who you gonna hit?"

"Nobody that could be any concern of yours, Joseph. This is a private matter." Tellios put a strawberry in his mouth.

"Using one of my people for a hit job makes it my concern!"

There was a longish pause while Tellios ate the strawberry, and while he considered how much to tell. "Somebody at the ranch," he admitted at last.

Januschka ran a mental finger down a short list of names: Riscatto, Shiffler, Downey, Kori, Ramsey. He slammed his fork down on the table. "The professor, right? That's why you were asking about Brichter! Him and Brichter are friends. So after all your talk about how you got the professor by the short hairs, he did just like I warned you, right? Went talking to Brichter! How much can he tell? You got to keep them civilians away from your business or they cause all kind of trouble. So all right. Whitlock'll love knocking off a college professor. I'll get hold of him and have him call you."

Chapter
4 †

He was early, but the sun was touching the horizon when Brichter turned in at the big mailbox that marked the Tretower entrance. A narrow gravel lane between the traditional white board fences showed the way. The place looked well kept; the verge was clean and the fences freshly painted. But Brichter's attention was focused on the collection of buildings at the end of the lane.

He had looked at them from afar whenever he happened to drive down Eerie River Road, speculating about the residents. All the buildings were clean-cut and substantial, but the main house was a beauty. Cream with green trim, it was a cluster of steep roofs, three tall corbeled chimneys, a mix of window shapes, and a big wrap-around porch. Shortly after the Civil War, some man had announced his arrival in the upper class with this house.

He or some later owner had built a one-mile racetrack that encircled the house, cottage, barn, and sheds. The effect was to make a fort of the settlement. Brichter drove his ugly purple car through the gates into the barnyard, stopping in front of the stone-and-stucco cottage that Ramsey lived in. The curving walk leading to the door was lined with nodding daffodils.

It was a mild evening, and the air was fragrant with freshly turned earth, new growing things, and equine scents. A big green pickup was parked outside a shed, flanked by an old, immaculate black Lincoln and Ramsey's little MGA. Brichter consulted his watch; he was nearly twenty minutes early. He considered standing around a few minutes; he disliked being early. There were lights on in the horse barn; impulsively, he turned away from the cottage and walked toward it.

The barn was a big, single-story, light-green structure, T-shaped, a big crossbar on a short, fat stem. Clean, weed-free gravel covered the barnyard in front of it. A smaller door was set into the big double doors. Brichter opened it and went in. And almost walked into a three-board white fence just inside the door.

Then he saw it was the gate to an enclosure that circled an arena. Overhead lights made pools of brightness on the dirt floor, and the warm smells of hay and horses filled his nostrils. The fence allowed for an aisle, and Brichter started along it. Near the other end of the arena was a dark-haired young woman in riding pants and a red shirt. She was slender but not angular, equipped with a long thin whip, and occasionally eclipsed by the passage of a magnificent stallion trotting around her at the end of a lunge rein. At a terse command, he spun on his haunches and began trotting in the other direction. She came around, following him, her pale face intent. Staring, Brichter slowed and stopped.

She had long, dark hair tucked into a complex knot at the nape of her neck, stray strands of it fine and curling. The line of her delicate jaw was well defined, and the harsh overhead light made shadows under her cheekbones. Her mouth was sweetly shaped. There was no tilt to her small nose. Her eyes were large and light-colored behind a thicket of lashes. She moved with a dancer's grace, turning in time to the horse in orbit around her. Brichter leaned on the fence the way a cold man will lean toward a fire.

The grunting stallion came around again. He had the high tail, offset head, and the delicate, dished face of the purebred Arabian. He was the color of polished walnut, with black legs, mane, and tail. Brichter searched his memory and came up with the word for horses colored like that: bay.

"Ho!" ordered the girl, back to Brichter, and the horse stopped short, ribs heaving. "Come," she said in a different voice, and the horse hurried in, patently to enjoy the way she stroked his nose, but then his head came up, nostrils flaring.

She turned and saw Brichter, immediately looked around. "Riscatto?" she called. There was no reply, and she looked again at Brichter, not curious, not anxious, not pleased or helpful, just waiting.

"How do you do," he said, as gently as he could.

"Who are you?" she asked.

Her voice was low and smooth, and he was ravished all over again. "I'm Peter Brichter, here to see Dr. Gordon Ramsey. I'm a friend of his."

"Gordon's in the cottage," she said, turning away, pushing at the horse's neck to turn him as well.

"Wait!" he called, and she turned back, her face a polite blank. "Are you Kori?"

"Yes."

"Do you ride that horse?"

"Yes."

"Ride him for me."

"I don't think so," she said, and turned away again.

"Why not? Is he tired?"

She stopped again, turned again and said, still politely, "No."

"Then just once around the floor?"

Was there the slightest flick of amusement across her face? He grinned, embarrassed at the vastness of his need to remain in her company, but would not take back his request. The horse nudged her shoulder. "Very well," she said. She unsnapped the rein from its ring on the horse's nose and dropped it in a coil on the floor. "Ho," she said softly, patting him on his neck. She jumped up to lie across his back, swung a leg over and sat up. Using voice and legs, hands resting on her thighs, she made him do a very collected canter around the arena. She sat erect, riding deep into the rocking gait, as if she grew out of the horse rather than sat on him. The circuit took just over a minute, and Brichter watched as if hypnotized.

She turned the horse in and stopped him just past the coiled rein. "Up, Baby," she said, and he reared. She slid backward over his rump to land precisely next to the rein, then turned to Brichter.

"Sensational," he said, meaning it, and this time the smile was definitely there, playing very briefly over her face.

She bent and picked up the rein, said, "Come on, Baby," to the horse, and they walked off.

Lighter than air, he went back down the aisle, the rhythm of the canter in his ears, the remembered arc of the horse's neck and curve of the girl's hip blinding him, so that he stumbled over the board threshold of the door.

"What were you doing in there?" came a sharp inquiry, and he shied, startled. It was Ramsey.

"H'lo, Gordie," he said. "I just met Kori."

"You bloody ass!" said Ramsey. "Come on, let's get you out of here, quick!"

They walked in silence past a small shed where two chickens clucked and cawed quietly to each other in the fading light.

"Why didn't you come straight to the cottage?" demanded Ramsey.

"She rode her horse for me, Gordie. She's very beautiful; why didn't you warn me?"

"Tellios made careful arrangements so you didn't meet her!"

"No wonder, looking like that."

"Shut up and pay attention! If he finds out what you've done, he'll have you thrown off the place! Then he'll question her, and if she can't convince him of her innocence, God knows what he'll do to her!"

"He won't hurt her; she's one of the magic ones."

"Well, I'm not! He may decide I'm at fault here! And if he does—"

"Take it easy, Gordie. Nothing's going to happen to anyone. All I did was watch her ride around the arena one time. She's terrific with that horse. Good hands, they call it. But with her it's more than hands—"

"You bloody great nit! Don't you remember why you're here? Nick Tellios will not hesitate to kill anyone who disobeys his orders! Including you, including me, including her!"

They started up the walk to the cottage, Ramsey leading. Brichter said, "All right; if it will make you feel better, I'm sorry. But Jesus, Gordie, you've got to find a way to let me talk to her. There's something about her— Have you been around her so long you can't see it anymore? How can you not be in love with her?"

Ramsey opened the door to the cottage. "I adore her. But I'm gay. That's the lever Tellios used to pry me out of academe." He started in, glanced back and saw he had finally broken the spell. Brichter was frozen, staring at him. "Oh, hell, Peter, do come in! I've been celibate for years!"

He led Brichter down a hallway to a very comfortable living room where two wing chairs were half turned in to a fireplace.

"Sit down," invited Ramsey, taking a chair himself.

"Thanks. You want to tell me about it?"

"I had an affair with a student. To that point, I had kept that side of my life away from the campus. But that one time, hmmm?" He sighed. "We used to leave notes in one another's campus mailboxes. Our affair didn't last long; he was very unstable. His father is a distinguished alumnus, which in university language means he makes substantial donations to the general fund every year. His mother, God help me, was and is on the Board of Regents. He went into politics; he's a state senator. And not only did he never come out of the closet, he married a fine woman and they have children."

Ramsey studied his clasped hands. "Always, there is the question: Was it seduction, or something better? Or something worse? I don't know how Tellios acquired it, but he has a letter the boy wrote me, making it perfectly clear what went on between us." He looked at Brichter. "You see now why this must never go beyond this room? It would destroy all of them if that letter were revealed. And, of course, it would immediately taint all the male friendships I have ever formed—including ours."

"What a load you've been carrying!"

"She's made it easier." Ramsey gave a little nod in the direction of the barn. "Hmmm? No matter what I've done, no matter what may be said of me, I can point to her as a wonderful accomplishment."

"Does she know?"

"Not about the blackmail, but I took the other weapon out of his hands some time ago."

"Gordie, it seems a little odd that a man of Tellios' type would have wanted a homosexual teaching his niece."

"He didn't. He wanted first of all a teacher he could control. Then he wanted someone who would not interfere with a beautiful child just starting to blossom. And I had the advantage of not being a woman, who might get the rest of his crew stirred up."

"She stirs me up. Tell me about her. Is she shy? She acted shy."

"It's more a deep reserve, complicated now by fright. Among friends she has a fine sense of humor to go with a subtle intellect. She whistles Bach and plays a mean game of poker. Tellios is leery about letting her out of his sight, so she's hardly been anywhere, and she has a badly skewed education, but I like to think she's doing well."

"Why is he like that about her?"

"Because he's the last Victorian? I don't know. She did suffer a breakdown on the death of her parents. If he'd sent her to a hospital, that might have been better, because she's unnaturally attached to him, and he to her. Fearing him as she does, it is nevertheless to him she looks for protection. She pretends to believe that her uncle is eccentric but well meaning and must be indulged." Ramsey made an odd sound meant to be a chuckle. "He's seventy-four years old; I've been waiting for him to die."

"You historians always take the long view," said Brichter. "I wish you'd told me about this setup a long time ago. Meanwhile I'm glad he got his hooks into you. I'm sorry, but I am. You saved her for me."

"For you? Perhaps you'd better consult her about that." Ramsey frowned. "Love at first sight doesn't seem like you; has this happened to you before?"

"No." Brichter's sideways smile appeared. "Well, once, in a different context. Have you ever seen an aircraft carrier? I remember the first time I saw the U.S.S. *Ranger*. I was walking along the pier to report aboard for duty, and found myself under this immensely high, curving wall of steel plates, bubbling softly to herself: a sleeping dragon, dreaming of adventure. I never got over that first impression and I still think fondly of *Ranger*." He shrugged. " But tell me more about Kori. The way that horse came to her—is she kind?"

"And good. And still innocent."

Brichter made a disbelieving face. "Come on! Looking like that? You can't mean it!"

"In a little while you'll meet a fellow with a bad limp and a humble grin. He's Mel Downey. He used to have a collection of magazines illustrating the possibilities in human sexual intercourse, hmmm? He let Kori spend an hour or so paging through his collection, and she let slip to Tellios some of her newly acquired knowledge. Tellios made her admit the source and Downey was dumped out of a moving car at County General Hospital with smashed legs, broken arms, and facial fractures."

"Jesus! When was this?"

Ramsey thought. "She was almost sixteen—about four and a half years ago. She never spoke to me about it, but she spent a long while reading up on the Christian concept of guilt. Meanwhile, Tellios keeps Downey around as an object lesson, and it works well." Ramsey glanced at his watch and stood. "Now, with that warning in mind, let's go up and meet them."

Brichter nursed his tiny goblet of sherry—he disliked sherry—and stood with his back firmly against the carved stone fireplace in the parlor. Things were not going well.

Each had been surprised by the other. Tellios, warned by Januschka's description to look at Brichter as a supercop, wasn't sure what to make of this quiet, stoop-shouldered individual with the cheap blue suit and sour expression. Tellios stood on the other side of the fireplace, his smile, pulled crookedly over his misshapen mouth, contradicting the look in his eyes.

Brichter, who knew what Tellios looked like, was thinking this a sad attempt to suborn him. He'd been expecting to be treated as if he were a long-lost friend, coaxed into conversation and his every statement received as relevation. But Tellios, in a hurry to find out what Brichter was really like, had asked some sharp questions. And Brichter, who had no talent for turning away nosiness with polite small talk, much less with the complex dissembling of undercover work, had retreated into monosyllables.

The others were of no help. Mel Downey, a little man with unevenly bowed legs and mismatched profiles, stood in hopeful proximity to the sherry decanter, glass empty.

Paul Shiffler, a thickset cowboy type with a broad red mustache and a suit of Western cut, sat on the neo-Victorian sofa, right ankle on left knee, regarding Brichter suspiciously.

Ramsey stood beside Tellios, looking like a proctor during finals who has just been told one of the students is armed.

"I understand you and Professor Ramsey enjoy long talks on intellectual matters," said Tellios.

"Sometimes," nodded Brichter.

"What sort of things do you talk about?"

"Everything." Brichter looked around the room, cop-eyes absorbing detail. He didn't think much of the fake ferns, but the room itself was as large and beautiful as the exterior indicated it might be. Downey was surreptitiously refilling his sherry glass.

"What did you talk about last?"

Brichter thought, recalled a conversation of a week ago. "Artificial intelligence."

"You mean computers? I bought Professor Ramsey a personal computer to help in his writing."

"Artificial intelligence is a very advanced sort of computer program," said Ramsey suddenly. "It has led to the science of cognition, which links anthropology, psychology, linguistics, philosophy, and computer programming in an attempt to formulate the rules of understanding. Apparently even vision can be expressed in mathematical terms." He tended to wordiness when nervous.

"You discussed the uses of such programs?" Tellios asked Brichter, flicking a repressive glance at Ramsey.

"Their uses are evident," said Brichter. "We discussed the definition of sentience, the possibility that computers using such programs might one day meet the definition of sentience, and whether destroying one might be murder."

Shiffler snorted contemptuously.

Tellios shook his head in admiration—and noted that when his attention was captured, Brichter could speak several sentences in succession. "Too bad that people seldom discuss matters of a philosophical nature," he said. "Our conversation here tends toward the practical. Buying hay. Selling yearlings."

Brichter had been wary of bringing up his new favorite subject, but could not resist this opportunity to move the conversation toward her. "I understand you have some very expensive horseflesh out here."

"And an extremely talented person to handle them," said Tellios. "You mean Kori?"

That came a little too eagerly, and the old man's eyes crinkled in amusement. "I mean Guy Riscatto. Though Kori does contribute. One would almost believe she has never been . . . ill. Of course, I'm sure that's because of the stability of her environment; an ordered routine can work wonders. All my employees know better than to allow her to meet a stranger without careful preparation. It's one of my strictest rules." His eyes flicked again at Ramsey, who swallowed hard, then glanced at his watch. "I believe we should go in to dinner now."

Tellios led the way out of the parlor and Ramsey took that opportunity to sigh and then shoot a pleading glance at Brichter.

Kori made two changes in the numbers, punched "Enter" and watched ramifications appear down all the lines. "Mr. Marcotte wants Storm Wind and her foal as a unit, but I think we should keep them until the baby's weaned, then sell just the baby. Stormy really seems to nick with Summer Wind; this is her second good-looking foal by him. This baby may shed out gray, and she looks very promising."

"Aw, you think all Summer Wind's foals are wonderful!" scoffed Riscatto. The two were sitting in Ramsey's study at the back of the cottage, both still in working jodhpurs. Riscatto was a dark man of medium size, very bald. He leaned forward in his chair to look over Kori's shoulder at the screen. "You're in love with Hurricane."

"No, if I really loved her, I'd sell her now, with Storm Wind, to keep you from fooling with her. You have a talent for spoiling a gentle disposition." The baby in question, a scant four weeks old, was a promiscuously friendly mite, currently a dark brown.

"No, I don't; I bring out a hidden spirit in them." Riscatto touched the top of his bald head with a flat hand. "You may not like my technique, but you've sat in the stands and watched me win a string of blue ribbons you don't mind bragging about in your ads." Tellios had told Riscatto to arrange this meeting to keep Kori out of the way until the visitor left. Which was fine with Riscatto; he'd heard a thing or two about Brichter.

The phone rang and Riscatto twisted around to pick up the receiver. "Yo," he said. "Yeah," he added with a glance at Kori. "Yeah. Okay, I'll tell her." He hung up. "Meeting's over. Nick wants you to hustle up to the house and change for dinner. I guess he changed his mind about you meeting the cop."

In an instant she shifted from competent businesswoman to frightened young woman. "What cop?"

"Didn't you know? That fellow you showed off your bareback riding to a while ago is Detective Sergeant Brichter."

The dining room in the big house was large, with cut-off corners, dark wainscoting, and another fireplace. On the walls were old paintings of sinewy horses showing the whites of their eyes at storms, at cougars, and at being ridden hard by ladies with improbably tiny waists. The room did not look like a restoration but as if it had never been remodeled. The table was long and massive, with carved wooden legs. Its linen was spotless, the service a legendary porcelain and an old, heavy silver. Tellios, in a little black suit, stood at the head of the table and directed them to their places: Brichter on his right, then Shiffler, across from Shiffler Downey, and on Downey's right Ramsey. An empty place remained on Tellios' left. The old man excused himself with a magician's portentous air and went out.

He came back leading Kori. She was wearing a very modest dress of blue silk. Her dark hair was in a precarious knot on top of her head, and she had the glowing look of a recent, hasty bath. She said nothing, looked at no one, as Tellios led her to her place at the table.

"Koritsimu, am I correct in saying no introductions are necessary?" asked Tellios.

Her eyes brushed Brichter and dropped again, but not before he saw they were gray, not blue, a shade darker than his own. "I saw him in the barn," she said quietly. "But he didn't tell me who he was."

"How rude of him. Koritsimu, this is Detective Sergeant Otto Peter Brichter, of the Charter police. Sergeant Brichter, this is my niece, Kori Price."

After the briefest of pauses, she said. "How do you do, Sergeant?"

He aimed a smile at her, which she missed. "I'm well, thank you, Miss Price."

Tellios took his seat and the meal began.

A few minutes later, "I trust you don't mind our unfancy cooking, Sergeant," said Tellios.

Brichter, who had taken his first bites without even noticing what they consisted of, so rapt was he looking at the girl, yanked his attention to the meal. Mushroom broth, a lean and rare roast beef, tiny new potatoes, fresh asparagus in a butter sauce—simple things, perfectly prepared. "This is delicious," he said, a little surprised.

Tellios smiled so proudly at this that Brichter realized who the chef was. Tellios, seeing his realization, said, "Professor Ramsey and I take turns in the kitchen, with occasional relief from Mr. Shiffler."

"Not Kori?"

"Kori is not much of a cook."

"Yeah, but she sure knows her way around a barn," said Shiffler, fitting a mouthful of potato under his Marlboro mustache.

"The professor lets her use his computer to keep track of business," offered Downey.

Tellios nodded and said, "I encourage her to make as many of the business decisions as she can."

"She's pretty young to be making business decisions, isn't she?" asked Brichter, unconsciously joining in the trend toward speaking of her as if she were not sitting in the room with them, stiff and silent.

"Consider, Sergeant," said Tellios, "she hasn't had the . . . plethora of distractions normal for her age and sex. Consequently, she is very mature for her years. She never shouts or weeps or loses her temper. Combine that with intelligence, and one should not be surprised to find her doing well. Of course, there was some luck involved in the acquisition of our champion, Summer Wind." He offered what was surely a family joke: "She bought him sight unseen."

"How do you mean?"

"She bought an 'aged mare,' I believe the term is, in foal to a famous stallion. The result was Summer Wind."

Brichter frowned. The stallion he'd seen in the barn was fully mature; Tellios was saying that she had been well enough to involve herself in business for at least three years—if the horse he'd seen was, in fact, Summer Wind. He said to Kori, "I don't know much about Arabians, but that one look I had at Summer Wind sure impressed me."

"Thank you," she said, without looking up. She had not touched her meal.

Shiffler asked abruptly, "You enjoy being a cop, Sergeant?"

Brichter shrugged. "Like most cops, I enjoy the exercise of authority. I resent stupid laws and stupid courtroom decisions that make my job harder than it needs to be. Do you enjoy your work, Mr. Shiffler?"

"Why not?" retorted Shiffler.

Brichter cut the tender top off an asparagus spear. "You're from Chicago, aren't you? I should think you'd find it kind of boring out here in the country." He glanced at Tellios. "As a matter of fact, you're from up there, too, aren't you? Don't you ever miss the action?"

Tellios shook his head. "Chicago's close enough that I can visit it whenever I feel the need. Which isn't often; I'm retired and I enjoy life here."

"Every Fourth of July," said Downey, "he sets up a pig roast." A crooked, malicious grin appeared. "Oh yeah, you might not like coming to a pig roast, huh, Sarge?"

Brichter raised one eyebrow. "I imagine that, sooner or later, just about everyone gets raked over the coals."

Shiffler guffawed.

"Quite correct, Sergeant," said Tellios approvingly, looking at Downey, who hesitated, then laughed too, but not happily.

Dessert was homemade ice cream with raspberry sauce.

"Perhaps Sergeant Brichter has some subject of intellectual value he would like to raise," said Tellios.

"Hmmm?" said Brichter, watching Kori. Wrapped in her controlled silence, she stirred her ice cream without eating any of it. Her complexion was flawless, naturally pale, with great swatches of pink on either cheek, doubtless a reaction to his stare.

"I can see you aren't interested in matters of the mind this evening," said Tellios. "We can try again some other time, if you don't mind coming out again."

This is what Brichter should have been waiting for, but he wasn't listening. He tore his eyes away from Kori with an effort and addressed his host. "Mr. Tellios, that was a wonderful meal.

Would you allow Kori to take a walk with me now to shake it down a little?"

"It's muddy out; I'm not dressed to go walking," said Kori quickly.

"Your wool cape is in the hall, along with your boots," said Tellios at once. "Go ahead." He looked at Brichter. "But don't be long."

Her feet were small and neatly formed, like her hands. Like her. He felt he could stand and watch her pull on an old pair of Wellington boots for the rest of his life. He would handle this case bravely, and she would find him admirable. A phrase come to mind: ". . . worship her by years of noble deeds . . ." Geoff's words. He was dismayed to think that he had sunk to Sir Geoffrey of Brixham's level of sentimentality, but then she glanced up at him with those great, immaculate eyes, and he yearned to do just one noble thing for her. He offered his hand to help her to her feet. She took the cape, which was long and a dull blue-green, from an old armoire, and fastened it about her shoulders. It had a hood, which he found terrific, and they went out the front door and down the three steps of the porch.

"Do you mind that I asked you to come along?" he asked.

"No."

"Positive? You're not just being polite?"

She said, "Gordon says never lie unless you have to," and it wasn't until he was in bed hours later, replaying the evening, that he saw the ambiguity of her reply.

They went down the slope of the lawn, fragrant with the scent of young grass and jonquils. The top of her head was just a little higher than his shoulder. She wore no perfume. He wished he'd worn his new suit. He wished he dared take her hand.

A brilliant light high up on a pole shed a blue-white cone down to the ground. They walked through it and into the darkness again on the other side. "Do you enjoy working with horses?" he asked.

"Yes." Said so flatly as to close that subject.

He tried another. "Gordon is a good friend. I learned a lot from him from his courses I took at the university."

"Yes?"

"He's said some nice things about you."

"He's very kind." Subject closed.

He stopped. "Look, what's the matter?"

"Nothing."

"I want to help you; that's what I'm really doing out here."

"Who told you I needed help?"

"Gordie."

She looked up at him, her eyes hidden in shadows. "Are you truly a policeman?"

He smiled. "Do you want to see my badge?"

"No." She looked away. "I think we should start back now."

"Could we talk a little first? I have some questions for you, if that's all right."

She took a step backward. "I have nothing to tell you, nothing! Please, can we go back?" Her hands were trembling, and when she noticed that, she pulled the cape closed over them.

"Hey," he said. "Hey, it's all right. You want to go back, okay, whatever you want, that's what we'll do. But don't ever be afraid of me; I'd cut off my right hand before I hurt you."

"Yes?"

He raised the hand. "I swear."

"All I want is for you to leave me alone."

He stayed a prudent three paces behind her all the way back to the house.

Chapter
5 †

Jilly Meade stroked the back of Tonk's broad neck. The two were sitting side by side on a luxuriously comfortable couch.

"That goddamn Brichter," he was saying, "thinks he knows everything. That's why he's always cutting down people. He even treats me like I'm some kind of clown."

They were in her place, which made his look like a rat's nest by comparison. He might've known she'd have a place like this, a girl looking like she did. She was really beautiful, tall, with dark red hair and white skin, and big, stand-up breasts. She was wearing a lavender dress with a trick top that seemed decent until you were in a position to look down it. Which he was doing right now.

She was high-tone and sexy, a neat trick. Her grammar was so good; when she used a dirty word, she made it sound classy. She said, "If he's that much of a shithead, why don't you just call him out? Beat him up?"

"Naw, I can't do that; Ryder'd can me." He fingered his blond mustache, which grew down past his mouth to near the edges of his jaw. "It's not up to me to do something, it's up to Captain Ryder. Both me and McHugh have let him know we wouldn't mind losing the jerk and working short-handed till he finds a replacement, but so far it's no go. Brichter makes good, solid cases, and plenty of them, so until that changes, Ryder's gonna keep him around. He may be God's gift to the department—just ask him, he'll admit it—but that don't mean I want to do him any favors."

"No, people who pick on my Tonker deserve no favors at all." She leaned over and blew gently in his ear. "Now, tell me what else you've been up to."

He sighed. She was always so damn interested in his work. She wasn't the first woman he'd taken to bed who turned out to be more interested in his job than he was. He knew all about her type,

49

turned on by the gun he carried. But Jilly was also the most accomplished woman he'd ever had. In or out of the sack—but especially in—there had never been anyone remotely like her, not ever.

She pulled her fingernails down the palm of his hand, her eyes making promises. "Tell me," she whispered, already excited.

"Oh, okay," he said, and scooted away from her long enough to turn and lie back, with his head in her lap. "What do you want to hear?"

She began unbuttoning his shirt. "Tell me about a secret operation, something nobody is supposed to know."

"Hmmm," he said. "Well, we got a tip the other day, about that broker we been looking for. I can't tell you his name but Brichter says . . ."

Per instructions, when Brichter got home, he called Ryder. "I've just come from Tretower. Things are moving along well, I think."

"Listen, we can talk about this on the phone if you like," said Ryder, "but why don't you come over? I've got some beer on ice."

Brichter didn't fraternize and automatically started to refuse. But then he reconsidered; Ryder was okay, and right now he sounded very friendly, as if he was pleased as well as surprised that this was working. "Sure," Brichter said. "Fifteen minutes?"

"I'll unlock the downstairs door."

Frank Ryder lived in a small, old-fashioned brick apartment building. His apartment, a front-to-back series of rooms, was a maze of couches, tables, and overstuffed chairs. Ryder, in plain white T-shirt, workpants and slippers, gestured around. "My wife got the house," he explained in a slightly blurred voice, "and stuck me with the furniture. The divorce was final two years ago, but I'm keeping it because maybe when I retire she'll let me come home." His faded blue eyes were sad. "Excuse me," he said. "I'll get the beer."

Surprised, Brichter thought, the man's drunk.

Ryder came back with two bottles that had glasses upended over them, and went away again to bring back a small bowl of shelled peanuts. "Sorry about that," he said, sitting down heavily. "Slipped up on me, talking about my wife."

Brichter also sat. He took his bottle and made a ceremony of tipping its contents down the side of his glass while he groped for something to say. "Why do you think she'll ask you home?"

"Aw, she probably won't. I hear she bought all new furniture.

But see, we only broke up because she couldn't take my being a cop. Stuck with it until the kids were grown, then threw me out. Twenty years of chewing her nails to bloody ruins if I was three minutes late getting home. That's no way to live." He poured his beer carelessly, putting a big head on it. "You ever been married?"

"No, sir."

"You will be, girls today will marry anything. When they start closing in on you, watch out for two kinds: the one that worries too much and the other that wants only the gory details, the gorier the better. There's no way you can keep either kind." He took a drink of his beer and produced a salacious grin. "There's also a third kind, that gets sexually stimulated by your job."

"Badge groupies," nodded Brichter.

"So you've run into them too." Ryder grinned. "Now if you're in need of a quick lay, they can't be beat. But don't marry one; they got the hots for the gun, not you, and you can come home from a long stakeout to find a brother on the force taking care of your business."

Brichter sipped his beer and wondered how he could bring the conversation around to Nick Tellios.

Watching him, Ryder said, "You don't need this lecture, do you?"

"No, sir, I don't think I do."

"Because you've picked your girl? Who is she? I've never heard about you being stuck on anyone in particular."

"I don't talk about my private life." That sounded colder than Brichter had meant it to, and he sought quickly to make it right. "I mean, I hope you're right. I just met someone tonight, and my brain is still spinning."

Ryder frowned. "You haven't been anywhere but the ranch, have you? Was there someone out there? A guest?"

Brichter put down his glass. "In a way. Kori—that's what they call Katherine, the niece."

"The crazy kid?"

"She's not a kid. Nor is she crazy."

"No? Did you talk to her?"

"Briefly. I happened to go into the barn and see her, and then Tellios invited her to join us at dinner."

"How bad is she? He had a doctor say she's schizo, didn't he?"

Brichter felt his jaw tightening. "Hey, is it raining? I think I left a window open on my car." He stood and made his way over to the big front window and looked out. It was not raining and his car

windows were rolled tight. A big pickup truck, the same kind and
color he'd seen at the ranch, rolled slowly by. He stood awhile, but
the truck didn't come back. Ryder waited in silence, and he turned
and asked with his painful sideways smile, "How many confes-
sions have you wrung from the quivering lips of suspects with that
goddamn talent of yours for waiting?"

"Hundreds," admitted Ryder. "What's the problem?"

"Tonight I met the most beautiful young woman I have ever
seen. Her eyes, her mouth, her hands, the way she walks, her voice
are all just what a woman's should be. She's young, of course—too
young, probably, but . . ." He didn't want to think about that. He
turned and looked out the window again. "After dinner I got to take
her for a short walk. I asked very politely if she'd answer a couple
of questions, and she jumped ten feet and landed shaking all over.
Ramsey says she's as bright and good as she is beautiful, so I don't
know why she's scared of me." He turned back. "I want to help her,
if I can. Ramsey's scared for her, but she told me flat she wants
only to be left alone. The whole setup out there stinks. Ramsey
wants out, but he thinks she needs to be taken away too. In the barn
and at the dinner . . . I agree with Ramsey that she's sane, but she's
too damn quiet and on guard to be normal."

"Didn't you used to be a paramedic?"

"Yes, why?"

"You're pretty good on head injuries; don't you know a stress reaction when you see one?"

Brichter snatched back his retort just in time, and thought that
over. "Stress," he murmured. "You know, that could just be it.
She's scared, she's under enormous pressure to stay on the good
side of that little bastard, and there's no place to run and hide."

"And she's been under that gun for years," said Ryder. "It must
at times seem like a prison. So, like a lot of experienced lifers, she's
learned to keep her head down and use routine as a substitute for
security. Only now here comes Sergeant Brichter, wanting her to
do things she may not want to do, offering to take away the only
authority she knows, disrupting her routine, scaring the piss out of
her."

"No wonder she warned me off, poor kid." Brichter came back
to sit on the couch. He grabbed a handful of peanuts. "Thanks. I
needed to hear that, Captain."

"You're welcome, I hope. So, having gotten that off your chest,
what else happened out there tonight?"

Brichter grimaced. "Tellios can come on like he's Morley Safer and you diagnose cancer by mail. We stood around giving each other slantwise looks. There are six people out there. Two are civilians, Kori and Ramsey. The others are Tellios, Paul Shiffler, Mel Downey, and Guy Riscatto. Riscatto and Kori were supposed to be having a business meeting, only she got invited up to dinner at the last minute. Tellios knew I sneaked into the barn and met her, so I assume there was someone else hiding in there who saw us. Maybe he wasn't hiding; hell, maybe he came marching by buck-naked playing 'God Save the Queen' on a trumpet. I doubt I would've noticed. Anyway, things got better over dinner, maybe because they tend to be nicer when she's around, or maybe because Shiffler expressed an interest in my job attitude and I showed him a bad one."

Ryder began to laugh. "For an undercover operative, you are one silly goof, you know that?"

Brichter's face shut down. "How am I supposed to take that?"

"As a piece of friendly criticism. That pretty lady saved your can for you. I warned you you were no good at role-playing, but you insisted on trying it out. Tellios got an accurate measure of you over cocktails—"

"Sherry."

"Sherry, then. And he didn't like what he saw. You are as ept socially as a wolverine, but you are not a crook; and I didn't think you'd be able to convince Tellios otherwise. But then you display this sudden, genuine passion for a woman he controls, and he thinks he's found a way to change you from a weapon in my hands to a weapon in his. Tell me, how far would you go to earn a kiss from her?"

Brichter constructed an image of her reaching up for him, eyes closing, mouth parting, and he grabbed his beer to drown the image in a strong series of swallows. "Pretty far," he admitted, eyes watering, wiping his mouth with the edge of his hand.

"And you can bet Tellios smells that on you. Fine. Now, like it or not, we're calling McHugh in on this. No, not to take over. As consultant. You're going to have to convince Tellios you'd go all the way."

"We haven't got much time for lessons; he wants to see me again at eleven o'clock tomorrow morning."

Ryder frowned. "He's moving fast. He must be afraid you'll get over her."

The image returned unbidden, and was again drowned in beer. Fat chance.

"He'll want you to do something incriminating as soon as he can manage it," continued Ryder, "so he won't have to depend on this infatuation to keep you in line."

Brichter put down his empty glass. "What are the ground rules here?" he asked. "How far can I go to convince him I'm won over?"

Ryder leaned forward and pulled a thick finger for each point. "First, you are not to do anything illegal; second, you are not to counsel him to do anything illegal; third, you are to keep me fully informed of everything you find out, everything you do, everything you plan to do."

"Kind of a short leash, isn't it?"

"Damn straight. Remember my friend on the Chicago cops? He was working undercover and got too eager to prove himself. He took part in a robbery where the victim got shot. He did nine years at Stateville."

"Jesus."

"So you be careful. I was wrong earlier today when I said I'd get you a cheap funeral. You're a good man and I'd hate like hell to lose you. So don't get cute, okay?"

"Yes, sir." Brichter wanted to say something nice back, but couldn't think of anything. Instead he looked at his watch and said, "It's getting late. So long as I'm this close to downtown, I think I'll go over to the jail. There's an arrest report from last week I forgot to sign."

Chapter
6 †

Brichter parked his car in the area of the underground garage reserved for peace officers. He had stood awhile on the sidewalk outside Ryder's apartment, letting the cool air take away the clumsiness too-rapid downing of the beer had brought on, and had stopped on the way to buy a package of mints. He bit down on the one in his mouth as he walked up to the glass cage where prisoners were turned over to the jail.

The basement booking area of Charter's jail had no bars, only lots of knobless doors and thick tinted slabs of bulletproof glass. The new Safety Building was a mixture of state-of-the-art peace-keeping and the cruddy features bid-rigging, bribery, and other old-fashioned practices can bring.

A man in the tan shirt and brown pants of the sheriff's department nodded at Brichter from the other side of the cage, then pressed a button on his console. The door unlocked with a loud buzz, but Brichter had to yank twice to get it open.

"Here to turn yourself in for felony smart-mouth, Obie?" asked the deputy, his voice distorted by the cheap audio system. The thick glass between them was smudged with handprints left by prisoners braced for a search.

"Why should I give you someone interesting to talk to for a change? There's an arrest report Terry says I didn't sign. Have you got it?"

"Not right in front of me," said the deputy, looking. "Hold on; I'll ask the intake sergeant." He turned and walked off.

Brichter looked around the tiny bright-yellow room, with its scuffed floor and stink of vomit and fear. More than six thousand indignant suspects passed through this room last year, he thought.

Thirty of them had been his. For a detective, that was a goodly number, particularly considering the solidity of Brichter's cases.

But Brichter had the unusual quality of being aware of his skills without being any more proud—or falsely humble—about them than if they belonged to someone else.

The deputy came back, turned the sound up and said, "He'll be here in a minute. It's not like you to screw up the paperwork, Obie."

"I know."

"Hi, Obie!" The intake sergeant on duty was Sergeant Oliver Asher, a square-faced Ojibwa Indian Brichter secretly admired for his military correctness in everything from his uniform to the way he ran booking during his shifts.

"Ollie, you got that report I'm supposed to sign?"

"Sure do. Though I'm kind of surprised at you—"

"Yeah, so's Tom. You want me to sign it or are you going to keep it as an oddity?"

Asher laughed. "Come on in; there's fresh coffee."

"Thanks." Brichter put his gun in one of the rows of small lockers in the cage. It was not possible to go directly from the cage to the room in which Tommy waited. He had to wait for the clack that meant the door to the interior was unlocked, go down a short hallway to the area where suspects were processed, then back up another hall, press a call button and wait while yet another door was electronically unlocked. He entered the sanctum where Tommy hovered over his controls, and Asher handed him a Styrofoam cup of black coffee. "Kind of busy tonight," he said, "but care to sit and talk awhile?"

Brichter sipped the beverage gratefully. "Thanks, but it's already past my bedtime, and I'd be rotten company. Maybe you better just bring me the report."

"I'll go get it."

Brichter sipped again. The coffee was almost too hot to drink, but it helped push away the last of the beer fumes. He sat down at a little desk at right angles to Tom, who was surveying TV monitors and operating his doors.

Ahead of Brichter was a very slender woman deputy sitting on a stool, her back to Brichter, filling in a form on an electric typewriter—the computer was down again. She was facing a thick glass partition behind which a suspect stood in a little booth, like the isolation booths on old TV quiz shows. Brichter was aware that this new method of booking was more secure, but he had a sneaking preference for the old way, where the captive sat beside a desk and breathed the same air as his captor.

"What is your date of birth?" the deputy was asking.

"July twenty-third—no, twenty-fifth. I mean, twenty—" He thought. "Eth." The suspect was a young white male almost too drunk to stand.

She didn't enter any of his guesses. "What year?"

The drunk rolled his eyes, obviously trying to subtract the age he had already given from the current year. "Sixty-four?" he hazarded. "No. Sixty-two."

Gently, the deputy asked, "Look, son, do you want to change your mind about any of the information you've given me so far?"

"No, why should I? Jus' gimme time, okay?"

But she whirled her stool around and called angrily, "Will someone hang this jerk?"

"Hey!" said the drunk, alarmed.

"I'll get him, June," said Ollie, coming back with an arrest report in his hand. "What's wrong?"

"Using someone else's driver's license, probably. Unless he doesn't know his own birthday!"

Ollie tossed the form at Brichter and walked toward the door in absolute certainty the deputy would see him in time to unlock it. Seconds later he appeared at the back of the booth to remove the confused suspect and explain that "hanging" meant his booking would be suspended while he sat in an isolation cell and thought things over. The suspension would end when he decided to cooperate.

Brichter shook his head, took out a pen and began looking the report over for other errors.

Meanwhile another suspect had stepped into the booth. "What's your name?" June asked neutrally, her fury of a minute ago gone.

"Daniel Wells Bannister."

Brichter glanced up. Bannister was a notorious teenager, a drunk and a thief, adamantly bad despite repeated efforts by the juvenile court and his upper-middle-class parents. A thin kid whose spiky, mud-colored hair was brilliant purple at the ends, Bannister didn't look very dangerous tonight. He looked as if he had a bad case of flu.

"Mr. Bannister, you are charged with possession and sale of stolen property, resisting arrest, and assaulting a police officer. Please read the information on that card taped to the window telling you the rules here at the jail." She began typing the charge and pertinent ordinance on the booking sheet.

Bannister bent to read the card. His unbuttoned flannel shirt opened as he stooped, revealing the life-size color photograph of a woman's bare breasts printed high on his T-shirt. Brichter grimaced, but if June noticed, she gave no sign.

"Mr. Bannister, do you have a nickname, alias, or other name you use?"

"Roach." The kid straightened and wiped his runny nose on his sleeve. He glanced over her shoulder and said, "Sergeant Brichter! Hey, can I talk to you?"

"What is your marital status?" asked the deputy sternly.

"I'm single. See that guy behind you, at that desk? It's real important I talk to him, just for a minute."

"Look—"

"Yeah, we'll finish your fuckin' paperwork! But ask him first, so he don't bug out on me, okay?"

She turned around. "Obie, do you wish to talk with Mr. Bannister?"

"Since he asked so courteously, how can I refuse?" Brichter's curiosity was roused; it wasn't like Roach to ask to talk to a cop.

Brichter finished examining the report and signed it while June got her information. Then he went into the back area and met Roach in the small medical examination room.

The kid had huddled himself into a gray metal chair beside the gray metal desk, his fingers still blackened from being fingerprinted.

"Something on your mind?" Brichter said.

"Yeah." Roach yawned hugely. "I tried to call McHugh, but he's not home."

"So?" Brichter walked around to sit behind the desk, his quick gray eyes noting the knotted hands, the sweating, the runny nose. "What have you been doing to yourself?"

"That's what I wanted to talk to you about. I got to get out of here, do something to get myself straight."

"I'm not going to pay your bail."

"No, my mom can do that. Just tell me the name of it, okay?" He crossed his knees and hunched forward.

"Heroin, from the looks of you."

Roach drew a trembling sigh. "Shit! But okay, I guess I have to tell you what it is to get you to help me."

"You want me to help you make a *buy*?"

"No, no! I want you to help me get off it!"

"The Detox Clinic at County is very good."

"No way! If I go out there, my old man will find out! I got to get off it on my own! Man, Dad would cut me off at the knees if he found out!"

"You want me to hide you someplace, hold you down till you quit screaming?"

"Hell, no! Look, you cops know things we don't. Isn't there some kind of pill I can take to zonk me for a day or two? I'm almost twelve hours overdue, and I'm not screaming, but I'm coming close! C'mon, Sergeant, help me out here, okay?"

Brichter studied the kid. "Who arrested you?"

"I dunno. A great big guy. Blond, with a mustache."

No one in Narcotics answered that description. "Sergeant Feltgen, from Burglary?"

"No, I know Feltgen. This guy's bigger. Got a name sounds like a hammer." Roach bowed his head and groaned softly.

"Tonk?"

"Yeah, that's what they called him in the cage. And it's a bum rap, honest! That TV ain't stolen, it's mine! He was supposed to give me some horse for it, but he arrested me, the son of a bitch!"

"You assaulted *Tonk*?"

"I was scared, man! The way he reached for me, I thought he was gonna wad me up like a sheet of paper! I hit him one time, on his arm. He laughed about it all the way down here, then stuck me with an assault rap. He said he got a tip I'd be selling stolen goods. Wouldn't listen to me or call my folks or nothin'!"

"That story about the TV can be checked out very easily," warned Brichter.

"So why won't anyone do it, goddammit? Listen, there's a big brown envelope in one of our kitchen drawers; it's got all our guarantees and warranties and shit in it. There's one in there for my TV, got the serial number and everything."

Brichter frowned. Roach sounded very sincere. So why had someone passed along a false tip?

And why give it to Tonk? A malicious prankster would have tipped Narcotics or Burglary, not OCU. "Where have you been getting your heroin up to now?"

Roach twisted in cramp. "Sheee-it!" The room fell silent as he rocked with pain. Brichter watched impassively. Finally the kid muttered, "Everyone thinks because my old man's an attorney, I can get all the money I want anytime I want. That's crap. If it was true, I wouldn't be hurting like this right now."

"You were able to buy enough to hook yourself."

"Huh-*uh!* I used to have this friend who was giving it away."

"For free?"

"Sounds like a crock, don't it? But I swear, it's true."

"This friend have a name?"

"Sure. Look, you gonna help me or not?"

"How about you help me some more first? Why did your friend quit giving it away?"

"He didn't. He just started wanting little favors and some of them were stinkers, like snitching, so I told him to stuff it. I was only skin-poppin'; I thought maybe I wasn't even hooked, y'know? But shit! I found another source, but I didn't have enough money, see? So he told me I could meet this other guy and swap my TV for enough horse to get me through the week. But that big bastard turns out to be a cop. So, please, okay? I swear I won't be such a jerk again. I just want to get clean and keep my folks from finding out. See, I'm eighteen now, and this is serious. If you won't help, do you know where McHugh is?"

"Not if he's not at home. Do you want me to try to find him for you?"

Roach considered this, then shook his head. "Hell, take you all night prob'bly. And he may be drunk when you do catch up with him. I'm gonna be in a bad way here pretty soon. You know McHugh's a good friend of my dad's, right? So you'll sort of be doing us all a favor if you tell me what I want to know! Oh, God; oh, shit!" He twisted up again.

Brichter considered the situation. Pushers seldom gave more than the first hit away, and it had taken a lot more than one to get Roach this solidly hooked. The kid's father was a well-known counsel for the defense, and a member of several commissions; and his son's addiction would be an embarrassing, even damaging, problem to be made public. Now he thought about it, Phillip Bannister's behavior lately had been a little erratic, as if he, too, had been acquired as a friend.

But Brichter knew better than to put a name into the kid's mouth. Roach had to say it first. "I need to know who your friend with the free heroin is."

"God, my head's all messed up! Can't you just tell me what to do? I can't go home like this! Help me and I promise I'll talk to you when I feel better!"

But Roach was far too unreliable a person for Brichter to accept that promise from him. "I'd like to, but you've got to cooperate with me now."

"I can't tell you who he is! Shit, you think I'm the only one he's got doing him favors? I could get killed or something! Okay? Please!"

"I'm sorry, Roach, the only thing I know of that makes withdrawal any easier is at the clinic." Brichter stood and closed his notebook. "It might help your case if you ask to go out there. I don't think you can hide it from the jail officer."

These were calculated, even Jesuitical, statements. The medicine at the clinic was Dilaudid, a powerful painkiller, and it was available via prescription or even on the street as well as at detox. Not that he needed it; Roach was probably not going to get much sicker than he already was. Many before him had gone cold turkey in jail; doubtless most of the deputies who had seen Roach already knew what was wrong with him. Withdrawal from barbiturates or alcohol is much more painful and dangerous than withdrawal from heroin. But Roach was already regretting his venture into heavy drugs, and with the help of some good counselors he might stay clean.

"So c'mon, Roach," Brichter said, "let me take you to County."

"Hell, no! Dad would kill me!"

Brichter said impatiently, "I think, you jerk, your dad already knows!"

Roach snuffled hard, pressing the heels of his hands into his eyes and rubbing. "You're lying to me."

"Am I? Someone's been getting him to do some weird things lately, like he voted to renew Chauncey's liquor license in the teeth of testimony that Chauncey's allows gambling, and he somehow failed to file the papers on time that would have stopped a fight over taxi licensing."

Roach shook his head and wiped his nose with both hands, his expression dull and ill—then sharpening. "You mean someone's blackmailing him?"

"Someone found some kind of handle on him."

"Blackmailing him over me? Are you sure?"

"Sure as I'm sure what's wrong with you. You want to tell me about your friend now?" Brichter's expression was very intent.

"Shit!" Roach shifted uncomfortably in the chair, looking even more stricken than before. He mumbled, "Look, how about I change my mind and let you take me to detox? I hurt so bad I don't know what I want to do. Except I don't want to answer any more questions, okay?"

Brichter gestured angrily, but said no more. Roach, like everyone else, had a right to silence, and once it was invoked any further attempts to question him were illegal and their product inadmissible.

Chapter

7 †

"It sounds like there's a minimum of role-playing in this game you're into," said McHugh. "That's good. Just be mostly yourself. If he says something that would normally make you sore, let him see you're sore. You're not the ass-kissing type, so don't kiss his ass, even if that seems to be what he wants you to do. On the other hand, be polite and be careful to never really lose your temper. I'm not sure what you did to make him think you're in love, since I've never seen you even like anyone before, but whatever it was, don't overplay it. Most people are good at picking up clues, and it makes them think they're smart if they figure out something for themselves. It also keeps them from realizing you're the one giving them the clues."

"Yeah," said Brichter. They were in Ryder's claustrophobic office, Brichter leaning back in the chair, seemingly not listening, McHugh sitting on a corner of the desk, unfolding a paper clip and winding it around his finger.

"Let him know you're poor," continued McHugh, "but don't overplay that, either. Say it like a joke, once, and don't repeat it."

"Right."

"Stop me if I'm boring you."

"That's never stopped you before."

McHugh tossed down the ruined paper clip. "Obie, when are you going to stop being such a goddamn prick?"

Brichter pulled an ear. "You know, it's a funny thing about that word."

"What word?"

"Prick. It's slang for the penis, of course, and by extension it means a pushy smart aleck, a know-it-all. Now the Yiddish word for penis, *schmuck*, by extension has come to mean a gullible fool. That's a cultural difference I find interesting."

"You're a cultural prick."

Brichter opened his mouth to say something, then shut it again. If he yielded to temptation and allowed a quarrel to develop, Ryder would be disappointed in him. And he was beginning to like Ryder. "So go on," he said, "tell me some more about working undercover."

"It can be your ticket to a funeral. Crooks don't like cops finding out what they're up to, and nobody likes to be made a fool of. Get caught doing both together and the reaction is likely to be blood, your blood, all over the place. How the hell did you convince Tellios you're in love with his dingdong niece?"

"First, maybe she's not a dingdong. Second, maybe I'm a better actor than you think."

"And maybe I'm Queen of the May. C'mon, what'd you say? I need to get a picture of what's going on out there between you and Tellios."

"I walked into the barn where she was exercising her horse, and I asked her to show me how she rides him, and she did."

"And?"

"That's it."

"That can't be it! What did you say to Tellios?"

"About her?" He thought. "That it was surprising someone so young could be running a horse ranch. And I looked at her a lot." His voice gentled. "She's worth looking at."

McHugh grinned. "Oh, I get it. Not that hard to look at, is she? And Tellios fell for it. That means he's got a blind side where she's concerned. Great!"

Brichter courteously refrained from shoving McHugh's teeth down his throat. "How do I deal with the three men who work out there?"

"What do you know about them?"

"Ramsey says they're pirates—crooks."

"Okay, you aren't a crook, right? Just"—McHugh put a hand over his heart—"a man in love. And why complicate things for yourself, trying to fool them too? Stay out of their way."

"All right."

"I told Frank to bitch to Tonk that he had you over to his place last night to try to straighten you out and you took it very badly. Tonk will love hearing that, and he'll spread it around. It'll get back to Tellios, and that will help him believe your defection. I'll make a crack or two myself about you." He grinned. "It'll be hard, but I'll force myself."

Brichter nodded. "I appreciate your efforts on my behalf."
"My pleasure."

Brichter parked his car by the jonquils, walked up to the big house,
and rapped on the beautiful front door. Downey opened the door
promptly and gave Brichter a sly grin. "Hi, Sarge!" he said.
"C'mon in."

Tellios was waiting at the door to the parlor. He offered his dry
little hand to Brichter, who engulfed it carefully in his own big one.
"Would you like coffee?"

"Yes, thank you."

The parlor was as he remembered it, a large room so beautifully
proportioned that its size was not startling to the eye, or even apparent until one began to estimate its distances. Tellios went to a
rolltop desk beyond the fireplace, filled a cup and picked it up by
the saucer, then a cake plate stacked with croissants. "This way,"
he said, and led Brichter to a little round table between two oval-
backed chairs. "Sit down. And try a croissant. Professor Ramsey
made them." He went back to fill his own cup.

Hungry, Brichter sat, chose a croissant, and ate it in three bites
before he tasted his coffee, which was strong and hot. Tellios sat
down, selected a croissant, and took a bite as Brichter reached for
seconds. "Good, right?" Tellios asked.

Brichter nodded. "Gordie always was a fine cook." He felt the
following silence to be uncomfortable, and filled it with the subject
most readily at hand. "You said Kori doesn't cook. I'm surprised
she hasn't learned culinary skills from him—or you."

"When she was fourteen she announced she had no interest or
talent for cooking and I didn't force the issue. I find allowing a
young woman her one rebellion prevents the urge from spreading.
She performs her schoolroom tasks for Professor Ramsey to the
best of her ability, which he says is considerable; and when I told
her she could keep her horses only as long as they paid their way,
she took me at my word—and still has the horses. Have you ever
owned a horse?"

"No, sir; I've done some riding, but a horse is a serious invest-
ment; I can barely keep myself in shoes. And you've seen my car."

Tellios laughed and drank his coffee. "Yes, despite all one hears
about a flourishing economy, there are times when a second income seems almost necessary. I'm sorry now I didn't invite you out
sooner, seeing you're so good a friend of Professor Ramsey's.
You've known him a long time?"

"Yes, sir."

"You consider yourself perhaps a close friend of his?"

Brichter tensed; the atmosphere in the room had abruptly altered. "Yes."

Tellios leaned forward and said softly. "Suppose, just suppose, we were to acknowledge that your behavior affects his happiness, even his well-being."

"No, sir, that won't do," said Brichter coolly. "I can't take responsibility for him, since he's your man. He obeys you because you control Kori. I command neither of them. In fact, since you control both of them, perhaps we should say I hold you responsible for their well-being. If something should happen to either of them, I just may come calling on you for an explanation."

"Brichter!" whispered the little old man savagely.

"The name is Sergeant Brichter, Mr. Tellios," said Brichter, "and having gotten that nonsense out of our systems, we can discuss the real terms under which I'll work for you." Brichter held out his hand, surprised at how steady it was. "More coffee?"

Tellios handed over his cup. "Thank you," he said. A spark glowed in the dusty eyes; he was murderously angry. Brichter took both little cups to the Thermos pot on the desk and filled them. As he returned, Tellios said quietly, "You've got more nerve than any cop I ever met."

Brichter's sideways smile appeared. "Then you haven't been arrested very often, Mr. Tellios."

"No. Not in a long while, either." Tellios took his cup from Brichter and put it down. "So tell me why you agreed to come out and see me today."

Brichter sat and said truthfully, "Because I want to continue seeing Kori. I don't think I've ever wanted anything so much in my life. If seeing her means coming to some kind of terms with you, so be it."

Tellios nodded. "But suppose she decides after a while she doesn't like you? Then what? You walk?"

"No, sir. I suspect this deal will have me doing something illegal, which will remove that option. I'm gambling that if I am patient and careful, she'll come to like me."

Tellios narrowed his eyes and said, "You're willing to gamble your whole career on the chance that a young woman may come to like you?"

"My position on the police force has almost always been in jeopardy. I have what is called a 'personality problem.' " Genuine bitterness swelled in Brichter's throat and showed in his voice. "I was sent to the Organized Crime Unit because they work individually and I couldn't get along with any partner. And now the other two in the OCU office are on my captain's neck to get rid of me because I'm such a pain in the ass in the squad room. I work a lot of hours, and I do damn good work. But last night I had to go over to Captain Ryder's apartment and listen to a lecture on getting along!"

Brichter saw Tellios relax very slightly at that and thought, the bastard did have me followed.

Tellios sipped his coffee. "I have heard some stories about you. Still, I warn you, I'll set out to learn if what you've told me is the truth."

"That won't be hard; I'm the subject of scrawls in the goddamn men's rooms! This negotiation isn't necessary, you know; just wait six months for me to be thrown off the force!"

"Bullshit, Sergeant," said Tellios. "The work you do is too valuable for them to throw you out. Later, perhaps, I may have to use my influence to keep your badge in your pocket. But now, are you prepared to take direction from me? For a supplement to your income—and Kori?"

"I was thinking of a thousand a week," Brichter said.

Tellios pulled his lips closed over his misshapen teeth. His eyes narrowed. "Don't you think that's a little high?"

"No, sir." McHugh had said it was a reasonable amount, considering what Tellios thought he was buying. "What do you want me to do for it?"

"The first thing I want you to do is dismantle that file on myself."

"What file?"

"Now, don't start off stupid. You've been adding things to it recently. I want you to remove anything that points to me as a drug broker. Put in harmless paper to replace what you remove."

"I don't know—"

"The day I receive a grand-jury summons is the last day you'll see Kori."

Brichter began a mental listing of all the people who knew he'd been working on that file. He caught himself and shrugged. "I'll do what I can, but as for the grand jury, I don't think that's fair. Others may have the same information I have in a file I know nothing about."

"Make it your duty to find out about them and let me know. Meanwhile, who was the person who phoned in the tip about me?"

Brichter felt his breath catch and turned it into a grin. "You sure know a whole lot more than I thought you did!"

"Who was the tipster, Sergeant?"

"Anonymous. And no, I don't want to try to find out who it was. You've heard the story of the goose and the golden eggs; I'm hoping to hear more from that source. But I knew you'd want something from me. I came all primed with an informant's name to show good faith, and now I feel like a jerk, because he isn't much, and I sort of hoped you'd do a favor for me when I told you."

"You intrigue me. Who is he?"

"A pimp. He's recruiting youngsters for his string in Chicago, using cocaine to turn their heads. Evidently Januschka hiked up the prices he charges for each girl this guy ships out, and to make it up, the pimp's been selling pushers to me. That fellow I arrested two days ago"—he was the one whose arrest report Brichter had failed to sign—"he was the second." The pimp had not been selling pushers, but he was stupid, greedy, and arrogant, and when Brichter told Tellios his name, there was belief on Tellios' face.

"And what was the favor?"

"I'm hoping telling you will get him run out of town. I don't approve of fourteen-year-old prostitutes."

Nor, apparently, did Tellios. "Very well, Sergeant, you've accomplished your goals. Your pimp will leave town shortly. You realize, I hope, that you've put yourself in my hands by telling me this. How about I pay you a thousand dollars a week for one month, after which we'll negotiate further payments based on the value you show to me? I'll get the first installment to you by this time next week."

"Fine." This won't take a month, thought Brichter. He finished his coffee and as he lowered the cup caught the tail end of a smug expression on the gangster's face and thought with a chill, the old man doesn't think so either.

Tellios stood. "You are a very unusual man, Sergeant Brichter. I don't feel yet that I've acquired a friend, but perhaps we may be able to get along, if neither takes the other for granted."

"Yes, sir."

"Would you care to visit Kori and Dr. Ramsey before you leave? She's at her lessons, but a minute's interruption shouldn't hurt."

He hesitated. How would he react if this agreement with Tellios was real? "No, I don't think I want to talk to either of them—I mean, I've got to get back; Captain Ryder will be wondering where I've been."

"I understand. Come back this evening if you like."

"Yes, sir. About seven?"

"Fine. You'll feel better about things by then. And in a day or so it will be as if nothing has happened."

"Yes, sir." Tellios walked companionably with him to the door, but Brichter felt a dusty brown stare on his back as he strolled down the sunlit lawn toward his car.

They were working on a numbers-theory program and Kori was not doing well.

"All right, take a break," sighed Ramsey, and she gratefully swiveled the chair around to put her back to the screen. "You really must concentrate more on this, pet," he grumbled. "I don't know how you manage the horse business when you're so bad at numbers."

"It's different when it matters," she said. "What do you suppose your friend is talking to Uncle about?"

"You. He's negotiating for the right to continue seeing you."

She stared at him. "Uncle will never agree to that!"

"He very well may. You see, Peter is pretending to allow your uncle to suborn him, with you as his price."

"No, I don't want that to happen! Gordon, I won't see that policeman again."

"Why not? He's here to help us."

"I don't need help."

"Yes, you do. Your uncle is a gangster, and things are going the wrong way for gangsters, thanks to Peter and his co-workers in the Organized Crime Unit. Your uncle may do something foolish if he feels he is about to be arrested, and I don't want that foolish thing to concern you."

"Uncle is not—" She stopped. "I want nothing to do with this. Besides, Uncle's far too clever to be fooled by your Sergeant Brichter."

"Your uncle is a frightened man, and Peter is extremely clever, and, in this case, highly motivated." She twisted the chair around so her back was to him, but he went on, "He knows Peter and I are friends. He must suspect that I have told him what I think is going on out here. Unless he can be convinced he has Peter under control, he will extract the severest penalty he can think of from me for betraying him."

"What penalty?" She turned back. "He wouldn't harm you! He

knows what I think of you, how much I—" She stopped. "How much I depend on you," she said, amending.

"He also knows that you and I discuss many things. Has he ever asked you about our conversations?"

She shook her head. "Just generally, such as what century am I studying, or have you given me any Cicero to read. Why?"

"He has never asked you what I've told you about your parents? Or my own past? Or what I suspect about his past?"

Her frown deepened. "No. Well . . ." she stopped again. "Now and then he will ask me to repeat as much as I can remember of a discussion we have had. I told him once that, if he is so curious, he should just come sit in on my lessons, but he said no, he didn't have time for that."

"What discussions has he wanted repeated?"

"He was very interested in that too-many-people-for-the-lifeboat discussion we had. And, oh, I forgot, he said to tell you that he agrees with you that Dante was right to put traitors in the deepest part of hell." She turned back to the screen. "But I'll make a bet with you. I'll see Uncle at lunch, and he'll ask me what I thought of Sergeant Brichter and tell me I won't see him anymore. Meanwhile, Eratosthenes was an ass, and his sieve is a humbug." She studied the screen. "Is seventeen a prime number?"

"Yes."

"Then why won't it fall through the hole?" She began to punch new instructions into the computer.

"Hello, Nick?" said Januschka's voice.

"Hello, Joseph."

"Say, I just heard from Jilly. Tonk Erickson came by her place at noon for a quickie and told her things are coming apart for Brichter in the squad room. Brichter's boss had him over to his place last night to try to straighten him out, which isn't gonna happen. Sounds like he'll be getting transferred out of there real soon."

"No, he won't."

Januschka cut off a chortle in midstride. "What?"

"I want him to remain where he is, at least for the time being."

"Oh yeah? Why?"

"Because Sergeant Brichter just left here, and for a grand a week he's agreed to see the light."

"You think—you *really think* you bought off *Brichter*?" Januschka's voice rose high in an effort to keep from shouting.

"Goddamn it, I told you what she told me this morning! He's on to you!"

"Of course he is; that's what brought him out in the first place. But he took one look at Kori and he thinks he's in love."

"You're not gonna let that son of a bitch talk to her!"

"He's already talked to her. He can hold her hand if he wants to. She's been quite well lately, and he's so smitten he ignores any small . . . anomalies in her behavior. It's only for a week or two, you know."

"You stupid old man! You're taking a hell of a chance! Who knows what she's picked up here and there about you and your operation? I told you, I've already got a pipeline set up through Tonk and Jilly. Why take that chance?"

Because Tellios fed on the exercise of power. He saw Brichter in a few weeks' time broken, obedient. He said, "It never hurts to have a backup, Joseph. By the way, Whitlock is coming to see me this afternoon."

"And you're gonna sic him on the professor the same time you try to make friends with Brichter."

"I know what I'm doing. Trust me."

Kori went upstairs to change into her oldest working clothes before coming down to lunch. She studied her face in the dresser mirror as she buttoned her shirt. It looked grave and pale—but she was a solemn kind of person, and naturally pale, so that was all right. She mustn't let Uncle see her looking different. Why was Gordon so frightened? It was his fear that had infected her, not her own worries, not the increasing tension she sensed in her uncle. Uncle could stand tension; he was a powerful person. And he loved her. Nothing else was important in her shrunken list of priorities. Uncle would not allow Sergeant Brichter to trouble her, so why should she be afraid? She looked down at her trembling hands. Stop it, she said, and watched them until the trembling stopped. There. She glanced at the clock on her dresser—Uncle liked his little girl to be prompt—and hurried out of her bedroom, down the back hall, down the back stairs and into the kitchen.

Tellios turned to greet her as she hurried into the kitchen. She was wearing old jeans and a faded chambray shirt, her foal-delivery costume. Tellios said, "Any time now, I see."

"Yes. This will be the last, thank goodness." She sat down, looking tired and subdued.

He picked up a dipper and a bowl. "What do you want on your half of the ham and cheese?"

"Mustard, I suppose."

He filled the bowl and brought it to her. "Beef and noodles," he said. "Your favorite. I made a big pot; I'll freeze it in those single-serving bags so you can have it whenever you like." She didn't reply, but began to make a production of spreading her napkin across her lap. He frowned. "Is something wrong with the mare?"

"Hmmm? No." She picked up her spoon.

"Arithmetic woes again, I take it?" He went back to the counter, put a slice of bread on a plate, then collected a generous yellow dollop from a jar on a knife.

"Yes. Well . . . no."

His elbow worked as he spread mustard on the bread. "Tell me what the problem is, Koritsimu."

She lifted a lumpy spoonful of soup and poured it back again. "It's not a problem, exactly. Just—questions."

He sliced the sandwich in half, brought the plate to the table, and sat down. "Questions?"

She glanced at him and down again. "Silly questions."

He smiled, reached for his half of the sandwich. "So, ask me a silly question."

She hesitated, and he wondered if she was thinking up a way to ask a difficult question or thinking up a silly question to comply with his request. She was not as easy to read as she once had been. He smiled to show he was just being friendly-curious.

"Have you ever been in jail?"

The smile vanished. "I would call that more an impertinent question. Who put you up to asking it?"

"No one. But Riscatto says you've been lots of places and done lots of things, and I wondered if you'd ever gone to jail." She looked at him, troubled and hopeful. She wants the answer to be yes, he thought, surprised.

He said, "Suppose I told you that I once spent a night in jail."

"What was it like?"

He considered. "A humbling experience. Why do you need to know?"

"Do policemen look for reasons to put people in jail?"

Ah. "Some do."

"Suppose—suppose a policeman should want to put me in jail?"

He wanted to laugh; instead he took a bite of his sandwich, and said around it, "I'm afraid I find that hard to believe."

"Just suppose."

He swallowed and quashed that fear firmly. "Under no circumstances would I allow anyone to take you to jail. Do you understand? So long as I am here, you are here. Now, what put that silly idea in your head?"

"Sergeant Brichter—"

He let the laugh out this time, made it reassuring. "You have nothing whatever to fear from Sergeant Brichter. I wouldn't allow him to come back for a visit if I thought there was any danger in him to any of us."

She could not conceal the dismay. "He's coming back?"

"Yes, this evening." He felt a stab of suspicion. "What has the professor been telling you?"

She hesitated. "That Sergeant Brichter is an intelligent person who means no harm."

"There, see? So you will be polite to him? Just for a few days?"

"Yes, Uncle."

Chapter
8 †

When Brichter went back to the office, he found Ryder and McHugh waiting.

"Well?" demanded McHugh.

"He offered me a thousand a week and conversation with Kori to gut our file on him."

"He's moving awfully fast," said McHugh.

Ryder, not sure he liked that, asked, "Did you agree?"

"Sure."

"So you're in out there," said McHugh.

"He says he's not sure we're friends, but maybe we can do business together." Brichter went to his desk and got out his notebook. He wanted to record all he could remember of the conversation while it was still fresh. He was a careful note-taker, the truth behind a street rumor he never forgot anything he saw or heard.

"So what's next?" asked Ryder, following him.

"I'm going out to talk to her and Ramsey this evening." He sat and opened the notebook.

"Don't forget to mix a little business with the pleasure," counseled McHugh.

The cold gray eyes swept him. "Haven't you got an operation of your own to run?"

"Hey, I'm on your side, remember?"

"If that means you feel you have to lead me by the hand, then get away from my side, okay? I want her safely out of there, oh, maybe six hundred times as much as you do. I have every intention of bringing her out with me tonight when I leave— Captain, I want to talk to you about a place we can hide her and Ramsey from Tellios."

McHugh blinked, then laughed. "You really are gone on her,

aren't you? You hear him, Frank? I guess there's something human inside there after all!"

"Lay off, Cris," said Ryder quietly.

McHugh snorted. "Are you saying he hasn't got it coming? After all his cracks about Tonk and his ladies?"

"I said, lay off, Cris," repeated Ryder. "Obie, when you finish with that, come get me; we'll talk more about this over lunch."

Brichter, writing, did not look up. "Yes, sir."

"Well, to hell with both of you, then," said McHugh, surprised. "I guess I know when I've worn out my welcome." And he stomped out.

Tellios reached out and pressed the "Stop" button on the little recorder. "I'm sure you can see, Mr. Whitlock, how anyone hearing this recording would vote to convict you on a charge of murdering Mr. Woodruff."

Whitlock, perspiring lightly, studied the recorder as if considering how fast he'd have to move to acquire it. He was a short, thick-necked, heavy-shouldered redhead, about thirty-five, with a densely freckled face.

"Perhaps you noticed the poor quality of the sound," continued Tellios. "That's partly because it was recorded during our phone conversation and partly because it's a copy. The original recording is not at the ranch, but in the hands of someone who has instructions concerning it."

"I sure hope you haven't let that someone listen to it," Whitlock said.

"Of course I haven't," said Tellios. "I have no desire to get you into trouble. You're a friend, Mr. Whitlock. Didn't I explain that to you when I offered to get your loan-sharking case dismissed?"

"Yeah, but I didn't think you had a recorder going when we talked."

"I'm sorry about the subterfuge, but I needed a way to encourage your sense of responsibility. Have I succeeded?"

"Oh, yeah. Sure."

"I'm about to offer you an important job."

Whitlock's little blue eyes shifted warily. "What kind of job?"

"I want to kidnap someone."

Still wary, but grabbing at an opportunity, Whitlock asked, "Do I get to ask for a ransom?"

"Naturally. Fifty thousand dollars. Only, as is so often the case, your victim will not be returned alive."

Whitlock relaxed. "A hit job, you mean. Shit, is that all? I can think of ten ways right off the top of my head to make someone disappear forever."

"No, you don't understand. I want the body to be found."

"Why?"

"Because I would be disappointed to pay the ransom and have your victim turn up at the Safety Building alive and . . . vindictive. I am going to treat this as an actual kidnapping; that is, I will call the police—"

"Hey, now, I don't think trading one murder rap for another is any kind of a deal!"

"Don't worry; I won't call them until I've paid the ransom and you are far away. And I'll be upset over this terrible thing, so I probably won't report all the details correctly."

Whitlock leaned back in his chair, stretched his short legs out in front of him and stuffed a freckled hand in a denim pocket. ''Is this person someone I know?"

"That would be extremely unlikely."

"Someone you know?"

"Yes, someone here at the ranch."

"You're going to a whole lot of trouble when you got a barnful of horses. Aren't horses all the time kicking people in the head?"

"No, they aren't."

Whitlock's little blue eyes squinched into a smile. "And anyhow, I heard that a long time ago you used to arrange fatal accidents. Up in Chicago, right? And the cops know it."

"I was never charged in connection with that."

"Yeah, but I guess you want to keep as far away from this as you can." The redhead raised his free hand. "Hey, okay, that's only being smart. And I'm willing. So what you want is for me to snatch this person, keep him around until you pay me the money, then kill him, right? And you lie to the cops about getting phone calls or ransom notes or whatever."

"You call me as soon as the victim is in your hands. The murder will occur immediately thereafter, quickly and cleanly, *before* the ransom is paid. You will place the body where it will be easily found. You have a reputation for facile promises, for lying and for reneging on deals. None of that is to happen this time. I will be angry if my instructions are not followed exactly as given, and anger may cause me to do something you will regret. Do you understand?"

Whitlock glanced at the recorder. "Yeah," he said.

"Fine. Now go about your business as if we never had this conversation. Don't try to contact me; further instructions will come from Mr. Januschka."

Whitlock grimaced. "I don't know if that's a good idea. He's not too happy with me right now."

"This is our way of giving you a second chance. It's important that you show him you know how to follow orders."

"Yeah, but he's not one for following the rules himself, you know. Like he says, if I wanna go on with my loan-sharking, I got to give him a share. That ain't the way it works; shies are independent operators. Are you gonna let him do that?"

"I don't give orders to Mr. Januschka; he's capo in Charter. I only advise him; whether he takes my advice or not is his business."

There was something in the way this was said that made Whitlock wink and grin, as if at a shared joke; and he responded to the tone, not the statement. "But maybe you'll advise him to change his mind?"

Tellios lifted his narrow shoulders into a little shrug. "If I am particularly pleased with the way you handle this job, I will speak to him about you."

Again Whitlock heard the tone as well as the old man's words. He nodded. "Okay, it's a deal. Who is it and how do I make the snatch?"

A few minutes later the pair came out onto the front porch to find a fine, cold rain sifting from the clouds. Whitlock shrugged himself into a blue windbreaker. "A shitty day," he observed.

Tellios did not answer; he was looking off toward the racetrack gate, where a girl on a wet bay was fumbling with the latch.

Whitlock leaned against a pillar of the porch, tucked one toe against the outside edge of his other foot, worked his fingers into a pocket and flapped an elbow at the girl. "That Kori?" he asked.

"Yes." Tellios waved and she waved back. "The rain must have brought her in early. Go on, leave now; she is not permitted to meet strangers unprepared."

Brichter made his way through the maze of fabric dividers to Geoff's cubicle and stood a minute, watching his friend and waiting for him to notice he had company.

Sir Geoffrey of Brixham was being Geoffrey Collins today, he of the three-piece suit and credit manager's job. Brichter watched as he punched customer numbers into his computer and checked their credit limits against orders salesmen had brought to him. He finished the last of a small stack and cleared his screen. When he sat back he caught the presence out of a corner of his eye and swiveled his chair around. "Hi, Pete!" he said. "How long have you been standing there?"

"Not long."

"What can I do for you?"

Brichter didn't like working his way up to a topic, and with friends didn't bother. "I've met a girl who's knocked me right over. But she's in a mess, and I'm not sure whether or not some of it is of her own making. She's not only out of my reach, she's scared to death of me."

"What do you want me to do? Talk to her?"

"No, I want you to teach me how to talk to her."

"I don't understand."

"Look . . ." He stopped, half turned away and tugged an ear. "All right, listen. There's this girl, and, for the first time, a boss I like. And the boss is leaning on me to get along with my co-workers, which for once I'd like to do. Only I don't know where to begin. You know me, I open my mouth and something smart-ass comes out. You're my expert on courtesy. Can you give me a simple rule to live by?"

"I dunno. But lesson number one: Say 'please' and 'thank you,' even to your friends. Especially to your friends."

"Please make up a rule even I can remember."

"Sure." But Geoff had to think about it for a minute. "Okay. Bite your tongue."

Brichter waited but there was nothing more. He asked, "That's it?"

"You asked for a simple lesson. Courtesy is the art of kindness, of doing good, of saying what others have to hear in as unoffensive a way as you can. To accomplish that you have to listen—really listen—to learn what they need. Once you start doing that, they stop being targets or an audience, and you'll stop insulting them."

Brichter thought that over. "Like when you arrest a heavy suspect, you watch everything he does and says for clues."

Geoff laughed. "Well, in a nicer way, of course. If you buy me lunch tomorrow, I'll let you talk my ear off about her."

Brichter reached for a sharp comeback, but then looked at Geoff and saw only sympathetic interest. "Okay," he said. "Yes, I'd like that." He started to turn away, then turned back. "Thank you."

† † †

Brichter found Nelsen after lunch, patrolling the River Street district. He signaled him over. Nelsen was riding alone. "This won't take long; I just want to talk to you about the night you went out to Tretower on the Price murder."

"That was a hell of a long time ago."

"I know. But there's no statute of limitations on murder."

"You thinking of reopening the case?"

"Maybe. What do you remember about it?"

"It was my first dead bodies. Jumpin' Jehoshaphat, that woman was a sight!"

"About the child you found—"

"Katherine, yeah. I remember her from before it happened. Her dad used to raise Welsh ponies, and she rode one in a Fourth of July parade, all of four years old she was, cool as ice, like a little princess."

"Tell me what happened that night."

"Sure." But Nelsen's account, though without all the "proceedings," differed little from his account in the report, and sounded perfectly straightforward. "Tellios was upset, I could see that. He was especially worried about the kid; I guess she was kind of his favorite niece or something. He just came right up to me in the kitchen and yanked her out of my hands, and walked out. I don't think he said a word, but she'd deafened me with all that screaming, so I can't be sure."

"I see. Well, thanks, Nelsen, you've been helpful."

Nelsen squinted a puzzled eye up through the squad-car window. Brichter was not known for his good manners. "Okay, if you say so."

Brichter headed for the ranch—as before, early. Just as he turned into the long driveway from the road, he saw a green pickup truck crossing the racetrack at the other end, heading out. He stopped and backed up, waiting. The pickup halted at the road and Downey, riding passenger, rolled down his window. "Hiya, Sarge!" he said cheerfully. He turned to the driver, a bald-headed man with piercing dark eyes, and said, "This's Sergeant Brichter, y'know."

"Yeah?" said the driver, unimpressed.

Downey said to Brichter, "This here's Guy Riscatto, another one of us."

"Uh-huh," said Brichter, remembering in time to forget his manners.

"Do somethin' for ya?" Riscatto asked.

"I'm here to see Dr. Ramsey."

"The professor's not home."

"Then I'm here to see Miss Price."

"He can do that, it's okay," said Downey.

"I know. Check in at the house first, okay?"

"Sure." Brichter parked his car just beyond the twin white maples marking the foot of the walk up to the big house. Grape hyacinths were blooming in the grass around their roots, perfuming the air. Ramsey's antique MGA was nowhere in sight.

He glanced up at the big house, decided another way to show contempt for the trio was to ignore their instructions, turned and went to the barn. The only sound was of contented hay-munching. Kori was not there.

Brichter left the barn and wandered around a little, afraid to be too obviously searching, noting discreet alarm boxes and the location of two more big pole lights.

Not far from the barn, against the racetrack's inner fence, was a kennel setup for five dogs. The dogs, large German shepherd crosses, were locked inside. They ranged in color from cream to mostly black, and watched him with a chilling professional interest. The door to each run, he noted, opened onto the track, and could be operated by a lever from this side. He didn't speak to the dogs, and they didn't bark at him.

A few minutes later he was walking by a green shed and a large chicken startled him by squawking out from behind a half-open door. He heard a low woman's voice coming from inside, and a horse's *huh-huh-huh*. He looked around the door. Kori, in jeans and chambray shirt, her hair covered by a red scarf, was behind a four-board fence, kneeling in deep straw beside a brown horse. The horse was lying down.

"Hello, there," he said.

She started. "Oh, it's you. Could you go find Riscatto for me?"

"I saw him leave as I arrived," he said.

Her mouth tightened, and she stroked the horse's face. "Was Downey with him?"

"Yes. Is something wrong?"

"Do you know anything about horses?"

"I read a book about them once, called *A Leg at Each Corner*."

A collection of cartoons about English children and their ponies, it was ludicrously inadequate to the present situation, but she was not amused.

He approached the fenced area with its deep bed of straw. "Are we going to become a mother?"

"Yes. Do your trousers wash?"

"Yes, I think they do," he said. They were brand new, bought to impress her. "How do I get in?"

"There's a gate down there." She pointed.

He took his jacket and tie off, laid them over the fence and entered the enclosure. "This her first?"

"Yes. I think it's mostly that she's scared."

"Has her water broken yet?"

"Yes, long since." She gave him a speculative look. "I don't remember that being in *A Leg at Each Corner*."

"Maybe it was in another book then. I read a lot of books."

"Look, can you help or can't you? Gordon said policemen deliver babies all the time."

He waded through the straw to stand beside her. "It's a funny thing, but none of the babies I ever delivered was a horse. What do you want me to do?"

"Go down to the other end and wait."

He did as he was bid and noted the mare's tail had been closely wrapped in coarse red sacking.

She said, "Watch it, here we go again."

The mare strained in silence, her belly distorting. "She doesn't seem to be in any great pain," he said.

"No, but she's tired, and nothing's resulted from all her efforts. Riscatto said an hour ago she'd be fine, but also that he'd check back before he went to pick up my grain order. I guess he forgot."

The mare strained again, and he stepped back out of the way as a tiny pair of legs in a filmy sac appeared—and went away again.

"Hey, first sighting," he said. "Two forelegs, I think."

"Oh, good!"

"They didn't stay out."

"That happens."

"So now you call the vet, right?"

"No, I'm— Not yet."

She's not allowed to make phone calls, thought Brichter, with a stab of anger. Give her rotten help and tie one hand behind her back. "Is there a phone in the barn? I can call."

"No, you'd have to go to the cottage or big house. And things aren't that serious yet, I don't think. Does Uncle know you're here with me?"

"Uh, no. He doesn't know I've arrived, probably. I'm early; I hoped to find you in the barn like I did that first time."

She stared at him. "Why do you needlessly complicate things? You're supposed to be so clever—" She stopped, dismayed. "Sorry, I didn't mean—" She thought. "Perhaps—have you been here long?"

"Fifteen or twenty minutes. I was looking around."

"Then he's probably seen your car. Is Gordon back?"

"No. Look, Mr. Tellios didn't seem angry when I came to the barn alone the first time. I didn't think it would be all that serious if I did it again."

"Everything with Uncle is serious."

"Sorry. But first things first. I think we've got a baby to deliver."

The mare's hind legs were stretched in spasm, and Brichter saw the two tiny legs reappear, one slightly in front of the other, encased in a wet, filmy sac strewn with blood. This time they did not go back in. Brichter squatted and patted the mare's rump. "Atta girl," he said. "What's Mama's name?" he asked.

"Bitter Wind."

"Is she related to Summer Wind?"

"No, I put some kind of 'wind' into all my horses' names."

He smiled. "The Arabs called them Drinkers-of-the-Wind because of the way their noses flared when they ran."

"I don't remember that from *A Leg at Each Corner*, either."

"I think it was in that other book. The Arabian is the world's oldest recognized breed. They average fourteen and a half hands in height, have one fewer vertebra in the back and two fewer in the tail than other breeds, and are the most human-oriented of horses."

"Yes, I know," she said.

The mare strained again. This time a small dark head emerged, lying on the upper forelegs, and, following Kori's instructions, Brichter broke the sac so the foal could take its first breath. Things progressed rapidly after that, and soon, there was a skinny, exhausted baby horse on the straw. "It's a boy," said Brichter, pleased.

The foal shook his head gingerly and blew a bubble through his nose. He looked very thin and frail. "Let's get him dry," she said and went for some more sacking. She gave Brichter a piece of it, and they rubbed the newborn down, both to dry it and stimulate its circulation and breathing.

"Well," she said critically a few minutes later, daubing iodine on the stub of its umbilical, "I was hoping for another filly, but he sure is pretty!"

"He looks kind of skinny to me," he said.

"They come like that," she said. "But look at that cannon bone!"

"Okay," he said, looking.

She smiled. "Well, at least you know where to look."

The two left the birthing area to let the mother sniff and lick her newborn and make gentle noises at it.

"That was neatly done," said Brichter. "Relatively speaking," he added, looking at his trousers.

They leaned on the top railing and watched the foal try to stand on its own. Brichter was charmed into smiling at the new life struggling to unfold, to stand on ludicrously long legs and stagger toward the big warm shape that was Mother. Bitter Wind was up now herself, and blowing warmly to encourage her baby.

The quick, rolling opening notes of Bach's "Jesu, Joy of Man's Desiring" in a lovely, liquid whistle began. Brichter had always fancied himself as a whistler, so when the appropriate place came by, he began the melody. She immediately stopped whistling and stepped away from the fence. "I have to go now, Sergeant Brichter," she said shyly. "They'll be all right for a while."

"Hey," he said. "I didn't want you to stop."

"I wasn't whistling for you. I do it sometimes without thinking."

"You do it very well."

"Thank you, Sergeant."

"You could call me Peter."

"I . . . don't think so."

"Look, my name is Otto Peter Brichter. My friends call me Peter, but you can call me Obie for now, if you like."

Diverted, she cocked her head. "Anything but Otto?"

"Yes."

"I think I prefer calling you Sergeant Brichter."

"Anyway, I enjoyed helping you."

"You weren't bad for a beginner."

"I'm not a beginner cop."

"No? Then Uncle should have more respect for you." Obviously reminded, she said, "Go to the cottage. I'll tell Uncle you're here. If he wants to . . . talk with you, he can call you on Gordon's phone. If not, then I—I suppose I'll see you again tonight." And she was gone.

Chapter
9 †

The door to the cottage was unlocked. Brichter made free with a towel and washcloth in Ramsey's bathroom, then went down and made a pot of coffee in the kitchen. The phone didn't ring.

He was in the living room, working on a second cup and reading yesterday's paper, when he heard the front door open. "Peter?" called Ramsey's voice.

"Here!" he replied. He got up and went to find Ramsey struggling to close the door while encumbered with two large sacks of groceries. He took a bag. "I hope you don't mind that I made myself at home."

"Not at all. Sorry I wasn't here; I went out to buy for supper and got carried away."

Brichter helped put things away in the kitchen, then stayed to chop greens for the salad.

The feature of dinner was steak and kidney pie. "Not bad, if you don't think too much about the kidneys," said Brichter. He described his assist with the birth of the foal. "It's messy and ugly in one sense—I ruined my new trousers helping out—but when it's over, there's this brand-new life trying hard to breathe and stand and suck, discovering he has eyes and nose as well as ears, and lots of space to fall down in. And there's first-time mama, snuffling at this strange, spidery creature, falling in love with it, and you begin to think instinct's not such a cold thing after all."

They moved into the living room. The evening was warm, and Ramsey made no move to close the two big latticed windows open to the fragrant air. The two men sat in companionable silence, sipping coffee.

Brichter spoke at last. "How come no one's ever gotten suspicious about this insanity story Tellios puts out?"

"Because virtually everyone who meets her has heard the rumors about her 'condition.' Naturally, they treat her oddly—and so take away the notion she's odd. What she thinks of them she doesn't say."

"Have you ever seen any sign of genuine psychosis?"

"I've never seen her lose her temper or cry, but you saw how Tellios boasts about those traits and so reinforces them. It's not that she lacks those emotions; I have seen her sad and I've seen her angry. She merely becomes silent until she gets over it. Like you do."

"Isn't it abnormal for a female in our culture not to display sorrow and anger?"

"Under normal conditions, yes." Ramsey wriggled uncomfortably. "All right, from what I saw of her the first year or so after I came, there was probably enough of a worry about her to at least give Tellios the idea for the psychosis tale. But if she was overwhelmed by what happened and escaped the only way she could, she has recovered magnificently. When I came to Tretower—" He stopped, remembering, and began again, in a different voice. "When I came to Tretower, I was angry that I should have been forced to leave a life I loved to become a . . . baby sitter. Hmmm? My anger frightened her, but I saw no reason to care. And then I became so involved with self-pity that I missed seeing her first subtle expressions of sympathy. When I did, it was a revelation. That this damaged and cruelly orphaned child should find it possible to feel sorry for me shook me to my roots. I don't know from what sturdy stock she springs, or what solid base her parents had already built for her, but it has been the greatest pleasure of my life to nurture and educate her. She saved me, Peter. She gave me back my self-respect."

"I'd say you saved her, as well."

Ramsey said, without a trace of pride, "Yes, that's true. It was so incredibly unlikely that we two should meet, and there was nothing else that could have done us so much good, that I am inclined to see the hand of God in it."

"Tellios found you and brought you here; you see Tellios doing the work of God?"

Ramsey shrugged. "I asked Kori in a test if she knew what God was about when He allowed a child to be born dying of cancer. She wrote a lovely little essay, saying in effect that assuming a mere human could understand the work of the Almighty was like assuming the horse that pulls the plow could understand land management."

"Fair enough. Does she ever hint that she understands more than Tellios thinks about what goes on at the ranch?"

"No. But if this were Elizabethan England, I'm sure she could adopt the Queen's favorite motto as her own: *'Video et Taceo'*—I see and am silent. No one but she knows what's stored deep in that lovely head."

"Would she tell me if you asked her to?"

"Perhaps. That's what you want me to do tonight, isn't it?"

Brichter nodded. "Yes." He asked, "Did Tellios ever try sending her to a regular school?"

"When she was eight, she was put into a class of first graders, children younger than she, and between that and the teasing—children can be even crueler than adults—she took it hard. Tellios pulled her out, but when he found her trying to teach herself to read using a favorite book, he decided she would benefit from private lessons."

"And no one ever came out to check on her?"

"I suspect the county was so grateful she was not dumped into its already overburdened system, it was content to leave things be."

"Captain Ryder said he has seen her in town a time or two."

"Yes, she's done a little shopping, but Tellios comes along, hovers and interrupts, and so she prefers to shop by mail. She goes to horse shows and auctions, but Riscatto is the one who goes into the ring or places the bids. She's been to Chicago two or three times to visit museums and the zoo and the Sears Tower."

"Movies? Theater?"

"No, Tellios rents video prints of things she wants to see. She reads the newspapers and subscribes to a number of magazines. She goes to church at Christmas and Easter. I take her; those are the two times a year she is permitted to leave the ranch without Tellios or Riscatto along."

"Yeah, but we've missed Easter and Christmas is a long way off." The companionable silence fell again, then Brichter asked, "Are you writing anything?"

"A monograph on fifteenth-century English nunneries."

"A nice, dry, respectable subject."

Ramsey smiled and replied, "A bishop once came calling on a royal English abbey—over which he had no jurisdiction, since it belonged to the crown—and tried to give the nuns a papal bull forbidding them to go gadding off on pilgrimage, as was their wont. Not only did the abbess have him ejected bodily from their property, she threw the papal document at his head to speed his journey. You may recall, Peter, that the term 'bull' comes from the Latin *bulla,* a large and heavy lead seal attached to such communications. Her choice of weapon was not only apt, it was potent."

Brichter laughed. "I had forgotten why I took so many of your courses; you made those historical figures live and breathe as real people. I bet that abbess was a tough old bird."

"She had to be; those were tough old times."

A knock signaled Kori's arrival. Ramsey went to the door and Brichter heard his anxious question, "Is your uncle angry about Peter's not coming to the house?"

And her reply; "No, but he's not pleased, either."

Ramsey showed her in to where Brichter stood beside his chair, and left the detective to entertain her while he went for more coffee and a cup of hot chocolate for Kori.

She was wearing a soft dress of pale green. Her incorrigible hair, so dark it appeared black in any but the strongest light, was done up in two braids wrapped around her head, from which fine strands of it escaped to curl in across her temples and down in front of her ears. She looked incredibly lovely in the soft light of the standard lamps, but there was an unnatural stillness about her, that same careful not-anything air he had seen about her at the dinner table last time. She doesn't want to be here with me, thought Brichter, unable to come up with words to change her mind.

At last she said, "I heard Gordon talking about medieval abbeys as I came up."

"Um," he said. "Yes. Would you like to sit down?" He indicated his chair, and she took it, curling up in it like a cat, and as watchful.

He leaned against the mantel and tried to think of a safe subject of conversation. He wanted badly to kiss that tender mouth. He wanted to know if she realized what kind of murderous bastard her uncle was. He asked, "You know something about medieval history?"

"My tutor specializes in fifteenth-century England. I knew who won the War of the Roses before I mastered seven times anything."

So this was her badly skewed education, he thought. Grateful he belonged to the Society for Creative Anachronism, he asked, "Who's your favorite English king?"

"Richard the Third."

He was surprised. "That 'bottled spider'?"

"He was a good man," she said warmly. "He was famous all over England for his justice. He was a brave soldier and a loving husband and father."

"Richard the *Third*?"

"When he was killed at Bosworth Field in 1485, the city fathers of York, who knew him very well, wrote in their official public record, 'King Richard was piteously slain and murdered, to the great heaviness of this city.' "

"Are we speaking of Old Crouchback, who murdered his brother's sons to secure his claim to the throne? What have you been reading?"

"Gordon has a book by Paul Murray Kendall. Kendall uses primary sources to show what Richard did and was like according to people who knew him. I don't know how policemen sort out these things, but the man Kendall discovers had such unbending ethics I don't think he was capable of a treason like murdering the king's sons. That they were his nephews only makes it less likely." She looked him full in the face and her courage failed her.

There are two kinds of German faces. One is round and jolly. The other Brichter had, lean and long-nosed, wide at the back of the jaw, with thin lips and pale eyes, cold in his sharply-drawn face. When surprised or doubtful or angry, an intimidating face. "I—I'm sorry," she stammered. "I must seem always to be scolding you." She began to get up. "Perhaps you should excuse me. Gordon may want some help."

"No, stay!" he said, accompanying the sharp order with a gesture that made her shrink back into the chair. He pulled an ear, then stuck the offending hand in a pocket, and when he spoke he had gentled his tone. "What you've told me would stand as evidence in any court."

"You're being very kind."

"No, I'm not," he said and the lie made him smile. The wry movement of his thin mouth made him appear much friendlier. He said, "Honest, you've about convinced me I should take another look at the last bud on the Plantagenet vine."

She smiled back, then appeared to cast about for something else to say. "Gordon told me you have a friend in the—" She paused to recall the name. "Society for Creative Anachronism?"

"Yes. Two friends, actually. Well, one's my cousin, Anne. The other is her husband, Geoffrey. I'm kind of a member myself—Lord Stephen Shutzman, that's my SCA name."

"There was an article about them in the Sunday paper around Christmas last year. They did a medieval feast, with a real boar's head. It looked like such fun."

"I was there, and believe me, a boar's head is much better to look at than to eat," he said and she laughed, a sound that delighted him.

"I'd like to introduce you to Geoff and Anne," he said. "You'd like them. Anne can sew any costume you can show her a picture of and Geoff—well, Geoff's a 'verai parfait gentil knight.' "

She smiled at him. *"Sans peur et sans reproche?"*

"Yes, but not snotty about it. You are very beautiful."

"Thank you." His abruptness made her uncomfortable again, though she tried not to show it, and even to return the compliment. "I—I like your hands."

He looked down at them, surprised.

Ramsey entered with a tray holding cups and a small plate of sugar wafer cookies. "Are you going to do a magic trick? Showing us nothing up your sleeves?" He put the tray on the coffee table. "Take my chair. Peter; I'll get another from the study." As he left the room he said over his shoulder, "She likes them large and square; I don't know where she got her taste in hands."

Brichter, whose hands were indeed large and square, with blunt fingers, looked at them as he sat down, then at her. He could think of nothing to say.

She looked away—he was staring, he caught himself at it and grimaced, and was glad she wasn't looking at him grimacing at her. She said, "I like medieval history, but I don't get so intense about other historical figures, only Dickon." Which was, he knew, the correct medieval diminutive for Richard. She was trying to recapture the pleasant mood of a minute ago; he wished Ramsey hadn't told him over supper that she was under orders to be nice to the policeman.

He said, "Anne takes the Middle Ages personally, too. Only she prefers England in the fourteenth century."

"An interesting time, the high Middle Ages, with its three Edwards; England in succession at its best, its worst, and best again. Castles and Chaucer and John of Gaunt. I'd like one day to visit—" She stopped, sipped her cocoa.

" 'This royal throne of kings, this sceptred isle, / This earth of majesty, this seat of Mars, / This other Eden, demi-paradise'?" he asked.

"The real thing is often a disillusionment," she said. "I've seen so much of it in books and movies, I'd probably be disappointed in the real place."

"Never!" declared Ramsey from the hall. "Disappointed in England? 'This happy breed of men, this little world'?" He appeared in the doorway, dragging a third wing chair, grunting with the effort.

" 'This precious stone set in the silver sea'? *If* you can tear yourself away for a moment, Peter," he added, and Brichter went to help.

" 'Against the envy of less happier lands . . .' " murmured Kori softly into her mug.

As the third chair was set before the fireplace, Brichter said, "I've been there. And everything you've read about it, every movie set there you've ever seen: they're all true."

"But Shakespeare, as always, says it best," said Ramsey, seating himself and reaching for a cookie. "Peter, would you close the windows? It's getting cool."

And if she heard us as she came up, so could another eavesdropper listen in, thought Brichter, drawing the curtains as well. The effect was to make a safe haven of the room. He wished it were not necessary to take them away from this friendly place.

"Where were we?" asked Ramsey, as Brichter returned to his place.

"I'd like to borrow a book of yours by Paul Murray Kendall," he said.

"Ah," Ramsey smiled. "Her good Dickon. Very well, remind me before you go home." He put down his cup and said carefully, "Pet, you know Peter and I have some things we want to discuss with you."

She said immediately, "I've decided I don't want to discuss anything with you I can't tell Uncle about."

"This isn't just for your sake, you know," said Ramsey. "Peter is investigating a serious crime in which he thinks your uncle is involved."

"He's not just involved," corrected Brichter. "He's in charge of an illicit dope operation being run right here from the ranch."

"I don't believe you," she said.

"Also," continued Brichter, ' 'I have reason to believe your uncle has some degree of authority over Joe Januschka, who is in charge of organized crime in Charter."

"What makes you think that?" asked Ramsey.

"When I asked him to do me a favor and help run a pimp out of town, he said to consider it handled. That means he either can arrange it himself or order Januschka to do it for him. He also said he was the one with the connections necessary to keep my badge in my pocket after I began following his orders."

"I don't understand; what orders?" asked Kori.

"For one thousand dollars a week and the right to visit you whenever I please, I am to remove any incriminating evidence I have against him from my files and prevent, so far as I am able, any other investigator from looking his way."

"But that means—" She stopped, frowning.

"That means he is a criminal!" said Ramsey fiercely.

"No, no," she protested. "Not altogether. You don't know, Sergeant." She glanced at Ramsey and away. "You don't know."

"What don't I know?" asked Brichter.

She appealed to Ramsey, "Please, Gordon, I don't think I want to continue this."

"There's nothing you can tell him he doesn't already know or suspect. Go ahead with what you were about to say."

"But it concerns you too."

"I know. And he knows. It's all right; go ahead."

"Well . . ." She put her mug on the coffee table. "I believe my uncle runs some kind of business that's against the law. The fact that he insists I not be curious about it, and that I stay away when he has certain visitors to the house, makes me sure of it. But there's this other thing about him: He takes dishonest people and makes them be good. Downey and Riscatto and Shiffler are crooks, but so long as they work for Uncle, they have to behave as honest people do. And—and Gordon. Uncle knows he did something—shameful. I have no idea what it might be, but I'm sure that's so." She looked at Ramsey, who sighed and gestured at her to continue. "So you're here now, and between writing books and articles, you are educating me, showing me how to explore the world without having to go out there. And I—" She stopped short.

"What about you?" asked Brichter.

"I've done some wicked things too. I betrayed Downey and—and—You know, don't you, Gordon? I told you the dreams, and you know what it is. You haven't told Sergeant Brichter about the dreams, have you?"

"Yes, he has," said Brichter.

She was very frightened. "Uncle was wrong then. I asked him and he said not to worry, that he wouldn't let a policeman arrest me, but now it's come, hasn't it?"

Brichter's heart sank. Was she insane after all? "What are you talking about?" he asked. "I haven't come to arrest anyone."

"Yes, but if you know about the dreams . . ."

"The dreams are of your parents," said Ramsey gently.

"Yes. You didn't tell me that; you didn't want me to know. Just like Uncle. But more and more memories are coming now."

Ramsey, bewildered, said, "You remember your father loving you, and you are beginning to remember the night they were killed."

"Yes, the night I killed them."

"Don't talk nonsense!" said Ramsey.

"You *remember* killing them?" asked Brichter.

"I remember coming down the stairs and hearing a big quarrel," she said. "And I remember them lying on the floor and the blood . . . And the man—Papa, it was Papa—saying 'Run away!' And I remember running and hiding from the police, and Uncle making the policeman let go of me, saying he would not let the policeman take me away."

"More dreams?" asked Ramsey.

"No, some of it's coming back as real memory. Just bits and pieces. Out on the porch with Uncle, who held me and petted me. I was desperately afraid, I remember. The policeman had dragged me out from behind some bowls. I thought that was a dream-part, but now I remember the bowls. They were tan and yellow and pink, and some had flowers on them. They're for making bread; there are still two of them in the pantry."

"They were in a kitchen cabinet," said Brichter.

"Yes. The policeman had been looking and looking for me. Calling, 'Come out, Kori,' in a horrible whispery voice . . ." Her eyes went stary as she looked back at the memory.

"I can't believe you killed your parents," said Brichter.

"I don't remember doing it," she said, "but I know I did. Why else was I hiding from the policeman? And why was he hunting for me?"

Brichter said, "Frightened children run even from rescuers. Anyway, the homicide report says a burglar killed your parents."

"A burglar who took nothing and was never caught," said Ramsey. "Peter, Kori has come independently to approximate my conclusion about Tellios: He catches people in a wrong and offers to protect them. If they agree, they find themselves trapped into obeying his every whim. The policeman whose report concluded a burglar was responsible may have been one of those. Or are you the only policeman he has attempted to corrupt?"

Brichter thought of Tellios' certain knowledge of that file and frowned. "No, I guess not."

"What will you do with me?" asked Kori. "Will you put me in jail?"

"No," said Brichter. "Of course not."

Her face was a white blank. She had been braced for an arrest, that was obvious. "Why ever not?"

"First, I have no evidence," he said. "You don't remember doing it, there are no witnesses to say you did it. I don't think your assertion of guilt at this remove is valid."

"Suppose I did kill them?"

"I can't imagine sending a twenty-year-old woman to prison for an offense, even a felony, she committed when a very small child," said Brichter. "And suppose you didn't? I wouldn't want to arrest an innocent person. The best suggestion I have off the top of my head is a hypnotist. A good one may enable you to remember all of what happened. But I don't know; you were only six at the time."

"Suppose she had been taken in charge at the time?" asked Ramsey.

"I've never done much with juvenile crime," said Brichter. "But okay, suppose. She would probably have been found insane or of diminished responsibility, put in a hospital, cured and released. Though I've never heard of it happening to a child under ten, if she'd somehow been found delinquent and put in a juvenile center, they couldn't have held her past her nineteenth birthday." He looked at her. "By almost any description, your uncle has been your jailer. So all right. You've done all the time you possibly could. More. At twenty, you're overdue for release. Time for the warden to receive a writ of habeas corpus and explain in court why you're still being held."

"Uncle? Oh no; he must never know of this! He thinks I don't know! If he found out, he might not want to protect me any more, and—" She gestured and said, more quietly, "I don't think I want that to happen."

"No, pet," said Ramsey, "this is not protection. This is a prison, and it's long past time you were set free."

"But—but I've been happy with Uncle!"

"Have you?" asked Brichter.

"Mostly!" She looked on the verge of tears, whether of relief or terror Brichter couldn't tell. But then she swallowed and the signs of incipient crying went away. "I will admit I've been unhappy the past few months. Uncle has been . . . less easy to live with. The others have noticed it too. Shiffler hardly speaks to anyone,

Downey drinks and is surly, and Riscatto is so hard on the horses I've canceled my plans to show them this spring."

"What do you think is getting to him?" asked Brichter.

"I don't know. He's had fewer visitors; perhaps his business is slacking off."

Brichter automatically reached for his notebook. "What do you know about your uncle's business?"

"Nothing. Oh, that he has visitors? Yes. But what of it? Anyone might conclude he's running some sort of business from the way the fly-in visitors are treated, more like customers than friends. Shiffler drives to the airport to meet them and takes them back again. He says their clothes are very expensive. I'd guess there is money involved; Uncle usually goes into town with a locked brief-case the day after they leave."

"So Shiffler is the man I need to talk to about this," noted Brichter, writing.

"No!" she said sharply, and he looked up at her, surprised.

"I said no such thing! Shiffler is . . . ignorant and stupid and, and—" She gestured as if waving a fly away from her face. "He's nobody."

"Downey," Ramsey mouthed at Brichter.

"I see," said Brichter, pretending to cross out Shiffler's name. "Do you ever meet any of these visitors?" he asked her.

"No—well, not these visitors."

"Does he have a great many?"

"What would constitute a great many?"

"Two or more a week, perhaps?"

"No. There are far fewer than that. Three a month would be closer to an average. That's including people from town. Twice a year, near Christmas and in the summer, there's a large party, which I don't attend. When guests stay late, I sleep here, in the cottage. Once we had a blizzard, and the guests couldn't leave, and I stayed with Gordon all the next day as well, except for chores." She smiled at Ramsey. "That was rather fun."

"Who have you met? Can you remember their names?"

"I met a lady from town. Her name was Mrs. Severance."

"The alderwoman?" said Brichter, surprised.

Kori bit her lip, but admitted, "Yes. She was very polite and just a little nervous."

"How many times have you met her?"

"Just once, last summer, though I think she's been here three or four times. And a Mr. Bannister. He's an attorney, Gordon says.

I've met him twice, though he's been here more often. He appeared sad when I shook hands with him. Not paying attention."

Brichter said, writing, "Who else?"

"His Honor the Mayor."

"Mayor Johnson?"

"Yes. He was here just once, I think. He was nervous too—almost scared. Of me, I think, though I can't see how that could be. His hand was wet with perspiration when he shook mine. He looked as if he expected me to spontaneously combust or something."

Brichter laughed. "I bet, the old cummerbund! It's a wonder that man keeps getting reelected, the way he lathers up in uncomfortable situations."

"Uncomfortable?" said Kori.

"Pet," said Ramsey, "there is a general rumor that you have never quite gotten over a mental breakdown you suffered after your parents were killed. Your uncle allows them to believe it is only the kindness of his heart that has kept you out of the hospital all these years."

"I see," she said blankly. "That explains many things, doesn't it? I thought it was—well, I never knew why people looked at me as they did. Or rather I did, but maybe—" She stopped, then began again, feeling her way. "I've always felt I had this terrible secret, that I was secretly a bad person. And that I had to be extra good, to please Uncle, who knew what I was, and to make up for being wicked.

"I remember a time of living inside myself, when everything outside of me was dark and slippery, except Uncle, who was very close and breathing on me all the time. Then there was a kitten. Small and funny, I remember, and I started to get well after that. Much later, when Summer Wind was born, and grew up better than anyone thought he would, and he was my choice and the result of my training, that seemed to mean I couldn't be so very awful. I've known for a long time Uncle was wicked, but I thought only a wicked person could love me." She looked at Ramsey with wounded eyes. "I'm sorry, Gordon, but you see, I knew there was something—something you were ashamed of."

"Oh, my very dear child," he said.

"So, you see, it would be almost better to find I'm insane than to know I did a terrible thing while in my right mind."

"That poisonous villain!" said Ramsey. "You did nothing wrong, nor are you insane! Tomorrow I'll explain to you why I came here. I had no idea you thought so badly of yourself, or I would not have allowed this to go on all these years. I'm sorry, I apologize."

"Dear Gordon," she said. She turned to Brichter. "What else do you want to ask me?"

He consulted his notebook and asked, "Is there any connection between Tellios' visitors and your horses? That is, could the horse operation be some sort of cover for the drug operation?"

"No. I handle the horses altogether. Uncle hired Downey, Shiffler, and Riscatto, so they're his, but they obey me in matters pertaining to the horses. I schedule the stud and decide which shows what horses are to attend. When people bring their mares to the ranch, Riscatto deals with them, sometimes with Uncle, but they are people I know about."

"Hasn't this ever bothered you, their taking all the glory?" asked Brichter.

"They don't take it all," she said. "Horse people know who I am. They know my stallion and his offspring, and know I deal honestly with them. Years ago, Uncle acted for me, because I was so young, but the decisions were mine. I do more of it now, but I've never insisted on taking over completely. He loves me and he's proud of me, and letting him pretend to be the one doing it was a delicious secret. Like our secret language."

"What secret language?"

"A kind of game we used to play. It started farther back than I can remember. Words like *kala* for 'good', and *kako*, for 'bad'; we used to argue over broccoli with those words and confuse Downey. And there is *see agga poe*, which means 'I love you.' Just silliness. Words he made up to have a secret meaning."

Writing, Brichter asked, "Was it a whole language, or just those few words?"

"Not a whole language, but more words than that. There was *ella* for 'come here,' and *Kook-lah* for 'doll.' "

"Do any of the others at the ranch know what these words mean?"

"No, just the two of us."

Ramsey said, "It's typical behavior. Tellios likes secrets, especially the kind you can display without anyone guessing. Like me. Like the dogs."

"There doesn't seem to be anything secret about the dogs," said Brichter. "I saw them."

"They aren't ordinary dogs, Peter," said Ramsey. "They are brutally trained killers. Shiffler turns them loose at night to roam the racetrack, as a backup to locking the gates, and they would tear apart anyone crossing in either direction, without a bark or growl of warning."

"Jesus!"

"That's another pattern of his behavior," said Kori. "Backups. He likes being doubly prepared. He installed a bottle-gas generator years back in case of power failure, and kept the kerosene lanterns anyway, in case the generator failed. He has two of every suit, in case he wants to wear one and it's at the cleaner's or gets soiled before he leaves. You should have heard him approving of the several backup systems on the space shuttle."

"Much good it did them. And as for the dogs and locked gates, the gates were left open when I came in last time, and they were open this time, too. I don't see why I can't sneak the two of you out when I leave."

"Oh no, that's impossible," she said. "He told me at dinner tonight that from now on, when you're visiting, the gates are to be locked, and you aren't to leave until I'm back in the big house with him. He said he doesn't mind you being impulsively early, but he doesn't want you to take me on an impulsive car ride."

"That'll teach me to be impulsive," said Brichter, who almost never was. He got up and went to the window. "The gates are closed," he confirmed.

"Oh, that's wonderful!" said Ramsey angrily.

The phone rang, and Ramsey went to answer it. "Hello?" he said, and glanced at Kori. "Yes, she's still here. It is?" He looked at his watch. "Oh my, yes, it is late. We were talking and didn't realize—" He was interrupted.

Brichter consulted his own watch. "It's quarter to eleven," he said, surprised.

"That's very late, for me," she said. "I'm up before six."

"I'd sooner cook three meals a day than rise before six," Brichter said.

She cocked her head at him, a gesture he remembered from the maternity shed. "Who told you I don't cook?"

"Tellios. He seems to think you deliberately chose that as a form of rebellion."

She smiled. "Does he? How interesting."

Ramsey hung up in a mild sweat and said, "Mr. Tellios requests that Kori come home at once."

She stood. "Then I'd better go."

"Was he angry?" asked Brichter.

"I couldn't tell. I hope not; it's important he not be angry with her."

"Or, more importantly, with you," said Kori. "He thinks of me as a child, more done to than doing, so he tends to blame others when I do something that annoys him. But if Uncle were really worried about you he'd have sent Downey, and if he were angry, he'd have come in person. Where's my cape?"

"In the kitchen," said Ramsey. They got it, Ramsey wrapping her in it as if it would protect her against any danger, and they walked her to the door.

"May I come and see you again?" asked Brichter.

"Uncle says you may."

"I'm not asking him; I'm asking you."

She studied his face a long, uncertain while, then gave a barely perceptible nod. "Very well; you may call on me again." She held out her hand for a brief handshake. "Thank you for an—interesting evening, Sergeant Brichter."

They watched her stride off into the night. Brichter said, "No wonder she was so scared of me, thinking I was going to arrest her. I hope she was right about being able to handle that malignant old man."

Ramsey murmured, "Judith."

"What?"

"Have you ever read the Apocrypha? There's a story in there about a brave lady named Judith who saved her city-state from an army by walking a very narrow line into the heart of the enemy camp. I must be sure to go to church this Sunday."

"Say a prayer for yourself, Gordie; I don't like you staying out here."

"I don't like it either. Call me tomorrow, preferably with an idea. If Shiffler answers, hang up."

"That isn't funny."

"It wasn't meant to be."

Tellios had had a visitor while Kori was at Ramsey's cottage. Joe Januschka sat on the medallion-back couch in the parlor and tried to stare down the little old man on the cane-bottomed chair across from him.

"You can't deny it; I saw his car out on the gravel," said Januschka.

"Why should I deny it?"

"After I warned you, you're still letting a goddamn cop on the place to talk to two civilians who know more about your operations than I do?"

"Koritsimu knows nothing, so even if she wanted to say something bad about me, she couldn't. And I *own* the professor; he doesn't have eggs for breakfast without checking to see if I think it's okay. I'd feel safe letting the chief of police talk to both of them alone."

"Shit, so would I! But we ain't talking the chief, we're talking that bastard Brichter!"

"Sergeant Brichter has been breathing funny ever since he met Kori. He thinks he has found the grand passion of his life. Inside a month I'll own him, too."

"He's running a con on you," said Januschka.

"If this were McHugh, I'd agree with you. But Brichter, for all his other talents, is . . . incapable of maintaining a deceit. That's why this is so amusing. He came out to see if what he had heard about me was true, but quite on his own and against my wishes, he met Kori. Now he knows the truth, but he no longer cares."

Januschka leaned forward and jabbed a forefinger at Tellios. "That's what you think. You're just like him, you know that? Think you know goddamn everything!" He was so angry he could no longer sit, and once up, he began to pace. "I've had it with you and your games! I'm calling for an end to it now! When Brichter leaves this place tonight, he's not coming back. You make your call to Whitlock first thing tomorrow and finish the professor. Then you call a mental hospital to come and get Miss Rosebud, and you put her away. Because you are putting this place in the hands of a real estate agent. Tell him to send the check to Florida, California, Arizona—wherever you want, so long as it's far away from here. Because this is it: You are out of here, as fast as you can move."

Tellios sat very still. The blood had drained from his sallow face, leaving it a pale yellow. "You can't order me—" he began.

"The hell I can't! You think you can forget who I am? You been poking and pushing your way into my business for over a year! Pretending you want to help me, giving me advice I don't need. Letting everyone know I depend on you. You want back in the outfit? Fine! But you either work for me, or you climb over me! I ain't gonna play dead and I sure as hell ain't gonna take you for a partner! I warned you a long time ago I knew what you were trying to do, but you wouldn't listen. So here it is, old man: You made it to seventy-four; you want to make it to seventy-five, you do it some-where else!"

Rage warmed Tellios' blood, which flooded back into his cheeks, but when he spoke, his voice was almost gentle. "You think you can make me go?"

"I got no choice, Nick! What you been doing is giving us—all of us—all kinds of problems. The cops are breathing down every-one's neck, TV and the newspapers are wondering real loud about Whitlock getting off, and the feds are gonna blow into town any day now. My people look to the boss for help, only they ain't sure who he is anymore! I'm sick of warning you; here it is in plain En-glish: You're gone. One way or another, you're gone."

"I've got friends in Chicago, Joseph."

"Bullshit. You were run out of Chicago, and now I'm running you out of Charter. Agree to go, *now*, or by God I'll shoot you my-self, *now*."

"You won't shoot me, Joseph."

Januschka's hand went into his pocket.

"Because your car is out there," continued Tellios. "Unless you bought it new today, I think Brichter will recognize it." While Januschka stopped long enough to sort out the implications of this, Tellios stood and went quickly to his desk. He picked up the phone and punched seven numbers. Someone answered and he asked, "Professor Ramsey, where's Kori? It's nearly eleven." He listened briefly. "Never mind, just send her home now. Thank you." He re-placed the receiver. "There. The front door will open in a minute and they'll all see your car in the drive."

Januschka began to laugh. "Nick, I got to admire you for that." His hand came out of his pocket.

Tellios came slowly back to his chair and sat on it as if his bones hurt. "On the other hand," he said, "I'm getting old. I can't fight an old-fashioned war with you with as few men as I have. Suppose I acknowledge that you are boss not only in Charter but over my op-eration. What kind of share are you after?"

"No, no shares, Nick. You just showed me you're too slick for me. I want you out of town. I'll give you a week."

Tellios frowned. "I don't think a week is reasonable, Joseph. Here, think about my counteroffer. I have an extremely profitable operation, you know. Between the two of us, we are about to neu-tralize the Organized Crime Unit, which means business will soon be back to its former levels. This is the wrong time for us to be-come enemies."

"We're already enemies! We been enemies since you came here, you and your stinking 'friends' and your high-tone notions of dinner with the mayor and concerts. You were born in the same gutter as me, Nick; and you made your bones the same way I did, knifing someone in the back! So now you're old, and you use words instead of a knife. Well, you made your words work tonight, but remember, a bullet may work on you next week. If you're still in town seven days from today, you're a dead man."

Januschka turned on his heel and strode for the door. Tellios watched him go. He wished he'd stayed by the desk; there was a gun in one of the drawers. It would have been interesting to have pulled it on Januschka, showed him he still knew the use of bullets. But the door slammed, and the opportunity was gone.

Tellios went to the window to watch the two men walk to their cars. Januschka was afraid of Brichter while Tellios was not; yet Tellios was afraid of Januschka, now.

Januschka was too unpredictable. He might decide tomorrow to call and accept the offer of a share in the brokerage. Or he might renege on his offer of a week's grace and, in a day or two, when the key was turned, six sticks of dynamite would turn Tellios' car into a fiery wreck. Januschka's famous temper was mostly for effect, a reflection of his style of governing—but when he was genuinely angry, as he appeared to be tonight, he was like a shark in bloody water.

Funny how Januschka assumed Tellios couldn't take Kori with him into retirement.

But he was right, there was no way. Those goddamn dreams, that name. He wished she hadn't told him about the dreams. It was almost like she was on Joseph's side, helping him declare the game over.

He heard the door open and went out to intercept Kori. "How was your evening?" he asked.

"All right." She turned so he could help her off with her cape and stayed turned away yawning while he hung it in the armoire.

"What did you talk about?"

"Richard the Third and the War of the Roses. Sergeant Brichter called him a bottled spider."

Tellios knew she liked King Richard. "You didn't quarrel with him, did you?"

She turned to face him. "No, of course not."

"Good, I'm glad you remembered to be nice to him."

"Is polite okay instead? It's easier to be polite than nice to some-one like him." He laughed in pleasure at this sharp appraisal that so meshed with his own. She yawned again and went on, "If it's all right, I'm tired and I'd like to go right up to bed."

"In a minute. What else did you talk about?"

She sat down on the stairs and began to remove her shoes. "Well, feudal England. Sergeant Brichter said he has a cousin who also takes history seriously, and the fourteenth century is her favor-ite."

"Anything else?"

There was a silence while she thought. "We talked about the foal."

"Have you named him yet?"

"Yes."

"What?"

A trifle reluctantly, "Copper Wind."

"Because the policeman helped deliver him?"

"No, it's for his color; he's even redder than his father."

"Do you like Sergeant Brichter, Koritsimu?"

She shook her head. "Sometimes he looked at me as if he were thinking like a policeman. He . . . made me uncomfortable when he did that."

He nodded. "Cops are like that, always poking their noses in where they aren't wanted." Still testing, he asked, "But this one isn't altogether bad, is he? The professor likes him; those two are best friends."

"No they aren't!" she said sharply. "I mean, I—I sort of think Gordon doesn't like him so much any more."

"Why not?"

She hesitated. "I don't know. But he doesn't, I'm sure he doesn't."

"Very well. You may go up now."

He watched her climb the stairs and vanish down the hall toward her bedroom.

She had never learned to lie. He would call Whitlock now.

Chapter
10 †

Early next morning, as was her custom, Kori rose, and just before seven, dressed in boots, fawn jodhpurs, black sweater and riding coat, she was crossing the dew-wet grass, casting a weather eye toward the risen sun. The sky was a clear blue; it was going to be a beautiful day.

She went into the box-stall area of the barn and flipped on half of the lights. Summer Wind poked his head over his box-stall door and thumped a hoof against it.

"Yes, I see you, baby," she said, smiling, and went to get his saddle and bridle. "Sorry, I'm late."

She led him out of his stall and snapped the end of a rope hanging from a wall onto his halter. He moved restlessly on the end of it. "Stand still, now," she warned. "We don't go until you're dressed." She smoothed the saddle pad over his back and put the saddle in place. "Uncle got up when I did this morning, which he almost never does," she said. "And he insisted I have a slice of toast and a cup of coffee with him. He was very nice and gentle with me, more than he's been for a long while. I'll speak to Gordon as soon as I can about it. Uncle scared me last night with those questions, and I don't like the way he was this morning. Pleasant but something else: Sad? Angry? As if he were preparing me for bad news." She pulled the cinch tight. "Maybe I'm being paranoid—which I understand after last night is what is expected of me by most of the people I've met—but I don't like this at all. Uncle watched me from the porch, so I couldn't go anywhere but here, but as soon as I get back I'll tell Gordon, who will phone Sergeant Brichter, who will find some way to get Gordon out of this. Which I think might be a good move." She pulled the stirrup down and smoothed the leather over the strap, then stopped to muse, "I wonder if I should go with him." Summer Wind pawed the brick

103

floor and looked around his shoulder at her. She smiled and said, "Well, all right, I'll ask if you can come, too. Do you think you can squeeze into the back seat of a squad car?" The horse looked away and blew a raspberry and she giggled.

She came around to his head with the bridle. "Such a big, bright baby you are," she said. He reached forward to accept the bit, and rattled it impatiently against his teeth while she unfastened the halter and buckled the bridle behind his ears. She went back to his left side, said "Ho, now," and mounted.

Much as she loved the stallion, Kori had thoroughly trained and disciplined him, and he sidled obediently back and forward as she opened the barn door from his back and closed it again, repeating his performance at the two gates of the racetrack, swishing his tail and blowing at the dog that stood nearby.

They followed the outer racetrack fence around to a trail that climbed a steep hill, where yet another gate needed to be opened and shut. Once that was done, there was no barrier between them and the east end of the ranch.

They set off at a trot, but, in an excess of energy, the bay broke his trot to dance and mock-shy at a rabbit that leapt out in front of them. She laughed at him, riding him through his antics easily. He was only permitted this misbehavior now, at the beginning of his morning ride, when there was no one to see him being less than perfectly mannered.

A few minutes later, when he was warmed up, she galloped him flat out in a big circle on the new grass of the meadow, drew flying up in rainbowed mist all around them. Then, both breathing hard, they slowed to a walk and came back onto the trail.

"Good baby!" she cheered, smacking him several times on his hard neck, and he nodded agreement.

In a minute he'd caught his wind and she pushed him into a canter, a pace he was holding as they approached the grove of old oak trees that marked the limits of the ranch.

Suddenly his head came up. She pulled him back into a walk and looked where he was looking, but saw nothing. "Alarmist," she scolded. "It's probably just a bird fight."

They were nearly at the grove when a redheaded man in a blue windbreaker walked out and waved at her. "C'mere, lady!" he called. He had a rifle cradled in his other arm.

After the briefest of startled hesitations, she whirled Summer Wind and started to flee, but there was a flat *whack!* and the animal went instantly into a somersault. His tumble was so abrupt she had no time to prepare for a fall. She went over his shoulder and landed on her left hand—which exploded in pain—and then on her head.

She was sick and dizzy. Something was in her eyes. She could not hear Summer Wind either up or trying to get up. Dazed, she tried to get her own feet under her. From behind, there was the sound of someone running toward her. She leaned on her left hand to look around, and pain darkened her vision.

Someone grabbed her, crowing with delight. "Hi, there, cowgirl!" He swooped her effortlessly into his arms and began to run.

"Horse," she managed to say. "Hurt?"

"Naw, he's fine."

The voice was unfamiliar. She tried to lean back enough to see his face, but he pulled her close to his windbreaker. "Hold still." A moment later he stooped; they were climbing through the fence.

"I'm not supposed to leave the ranch without Riscatto or Dr. Ramsey," she said, for the first time frightened.

"That's all right; you're with me." Which was nonsense. Was she dreaming?

She got a glimpse of the back end of a car, trunk open, before he put her down in it. He put a hand on her shoulder to hold her still and said, "Quiet down. Everything's gonna be just fine."

He released his hold and she immediately twisted around enough to wipe at the sticky stuff in her eyes. She glanced at her hand, not surprised to see blood, then looked up, blinking, half blinded, to glimpse a strong-looking man whose blue jacket was smeared with red. He was flipping a handkerchief over to form a triangle.

"Why did you shoot my horse?" she demanded.

"Here," he said, "let me put this around your head." He tied the handkerchief around her forehead, pulling the point of it down over her eyes. "Can you see?" he asked.

"No. I don't want to go with you."

"Duck back," he warned. "I'm closing the lid."

"Did you kill Summer Wind?" She felt a rising panic.

"I just winged him a little. Get down." She cringed back as the lid slammed shut.

A few seconds later the car's engine roared, and they bumped and waddled briefly down a bad road to a good road, then accelerated along it. It felt as if they were flying. The man had lied, she was sure. Summer Wind was hurt, maybe dead. When Uncle found out, he would be furious.

After a long time on the road, there was a series of stops and turns before the car stopped for good and the engine was shut off. She heard the car door slam and gritty footsteps, and then the trunk opened. "Hi, there," he said, cheerful as if she'd accepted a friendly offer of a ride in his trunk. He helped her out, keeping hold of her more tightly than she felt was necessary. He led her to a door, inserted a key, and took her in. The room was big, hollow, and smelled of dust and mildew.

He led her up three steps, then across a wooden floor, pulling her now and then to avoid obstacles, and sat her on a bench whose seat was curved for comfort. It had a smooth back.

"Now," he said, "let's have a look at you."

She sensed the shadow of his hand in front of her face, then the end of the handkerchief was raised so she could see. He was bending over her, as curious about her as she was about him. Except he was not afraid.

"Hi," he said.

"Who are you?" she asked.

"I ain't gonna tell you."

"Are you going to let me go then?" she asked.

"Now why would I let a nice lady like you stay in a place like this?" he replied.

His voice was mocking, false. She looked beyond him at the room they were in. It was a church, a small, shabby one. The pointed windows were not stained glass but some pebbly stuff that permitted light but no vision. There were only three pews left, and one of them sloped to the floor, its end broken off. A lot of floor space was taken up by large boxes full of clothes and rubbish, which explained the weaving necessary to get her from the door to here. They'd come in by a side door; she could see it at the bottom of its little well across the room. In the front, where the altar used to be, was a large round table and six mismatched chairs, two of them wooden. Empty beer and soft-drink cans, cards and a shiny-new cordless phone were on the table.

"Not much, but it keeps the rain off," he said.

"My wrist really hurts," she said.

"Lemme see."

She held out her left arm, and it was taken in a strong grip halfway up the forearm. She gasped with pain and began a reflexive struggle to pull loose, but he tightened the grip and pain became a flashing, whirling thing. "Let go; please let go!"

"Quit fighting and it won't hurt so much," the redhead said

calmly, watching her. With a mighty effort she relaxed her pull and
he loosened his hold a little. "See?" he said. But then he turned her
arm sideways to look at it, and the pain flashed anew. Don't pull,
don't pull, don't pull, she thought. "This arm looks broke all right.
But that head may not be as bad as it looks. Anything else broke?"
The grip tightened again. "You hear me?"

"Yes," she whispered.

"Answer when you're spoken to, hear?"

"Yes."

"Anything else hurt?"

"No."

"I don't want any trouble out of you while you're here. You understand, Kori?"

He knew her name. "Yes."

"Good." The grip abruptly loosened.

She said, "I want a doctor." She would tell the doctor to call her
uncle.

He laughed. "Aw, you won't die from a busted arm!"

"What do you want with me?" she asked.

"You'll see," he said. "Take your boots off."

She didn't want to do that. "I can't one-handed."

"Sure you can." There was a hint of ambiguity, as if, were she to
insist she couldn't manage, he would take them off in a way she
would find unpleasant. She began to push at the heel of one boot
with the toe of the other.

He took several steps back, until he came up against one of the
narrow wooden pillars that supported the ceiling. He leaned
against it carelessly, hooked the toe of one foot against the outside
of the other, shoved a hand into a denim pocket and watched her
struggle with the boots until she managed to get her feet out of
them. "See?" he said, smiling, flapping an elbow at her. "You
never know what you can do until you try." His hand came out of
the pocket with several lengths of twine. "I'm going to tie you up,"
he said, approaching. "If you try anything stupid, I'll break your
other arm." No ambiguity this time; she was sure he'd do it.

He tied her feet first, tightly and efficiently, then studied the broken arm for a few seconds before laying it on top of the good one
and tying one to the other. "See how good I am to you when you
behave?" he asked. "Splinting your arm and everything. You be
sure to tell your uncle that when you talk to him."

"When will I get to do that?" she asked eagerly.

"Soon's I call him up," he said, looking up in time to catch her dismay.

"Oh no, you're a long way from going home," he said with that terrible grin, and she began to realize she might never go home at all.

Tellios filled a Thermos jug with coffee and took it and his cup into the parlor, where he sat at the rolltop desk. His face, with no one to see it, was bereaved. *No other way*, he thought. *I should have known; it had to happen sooner or later. I hope she's not afraid.*

At seven-fifty the phone rang and he snatched up the receiver. "Hello?"

"Mr. Tellios?" It was Whitlock's voice.

"Have you got her?"

"Kori's right here with me."

"She can hear what you're saying?"

"That's right."

"Is she all right?"

"Pretty much. I mean, she tried to get away on her horse, and I had to shoot it."

"You shot her horse?" Tellios escaped eagerly into anger. "Goddamn you, that horse was worth almost a hundred thousand dollars!"

"Well, I didn't know that, did I?" said Whitlock without regret. "Oh, and by the way, she fell kinda hard."

His heart lurched. "Is she hurt?"

"Her arm's broke. She's taking it real brave, not crying or anything."

"She never cries. Let me talk to her."

"Sure." The phone was put down and footsteps walked off. There was a silence, then Whitlock could be heard. "I'll hold the phone for you. Remember, you be careful what you say."

Silence again, then, "Hello, Uncle?"

She spoke with that unnatural calm that meant she was scared. "Koritsimu! Is he hurting you?"

She hesitated and he thought, *Whitlock is a dead man.*

"I want to come home, please, Uncle," she said.

"Of course. This will all be over very soon. I want you to be brave, as you always are."

"Yes, Uncle."

The receiver was taken away and Whitlock said belligerently,

"See? She's here and she's alive. You want her back the same way, you do like you're told."

"Very convincing, Mr. Whitlock," Tellios said.

"Hang on a second." The phone was dropped, hard, then he heard a grunt as if something substantial were being lifted and footsteps as it was carried off. After a minute the footsteps came back and Whitlock said, "Now, it's time we talked."

"I don't like the broken arm."

"Don't worry about the arm; I tied it up some trick way that's supposed to help. This is gonna cost you fifty? Yeah, fifty big ones or it'll be more than her arm gets broken."

"If I see any evidence whatsoever of violence done to her, you will spend a long and unhappy life regretting it."

Whitlock paused, obviously trying to think of some way of saying what he felt needed to be said without giving the game away. "Don't you worry about a thing. She'll be fine. You worry about getting the money. I'll call you back at four this afternoon to see if you got it."

"See that you do. Meanwhile, go take care of her. Do it now, make it quick and clean. When you call again, I'll give you instructions on where to deliver the body."

"You do that."

Whitlock put the phone down again and turned to look at her. From the way Tellios talked about her, he'd expected something different than this skinny thing with too much hair curling wildly wherever it could break loose from its braids. The bloody handkerchief around her forehead didn't help, nor the swollen and purple arm. He didn't mind turning people into wrecks, but she had wrecked herself, which was different. And he was strictly forbidden to continue the wrecking, which filled him with aimless fury. He'd kill her and be glad; there was nothing in her to make it worth even talking to her about it.

"He told you to kill me, didn't he?" she said.

He stopped, his thoughts haring in seven directions at once. How did she know? Then he grinned. Because it didn't matter; she was dead meat. "What makes you think that, little lady?"

"I saw you talking to him yesterday, on our front porch. You were leaning against a pillar then, just as you were here when you watched me take off my boots."

The grin faded and he shrugged. "I thought you were too far

away to see me. But, how does that get to him telling me to kill you?"

"Because you would never dare to visit him one day and kidnap me the next. You have a distinctive voice, which you made no attempt to disguise when you spoke to him just now. That means he knows who you are. Either you have no idea with whom you are dealing, or he knows who took me away, and does not object to it."

"Yeah? Who is it I'm dealing with?"

"He's a member of the Mafia. You know that."

"What makes you think that?"

"Because he arranged for you to visit while I was out riding. If you were just an ordinary person I would have been introduced to you. But when I came back early from riding, Uncle sent you at once to your car."

The redhead's chin came up. "Suppose you're right? What makes you so sure you're supposed to end up dead?"

"What else am I here for?"

"You heard me on the phone just now: money. Or maybe I just wanted to talk to you. You're pretty sassy for a lady all tied up and nowhere to hide."

"All right, let's talk. Maybe I can make you a better offer than Uncle did."

He laughed then, genuinely amused. "Oh, my," he said. "That's fine, that's real fine. What kind of offer can you make me?"

"Freedom."

The laughter turned to chuckles, and they rang false even in his ears. "I don't get it."

"Sometime in your past you did something illegal and Uncle knows about it."

He felt his hands itch to go around that slender throat. "You lie."

"I never lie." She leaned back against the pew, looking comfortable and unafraid. "You see, the men at the ranch each have secrets, only Uncle knows all about them. There are people in our city government he controls the same way. He has the proof of what they did, and if they don't obey him, or if something happens to Uncle, the proof goes straight to the police or the newspapers, whichever will do more harm."

"Oh, yeah?" He stuck both hands in his pockets as he swaggered closer. "What's he got on me?"

"How should I know? He is a man of his word, and keeps his secrets just as he says he will."

"Then how come you know about them?"

"I have lived with Uncle most of my life; I know a great many things about him."

"And he knows something about you!" said Whitlock. "Right?" He saw her face change and laughed in triumph. "*That's* why you're so damn sure!" He raised an arm high to point downward at her with a stiff forefinger. "You're on a string just like the rest of us!"

"Yes," she said, unafraid again. "And so? That means you can trust me. I won't go to the police about you, because you can go about me."

"So what is this, playground time? 'You show me yours and I'll show you mine'? No way; I ain't telling you nothin'!"

"I'm not asking you to. But knowledge of its existence could set the police looking. And they can be very clever."

He lowered his arm. "Ain't that the truth? So all right, he's got us. How does that bring us closer to some kind of a deal?"

"I don't know."

"Well, you stupid, silly bitch! All this was just talk, then?" He turned and looked around him. "Where did I put that stuff?" he asked. "Heroin, heroin, heroin, to OD the pretty lady." She watched him begin to search the room, looking on top of the over-flowing boxes, on the chairs around the table, under the broken pew. She sat in silence, watching, not crying or begging, not even looking nervous, though he stretched the looking out as long as he could, trying to get on her nerves. When he had looked twice in all the obvious places, he straightened from the last one and looked at her. "You got one cool head, you know that?"

At eight-thirty, Ramsey, puzzled because she had not come in for a computer lesson, went to check on her at the barn. She wasn't there. The horses were complaining they hadn't been fed, and Summer Wind was not in his box. Alarmed, he went to the big house and was shown into the office-parlor.

Tellios, still in his bathrobe and looking very angry, stared at nothing from behind his rolltop desk, clenched fists in his lap. Guy Riscatto stood with his back to one of the tall windows, his attitude respectful.

"Has something happened to Kori?" asked Ramsey.

"That bastard took her," Tellios said tightly.

Ramsey tried to hide a sudden hope. "Who?"

"Some goddamn stupid jerk! She's been kidnapped!"

"What?" Ramsey sought a chair and sat down carefully. "Has—has he killed her?"

"No, I just talked to her."

"What does he want?"

"Money, of course! Fifty thousand dollars!"

"You'll pay the ransom?"

"Of course! I have no choice!" He glanced at Riscatto, then past Ramsey. "I just hope they don't kill her. She's injured already."

"Injured?"

"He says he shot and killed Summer Wind to get her and she broke an arm falling off him."

"Oh my God!" Injured and her beloved horse dead. What must be going on in her mind? "How soon before she's home again?"

"Tonight, tomorrow at the latest. I'm going into town in a little while to raise the money. I'll talk to him again late this afternoon. Meanwhile, I want you to go back to the cottage and wait."

"But I—"

"Whatever it is, it's canceled. If anyone calls here, we'll handle it, and if there's a message, I'll send Riscatto."

"Send?"

"Yes, your phone's out of order. Good thing, too; I don't want you tempted to call the cops. Give me your car keys. You're to stay on the ranch until she's back home safe with me."

Ramsey fumbled for his keys, and was ashamed of the way his hand trembled as he gave them to Tellios.

"Good. Go now, please. I'll talk with you later."

Ramsey got out of the house somehow and stumbled back to the cottage. He went to his study and sat before the blank screen of his computer. Too shocked to weep, he tried to pray. But the only prayer that came to mind was a militant one: "Saint Michael the Archangel, defend us in battle. Be our safeguard against the wiles and wickedness of the devil. O prince of the heavenly host, cast into hell Satan and the other evil spirits who prowl about the world seeking the destruction of souls. Amen."

Chapter
11 †

"I don't think it's fair, your pulling me off the case!" said Brichter, coming into the squad room on Ryder's heels.

"I don't give a good goddamn what you think; I looked in your file on Tellios and for all those hours you've got nothing! I could build a better case against you for wasting time than against Tellios for anything! No, Obie, it's time to cut our losses and go back to what we know: Januschka and company."

Brichter headed for the coffee urn and his first cup of the day. "Well, all right," he grumbled. "But I don't like it."

"What you like has nothing to do with it either. Forget Tellios; I want to see some action on Januschka." Ryder went into his office and closed the door.

"Ha, I see the computer-brain struck out for once," said Tonk, who had been an avid witness to the exchange.

Brichter turned cold gray eyes on the big, fair-haired man. "Is that a head on those shoulders, or some kind of extra-large pimple?"

"One of these days, smart-ass," said Tonk, rising, "you're gonna make one crack too many, and wake up in the hospital. In the meantime, I got better things to do." He walked out of the squad room, slamming the door hard enough to rattle its frosted-glass insert.

"Whew!" said Brichter, filling his cup and taking it to his desk. Ryder and Brichter had staged that conversation about Tellios here and in several places, for the benefit of people who might spread the story so that it would get back to Tellios. But only here had the eavesdropper come forward with such malicious pleasure over Brichter's seeming defeat. And only here had Brichter struck back. It wasn't that Brichter hadn't been listening; he'd heard only too well the malice in Tonk's voice. Was it envy that made Tonk so quick to anger? Brichter shook his head. Meanwhile, he stored the pimple analogy away. It was too good to use just once.

He made a couple of phone calls and found that the child-pimp had abruptly left town, an event he must remember to thank Tellios for. He pressed the button down and was about to dial Ramsey's number to hint for an invitation to lunch when the squad-room door opened and McHugh came in. He stood awhile in the middle of the room, then said cautiously, "Mornin', Obie."

"Morning," replied Brichter.

"I hear Frank told you to lay off Tellios."

"So rumor would have it."

"I see." McHugh nodded—gingerly—as if that confirmed an idea of his own, and went to his desk. "Sorry I'm late; any calls for me?"

"No."

McHugh sat down. "Christ, don't ever be a cowboy. Between that shit-kickin' music and the bourbon and branch, you'll be sick as a dog." He glanced at Brichter, who said nothing, and sighed. "I thank you for not taking advantage of a dying man."

"Maybe later, when you're feeling better. Or not."

"So Frank spoke to you too, did he?" McHugh opened a drawer and began to paw through it. "Got any painkiller?"

"No." Brichter again started to dial Ramsey's number when the door opened again and Lieutenant Colly came in.

He was a middle-sized black man with a short natural hairstyle and a worried expression permanently engraved on his round face. Raising his hand, he said, "Obie, can I talk to you?"

"What about?" asked Brichter warily. Colly had been his boss before Ryder, and their parting had not been amicable.

McHugh, at the urn, said, "Coffee, John?"

"No, thanks."

Brichter took a drink from his mug. "What's on your mind, Lieutenant?"

Colly dragged the chair from Tonk's desk to beside Brichter's and sat down on it with a sigh. "It's about Whitlock."

"That's my case," said McHugh, before Brichter could.

Colly looked around. "I know. But my Sergeant Hinckley's been working on him, too. And he's gonna bust him in a few hours."

McHugh came over. "For what?"

"Dealing. He's been selling heroin and cocaine out of an abandoned church he's got the keys to."

"So why come to me?" asked Brichter.

"Because I want you to help Hinckley run the bust."

"Like hell!"

"Now don't start, dammit!"

"You're the one starting! I don't work in Narcotics anymore, remember? And I don't have to save Hinckley's ass for him anymore!"

"I'm not talking Hinckley's ass, I'm talking lives! I didn't have to come down here, you know; I could have told you on the goddamn phone!"

Brichter was silent; the old angers had leapt to life with shocking suddenness. "I'm sorry," he said at last. "I didn't mean to come at you like that."

Colly, surprised, raised an eyebrow and said, "Hell, Obie, you always did have a mouth on you."

"So how come Obie and not me?" asked McHugh. "At the risk of sounding like a nag, it's my case."

"Because Obie's got the kind of mind we need for this. Hinckley's got a plan so bad it isn't even half-assed." He grimaced and said to Brichter, "So all right, you'll be saving his keister again. But someone needs to; he hasn't got any kind of head for logistics. The only thing he did right was get a lot of men all committed."

"Okay, but a raid takes planning. How much time do I get?"

"None. Almost none, anyway. But he does have a plan, sort of. And he found someone who's been in the church and knows what it looks like in there. I thought he was doing okay; I didn't get a look at what he has—or hasn't got—until a few minutes ago. I'd call it off, but like I said, the men are gonna be there. And Whitlock's pure poison. He's already got a couple of handguns and he bought a deer rifle yesterday. Building an arsenal, we think. He beat that loan-shark rap and thinks he's got a license to do anything he damn pleases. He beat hell out of a customer a couple days ago, who they still think might not survive."

"Do I get a piece of this?" asked McHugh, in a voice indicating violence if Colly said no.

"Sure," said Colly. "The more the merrier. Will you do it, Obie?"

"When is it scheduled for?"

"Gather at ten-thirty, go in at eleven."

"Tonight?"

"This morning."

Brichter was so surprised he couldn't think of anything to say.

Colly said softly, "From what I just told you, how many cops can we kill if we don't do this right?"

Brichter stood and walked away. He stood with his back to Colly for a long fifteen seconds, then tugged his ear. He checked his watch: half past eight. "All right." He sighed. "You want to tell Ryder or shall I?"

Colly raised both eyebrows at this evidence of a new and more flexible Brichter. "I'll talk to him. And thanks." Colly stood, and said, in the closest he had ever come to an apology, "How about we don't let Hinckley hog all the credit this time, okay?"

"There's only one way I know to keep you quiet for sure. And I got to do it. If I kill you, I don't go to jail. If I don't, I will."

"I won't tell."

"Huh. You talk pretty while you're scared you're gonna die, but what happens if I let you go? You get back home, safe and warm in bed, and the cops being nice to you, and your uncle screaming and hollering about how his precious niece had her arm broke by this terrible man, then what? And especially once you find out that horse of yours is dead?"

Kori's heart sank. "You did kill him, didn't you?"

"Yes, ma'am, I did. Shot him one time, right in the head; he was dead before he hit the ground."

She closed her eyes. "You're sure?"

"See, now you're all mad at me, aren't you?"

"I've been afraid we might have left him hurt and frightened."

"No, he went down like a ton of bricks and never wiggled an ear after that."

She nodded, believing that; she hadn't heard Summer Wind even breathing after their tumble. Still, she couldn't hide her grief. "You shouldn't have shot him," she said.

"Well, if you'd come to me like I told you, he'd be just fine."

"That's true." She nodded again, accepting the crumb of guilt because she needed not to scream in fury at him for killing her lovely, her gentle, her beloved Summer Wind.

"But you see, it don't matter now. Nothing matters, not whether you are the kind who keeps her word or not. Because there's still Nick. I got to do whatever he says so long as he's got that something on me."

She looked up at him to find again that look of terrifying curiosity about her reaction to his prodding. So long as that was not satisfied, the game could continue.

She pushed Summer Wind into that room in her head where she kept things she did not think about and closed the door. She said, "If we put our heads together—which will be the last thing Uncle expects us to do—we may come up with something that will help you. Then maybe we can think of some way to help me."

"I'm already helping you, ain't I? You're supposed to be dead by now. But I'm kind of hoping you really can help me get off the hook with Nick. So come on, talk to me."

She put her head back until it touched the top of the pew. "It's a recording, you say. And the original copy is not at the ranch."

"Yeah. Where is it? That's the question."

"He would never trust it to someone who might listen to it and use what he hears for himself."

"Shit, who could he trust not to listen to it?"

"But he did say that if something happens to him, it goes to the police, right?"

"Yeah, he did."

"So someone must have it, or can get access to it. If it were mine, I'd put it in a safe-deposit box." Which was a lie; if it were hers, she wouldn't bother to keep it at all. There was nothing hidden that couldn't be found, and the object here was not revenge from the grave, but to keep out of the graveyard. So long as Whitlock couldn't find the evidence, Uncle was safe; and how better to guarantee it wouldn't be found than to destroy it? But better keep that idea away from Whitlock. She frowned, trying to think what the rules might be about safe-deposit boxes. "I'd give the key to someone and give him some kind of legal paper so he could get in if I died. A lawyer would be good—" She stopped.

"What?" prompted Whitlock.

"There's a lawyer who comes out to the ranch. From the way he behaves, I think he's another on Uncle's list. His name is Phillip Bannister."

"Holy sufferin' Christ!" breathed Whitlock. "Are you serious?"

"Yes, why?"

"Don't you know who he is?"

Yes, but let Whitlock contribute. "No, who?"

"Big-time lawyer. Sits on county boards. His old man was a judge. And you say he's been out to the ranch?"

"Yes, four or five times. Maybe more. If you could get the key from him, could you use it to get into the safe-deposit box?" Kori thought there was probably more than possession of a key that got you access to a safe-deposit box—but they were sitting like con-

spirators now, heads together, which was much better than the
captive/captor relationship of a few minutes ago. Whitlock's sudden shifts in emphasis, tenor, and mood made him far more difficult to deal with than Uncle. She wondered if he had a boredom
threshold, and how high it was. The only reason he hadn't killed
her was his enjoyment of her struggle to keep it from happening.
When he got tired or bored, and certainly before it was time to call
Uncle again, he'd end it. It was just a matter of time.

Brichter dropped the receiver and tugged an ear. And thought hard.
Finally he stood and drifted over to McHugh's desk and stood patiently until McHugh chose to look up from a file he was putting
together for the county prosecutor.

"You want something?" McHugh asked.

"I need your help."

"I already told you I was coming along on that raid."

"No, this is a different problem, something we need to do right
now. It's as much up your alley as the Hinckley thing is mine."

"What is it?" McHugh put his pen down to listen.

"Ramsey's phone is out of order, and when I called the big house
I was told they don't know where Kori was, which is bullshit; they
know at all times where she is. I was also told Ramsey's working
on a manuscript and doesn't want to be disturbed. Tellios isn't out
there, apparently. I want us to go out there."

"Why drag me along? You're the one with the standing invitation to visit any time."

"Remember the time you got into your car but didn't start the
engine? And when you looked, there was a bomb wired to the igni-
tion. You said you didn't start the engine because you smelled gel-
ignite."

"And you smell . . . ?"

"I'm not sure. But I don't like it. All right, don't come. But
you're the con artist; tell me how to get in there, find out if there's
a problem—and if there is, yank Gordie loose without getting him
caught in a firefight."

McHugh considered the problem. "You really think it may be
serious?"

"Hell, I don't know. Probably not. But if it is . . ."

"Okay, draw up a search warrant, for stolen property. Take a
crew along, do a real search. Take evidence along to plant, so you
can make an arrest."

"I don't see how arresting one of them is going to help Gordie if he's in trouble. And a whole crew? Look, I've got this other raid to plan—"

"Use the same crew. Hinckley's got one put together already, right? And you don't arrest one of Tellios' boys, you arrest Dr. Ramsey."

Brichter appeared to hold his breath while he considered this. Then he smiled. "You are wonderful, you know that? By God, we could waltz Gordie right out from under their noses, and they couldn't do a thing about it! But what kind of evidence should I take? And how do I plant it?"

McHugh sighed in an exaggerated way and said, "Okay, if you do decide to bust him, just say, 'Find anything yet, Cris?' and I'll find it. Judas Priest, you will never make any kind of confidence man!" He grinned. "For evidence, we want something small, like a piece of jewelry." He picked up a pencil and made it vanish into the palm of his hand—he'd taken lessons from a magician a few stings back. He stood, reached over and retrieved it from Brichter's ear. "Maybe that Felchek ring is still in the property room; let's go see. And smile, Obie! This is gonna be fun!"

A line of sedans and a squad car drove up the lane to Tretower Ranch and stopped at the double gates.

Brichter got out of the lead car with a legal document in his hand. "Good afternoon, Mr. Riscatto," he said. "Will you open the gates?"

"Can't. Mr. Tellios ain't here." His puzzled dark eyes kept flicking in the direction of the cars. "What's this all about?"

"I have a search warrant for the cottage," said Brichter, displaying it.

Riscatto stared at it as if it had rows of tiny sharp teeth. "Don't tell me you've never seen one before. Where's Dr. Ramsey?"

"The cottage. But he don't want to be disturbed. He gave strict orders."

"I'm countermanding his orders. Open the gate."

"No way! What kind of shit do you think you're pulling, anyhow?"

"A legal kind of shit. I wouldn't recommend obstructing police officers in the performance of their duty; you could get arrested."

Riscatto glanced again at the line of cars and the patient, watchful men in them, then at Brichter's grim expression, and went to do as he was told.

Brichter walked back to his car and drove across the racetrack, the others following. They parked in a double row beside the cottage and got out to a chorus of door-chunking.

"So far, so good," said McHugh to Brichter. "Nice-looking place they got here. I wonder where the others are?"

"Shiffler is chauffeur, so he's with Tellios. If I know Downey, he's hiding in the barn. And there goes Riscatto up to the house, probably to try to get hold of the boss."

The pair led the way up the curving walk to the cottage door. Brichter knocked, and the door was opened by Ramsey looking frightened and relieved. "What are you doing here?" he asked.

"Search warrant," said Brichter, showing it. "We're here to search the cottage." Ramsey stared at the document. "Ask us in, Gordie."

Ramsey looked over Brichter's shoulder at the young army standing on the walk. "I don't know if there's room," he said. "But do come in." He stepped back into the hallway and Brichter led McHugh, seven plainclothesmen, and six officers in uniform into the living room. They stood shoulder to shoulder around two walls of the room.

Downey, standing beside a wing chair, gaped at them. "What are you doing here?" he asked. "What do you want?" There was a chess game on the coffee table, and he held a knight between thumb and crooked forefinger.

Brichter thought, *I wish Gordie had mentioned he was here.* "We have reason to believe a stolen diamond-and-sapphire ring is in the cottage," he said.

"C'mon," said Downey. "You know there's nothing like that around here."

"Maybe. As soon as we prove that to our own satisfaction, we'll go away. Why don't you go up to the big house and wait while we look for it, Mr. Downey?"

Downey started to move, then thought better of it. "Mr. Tellios sent me over to keep an—to keep the professor company. I don't think he'd like it if I left him alone with your people."

Damn. "We appreciate your loyalty, Mr. Downey, and your willingness to risk being arrested as an accomplice. Sure you won't change your mind?"

Downey cowered but muttered, "Huh-uh."

"Fine. Sit down."

Nervously, Downey sat.

Brichter looked around. "Dr. Ramsey? Come and sit across from Mr. Downey."

"All right." Ramsey broke through the crowd and crossed the little open space to his chair.

"First question," said Brichter. "Are there any weapons in the house?"

"No," said Ramsey. "You know I don't like guns."

Brichter turned to address his crew. "Decker, you and Chase take the front bedroom upstairs. Sunderland and DeCoyne, you've got the back. Whoever finishes first, get the bathroom. Baum and Shackley, get the kitchen. Englund and Feltgen, you're in the library, downstairs back. All of you, take turns, watch each other search, and don't miss anything. You know the rules; if you find something, don't touch it; sing out and I'll come look.

"McHugh, you and Gresham search right in here. Inkvist, you're inventory; sit in this third chair. Here's the warrant; get ready to list anything we find. You can also help me keep an eye on our two friends. Questions? Good, let's get started."

The room slowly cleared and Ramsey asked, "Is having elderly underwear in your dresser drawer as bad as getting caught at the hospital in it?"

McHugh laughed. "It lowers your grade half a point," he said. "I'll go first, okay, Gresham?"

"Yessir," said the uniformed cop. He leaned against the doorjamb and watched. McHugh scanned the room briefly, then began his first pass, a search of everything at a level above his ankles and below his waist.

Brichter stayed out of McHugh's way, moving as required, but trying to be always in Ramsey's line of sight. McHugh opened an umbrella, shook out magazines, ran his fingers under windowsills. He came to a sideboard, opened a drawer and began to unfold and toss out tablecloths, napkins, and place mats.

"Here, now!" objected Ramsey, but no one paid any attention. Except Brichter. His attention was almost entirely riveted on his friend. But so far Ramsey had offered no clue to his situation apart from nervous tension—which the presence of the police alone might have caused.

McHugh pulled a sideboard drawer entirely out and went poking around the interior. Sounds of things being disturbed came from all over the cottage.

Ramsey said, "I hope they're being careful in the library." Someone dropped a large pan in the kitchen and he winced. "Peter, what is all this in aid of? Do you really expect you'll find something incriminating?"

"We could. If we do, I'll arrest you and take you downtown for questioning. If not, we'll go away again. It all depends on you."

Ramsey's face cleared. "I see," he said. He thought for a moment, then said, "We're friends, aren't we, Peter? Doesn't that mean anything? Remember the birthday gift I gave you last year?"

Brichter considered the question, then nodded. "I remember," he said with a trace of a smile. "Find anything yet, McHugh?"

"Not yet." McHugh worked the drawer back into place and walked over to Downey's wing chair. "On your feet," he said.

"Sure." Downey rose and went to stand beside Ramsey. McHugh looked the chair over, then stuck a hand down the cushion and moved it slowly leftward. "Ah," he said. He wiggled the hand and came up with a prickly gold ring embellished with lots of small blue and white stones. "This the little gypsy?" he asked Inkvist.

Inkvist, a fat man with yellow hair, took the ring and looked it over carefully. "Indeed it is," he said.

"Hey!" protested Downey. "You planted that!"

"How could we?" asked Brichter. "You've been guarding that chair since we came in." He started toward them, and Downey misinterpreted the move.

"Don't you touch me!" he said, moving behind Ramsey. "This is a frame!"

"Let him go," said Ramsey. "I know how the ring got there."

"A nice, incriminating statement," said McHugh, smiling.

"Suits me," said Brichter. "Gresham, go call off the search, will you? Send them out to their cars. Inky, you go, too."

"Right."

Brichter said to his friend, "Gordon Douglas Ramsey, you are under arrest for being in possession of a stolen ring valued in excess of one thousand dollars."

"All right," said Ramsey calmly. "Do I rise?"

"Yes, and go lean on the mantel. I have to search you."

"Very well." Ramsey went to brace himself against the mantel. He was smiling.

"Mr. Downey, you're free to go now," said McHugh.

"I ain't goin' till he does," said Downey. "And if he does, Mr. Tellios is gonna be pissed."

So Brichter had to give Ramsey an official frisk. He ran both hands up Ramsey's right arm, saying, "You have the right to remain silent." As he traversed the back of his neck, he continued. "If you give up the right to remain silent"—he patted along the left arm—"anything you say will be taken down"—he began exploring

Ramsey's back and ribs—"and may be used against you in a court of law. Hold still."

"I'm ticklish," said Ramsey humbly. "Sorry." But he was still smiling.

Brichter stayed behind Ramsey and patted down the front of his shirt. "Where was I?"

"Repeating to a jury anything I say," said Ramsey.

"Ah, yes." Brichter explored Ramsey's circumference as marked by his belt, but with entirely unrecommended propriety ignored the front of his trousers and began going down his right leg. "You have the right to an attorney's presence during questioning," he said. Starting up the other leg, he added, "If you want an attorney and can't afford one, we'll appoint one for you." He stood and reached for his handcuffs. "Do you understand these rights as I've explained them to you?"

"Yes, you made them very clear."

Brichter clasped Ramsey's right wrist with the cuff, then pulled him upright. "Are you willing to waive your right to silence at this time?" He took Ramsey's left wrist and fastened it to the right behind the man's back.

"Well," said Ramsey, looking at Downey, "could we go downtown first? For one thing, I don't think my shoulders were designed to hold this position for very long."

"All right. Let's go."

Downey followed Brichter, Ramsey, and McHugh outside and stood, a lonesome figure on the curving walk, watching them leave.

As they drove down the narrow lane, McHugh asked Ramsey, "What was it you gave Obie for his birthday last year?"

"Two tickets to a play."

"Play?"

"A local production of the old Broadway show, *Take Me Along*."

McHugh laughed loudly. As soon as Brichter made the turn onto the main road, he unlocked the handcuffs on Ramsey's wrists.

"Thank you both," said Ramsey, flexing his arms. "That was exquisitely done."

"It was Obie who figured you were in trouble," said McHugh.

"Yeah, but it was McHugh who suggested the raid and whose magic made it work," Brichter said, "How's Kori?"

"Don't you know? She's been kidnapped, Peter."

"What?" The car swerved violently and recovered. "By who? When?"

"Early this morning. Tellios says a 'jerk' took her. It seems to be a genuine kidnapping; he's very angry. The kidnapper is asking fifty thousand as ransom, which Tellios says he's willing to pay. But he's afraid the kidnapper may kill her, which I can't help thinking might suit him, God damn his black soul forever."

"Oh, shit!" growled McHugh, slouching back.

"No!" Brichter thumped the steering wheel with a big fist. "He won't kill her. Tellios won't pay if they do. And he can't refuse to pay now that we know about the kidnapping. It'll take him a few hours to pull together that wad of cash; maybe we can find her first." He pressed down on the accelerator. "What else did Tellios say? Does he have any idea where she is?"

"I don't think so. He says Summer Wind was shot out from under her, and she broke an arm in the fall."

"Damn!" He pulled out to pass a squad car in front of them.

"My phone was put out of order so I couldn't call you. I thought you'd found out somehow when I saw you and that long line of men behind you at the door. Why did you come?"

McHugh said, "Obie knew there was something wrong when he couldn't get hold of you. He got me to put together a search team while he got the warrant signed—I bet the judge's ears are still flapping in the breeze. Funny thing," he added, smiling at the back of Brichter's neck, "I've seen this boy around the squad room a lot, but now I think maybe we've never been properly introduced. Sergeant Brichter, my name's Cris. How about we go get drunk together, to celebrate, after we find your girl?"

Brichter glanced back at McHugh. "All right," he said, "Cris." He pulled out to pass another car. "My friends call me Peter."

Chapter
12 †

Ramsey walked into the OCU squad room, followed by McHugh and Brichter. "Frank?" called McHugh.

The door to Ryder's office opened. "Got him?"

"Kori's been kidnapped," said Brichter.

"Oh, Christ! When?"

"Early this morning," said Ramsey. "He took her as she was riding. Mr. Tellios says he wants fifty thousand dollars for her. I believe he's out raising it now."

"This is Dr. Ramsey, Frank," said McHugh.

"I'm pleased to meet you, Doctor," said Ryder. "But I'm damned sorry about Kori."

"Captain," said Brichter, "since Kori's existence isn't widely known of outside the area, the kidnapper is probably a local. They may be right here in town. I want to go shake a few trees and see what falls out."

Ryder checked his watch. "No time; you've to go right now and help Hinckley with that raid. He's called twice in the last ten minutes."

"I'll take the raid," said McHugh instantly.

"This is where Obie shines, not you," said Ryder. "You go look for Kori. Take whomever you can find, use my name to get cooperation. But Obie's got this other thing to do. They're expecting him and he's already late."

"I'm gone," said McHugh, and was.

"You too, Obie," said Ryder.

Brichter said nothing for several moments. His face was the color of ivory, and looked carved from that substance, except his eyes, which glittered like ice. Then, very softly, he said, "Yes, sir." He turned on his heel and went out.

"Perhaps I can be of some assistance," offered Ramsey.

Ryder said firmly, "You're going to ground right here. Tellios may try to get you back, but I know some tricks from back when Miranda was a twinkle in his daddy's eye. Come with me, Dr. Ramsey."

"Poor devil!" said Ramsey, following Ryder into his tiny office.

"Yes, but he's an obedient devil, thank God. I'm bleeding for him, but they'll want his cool head at that raid to keep anyone from getting killed. McHugh can be like Paul Revere; anyone within sound of his voice will join in the search. As soon as the raid is over, Obie can join them. We'll find her. Sit here; I want to make some calls."

Ramsey sat. Ryder picked up his phone and punched four numbers. "Mitch? Yes, Ryder. Look, we got Gordon Ramsey hidden away down here—yeah, my boys can be pretty damn slick—but Tellios may send someone for him. Right. So tell him Feltgen or whoever isn't present up there is handling the case, and you don't know what he did with Ramsey. You remember the routine. Yeah, those were the days. Thanks."

Ryder pressed the button down, sighed and said, "We used to keep suspects from being bailed out this way, if we weren't satisfied they'd told all they knew. The corruption smells different nowadays." He punched four numbers again. "This is Captain Ryder. Intake sergeant, please." He waited. "Hi, Terry. Look, if anyone comes to bail out one Dr. Gordon Ramsey, say he never finished booking, that he had a heart attack, and got taken away in an ambulance. R-A-M-S-E-Y. A Ph.D. doctor. In receipt of stolen goods. We're keeping him here for his own protection. Yeah. Thanks." He pushed the button down, then released it and punched in four more numbers. "Sorensen? Ryder. If anyone comes up there looking for a Dr. Gordon Ramsey, say you heard the feds wanted to talk to him. This is important, we may be saving a life here. Yeah, anyone—If I hear one more cop-snitch story, I'm going to suggest the city bill Januschka for our salaries." He laughed. "Yeah, thanks." He tossed the receiver down, abruptly serious. "And if that doesn't hold him, there are parts of this building the public simply doesn't have access to. You're safe now."

"Thank you. I wish we could say the same for Kori."

"That goddamned Brichter!" said Tellios. He wheeled away from the window to face the hapless Downey. "You worthless piece of garbage, I thought I told you to keep an eye on the professor!"

"I did!" said Downey. "I stayed for the whole search. Once they took him away, there wasn't nuthin' more I could do. I thought they was after me; they found that ring right in the chair where I was sitting!"

"They planted it, right?" asked Riscatto, from the couch in front of the fireplace.

"I don't see how, nobody came near that chair till the cop found it!"

"Brichter found it," guessed Tellios.

"No, sir, Brichter just watched. It was that other one, McHugh."

"That bastard's almost as bad as Brichter," said Tellios. "And a whole lot smoother. McHugh palmed it on you."

"I don't see how," objected Downey. "And anyhow, the professor saw they was gonna arrest me and he confessed. They put him through the whole routine, warning and search and handcuffs."

"The professor wanted to be taken away, dipstick," said Riscatto. "He'd've confessed to anything."

"He wanted to tell the cops about Kori," confirmed Tellios. He rubbed his hands together restlessly. "So let him. It's too late, it's been too late for hours. I just wish I knew why Brichter came out."

"He called earlier," said Riscatto.

"What did you tell him?" asked Tellios sharply.

"The story we agreed on. That the professor's phone was out of order and we were getting it fixed. But that anyway he was working on some manuscript and didn't want to be disturbed. Brichter said okay and that was that."

"We should have taken care of Ramsey as soon as we knew she was gone," said Tellios. "He's a loose end, and I don't like loose ends." He walked to his desk and sat down, his dusty brown eyes distant. Then he began to smile. "So let's bring him back. He was so glad to be arrested, let's see how he likes being bailed out." He picked up his phone and began to dial, as Riscatto and Downey watched.

He stood, stretched and yawned, moving his shoulders and doing a little dance as if to resurrect tired muscles. "Well, purty lady," he said, "it's been fun. But the day is moving on, and if your body is still warm when they find it, your Uncle Nick will know I didn't obey orders. He may even start to think I messed with you some after he told me not to. So I guess the party's over."

"But we were nearly there!" she protested. "The plan—"

"There wasn't any plan. You were just trying to hold off the real plan, which was to put you away nice and neat so your old uncle wouldn't put me in jail. You're a smart one, all right; you nearly had me thinking a time or two we could pull it off." He walked across the room to the sanctuary, talking as he went. "But smart as you are, Nick Tellios is a whole lot smarter. Plus he's been at this game a whole lot longer." He opened a tall, narrow cabinet door in the arch and took out a gallon-size Ziploc bag about a third full of little plastic bags. "But he did say to ease you on out as smooth and nice as I could, and I think a short, sweet trip on a pink cloud will make him happy. It'll even make you happy, send you on your way with a smile on your face." He reached in again and came out with a candle, spoon, and syringe.

"Listen," she said. "I don't think the tape is off the ranch at all. I think Uncle has it right there with him. It isn't like him to trust anyone with information as valuable as that." She was gabbling; he wouldn't believe her. She stopped and tried to take a long, slow breath to ease her pounding heart, but it didn't work; he would see how terrified she was and that wasn't good; she had to calm down.

"I talked to a policeman last night," she said. "He's going to arrest Uncle."

He paused in the act of opening the plastic bag. "Ol' Nick would never allow his little girl to talk to a cop."

"But he did, he thinks Peter is going to be added to his list. Peter is pretending to let Uncle bribe him for a thousand dollars a week and the right to talk to me whenever he likes."

Whitlock grinned. "You expect me to believe that? Nick wouldn't let a cop within a thousand yards of you!"

"He let me talk to Sergeant Peter Brichter over dinner night before last and all yesterday evening."

Whitlock's pale eyebrows rose high on his freckled forehead. "Brichter?" Then they came down. "You lie. His front name ain't Peter. You never even saw him, much less talked to him."

"Yes, I have."

Whitlock reached back into the cabinet for a peanut-butter jar half full of water. He unscrewed the lid. "Describe him," he said.

"He's not really tall but tallish, and thin, and his hair is a sort of light brown. He's got pale gray eyes and a strict face. His voice is deeper than you expect and he's got big hands. His real name is Otto Peter Brichter. Obie is his nickname, but his friends call him Peter."

He was staring at her, surprised. "He has a thick notebook he writes everything down in," she continued. She thought. "His hair is starting to come out in front. He can whistle. He's very bright and—and he rather likes me." She looked down at her tied wrists.

"Well, I'll be dipped," murmured Whitlock. "You have seen him, haven't you?"

"Yes, and if he came in right now, you'd be very sorry!"

"Yeah, but he ain't. Nobody even knows who took you from the ranch, much less that I got you here." Whitlock pulled a Bic lighter from his pocket and lit the candle. He took a plastic bag from the big bag and opened it. There was a small amount of brownish-white powder in the bag. He looked over at her. "Here, whyn't I bring you over so you can watch how it's done?"

"I'm fine, thank you," she said, but he came and carried her to the table, sitting her on a rickety wooden chair.

"This's heroin," he said, holding up the bag. "I'll dissolve it in some water and put it in the syringe. I'm not sure what strength it is, so I'll put a couple of bags in."

He tilted the jar a little and dipped the spoon in to fill it with water. He held it over the candle and carefully tipped the contents of the little plastic bag into it. "See?" he said genially. "Nothin' to it. You ever had a shot?"

"Yes." Her mouth felt dry and she licked her lips. "Peter will be very angry with you for doing this," she said.

"I reckon he will."

"On the other hand, he'll be grateful if you don't."

"If he's messing with your uncle, what he is or isn't won't amount to a hill of beans pretty soon. In fact, if I *don't* do this, it may end up with your uncle killing the both of us."

"Peter listens to me."

"I just bet he does, when it suits his purpose."

"What does that mean?"

"I mean he's wising up. If your uncle wants him to be nice to a crazy girl, he'll do it, because he wants in on the action."

"No, I told you, it's a trick he's playing on Uncle."

"No, no. Now if you told me it was that Cris McHugh out there playing head games, I'd say maybe. That bastard is sneakier than hell. But Brichter is all up front; he can't pretend worth shit. So how can he all of a sudden convince someone like Nick Tellios he's selling out when he isn't? The answer is, he can't. Nice try, little lady."

† † †

When Hinckley pulled into the parking lot with Brichter, there were already six men waiting. As they got out, two more squad cars arrived.

In a couple of minutes a dozen men, evenly divided into uniforms and plainclothes, gathered around Hinckley's car. They were five blocks from the site of the raid.

Brichter unrolled a big sheet of heavy white paper on the hood of the car. "This is a sketch I made of the site, which is a small church. There's a double front door, here, and a side entrance, here, which opens into an alley. There are four gray Lexan windows along each wall, which may or may not open. Sergeant Feltgen's been watching it since about eight this morning; at last report there have been no visitors. There are, however, at least two people in there, to judge from voices overheard. Whitlock habitually carries a handgun."

"And he bought a deer rifle two days ago," offered Hinckley, and there were muttered expletives.

Hinckley was a stocky man with a shining dome of forehead and teeth filed down short and even. He gestured at the drawing. "I been in the place once, to make a buy. It's a pigsty; there's eight or nine big boxes full of trash and some old metal folding chairs, maybe a dozen, scattered around. There's a pew across the front, here, another along this wall, and a broken one here. Everyone goes in and out only at the side door, so if whoever's in there breaks and runs, it'll probably be for that. There's a big round table up front in what used to be the sanctuary. That's where Whitlock sits to sell his shit. He takes it out of a shelved closet right next to it, here."

Brichter said, "I want you four"—he nodded at four uniformed patrolmen—"to stay outside and take the four corners. They may come out that door, they may come out a window. They are not to go any farther, understand?" The four nodded. "The rest of us will go in the front; it's a double door and we can get in faster that way."

"Who goes in first?" asked Hinckley.

"Since this was your idea, how about you?" said Brichter. "You and Nelsen and me."

"Uh," said Nelsen, "me?"

"Yes, you," said Brichter irritably. "And since you're the one with the shoulders, you carry the maul. Two good hits should break the lock.

"Gresham, you come in right behind us. With you and Nelsen up front, showing the uniform, they can't shoot and say later they didn't know it was cops. The rest of you follow close behind.

"We go in hard, and the first thing said is, 'Police, search warrant!' Hinckley, you be responsible for that. After him, we all yell 'Freeze' and 'Don't move' and 'Hold it.' Say it like you mean it, let the adrenaline flow, so it never even occurs to them to pull a gun or grab the evidence and eat it. The secret of not having a shootout is to take immediate control."

Gresham, a tall rookie, resettled his hat on his head and said, "And I suppose the next thing is Miranda. We tell them individually or together?"

"Neither," said Brichter. "The suspects aren't under arrest yet. First we look for evidence so we can make the arrest."

Hinckley added, "And when we do arrest 'em, we still won't give 'em their rights. To quote the assistant county attorney, if you ain't gonna ask 'em no questions, you don't gotta warn 'em to shut up. It's a technique that may work; they'll expect us to come on hard with the questions, so we won't. We won't even talk to 'em. This will make 'em nervous, and maybe one will say something damaging. Now, to make this legal"—his blunted finger raked the men—"be damn sure not to say anything that could be construed as a question. That includes cute speeches about how a kid could get in and find some leftover dope and kill itself. I don't know the chapter and verse of the Supreme Court ruling—"

"Harris versus New York, 1971," said Brichter, forgetting he wasn't going to do things like that any more. "Statements voluntarily made before the Miranda warnings are given were ruled admissible."

"—but it doesn't matter," said Hinckley, giving Brichter a look. "Gresham, hang around 'em after we take 'em, and write down who says what, if anything. Any man who spoils the plan goes on Eerie River boat patrol all of Memorial Day weekend. I think that's it from me. Does Captain Colly have anything to add?"

The black man shook his head. "You two are running this." Colly was there in his role of SWAT-team leader, and hoping he wouldn't be needed.

Brichter said, "Everyone's to be vested, even the point men." He rolled up the paper and said, "We go in at eleven o'clock exactly. Time check." The men grabbed for their watches. "It's ten forty-nine as of . . . now. Okay? Let's roll."

Chapter
13 †

The white clapboard church stood on a small, weedy lawn. Hinckley parked across the street, and he and Brichter got out. Other men were approaching the church from other directions. All, whether in uniform or plainclothes, were wearing a blue garment reminiscent of the torso protection worn by baseball umpires, only thinner. Some were carrying shotguns.

Brichter and Hinckley climbed the three crumbling cement steps to the double front door of the church, where they joined Gresham and Nelsen, who was carrying a short-handled sledgehammer. The others took their places on the lower steps and at the four corners of the building. Brichter pulled his gun; the others followed suit. He checked his watch, waited, then nodded at Nelsen.

The ten-pound hammer slammed into the lock, which broke at the blow. Brichter and Gresham grabbed the doors and yanked them open.

"Police! Search warrant!" shouted Hinckley, stepping inside, pointing a shotgun at a startled man and woman at the table up in front. The man quickly dropped something under the table.

"Freeze, both of you!" yelled Nelsen, as everyone stormed into the church, shouting orders to hold it and not move.

"You or the bitch even breathes funny, I shoot," announced Colly with a worried frown, pulling even with Brichter and displaying a big Magnum that glittered with chrome.

"Stay where you are, Whitlock!" ordered Brichter, approaching the table. Then he saw who the woman was. For a moment he could not breathe.

"Peter," said Kori in a faint croak. She looked terrible, with a bloody handkerchief around her forehead and one arm, swollen and purple, tied on top of the other. Her clothes were dirty and her

132

flyaway hair was standing up in a mist all around her head. There was no color in her face at all.

"Now take it easy," said Whitlock, holding his hands straight up over his head. "This ain't what it looks like, and she's fine, she's hardly hurt at all."

Behind him, Hinckley said, "You know her, Obie?"

"Yes, I do. She's Katherine McLeod Price, sometimes called Kori." He made a caress of the words, and color flooded her cheeks. He added, more businesslike, "She's a kidnap victim."

Whitlock offered placatingly, "See how I tied up her arms? It's because her arm's broke. I learnt that trick with her arms from a medic. It keeps everything steady till she gets to a doctor. And I put that handkerchief around her head, too. She's a real brave lady, and I'm glad I was able to help her out until you boys got here."

Brichter said, "Hinckley, will you get this person out of my way so I can see to the lady?"

"Sure. Okay, Whitlock, keep your hands up like you got 'em and move this way nice and slow."

"Hey, now, I think you're reading this all wrong," said Whitlock, nevertheless obeying.

Brichter tucked his gun away and went to bend over Kori. "Are you okay?" He checked her eyes and looked into her ears for signs of bleeding.

"Yes. How did you know where I was?"

"I didn't." He very gently lifted her bound arms and frowned at the state of her left wrist. "I found out less than an hour ago you were kidnapped. God, I wanted to go turn over buildings looking for you, but I had to come here to arrest some two-bit dope pusher instead. And surprise, here you are." He put her arms down, saw her tied ankles and knelt to tug at the ropes. "Damn, these knots have pulled tight."

"You came for me by *accident*?"

He worked at the knots. "You could say that. I can't get these—" She bent forward sharply, making him duck back. "Hey!" he said. "Did I hurt you?"

"No, no. I just thought you came to my rescue. Peter, he shot Summer Wind—" She stopped, swallowing, then went on. "And he was going to kill me in another minute."

"*Kill* you?"

"With a syringe of heroin. He said I would die very pleasantly."

"Jesus!"

"I've been talking and talking, trying to hold him off until you got here."

"You knew I'd come?"

She was still bent forward. "I'd been praying you'd come, so when the door broke open, I was sure it was you."

He had never been so literally the answer to a maiden's prayers. He put a hand on the side of her face, expecting to wet his thumb on her tears, but her cheek was dry. "You're safe now," he said. "I'm sorry about the horse. And that I didn't rescue you on purpose."

She straighted, and managed a tremulous smile. Color had pinked her face into nearly a blush. "Damsels in distress shouldn't be picky. I'm all right now."

He smiled back and was startled when Colly murmured over his shoulder, "Ah, shall we begin the search?"

"Yes," he said, recalled to his duty, and turned to call, "Report anything you find to Hinckley, and make sure it gets put on Mallory's inventory!" He braced a hand on the floor and looked under the table. "Mallory?" he called.

"Yup?"

"Under this table you'll find a loaded syringe. Make sure it goes on your inventory and note it as intended for use as a murder weapon."

"Hey, now!" called Whitlock. "It wasn't me gonna use it on her! It was them other guys, the ones who went out the side door ahead of you."

Brichter lifted an inquiring eyebrow at Kori. "There weren't any others," she said. "He came to the ranch to get me and there's been no one else in here until all of you arrived. He took the heroin out of that cabinet over there." She nodded in the direction of a closed cabinet door inside the arch of the sanctuary, and Colly went over to take a look.

Brichter got to his feet and dusted his hand against his trouser leg, then gently lifted an edge of the handkerchief to see what he could of the head wound. "Both wrists broken?" he asked.

"No, just the left one."

"Good." Brichter turned and called, "Anyone got a knife?"

"I do!" Nelsen, who had been taking items of clothing out of a big, sagging box, stopped and strolled up, garrison belt creaking. "Is this really little Katherine?" he asked.

"Nelsen—" began Brichter.

"My name's Officer Nelsen, ma'am," he said to her, touching the bill of his cap in a salute. "We've met before, though I bet you don't remember me. I'm pleased to be of service to you." He was a large man, looking even larger in his dark blue uniform, eyes hidden under the shadow of his hat. Kori developed an interest in the room beyond him, where a search was getting underway. He produced a red Swiss Army knife, pulled a blade out of it and asked Brichter, "Want me to cut her arms loose?"

"No, her feet. Leave her arms alone." He asked her, "Did he bring you straight here from the ranch?"

"I think so. I was in the car trunk. May we go soon?"

"In a minute."

Nelsen sliced the rope in one place, put the knife away and carefully unwrapped her ankles. He straightened, looping the rope around one hand.

"Hinckley?" Brichter called, and Hinckley and Colly both came over. "Her arm's broken and there's a head injury. I want to take her to the hospital, but I need a ride."

"Nelsen," said Colly, "give that rope to Mallory, then take Sergeant Brichter and this young woman out to County General and wait there to bring them to the Safety Building." He looked at Brichter and said in a carrying voice, "You're doing an excellent job for us, Sergeant Brichter. Thank you."

Hinckley waited until Colly was out of earshot to mutter, "And I'm a horse's behind, I suppose."

Kori said softly, "May we please go now?"

"Yes, right now."

Nelsen said, "She's got no shoes; want me to carry her out?"

"I can walk, thank you," she said quickly.

Brichter helped her onto her stockinged feet, knowing they were either without feeling or on their way to shrieking new awareness.

Outside, she paused on the stoop to look around at the decaying neighborhood's sagging duplexes and filthy, potholed streets. A cracked glass sign bearing a brewery's logo hung above a small-windowed tavern on the corner. It was changing internally from white to yellow and announced Billy's Tap. Next door to it was a severely plain old house whose brown paint needed redoing and whose tiny yard was barren of grass. A little black girl, clad only in underpants, hair done in a dozen threadlike braids each ending in a bead, stood on the porch. The door opened and a large dark hand came out and yanked her inside.

"Come on, let's go." Brichter helped her down the steps. Nelsen was already in the squad, starting the engine. She let Brichter support her on the short walk to the car, and got in the back seat ahead of him. There was very little leg room and the doors inside had no handles.

Lights flashing, Nelsen drove swiftly, using his siren only to clear the way at crowded intersections. The neighborhood improved, and Kori stared out the window at a stream of storefronts, people, houses. Cars slowed and pulled over to let them pass, their passengers staring as they went by. "There's more to Charter than I thought," she said. Then, turning to Brichter, she asked, too casually, "Peter, do you know where Gordon is?"

"Gordon's okay. He's the one who told me you were kidnapped." His sideways smile appeared. "I rescued him on purpose."

"You rescued him—he's all right?"

"We went out to the ranch and pretended to arrest him."

The look she was giving him would have polished the rustiest armor, so he expanded on that, keeping the tale light and short.

"Thank you!" she said when he finished. Then, "Do you always carry that gun?"

"Except when I'm at home. Does it bother you?"

"I—I guess not. You need a gun to arrest people like Whitlock." She looked out the window. Nelsen had turned onto a frontage road lined with chain restaurants and car dealerships. "Have you ever shot anyone?"

"Hundreds."

Sensing rebuke, she fell silent. But then, she said, "You know, Peter, I've seen Mr. Whitlock before."

"When could you have seen him?"

"I came back early from a ride yesterday because the rain was so cold. He was standing on the front porch, talking to Uncle."

"Whitlock was? What was he doing out there?"

She bowed her head. "Uncle was hiring him to kill me."

"Are you sure? How do you know?"

"Whitlock said so."

"You mean the kidnap was a fake? Oh, hell! Why didn't you tell me this back at the church?"

"I thought you knew," she said.

"Here we are," announced Nelsen as the car made a sharp left turn. Kori leaned involuntarily toward Brichter, who put a hand out to brace her. Nelsen touched his siren to warn the emergency room people they were coming, braked to a hard stop and hopped out to open the door for them.

Brichter said to him, "Go park the squad and come in." He

helped Kori into the reception area of the emergency room. The nurse saw them coming and picked up a form, her face showing concern at the state of Kori's arm and head. But Brichter asked, "Is there a phone we can use?"

"Out in the hall," the nurse said, surprised, pointing, and Brichter led Kori to a pay phone in a wide, deserted corridor.

He dialed his squad room. "Captain? Has Colly got back yet?"

"Yes, they're booking Whitlock now."

"Hell, already?"

"He's invoking his right to silence. What's the matter? Something wrong?"

"Yes, sir, I think we may have a problem. The kidnap was a scam, run by Tellios, and Kori was not supposed to come out of it alive." Kori started to move politely out of earshot, but Brichter hauled her back and bent an elbow around her neck in a gesture both custodial and comforting.

"You sure?"

"Kori told me Whitlock admitted it."

"Son of a bitch!"

"Yes, sir. If Whitlock's made his call, and it was to the ranch, I'll start feeling awful damn lonesome out here."

"Hang on." Two minutes later Ryder was back. "He made his call first thing, but no one watched while he did it."

"Jesus Christ!"

"So I'll call Colly and let him round up the SWAT boys. Go ahead and get Kori taken care of. We'll be waiting for you in the parking lot by the north entrance. How'd you get out there?"

"Mickey Nelsen. He's parking the squad."

"Well, he's better than nothing. Keep him close by you. I agree, Tellios tried it fancy and it didn't work. So he may try it plain."

Chapter
14 †

Jilly Meade asked, "Is something wrong, Mr. Januschka?"

"No, nothing," Januschka said. "I'm listening; just keep on talking." He had called her in for a personal interview on Tonk, but gotten sidetracked onto other subjects. She was more attractive and intelligent than he'd expected; and while he distrusted what he thought of as a contradiction, intelligence in women, this one was also charming and funny. But then had come the call about the kidnapping. He hadn't wanted to send her away abruptly, so he'd brought the subject back to Tonk and asked the kind of questions it took a while to answer while he tried to figure the angles of this new situation.

Her voice, light and pleasant, its words utterly unheard, took up its tale. He walked around the plush living room, absently stroking the furniture. He wandered by her chair and just as absently caressed her shoulder. Her head promptly came back to rest against his stomach and he moved away.

The phone rang, and he took big steps across the room to answer it. "Hello, Guy! What? Who is this?" He listened. "Shit! Hold on, hold on!" He put a hand over the receiver and said, "I'm gonna take this in the den. When I yell, I want to hear you hang up."

"Certainly," she said, surprised. She rose in a sensual movement he failed to note and came to take the receiver from him. He hurried out. A few seconds later she heard him say, "Bye, Jilly!" So she rapped the receiver against the base with enough force to make him wince—then pressed the privacy button and began to listen.

"How the hell did that happen?" she heard Januschka ask.

"We raided a dope pusher in an abandoned church and she was there. We didn't even know she was missing."

"She alive?"

"Sure. We're at County General Hospital, me and Brichter, with her. Her arm's broken and her head's banged up, but she's not hurt too bad. After they fix her up, she's going to the Safety Building to answer questions."

Jilly had by now recognized Nelsen's voice. He was both an open friend of Januschka's and—at a price—a secret supplier of information. But who was the girl with the broken arm?

"Listen, Mr. Januschka, Kori says the kidnap was a phony, that Tellios arranged it."

Kori, the loony at the ranch Tonk said Brichter had fallen for.

"No shit! What makes her think that?"

"Hell, she says the kidnapper admitted it—and guess who he is? That loan shark the papers are screaming about: Whitlock."

"She said that? To who?"

"Brichter. In the car on the way to the hospital. She talks to him like she likes him, and he comes on like he owns a controlling interest in her."

There was a pause, then Januschka said, "Nelsen, how'd you like to earn yourself a big chunk of money? Say forty G's?"

Nelsen asked cautiously, "What would I have to do?"

"Off her."

"No way! The world isn't a big enough place to hide from both Tellios and Brichter!"

"So take Brichter out too. I'll give you eighty grand to kill them both."

"You're nuts, if you'll pardon my saying so! Is this some kind of joke?"

"I'm serious. Nick wants Kori dead; I want Brichter dead. Here's your chance to do us both a favor. You're out there with them, pick a time and place to do it, and stop by the ranch for your money. I'm calling Nick right now about where they are. Do I tell him you've agreed?"

Dumb, Joe, Jilly thought. And Nelsen's even dumber if he agrees to it.

"I'm sorry, Mr. Januschka. This place is too busy for me to get away with something like that. Anyhow, I'm just an information collector, not a hit man. Look, they'll wonder where I am if I don't get back. This one's a freebie, since it'll probably be all over the papers in the morning. Okay? So long." He hung up without waiting for a reply.

Januschka slammed the phone down; Jilly quickly replaced the receiver and returned to her couch.

When he didn't come back, she went again to the phone, held

down the forks of the cradle, lifted the receiver, pressed the privacy button and very carefully released the cradle.

Januschka was saying, "If you'd told me the plan, I could've told you it wouldn't work! She had a chance to talk to him, and Whitlock always listens to the last person he talks to! Dammit, I warned you he wasn't reliable! And so now he's in jail and she's not even seriously hurt!"

"Are you finished, Joseph?"

"Not by a long shot! You said she didn't like cops, so why the hell is she singing to Brichter? How much can she tell him? Does she know anything about me? Christ, you and your goddamn Rube Goldberg plans! If Nelsen wasn't so goddamn chicken, I'd've finished this for you! What do you plan next? Bomb the hospital?"

Tellios said, "Calm yourself, Joseph. Things are far from over. I have a contingency plan already in motion. You stay out of it; let me handle it."

"You goddamn better handle it! Or I'll handle you!"

Kori was taken to a small treatment room. A young man with a mop of black curls introduced himself as Dr. Speigel, an intern. He clicked his tongue at her arm, removed the handkerchief from her forehead with gentle, deft fingers to look at the wound. "This will need stitches," he said to a nurse hovering nearby. He cut the twine binding her arms and helped the nurse put a gauze-covered card-board splint on. The nurse eased Kori out of her sweater and got her into a hospital gown, Brichter politely looking the other way while the change was made. The arm was X-rayed and she was seated on the end of a wheeled cart while her reflexes were tested for evidence of concussion.

"No skull fracture," said the intern. "And I'm afraid the chance of a small, interesting scar on your forehead is nil." The injury was cleaned, stitched, and bandaged. The intern and nurse were professionally kind throughout, and Kori behaved with her usual courage, but she glanced often at the continuing, silent, comforting presence of Brichter.

When she saw how they proposed to set her arm, she raised her first objection. "Do you have to do it this way?"

"Both the long bones in your forearm snapped," said the intern, "and the ends have slipped past each other. Your broken arm is an inch shorter than the whole one, see? We can't leave it like that."

"I understand that," she said, aggravated at his condescending tone.

"Well, rather than manually pull the bones apart, which I admit is quicker, but can tear the flesh, I want to use weights on the arm to make it set itself, slowly."

She turned to Brichter. "Must I allow them to do it this way?"

"The arm has to be set; this is a safer and more reliable way," he said. "Better than the other, in my opinion."

"It won't hurt a bit," explained the intern, already fastening a black cuff around her upper arm. He squeezed the bulb, inflating the cuff to cut off circulation. "See? Now I'll inject painkiller into your forearm so you won't feel a thing."

"So you say," she murmured, trying not to wince at the needle's prick, or think of the far more deadly prick barely escaped. Then the intern slipped her fingers into tubular finger splints hanging from an overhead frame, and draped a sandbag over the crook over her arm. The procedure struck her as unmedical, even grotesque, and she again looked at Brichter, who nodded reassurance.

Dr. Speigel said he would check back now and again as they waited for the oxygen-starved muscles to relax and the two broken bones to pull back and align themselves.

The room fell silent, but it was an unhappy silence. Brichter, sympathizing with her distress but unable to think of anything further to say, sat down on a metal chair in the corner, put his notebook on his knee and began writing up his notes on the recent occurrences.

She could not bear to look at the arm, though anxiety focused her attention on it. After a couple of minutes she began to whistle Bach's Fugue in G Minor, whose plaintive notes and roundlike complexity had often served her when she needed distraction.

Brichter looked up and smiled. Of the fugues, the "Little" was his favorite. He closed his notebook and when the time came in the piece, began the second part. This time she didn't stop whistling, but kept going, dropping the lead and picking up the fourth part as he began the third. They picked their way through, switching parts as expedient, he following her. They came to a rousing, harmonized finish, and she smiled at him, pleased and grateful.

The door to the little treatment room opened and Nelsen came in. "Was that you two whistling?" he asked. He was carrying a big, gunmetal-gray transceiver that was talking in a gritty female voice to itself.

"Yeah," said Brichter, without taking his eyes from her. "Where have you been?"

"Phoning in. That was really nice. I don't usually like classical music, but that was pretty nifty."

"Thank you," said Kori politely, not sparing more than a glance at him.

Nelsen noted the torture apparatus attached to her arm. "What are they doing to you?"

"They're setting her arm," said Brichter. "It should be finished soon. You go wait out in the hall, and keep an eye cocked for uninvited company."

"Yes, sir," said Nelsen, and went out.

"You seem to be afraid of him," said Brichter.

"He makes me think of that policeman who dragged me out of my hiding place."

"That's not surprising; he's the one."

She glanced at the door. "Does he remember me?"

"He remembers trying to help you. Has he ever been a guest of your uncle's at the ranch?"

"No, he's not one of Uncle's . . . friends. But I'm afraid of him. I think it's the uniform; I couldn't bear it if you wore that uniform."

"I started out in one."

"Did you?"

"All cops do. It's a rule."

Silence. Then she asked, "Are you going to arrest Uncle?"

"Yes. Don't you want me to?"

"Oh, yes. Even if you are a policeman, you're a better bargain than Uncle."

The intern and nurse came back and agreed her arm was set. They let it down and a fiberglass cast was put on. "It's lighter than plaster, and it won't hurt to get it wet," the intern said. "You can even go swimming in it." They X-rayed the arm again to make sure the bones were still properly aligned, then helped her back into her sweater. The intern said, "How about you go out in the hallway and sit awhile, and and let this harden."

Brichter took her out and seated her near the end of a long row of gray plastic chairs. He said, "Stay here; I have to go talk with Nelsen."

Nelsen apprehensively watched Brichter approach. He's going to ask me who I phoned, he thought. But the detective leaned over and said quietly, "Captain Ryder and Captain Colly and his SWAT boys are gathering in the parking lot. Be ready for a shootout."

Nelsen felt his mouth sag open. "Shootout? Why?"

"Tellios may want to finish what he started, if he's found out where she is." Nelsen was sure Januschka had called Tellios, but he didn't volunteer this information.

"Colly'll call you on your transceiver when they're set up," continued Brichter. "They're going to try to get us into a car."

"Yes, sir," he said.

"Whatever happens, take care of the girl first, got that?"

Nelsen looked away from those piercing gray eyes. "Yes, sir."

Nelson heard Brichter walk away and wiped his lower face with one hand. Shootout? In all that open space? Massacre, more like. We won't get a chance to shoot back. I shouldn't have called Joe. I might have known doing him a favor would end up killing me. I bet Brichter suspects; that's why he was so nice to me yesterday. So even if I don't die, I'm going to have to face that. They'll take away my badge, and the newspapers and television will crucify me right in front of my wife and daughters. Please, no. I swear, if I get out of this mess somehow, I'll be the best damned cop in Charter. You hear me, God?

Chapter
15 †

Brichter went back to sit beside Kori. He said quietly, "There may be trouble when we leave."

"What sort of trouble?"

"We got to you before Whitlock could kill you. So your uncle may try again."

"You think he'll send someone here."

"Not in here, but maybe waiting outside. We'll know when we walk out the door. We're being as careful as we can, and the SWAT team is stationed out in the parking lot, but there's still a chance there will be some danger. I need for you to do exactly what I tell you to do. Stay calm and we'll be just fine."

"All right. Where do we go from the parking lot?"

He smiled. "To the Safety Building, where a large number of forms wait to be filled out."

"Peter, could you take me to a bath and a change of clothes first? I'm very grubby; they only washed my hands and face here."

"Sorry, *fy'n galon*, paperwork first, bath later." He bit his tongue, then asked, "May I call you *fy'n galon*?"

She frowned. "It's a love-word, Gordon says," she said, glancing at Nelsen, who was sitting some distance away and holding his transceiver to his ear.

"Yes." Brichter clasped his hands and looked at the floor. He didn't want to alarm her by speaking of this now, but having begun he continued. "Pretty soon I won't have any official excuse to come calling on you. But I want to come out anyway, to see those beautiful horses on your ranch—it's yours, you know; your uncle was only your trustee.

"And I want to see you.

"I know what *fy'n galon* means, and I want you to allow me to call you that. It's an endearment, and it describes how I feel about

144

you. Because you are special to me. In the weeks to come, I'll try to think of prettier speeches, but you're here now, and you're listening, and this is the best I can do off the top of my stupid head."

He looked so wretched, she said gently. "That was a lovely speech. Please, call me *fy'n galon*." So he took her good hand and held it until the nurse came out and said they could go.

At the end of the corridor was a pair of heavy wooden doors that led to the parking lot. Brichter and Nelsen, now very tense, stared out the small square windows in the doors.

Nelsen's transceiver cleared its electronic throat and said, "One-seven-five Remote, this is Colly. We're in place. Are you ready to come out?"

Nelsen held down the button and said, "Yes, sir, we're waiting at the door."

"Stand by, one-seven-five Remote. The car is coming."

They waited. "See it?" asked Brichter.

"No," said Nelsen. "Wait a minute; here it comes, a station wagon, with a uniform driving. God, that thing's a yacht!"

"I wish it were a tank." Brichter turned to Kori. "Here's what will happen. He'll stop right across from here and open the front and back doors on our side. There's a veranda out there we have to cross. Walk fast, but don't run. You and I will get in the back seat, Nelsen in front. You get down on the floor and stay there until I say you can get up. Understand? They'll tell us on Nelsen's transceiver when it's time."

She nodded calmly. "May I look out the window? I want to see how broad this veranda is."

Brichter, uneasily admiring her nerve, said, "Sure." He stepped aside.

The veranda ran the length of the hospital and was about twelve feet wide. Beyond it was the parking lot. It looked perfectly ordinary in the thin spring sunlight. An old station wagon was slowly approaching. She stepped aside. "I don't see anyone out there."

"They're there, but I hope we don't need them," said Brichter. "I'm hoping we feel very silly about all these precautions in a few minutes."

"You and me both," said Nelsen.

The transceiver said, "One-seven-five Remote, let's go!"

"Ready?" asked Brichter. "Now!" They pushed against the panic bars of the doors and walked quickly across the airy veranda toward the waiting car.

They were nearly there when there was an uneven series of pops; tiny objects ricocheted off the pavement around their legs. Brichter shoved Kori into the back of the station wagon and fell prone beside the car, partly hidden behind a fat pillar. Nelsen ran around to the front of the car as the attackers fired again. Both men drew their weapons and returned fire. The station wagon rocked under the impact of a large-caliber bullet and Brichter spared a fleeting instant to hope the gas tank wouldn't blow up. Not only was Kori inside the car, the tank was inches from his head.

There was gunfire from all around the parking lot now. The big gun spoke again and the back window of the wagon exploded, showering the interior with tiny cubes of glass. *Please*, prayed Brichter.

A man came partway around the end of a van parked on the street and shot three times at them with something that took large pieces out of the column Brichter was crouched behind. Brichter and Nelsen fired back twice in almost exact rhythm. The man screamed, a horrifying sound, and fell—and, as suddenly as it had begun, the gunfire stopped. Brichter heard Colly say distinctly, "Jerks!" And then, louder, "There are policemen moving in from across the street, behind you! You can't escape! You ready to quit?" He sounded disgusted.

After a moment, a reedy voice called, "I am!"

"Throw out your gun, then!" Colly ordered. There was the sound of heavy metal impacting and sliding on blacktop. "Come on out with your hands over your head!"

"Okay! Here I come! Don't shoot!" Downey, thought Brichter.

Colly called, "How many are you?"

"Only me; Shiffler's dead!" Limping footsteps approached the wagon from the other side.

"Hold it right there! On your knees—that's good! Now, lie down, face down! Arms out, straight out! Are the others going to come out?"

"Shiffler?" called Downey, falsely bright. "You better come out! Every cop in town is here!"

There was a silence that stretched and broke. Downey said, almost to himself, "I told you he's dead."

Colly asked loudly, "Who wants to go take a look?"

Nelsen scrambled out from behind the car, startling Brichter. "I'll check, hold your fire!" he called. A minute later, he said, "There's someone here; he's dead."

Brichter heard the door to the wagon open, and he jumped to his feet. He ran around the car to see Kori coming to a halt a few yards from the man on the ground, her face tight and angry. Downey, his thin, lumpish arms stretching out of his short-sleeved brown shirt, offered his most placating grin.

"You, the girl with the arm!" shouted Colly. "Don't move! Get her out of there, someone!"

Brichter went to her and took her by the shoulders. "Let's get out of their way, okay?" He began to lead her off. "Are you hurt?"

"No. Are you?"

"No." They stopped a little beyond the station wagon and he began possessively to straighten out a twist in her sling. That's far too cool a head you've got, he thought, noting his own still trembling hands.

Ryder hurried up to them, breathing hard, putting his gun away. "Just got here; I guess I missed the action," he panted. "Anyone hurt? Where's the other two? Hinckley said he thought there were three of them."

"One of them is dead." Brichter thought and said, "You know, I thought at the start there were three, too."

"So where's the third man?"

"I didn't notice anyone running off, but I was busy ducking."

Ryder turned around and called, "Colly?"

The black man disengaged himself from a group of cops standing around the man on the ground, and walked over. "Yeah, Frank?"

Ryder asked quietly, "How many of them did you think there were?"

"Well, I thought I saw three separate points of fire to start with, but later I saw only two. Why?"

"So did Hinckley," said Ryder. "And so did Obie. That's three different angles, all seeing the same thing. You got a suspect and a body. Where's the third?"

"Shit," said Colly unhappily. "Are we going to have to do a door-to-door?"

Brichter said, "Let me talk to Downey a minute?"

Colly nodded. "Okay."

Ryder said, "Here, your girl's in her stocking feet. I'll put her in a car."

Brichter looked down at her doubting face and said, "It's okay. This is Captain Ryder, my boss. You go with him. I'll be back in a couple of minutes."

"All right," she said, stepping back from him.

The cops had fastened Downey's wrists behind his back. Brichter walked up to him and took him by the arm. "Excuse me," he said to the cops, and pulled the prisoner far enough away to be out of earshot.

"You remember me, don't you, Mr. Downey?" he asked.

"Sure," said Downey, adding hopefully, "You're a friend of ours, right?"

"Wrong, Mr. Downey. Your boss is going to be charged with, among other things, attempting to bribe a police officer."

Downey studied Brichter's face, looking for a hint this wasn't true. "Damn," he muttered. "I might've known."

"Now I'm going to ask you some questions. You don't have to answer, you have the right to remain silent. You have the right to consult with an attorney, and to an attorney's presence during questioning. If you want an attorney but can't afford one, we'll arrange to supply one for you. Do you understand?"

The words put Downey into a familiar role. He shivered. "Yeah."

"You know you're in a hell of a mess right now."

"Yeah. Yeah, I guess I am."

"You're going to be charged with attempted murder."

Downey winced. "Yeah."

"So maybe you can make it easier on yourself by talking to me. No promises, but your cooperation will be noted."

Downey squinted at him. "You gonna write it down that I cooperated?"

"I write everything down." Brichter got out his big notebook and printed the name, time, and place while Downey jittered impatiently. Brichter, noting the shivering, suddenly shouted, "Someone bring me a blanket!"

"Thanks," muttered Downey. A minute later a patrolman appeared with a dull-green wool blanket that smelled of spare tire. Brichter hung it around Downey's shoulders.

"Can I change my mind and not talk to you?" asked the cripple.

"Yes." Brichter waited.

Downey closed his eyes to think briefly. "God, I dunno. Did we hurt any of you?"

"I don't think so. I've talked with the man in charge of our SWAT team; he didn't mention anyone being hurt. There may be some minor injuries. But Shiffler's the only one dead."

"I told him to keep his goddamn head down."

"Was it your idea to come ambush us?"

Downey looked startled. *"Me?"*

"Then someone told you to do it? You were acting under orders, maybe. From someone you felt you had to obey."

"Well, yeah."

"So all this wasn't exactly your fault."

"No—no, I guess it wasn't." Faint hope dawned in Downey's eyes. He straightened a little.

"Who was it sent you?"

Downey hesitated. "Shiffler told me I better come along."

"Shiffler tells you what to do?"

Downey drew up his shoulders. The tiny rapport of a moment ago had vanished. A breeze trickled through the open front of the blanket, and he shivered. "Well, maybe he passed the orders along."

"From who?"

Barely moving his lips, Downey whispered, "Mr. Tellios."

"Mr. Tellios told you to meet us at the hospital."

"Yes, sir."

"It wasn't Shiffler at all. It was Mr. Tellios."

"Yes, sir."

"He told you to kill us."

"No, not you, not unless we had to," said Downey. "We were supposed to kill Kori." He continued hastily, "I didn't want to, honest! She ain't a bad kid; she's always been nice to me." He glanced up at the little group near the station wagon and asked bitterly, "But what the fuck can you do?"

"I don't know, Mr. Downey," said Brichter. "So Mr. Tellios sent the three of you to shoot Kori."

"Yeah—no! I mean . . ." Downey gathered his few wits. He was shivering harder now with shock and cold; with his arms fastened behind his back, he could not hold the blanket closed.

Casually, Brichter rearranged it, tossing one end across Downey's shoulder. "There were three of you, weren't there, waiting to shoot Kori as we came out of the hospital?"

"All right, there were three of us. What the hell. The shithead ran off soon as he saw you ambushed us back."

"Who was it?"

"Riscatto."

"Tellios sent you, Riscatto, and Shiffler to ambush us."

"Yeah."

"Where is Riscatto now?"

"Halfway to Chicago, probably. He's always bragging he's got friends there."

"What's he driving?"

"Pontiac. Midnight blue, brand new. A rental. He was going on vacation tomorrow, and he was pissed Nick told him to use it for this job; he had this credit card nobody's reported stolen he put the car on, and he was gonna use it for his vacation."

Writing, "What name was on the card?"

"Mason. Andrew Mason."

"Thank you, Mr. Downey; you've been very helpful. I'm going to take you back now."

Brichter found Ryder talking with Colly and a couple of detectives. "What'd you find out?" Colly asked.

"Downey says Tellios sent him, Riscatto, and Shiffler to kill Kori. He says Riscatto cut out as soon as the rest of you started shooting, possibly for Chicago. He's got a cold credit card with the name of Andrew Mason on it, and he drove off in a new midnight blue Pontiac rented under the name. Captain, I want to cut out for Tretower, if it's all right. Where's Kori?"

"In Nelsen's squad," said Ryder, pointing. "It's okay; Nelsen's with her."

"God damn it!" Brichter walked quickly to the squad car and bent to peer in the window on the passenger side.

Kori was pressed hard against the door. The window was cracked open, the motor was running, and warm air was drifting out. Nelsen was speaking, his voice cautiously friendly. "My oldest, she's thirteen, she's getting too big for her pony. She's been saving for a horse. She rides her pony hard, and likes overland treks. What do you recommend?"

After a pause Kori said stiffly, "A Morgan." She became aware of a shadow against the window and looked around and up. When she saw his face she mouthed, "Peter."

Nelsen said, "I've heard of them. Kinda on the small side, but—" Brichter opened the car door and Nelsen stopped. He saw who it was, immediately got out on his side, and started in, "Now, don't fly off the handle at me! I know she's scared, but it wasn't anything I did! I was just talking to her. Captain Ryder said stay with her, so I did."

"Yeah, I heard," said Brichter, his voice gentle. "It's all right." Kori had put both arms around him and clung to him tightly, burying her face in his neck.

Ryder appeared and asked, "What the hell's wrong?"

Brichter replied, "She's scared to death of uniforms."

"Well, why the hell didn't she say so?"

"I don't know. *Fy'n galon*, why didn't you tell him?"

"I didn't want to cause trouble. I thought maybe it wouldn't be too long." She turned around to face Ryder. "I'm sorry, please don't be angry." She bumped back against Brichter, and they were embarrassed to notice she was near exhaustion.

Ryder said kindly, "Don't be afraid to tell us things in future. Now, let's get you downtown. Obie, I sent McHugh for a warrant on my way here. Sorry to take that pleasure away from you, but I figured we should move fast on this one."

Tellios sat impatiently in his office, waiting for his men's return.

Why were they late? They could have done it, dumped the rental, and been home long ago. Unless something had gone wrong again.

No, not this time. Not even Brichter could have stopped this. He went to the window and looked out. Where were they?

Restlessly he wandered around the big room. He stopped by his desk and, on impulse, unlocked and opened a bottom drawer. The ransom, now never to be paid, lay in neat, banded stacks. He lifted up two and uncovered a little pistol. He put the gun in his belt, replaced the money and locked the drawer. He resumed his circuit of the room, stopping again at the window.

Ah, a car. It was coming up the lane fast. The rental Pontiac—which was wrong; they were supposed to have dumped it and come home in the pickup. The car stopped at the gates and Riscatto got out to open them. There didn't seem to be anyone else in the car. Alarmed, Tellios went to the door.

The Pontiac jumped across the track, did a messy U-turn in the barnyard and stopped, headed outward. Riscatto hopped out, waving. "Come on, come on!"

"What happened?"

"You got to get out of here!"

"What's wrong?"

"Cops ambushed us! Caught everyone but me. For Chrissake, hurry!"

"Let me get some things."

"No, no, no! No time! The cops are right behind me!" He looked over his shoulder toward the road, then moved to get back in his car. "I can't wait; are you coming or not?"

Tellios came down the steps and hurried across the lawn. But when he reached the car, he stopped. "Kori?" he asked.

"Dead. I saw her go down." Riscatto got in on his side, leaned across to open the door for Tellios. "Get in," he said.

Chapter
16 †

Charter's Safety Building looked like a step pyramid of five "steps." It was formed of pebble-crusted concrete slabs; at the base of each step a long, narrow strip of darkness caught fragments of the unwarmed sunlight—windows. Nelsen drove up to a concrete wall and abruptly descended a steep ramp. At the bottom an articulated steel door rose to the clanging of a bell.

They entered, parked at the end of a short row of squad cars and got out.

Nelsen, still proving himself friendly, pointed out features of the building to Kori. "We've got our own power supply in here, water supply, too. It would take an army to bust into this place. The top floor is the jail, so getting out is even harder. See that glassed-in place over there? That leads right into booking, and there's a special elevator that goes from there up to the jail. They'll bring that guy who tried to shoot us into there; you won't have to see him at all."

Nelsen didn't mention the elevator often stopped between floors, sometimes because a cop wanted to hold a brief, unregulated interrogation or teach a prisoner some manners, and sometimes because the building contractors had been cousins or brothers-in-law of city council members.

They went through a yellow metal door into the basement corridor. Its unfinished walls were painted a harsh yellow; floor tiles and the overhead with its pipes and conduits were a rich shiny blue. It smelled faintly of cement.

"Thanks for the ride back, Nelsen," said Brichter.

"You're welcome, Sergeant," said Nelsen. "See you later." He crossed the corridor, opened a door and disappeared into a stairwell.

"This way, *fy'n galon*," said Brichter, leading her to a door down

153

the hall, a wooden one with a frosted-glass inset. She entered the room ahead of him with the careful curiosity of a new cat and looked around.

"Here's where I work," he said, flipping on the lights. He looked at the room through her eyes, saw the raw colors on the rough walls, the cheap old furniture, and for the first time wished it could be different. Kori's first look at the world of law enforcement must be seriously disappointing.

"Where's Gordon?" she asked, walking into the middle of the room.

"Here, pet," said a familiar voice. Captain Ryder's door had opened and Ramsey stood in the doorway.

She turned and walked in the straightest possible line toward him; by the time he had taken three steps out of the room she had reached him.

"Oh, I was so worried about you!" she said, putting her arms around him.

"Yes, I was a bit fussed about you as well," he confessed, pressing one cheek to the side of her head as he embraced her. "Are you all right?"

"Peter came and got me," she said. "Then there was some shooting at the hospital, but I'm all right, I'm fine. Are you all right?"

"Wonderful." There was a single tear making its slow way down Ramsey's cheek. "Good, reliable Peter."

Brichter let them have a minute, then asked, "Gordie, where's Tonk?" He was supposed to be guarding Ramsey.

"He's gone to fetch Whitlock, who has changed his mind about being interrogated. He should be back soon." Ramsey loosened his hold on Kori and said, "I expect you want to talk to her."

"Yes. I'll try not to be long."

"Where will you go from here?" asked Kori, turning around to face him, but keeping hold of Ramsey's hand. Her tired face was radiant.

"Captain Ryder said he'd arrange a safe place. I don't know where, but it's in town, I think."

The door to the squad room opened, and Norman Whitlock was shoved forward, then brought up with a jerk. His red hair stood up like wet feathers; he was furiously angry. His hands were cuffed behind his back and his shirt was unbuttoned nearly to the navel, evidently because a bunch of it had been grabbed up from behind. By Tonk.

"You goddamn son-of-a-bitchin' pig!" Whitlock shouted over

his shoulder. "Quit shovin', hear? You ain't got no right to be shovin' me around! I'm gonna—" He stopped speaking as he saw the others. His electric-blue eyes snapped from face to face, then came back to rest on Kori. With preternatural suddenness he was calm and friendly.

"Hey, there, pretty lady! Remember me? I see they got your arm fixed an' all! I bet you were really scared there for a while, but things are just fine now, right? I mean we're all nice and safe here in the police department, and we won't let them niggers try an' hurt you anymore."

Tonk took Whitlock by the arm and said warningly, "Don't you be talking to her." He said to Brichter, "Since you're back, I guess I can take him upstairs to an interrogation room, right? C'mon, Whitlock." He began to reverse directions.

"Hey!" Whitlock protested, resisting movement. "I got a right to talk to my friends!"

"You got no friends in here I can see," said Tonk, beginning to push.

"Sure I do! Hey, I think you all ought to take it easy on the purty lady. After all she's been through, if you try to talk to her now, she'll get ever'thing bass-ackwards! Maybe even say it was *me* who kidnapped her!" Tonk reached around his prisoner and opened the door. "You should maybe just take her home"—Tonk pushed him through the door—"put her to bed and—" The words were cut off by the closing door, though the sound of them continued, fading, up the hall.

Brichter stared awhile at the closed door, a speculative look in his pale eyes.

Kori asked Ramsey, "Was that Tonk?"

"Yes, pet. Is that vicious animal with him the man who kidnapped you?"

"Yes, but, he wasn't ever angry like that, just . . . nasty."

"Clever of him to suggest that questioning you now, when you're tired, could produce a distorted account. My dear pet, I want you to answer all of Peter's questions. And if he misses something, I want you to volunteer information. Can you do that?"

She said warily, "I'll try."

"Good," said Brichter. "Come over here to my desk." He seated her, sat down himself and rolled a yellow form into his typewriter.

She picked up his orange mug, which had a small dried brown puddle in its bottom. *"Illegitimi non Carborundum,"* she read. "Did you letter this on here?"

"No. Do you know what it means?"

" 'Don't let the bastards wear you down,' I suppose. It's not very good Latin." She smiled. "But it's an . . . interesting sentiment."

"Glad you approve," he said, and added, mock-solemn, "what's your name, ma'm?"

"Kori."

"Katherine McLeod Price," he said, as if repeating her, typing. "Address?"

"Tretower Ranch. What are we doing?"

"Getting a statement. I also want to ask you why your uncle went to all that trouble—" He was interrupted by his phone ringing, and he swooped up the receiver. "Organized Crime Unit, Sergeant Brichter— Who? Hi, Cris; no, Ryder's not back yet! *What?*" He listened very intently. "Oh, Christ!" He turned the receiver away and pressed the back of his hand against his forehead. Then he sighed, turned it back around and said, "Hold on." He punched the "hold" button and looked at Ramsey and Kori. "Tellios is gone."

"He got away?" asked Ramsey.

"Well, maybe. His car is still out there. McHugh found the gates open, the house lit up and unlocked, and no one there. They're searching the grounds for him."

"Oh, hell," muttered Ramsey.

"Mind the dogs," warned Kori.

"Jesus!" exclaimed Brichter, punching the button. "Cris, there are five outsize German shepherd types that guard the racetrack. Check the kennel near the barn; if they're not in there, for Christ's sake cross the racetrack only in your car. They attack without warning, and they're killers. Hold again for just one minute, okay?" He punched the red button. "Where the hell could Tellios have gotten to without a car?"

"Riscatto took him," said Kori.

Brichter considered the idea. "No," he said, "I don't think he'd have any desire to save his boss."

"I'm sure he wouldn't," she said. "But he thinks he has cause to take him away and kill him."

Brichter punched the extension button and asked, "Sorry to hold you up like this, but we're talking something over. Is Dr. Ramsey's car out there? Yeah, that little old-fashioned one is his. Okay. Hang on a second again." He pressed the red button and said to Ramsey, "We spotted the pickup a few blocks from the hospital. Are there any other vehicles he might have taken?"

"No."

Brichter put McHugh back on. "All right, look around very carefully. But we're talking over the idea someone came and took him away." He listened. "Yeah, I know. Look, I've got some things to do here, then I'll be out to help. Your warrant cover a search? Fine. Right. Bye, Cris." He hung up, leaving his hand on the top of the phone while he thought.

"I'm sorry," he said, turning to her. "I thought we'd finish this up tonight. Arrest that old man and set you free."

"It's all right. Peter, may I go home tonight?"

"No, we'll want to keep you in town until we find your uncle."

"But what if Riscatto buries the body?"

"You really think he'd like to kill him?"

"Oh, yes. They all hated him. I'm sure that's why Riscatto came and took him away. Uncle's game is over, now he's shown he's not omnipotent. Riscatto has been working on breaking loose, I think. Used to be, he stayed close to the ranch and treated me very nicely, but lately he's turned rude, and he's been missing meals to go into town. And he's been inflated with some secret pleasure. I was wondering if he had a girlfriend." She turned in her chair to look at Ramsey. "Aren't I right? Haven't you noticed him like that lately?"

Ramsey overturned both hands in a shrug. "No, but I don't work with him every day, as you do."

"I don't think he rented that car for a vacation," she said, turning back. "I think he thought he'd found a way out."

"So why not just take it? Why come out and kill Tellios?"

"I don't know." She reached up to rub her forehead, but her hand glanced away in surprise when it encountered the bandage, as if she'd forgotten it was there. "Is Joe Januschka really the boss? Or is Uncle?"

"Januschka."

"Was there a power struggle?"

"I've heard rumors to that effect," said Brichter, also remembering the angry look to Januschka's walk as he left the big house the other night. "Why do you ask?"

"The men at the ranch spoke disparagingly of Joe Januschka. Except . . . This is a very small thing, but recently I've heard Riscatto call him Mr. Januschka. Not around Uncle, but in conversation with Shiffler and Downey. Before, whenever Januschka's name came up in conversation, he was called Joe. Then all of a sudden it was Mr. Januschka. At dinner he said, 'I see Joe's back from Vegas.' But the next morning I heard him tell Shiffler, 'Mr.

Januschka's going to fight that traffic ticket on grounds of harassment.' Could it be that Riscatto went to Mr. Januschka for help?"

"Why would Joe Januschka even talk to Guy Riscatto?"

"Maybe because Guy was looking for a way out, and offered to switch sides in the power struggle."

"Have you seen or heard anything else that might indicate that?"

"Well, the story in the newspaper only said Mr. Januschka had gotten a parking ticket, his ninth. It didn't say he was going to fight it."

Brichter beamed all over her and wrote something in his notebook.

Kori smiled back and asked, "How long do I have to stay in town?"

"Only a few days, probably."

The smile vanished. "Days? I can't stay for days!"

"Why not?"

"The horses have to be taken care of!"

"Don't worry, *fy'n galon*, we'll take care of them." He made another note in his notebook. "Somehow." He turned again to the form. "How old are you?"

"Twenty," she said, her eyes concerned and unhappy. " 'Somehow' isn't good enough."

"Trust me. But first things first. What's your phone number?"

"You know my phone number. Peter, I need to go out there, and stay until I can arrange for someone to take over. Blue's off fore is tender, Coppy needs to be handled, and the farrier's coming day after tomorrow—"

"None of which is as important as your safety," interrupted Brichter.

"I'm not in any danger. Riscatto will see to it I never see either of them again." She lifted a hand against another interruption. "All right, just tonight and tomorrow morning? Tonight will be safe enough; you and your fellow police will take all night searching the place; there are a lot of places to look. I could sleep in the cottage . . ." She turned in her chair. "Couldn't I, Gordon?"

"Yes, if you like."

"Don't encourage her, Gordie."

She turned back to Brichter. "And you could watch while I feed the horses in the morning and help me write instructions for whoever comes to take care of them."

Brichter tapped the notepad with his pencil. "About the kidnapping: Do you remember them shooting Summer Wind?"

She turned away, caught off guard, then brushed at her tearless eyes with the back of a hand. "No."

Ramsey caught her eye and raised his eyebrows warningly.

Making an effort, she said, "I was riding along toward the east fence and we both—"

"Both?" interrupted Brichter.

"Summer Wind and I. We both thought maybe someone was among the trees by the fence. Then a man with a rifle came out and—and then I was dizzy and sick and being carried through the fence by a someone. He was very pleased with himself. He tied that handkerchief around my head and fixed it so I couldn't see. He said he'd only winged Summer Wind, but even then I thought maybe he was dead. He put me in the trunk of a car and drove me away."

"Did you see or hear anyone else during the time of the kidnap?"

"No. He drove what seemed a long way, then he helped me out and into a building. Inside, he lifted the handkerchief so I could see, and it was the church you found me in. I said I thought my arm was broken, and he took it as if to look, but squeezed hard. I cried out, but he just kept squeezing, saying if I'd quit pulling it would stop hurting. He was—interested in the way I reacted, in a scary and disgusting way. He made me promise to answer when spoken to and behave; then he tied my hands and feet."

"Then what happened?" Brichter made a brief note.

"He called Uncle on a cordless phone and carried me over so I could talk to him. Uncle told me it would be over soon and to be brave. Whitlock made threats about my safety if a ransom of fifty thousand was not paid, but when he hung up I told him Uncle had said to kill me, right? And that surprised him."

"I bet!" said Brichter. "Were you sure or just guessing?"

"I was sure. I said I knew Uncle had hired him because I'd seen him at the ranch the day before, standing on the porch with Uncle. And that he shouldn't kill me because maybe I could help him."

"Did he believe you?"

"He didn't believe, which was good enough. We talked about it, then about anything else I could think of, about how it was my fault he had to shoot Summer Wind, and about what Uncle held over him—he said it was a recording Uncle had made during a telephone conversation, but he wouldn't say what it was about. Except later he let slip it would involve him in a murder charge. We tried to work out a plan to retrieve it."

"Did you come up with one?"

"Nothing workable. I wasn't trying to come up with one, really;

I was only trying to keep him from killing me until you could arrive." She smiled. "It was close, but you made it. Am I under arrest?"

"No, of course not!"

"Then I could go home if I wanted to."

"For your own protection, I could prevent that."

"Would you?"

"Yes. Did Whitlock mention Joe Januschka at all while you were with him?"

She thought. "No."

The door opened and Ryder came in. "What the hell's this about Tellios?" he asked.

They glanced around, startled. "He's gone," said Brichter. "Who told you?"

"Cris called Dispatch to ask for more men and said Tellios isn't out there. It's all over the building."

Brichter said, "As soon as I finish up here with Miss Price, I'm going out to help."

"He could finish up with me on the way, or out there, if he likes," said Kori.

"What?" Ryder frowned at her.

"I want to go home, Captain."

"Nonsense. I've arranged safe accommodations for you and Dr. Ramsey right up the street."

Kori said nothing, but her manner as she turned away from him spoke of a rebellious heart.

Ryder came toward the desk saying, "Now, Miss Price, you don't want to go out there; they'll be turning the place inside out from now till noon tomorrow; you wouldn't get any rest."

She turned back to look up at him. "Captain, I'm very tired. It will take a certain amount of time to go out there and bring back clothing and other necessary articles for me. Surely it would be more efficient to let me ride out with Peter. It's nearly suppertime and I'm really tired. I could get something to eat in my own kitchen and go right to bed. You could line my horses up on the porch and shoe them in the hall and I'd sleep right through it." She raised a forestalling hand. "And if you're so concerned about someone coming back to harm me, simply leave the dogs out. If that's not enough, let Sergeant Brichter remain there with us. I want to stay out there until we find someone who can take care of the horses in my absence."

Ramsey smothered his mouth with his hand.

"No, no, Obie won't want to stay out there," said Ryder, aggravated.

"Why not? He's going out there anyway; he said so himself.
Why can't he stay? We have plenty of empty beds." She appealed
to Brichter. "Tell him, please, Peter."

"Maybe it would be less bother all around," Brichter said, surprising himself as much as anyone. "We can stop off at my place on
the way so I can get my razor."

Ryder threw up his hands. "Oh, hell, all right, go! Finish that report and get out of here! I've got my own work to do!"

Riscatto slowed as they capped the top of a steep hill—he had no
wish for another encounter with a slow farmer pulling something
that looked as if it came from outer space. Maybe it hadn't been
such a good idea to avoid the freeway on this series of back roads;
beyond the occasional hilltop startle, it lengthened the trip by
hours.

On the other hand, they'd be far less likely to encounter a cop
out here in the sticks.

"Where are we going?" asked Tellios.

"Chicago, for now. I've got contacts up there; they'll hide us until we figure out what to do next."

"I don't understand about the shooting. You say the cops were
right there, waiting. How the hell did they know?"

"I dunno. It was like going up against an army. They came at us
from all sides. I was lucky to get away."

"Brichter get hit?"

"I don't think so."

"But you think Kori was. Are you sure the radio doesn't work?
Maybe we should stop in the next town and call—"

"Relax," Riscatto ordered. "I don't think; I know. Must've been
four, five bullets hit her. Shiffler got her once with that goddamn
cannon, and I got her twice myself. There's no way she could've
survived that. There's no need to call."

But Tellios couldn't relax. He was beginning to regret coming
away with Riscatto. There was a funeral to plan for, a burial to arrange. He wished he'd brought some of that money with him, or
his checkbook. He'd have to borrow plane fare back. He began to
think up a story to tell the cops about why he ran. A respected man
like himself shouldn't have to go to jail.

† † †

There seemed to be people everywhere—house, cottage, barn, and sheds. Some were in uniform.

"When McHugh asks for reinforcements, that's what he gets," said Brichter.

"Perhaps with Tellios gone and the *Clarion* starting to call for reform, they feel it's time to make a show of decency," said Ramsey, and Brichter cringed at the bitter tone in his voice. Ramsey had never before voiced any criticism of Charter's finest.

Brichter got out and they did, too. "I want to go check on the cottage," said Ramsey, marching off down the lawn.

"They'd better not be searching through his things again," said Kori. Brichter led her across the lawn, up the steps onto the big old porch. The door was not locked. He opened it for her and they went into the hall. A policeman was on his knees in front of a benchseat that formed the base of a mirrored coatrack. He was methodically removing and inspecting old overshoes and riding crops while another policeman watched.

Brichter took her into the parlor. McHugh was sitting behind the rolltop desk, lips pursed, counting money. He stopped when he saw them and got to his feet.

"*Fy'n galon*, this is Sergeant Cris McHugh, one of the men I work with. Cris, Miss Price."

McHugh's eyes crinkled in a pleasant smile. "Pleased to meet you. I'm afraid we're sort of taking the place apart right now."

"That's all right," she said. "I don't mind."

"We're sure Tellios is not in the house or anywhere around it," said McHugh to Brichter. "But it looks like he left without packing so much as a toothbrush."

"Then maybe he was taken away." Brichter put a hand on Kori's shoulder with the air of a man taking a permitted liberty. "She needs to be in bed," he said. "Has her room been searched yet?"

"No, we've just done a walk-through upstairs. Go find Logan if you want to do it now; he's in the library with Erdahl—off the dining room."

"Okay, I'll be as quick as I can," Brichter promised her, and went out.

Kori stayed shyly near the door. Her braids were nearly hidden in the mist of hair that stood up around her head or curled down around her ears. The bandage across her forehead was only a little whiter than her exhausted face. She cradled her broken arm in the good one as if it pained her.

McHugh moved away from the desk. "Sit down here. You look about whipped."

"Yes, I am tired," she said in her pleasant low voice, taking the swivel chair. "Thank you. What's this money?"

"We're not sure. Was your uncle in the habit of keeping large sums of money in his desk?"

"Sometimes. How much is it?"

"Fifty thousand dollars, on first count."

"Oh," she said, "it's my ransom. No, my blood money." She reached out a forefinger and gingerly touched a stack. "I don't suppose many people get to see their own blood money."

"I did, once," McHugh said. "It was evidence at a trial. Someone paid this guy sixty dollars to kill me, but made the mistake of paying him off ahead of time, and the guy used some of it to buy brandy. I found him passed out in the back seat of my car." McHugh's tone was as much indignant as amused.

Kori looked at him in surprise, then her face lightened and she laughed. Under the tiredness and grimy clothes, McHugh thought, there was a wonderfully pretty young woman. No wonder Brichter went for this.

"What was that name Peter called you?" he asked. "Vin-something?"

"*Fy'n galon.* It's Welsh, a piece of evidence he's taken to using as a private nickname."

"Evidence?"

"My father called me that, and I think it was my remembering it that helped Uncle decide I had to die."

"Nice man, your uncle." He grabbed for a wicker-bottomed chair and sat down. "I'll bet you're glad he's gone."

"I'd rather know where he's gone to," she said.

"Any idea where we should look?"

"No, but I think Riscatto took him away and shot him." She closed her eyes and murmured, "I wonder what he told Uncle to get him into his car? I would have thought it terribly hard to frighten Uncle into fleeing." Her eyes opened. "I'm sorry, I'm drifting away."

"You've had a hard day."

"Yes, and in only a little over half the normal time, too." She sighed and gathered herself. "Thank you for helping Peter rescue Gordon." The amused look was suddenly back. "Gordon told me about your putting the ring into the chair. How nice to have such clever hands."

"We worked out the scam together. Peter's a bright guy."

"Yes, he is," she agreed.

"And he's really crazy about you."

Her face went still. "Yes."

"Don't you like him?"

"Oh, yes," she said lightly, and changed the subject. "What do you do when you're not being a policeman?"

"Pub crawl. Fish. Search for a really good jazz band."

Kori asked, "Are there some good places to catch fish around here?" she asked.

"There's a lake not twenty miles from here that offers great bass."

She nodded. "I'd like to try fishing sometime. There's a man on television Saturday mornings who sits in a boat fishing. He talks very quietly and it seems somehow like Christmas Eve, peaceful and yet full of anticipation." She caught his smile and apologized, "Gordon says I intellectualize things."

"You'll start getting over that now you're free."

"Free?" She liked that idea. "Yes, perhaps I will."

The door opened and Brichter was back. Kori's face brightened further and she went to him, took his hand and turned to smile at McHugh.

"Thanks for keeping me company," she said.

"My pleasure," he said, and thought, Nevertheless, there's no way Obie Brichter will be able to hang on to this one.

As they went up the stairs, Brichter said, "I'll see if I can rustle up a sandwich and bring it to you."

"No, I've changed my mind about supper, thank you."

Her room's elegant outlines were blurred by a superabundance of white furniture draped with white eyelet lace pinched into ruffles. The only color came from a blue carpet on the floor and a number of embroidered pillows on the bed. "Everything looks the same," she said.

"We tried to put things back; you'll notice some out of place in the morning."

"I almost wish you had torn it all down," she said. "It's Uncle's idea of a good little girl's room, and I don't much care for it."

He thought it was her guilt stepping out again, then realized a young businesswoman engaged, not only in the delivery of baby horses but in the other end of the pregnancies as well, might find this frosted confection silly. "Are you sure you don't want a sandwich or something?" he asked.

"Yes, thank you," she said, "but I think I'll take one of those pills the doctor gave me. My arm hurts."

"The painkiller's worn off. Or did I hurt it pushing you into the car? Let me see."

Obediently she took her arm out of the sling and held it out to him. He flexed her fingers and looked for signs of swelling and blueness. "Sometimes you act almost like a doctor," she said.

"That's because I was a paramedic for a while. No, this is fine." But he did not release the arm, nor did he move away.

She became aware that he was looming over her, and that he was male; and when she looked up at him, he cupped her pointed chin in his big hand and gently kissed her.

It wasn't much of a kiss; she wasn't used to being kissed. So he tried again, with more success, but then she pulled away and went to stand at the room's lovely oriel window, back to him. "I think you had better go downstairs now," she said.

"All right. Shall I send Gordie up to help you into bed?"

"No, I can manage."

"Sleep well, *fy'n galon.*"

"Thank you."

Later, Ramsey came in, a bowl of soup in one hand. She was already asleep. He held the bowl under her nose, which, after a few moments, twitched. Her eyes blinked to half-mast.

"Hello, I thought you needed this more than you need to sleep."

"No, 'm fine," she murmured.

He kept the bowl near her cheekbone. "Did you have a bath?"

" 'm-hmmm."

"That reminds me: Where's the linen closet? With Peter staying the night, I want to lay out extra towels."

"End of the hall. What kind of soup is that?"

"Beef noodle, your favorite." He helped her sit up and handed her a spoon.

She took a tentative bite, then another, larger one. "I guess I am hungry." She ate a few more bites, then said, "They didn't unplug my alarm clock, did they? I don't want to sleep too long; there's a lot to do tomorrow. With this arm, I wonder how I'll saddle . . ." Her feet moved under the covers. "I forgot. Where is he?"

"Downey said your uncle called Jack Clark to come with his

backhoe. He's being buried where he fell, saddle, bridle and all. Pet, I am so sorry about Summer Wind."

"I know. Thanks. But how am I going to do chores with one arm and no Downey or Riscatto?"

"We'll have to hire a hand straightaway. I'll try, but I won't be much help."

"Yes," she agreed, "you never did learn which end of a pitchfork to pick up." There was a silence while she ate some more. "Gordon, may I move into the cottage tomorrow? Just for a while, until I get used to things."

"Of course. I was going to suggest it if you didn't ask. And Peter and I will be here tonight, in case you wake up afraid."

"Thanks." She tilted the bowl in his hand to get the last of the juice. "I wonder if that money downstairs is mine."

"Money?"

"There was fifty thousand dollars in Uncle's desk. My ransom."

"I should think it's probably evidence."

"Oh. Yes, probably." She dropped the spoon into the bowl with a clatter and lay back. "Well, I'll get out the checkbooks tomorrow and see where we are. Enough to last until insurance is paid on Summer Wind, I hope. His next foal's not due until July, so unless we find a buyer for Blue Wind's filly, we've no income until then. How much does one pay for a hired hand?"

"I suppose it depends on how much skill he has," said Ramsey, not very helpfully.

"Well, bring on the problems," she murmured. "We're free, Gordon; we made it."

"Peter doesn't think it's over yet."

"Bother Peter! And thanks for the soup."

He bent to kiss her pale forehead. "God bless Peter," he contradicted firmly. "And you're welcome."

The car slowed and turned off the highway onto a gravel road. Tellios stirred from a doze, looked out the window, saw in the near-darkness giant clumps of white. "Where are we?"

"The end of the road, old man." The car bumped and jounced along. Tellios gripped the door handle to brace himself. It was an orchard they were driving into, the trees all in bloom.

"What is this?" he asked.

The car stopped, and Riscatto shut off the engine. "Like I said, the end of the road. Get out."

"The hell I will!" Tellios' head came around and he saw the gun, a nickel-plated automatic.

Riscatto grinned at his start of surprise. "C'mon, out!"

"Why are you doing this?" asked Tellios.

"Get out and I'll tell you."

Tellios opened the door with his right hand, at the same time reaching for the buttons on his suit coat with his left. He got out slowly, much more angry than afraid, hand on the little pistol in his belt.

He whirled and fired at the same instant Riscatto did, and felt himself blown backward by a blow to his chest. He rolled once and lay still, not dead, not even unconscious, but unable to move. He waited for Riscatto to get out of the car, to come and fire the make-sure shot into his head. But Riscatto didn't come.

He heard a whining sound coming from the car. I got him, he thought with savage satisfaction.

After a minute the pained breathing turned to a groan, which was terminated by a car door slamming. That's the door to my side, he thought. He waited some more, but the other door didn't open; Riscatto still didn't come.

I hope he's dying in there, Tellios thought. Suddenly the car's engine picked up and headlights swept jerkily over him, and stopped. He found himself staring right into the headlights. He still couldn't move, deliberately didn't blink. The headlights stared a long time, then moved away.

He listened while the car moved unevenly out of the orchard and its engine noise faded away. Goddamn amateur left me here to bleed to death. Stupid jerk didn't know enough to make sure.

He waited, feeling himself grow light and hollow. When he was only a shell and therefore light enough to move, he rolled onto his back and looked up, and saw, beyond the white cloud of blossoms, a single star. Not yet, he said. Not with her blood so fresh on my hands. I'll go to hell for Riscatto, but not her. Let me live long enough to find out why he did this to me, and kill him for it. But he continued to grow lighter until he felt himself drifting up and away.

Chapter
17 †

Brichter lay heavily asleep in the narrow wooden bed. Kori knocked twice, softly, and when he did not respond, opened the door. "Peter? Wake up."

"Whosit?" he demanded, startled.

"It's Kori."

He lay back down, grabbing at the blanket. "Wha' timesit?"

"Seven-fifteen. Breakfast is almost ready."

He rubbed his eyes and got them open. She was wearing jeans and a red sweater, and looked remarkably well and fresh, despite the sling and head bandage. She asked, "Are you really awake?"

"Uh-huh. But I can't get up till you go away."

"Ah," she said, suspicions confirmed, and the door closed.

With an effort he got to his feet. Three hours' sleep was hardly worth going to bed for, especially when one hated the waking-up process as he did. He wrapped a towel around his middle, checked the hall for pedestrians and hurried across to the big bathroom, a beautiful green-and-gray Victorian restoration with dolphin-shaped fixtures. And no shower, he noted glumly. But the boxed tub was enormous, the supply of hot water ample, the big new bar of soap fragrant without being feminine. Halfway through his bath he began to whistle.

He put on his second-best suit, a blue gabardine, and came down to the cheery orange kitchen. Kori and Ramsey were deep into a mushroom omelet, with marmalade toast and cups of rich, fragrant English tea. Ramsey had made a half-pot of coffee for him and Brichter gratefully poured himself a cup. He sat down and said, "Good morning."

"There's a paper, if you like," said Kori.

"Thanks," he said, reaching for it. He folded it so he could read the headline story, and reached for a piece of buttered toast.

168

"Marmalade?" offered Ramsey.

"No, thanks. How long have you been up, anyway?"

"She got up before I did," said Ramsey.

Kori said, "I've been out in the barn, discovering how difficult it is to muck out one-handed."

"I wish I could stay out here and help you."

She smiled at the sincerity in his voice, and he felt, not for the first time, that there was something to be said for men who could not spout blarney.

He drank his coffee and looked at the paper.

The Charter *Clarion* was trumpeting news of the events of yesterday. Kidnapped woman rescued. Shootout in hospital parking lot. Ex-gangster missing—Tellios' unsavory past, heretofore ignored by the press, was now played up. Whitlock was described as a vicious low-echelon hood, and the story of his beating a loanshark rap was retold (editorial page 12, noted the editor). Reports from the scene of the shootout were "confused." Brichter's part in the rescue was described as "brilliant detective work," and his participation in the shootout as "heroic." He snorted and turned to page 3, where several people prominent in city politics were quoted as saying they had never really been friends, exactly, with Mr. Tellios. He snorted again.

On the editorial page the county prosecutor's head was again demanded, and the police department was savaged for not having taken an earlier interest in Nick Tellios; though the sentiments were his own, Brichter didn't read past the first sentence of either editorial.

Brichter said, "The press is going to ask for an audience. Do you want to say anything to them?"

"Not I," said Ramsey.

"No, thank you," said Kori.

"Well, if you don't want to be bothered, why don't you turn the horses out to pasture now and come with me to the Safety Building? Both of you."

"I can't," she said. "Copper Wind needs a leading lesson today and lots of my company. He's got to be started now on the bonding process."

"You're keeping him?"

"Yes, now that Summer Wind—" She stopped, grabbed blindly and warmed her cup of tea with coffee. "Would you like some more coffee?"

"Yes, please."

She put the coffeepot down, reached for the teapot, looked with distress at her own cup. "I'm sorry, I'm all anyhow this morning," she said.

"Can I do anything to help?" he asked gently.

"No." She filled his cup with coffee. "Well, yes, maybe. I can't manage alone; I need a hired hand. Is there some way you can find me someone right away—today?"

He thought. "There's a labor pool in town. I'll call them, ask them to send out some candidates. Maybe you can pick a temporary hand from among them."

She gave him the speculative look she'd given him when he'd proved to know something about cannon bones. "Thank you."

He finished his coffee, checked his watch, stood. "I'd better get going. Thanks for the breakfast."

"You didn't eat much," worried Ramsey.

"I'll make it up at lunch."

"And then come to supper," offered Kori. "Is six-thirty too early?"

"No, that would be fine. Thank you. Um, would you like to go somewhere after supper?"

She looked at Ramsey, who said generously, "I think I'll stay home. You two go."

"Thank you, I'd like that," she said to Brichter. She stood. "I'll walk you to your car."

The morning sky was leaden. "We could use a soaking rain," she said, casting an agricultural eye at the clouds as they crossed the sloping lawn. A squad car was parked a little down from the outside gate. "He's rather ostentatious, isn't he?"

"We call it the halo effect; his presence alone is a deterrent. But he won't let anyone past without checking who it is."

"Will he be there all the time?"

"He or another. Ryder ordered a man on around the clock, until we find your uncle."

"But there's no real danger, is there? Even if Uncle's alive, he's with Riscatto, too busy hiding to come back here."

"Maybe. But his pattern thus far has been to send someone else after you. Do you know why? I mean, why he's so anxious to have you dead?"

She shrugged and looked away. "No. He was always so good to me, so protective. This is like a nightmare; I'm in danger without knowing how I got there."

He put an arm around her shoulders. "We're doing everything

we can to keep you safe." He got in his car and rolled down the window. "But leave the dogs out too, okay?"

She looked at a black-and-bronze animal standing near a railing, watching them. "I have to; I don't know how to get them in. Will you see Downey today?"

"Yes, first thing, I hope. Why?"

"They won't eat or drink on the track. I'll need to get them back in the kennels long enough to be fed and watched. Shiffler was in charge of them; maybe he told Downey how to do it."

"I'll ask."

"I'll open the gates for you." She walked over and pushed the gate open, walking it right out in front of the dog.

"Be careful!" he called.

"It's all right. I've done this before. If you open the gate and make a fence of it toward him, it's safe. It's finding yourself afoot on the track with nothing between you and him that means trouble." She opened the second gate, pulling it inward, making a bridge across the track. The squad car started up and moved out of the way. She came back to look through the window of his car.

"And yes, I'll fasten them shut again after you go," she said, smiling at his obvious concern. "I look forward to this evening," she added.

"Meanwhile, go back to bed; you need more rest."

"After you call about the dogs, I promise."

He looked in his rearview mirror as he started down the lane and saw her waving at him. At the end of the lane he turned onto the road and, with a single glance back at the beautiful house rising above its cluster of buildings, he roared off to town, making wishes he dared not express, even to himself.

A cool breeze touched Tellios' face and something tickled his ear. He moved his fingers and touched grass. He opened his eyes and saw a mass of blossoms.

Apple blossoms. He was in an orchard. Riscatto had shot him, that's why he hurt.

But he was alive.

Very slowly he got to his knees, then remembered something. He began to search in the grass. His upper left chest was stiff and painful. He was light-headed and very thirsty. He could use his left arm, if he was careful about it. Ah, there it was. He picked up the pistol and pushed it into his belt. Carefully, with stops to rest, he got to his feet.

He checked his watch. Eight o'clock in the morning. He had to get out of here, find a doctor. No. Gunshot wounds were reported. If a doctor saw that wound in his chest, he might know it wasn't self-inflicted, and next thing he knew, Brichter'd be up here asking to take him to jail. No doctor.

He'd go home. Nobody was there now; who would think he might circle back? Home, with the secret stash and his bed and a tame doctor from town. How far was it? He needed a car. If he could get out on the highway, he could commandeer a car. The breeze stirred his hair. Better get moving; it felt like rain.

He looked around. Which way was out? That way.

The left front of his suit coat felt stiff. Good thing it was black; cars didn't like stopping for people whose fronts they could tell were all bloody.

The walking cleared his head a little. Why had Riscatto done it? He'd been a little insolent the last few weeks, something Tellios had noticed but been too busy to do anything about. Busy fixing other things gone wrong, making hasty new deals, reassuring old friends, until he had begun to feel like that cartoon character in the boat that keeps spouting new leaks.

Funny, though, he wouldn't have thought Riscatto would have the nerve to come after him like that, not after all those quiet years. It would have been more like him simply to clear out. Maybe somebody nudged him in my direction. Joseph's angry face swam up in his memory, and he nodded to himself. Riscatto had spent a lot of hours away from the ranch lately—in Joseph's house, probably, drinking Joseph's whiskey and allowing Joseph to mutter in his ear.

So Riscatto, if he didn't die of his wound, would report to Joseph that Nick Tellios was dead. Good, he wanted to be dead, at least for now. When he was safely far away, he'd send Joseph a postcard. Riscatto would be hard put to explain a postcard from a dead man. Though it was unlikely Joseph would give him a chance to try. Tellios stopped to decide whether he preferred the amusing image of Riscatto trying to explain or the deadly image of him being shot in the head without knowing who or why. In a minute he set off again. Which way had he been going? That way.

A few minutes later, he stopped again to rest. The trees in the orchard were all alike and formed rows no matter which way he looked. Maybe he'd been going the wrong way. He started off in a deliberately different direction. Soon, his chest one gigantic ache, he had to stop again. This must be the biggest apple orchard in the state, he thought angrily.

When he was able to resume walking, he no longer tried to follow a row of trees, but simply went from one to the next.

After a long while he felt gravel under his feet and looked down, surprised. A lane. He stumbled to the right and kept going in that direction, moving slowly. Soon he came across an old, flimsy-looking shed. On the other side of it was parked a dusty Volkswagen Rabbit. He looked around, but there was no sign of its owner. Cautiously, he approached it. If the car was unlocked . . . It was. He got behind the wheel and sat a long minute, relieved and regrouping. He was incredibly thirsty.

At last he stirred and looked around the interior. Standard transmission, on the floor. He moved the stick experimentally. No keys, but once upon a time that had been no problem. He leaned sideways, groped for wires under the dash. He pulled two loose and twisted them together. The little car started promptly and he smiled in satisfaction. He put it in gear and drove off down the lane, testing brakes and clutch as he went.

The lane soon emptied onto a narrow blacktop road—not the main highway. He looked both ways, made a guess and turned left.

When Brichter walked into the squad room, his phone was ringing. He picked it up. "Organized Crime Unit, Sergeant Brichter. May I help you?"

"Hi, Obie, it's Max Dussault of the *Clarion*. Say, could you give us a statement about that girl you rescued? I hear she and you had a thing going before all this happened, and—"

"No," interrupted Brichter.

"Say again?"

"No statement. No comment." He hung up and went to start the coffeepot, taking it up the hall to the deep sink where it was rinsed—not washed; Brichter had learned to make coffee in the Navy—and filled, and brought it back. He put in one more scoop of grounds than the recipe called for, plugged it in and went to pull what information was in the file cabinets on Riscatto, Downey, and Shiffler.

Guy Riscatto was thirty-five and, according to an informant of McHugh's, knowledgeable about horses. He'd been seen having a drink with Joe Januschka in Chauncey's six or seven weeks ago. He was not known to be a drinker, womanizer, or brawler. He had been a racehorse trainer, but was barred from several tracks around the country, no reason available.

Paul Michael Shiffler, surprisingly, had a record right here in Charter—an arrest for drunk driving. That had happened almost eight years ago. Shiffler had served two days, paid a stiff fine, completed a safe-driving course, and helped out seven nights at the emergency room at County Hospital before having his chauffeur's license returned. That must have been an accident plea-bargained down to DWI, thought Brichter; people weren't given that kind of sentence eight years ago for simple DWI. He had no other record.

The door opened, McHugh and Ryder came in. The exchange of greetings was halfhearted; they'd parted too recently. Ryder sighed when he saw the coffee wasn't ready yet and went into his office. McHugh sat at his desk massaging his face and yawning.

Nothing was known about Downey beyond the fact that he'd spent twelve weeks in County General Hospital several years back for treatment of multiple fractures suffered in a beating by assailants he could neither name nor describe.

"Mornin', heroes!" said Tonk, tossing the door to the squad room open so hard it ricocheted off the wall. Evidently his interrogation of Whitlock hadn't lasted nearly as long as the search at Tretower; he was looking very fresh. He hadn't come out to help, either, and both Brichter and McHugh aimed resentful glances at him, which he ignored. "Hey, Obie, can I talk to you for a minute?"

"I don't think so," said Brichter. "Or is there some topic you can talk on for a whole minute?"

"Hey, smart-ass!" said the big man.

Brichter grimaced. "You're right; that was uncalled for."

Tonk hesitated, his head turned a little off-center, while he tried to decide if this was a more subtle insult. He shrugged and said, "I think I got some important information last night."

Brichter put the file folder down. "From Whitlock?"

"Naw, Whitlock's no good. He lies till you catch him at it, then he lies in another direction. It's about Downey. I put out the word on the Teletype asking if anyone knew Whitlock, Tellios, Downey, Shiffler, Riscatto—" Tonk had been counting them off on his big fingers, and he stopped to look at them while they wiggled, thinking. "That's all, I guess. And by God, Downey's an escaped convict. It came back in like five minutes."

"From where?"

"Stillwater, up in Minnesota. Doing twenty to life for burglary, arson, and murder."

"Downey?"

"Yep. Melvin P. Downey, age forty-six. Been gone ten years, almost, they said. And would we please keep hold of him; he's got fifteen years left to do up there."

A vision formed, of Downey clambering over a high stone wall, searchlights, blurred in a whirl of snowflakes, wiping over him, sirens bawling, but Brichter, smiling, shook his head and dismissed it.

"Good work," he said to Tonk. "Anything else?"

"No. I told the ME I wanted Shiffler's fingerprints to send out, too."

"Well done," said Brichter, surprised.

"Huh," said Tonk expansively. "There's more."

"Good. Sit down, will you? You're giving me neck cramps."

Tonk sat. "I got this new informant and he says—" Tonk backed up a little and repeated the phrase, emphasizing the pronoun. *"He* says Januschka booted Whitlock out about the time he got arrested, before this kidnap thing ever happened."

"What kind of informant do you have, for Christ's sake?"

Tonk frowned. "Jeez, I been hearing for weeks Januschka's pissed at Whitlock."

"So have we all. But not that Januschka threw him out of the Charter gang. Was this the same informant who gave you Roach Bannister?"

"Sure, why?"

"Because that also may have been a bum tip; the TV set was probably his own. Check it out; you'll look like a real jerk if you wait to let him prove it in court."

"Hey, he wanted to buy dope, didn't he? That was right. And he hit me, that's battery. Two out of three's not bad. And how do you know about Roach, anyhow?"

"I talked to him at the jail. Who is this informant of yours?"

"He's someone who knows someone who works for Januschka. I'll tell you his name some day."

Brichter tried it out. "You should write her name down somewhere, in case we ever need to reconstruct what you've been doing."

"His name, Obie; it's a guy!"

"Oh. Okay, his name."

Satisfied, Tonk rose and said, "But you can see we can't tie Januschka into this kidnap thing. Now I gotta go; a lady wants to talk to me. I'll be back after lunch." He strode out, slamming the door.

Brichter took the elevator to the top floor, was recognized and allowed to enter the jail's anteroom. The room was small, supplied with two rows of cheap plastic chairs and a few sad-looking visitors waiting to see prisoners. He paused by the counter to check his weapon. "I'm here to see Mel Downey."

Woody, a plump, boyish-looking deputy, reached for a phone and said, "I'll have him brought right out."

"Thanks." Brichter took the clipboard and drew the illegible line that was his signature.

While they waited, Woody volunteered, "You know he's awful cranky for someone who's never been to jail before."

"Yeah?" Brichter threw down the pen. "Where do I go?"

"Interrogation B's open. Holler if you want a stenographer. That'll be me. The pop machine only gives grape and ginger ale, sorry."

"Hell. Bring us some coffee."

Interrogation B's cement walls were painted a soothing blue, but the soft-drink machine was wrapped in heavy steel mesh and the table and chairs were bolted to the floor.

Brichter hauled out his notebook, found an empty page and wrote down the date, place, and name of the man he was about to interrogate.

The steel door opened and a short, heavily muscled black man in county khaki pushed a non-resisting Downey into the room. Never a prepossessing person, he was presently a sorry sight. They had apparently no jailhouse denims in his size; the ones he wore hung off his shoulders and draped over the tops of his shoes. His hair had been combed without benefit of mirror, and there was a smear of egg on his upper lip. He needed a shave. He stood, small and scared, just inside the door until someone should tell him what to do.

Brichter let him stand until he was finished writing, then gestured at the table's two remaining chairs. "Sit down, will you, Mr. Downey?" He kept his voice neutrally pleasant.

And Downey unerringly chose the chair at the end of the table, positioned crosswise to it. He sat with both feet flat on the floor and placed his trembling hands on his thighs. The deputy shot Brichter a significant chin-lift and left.

"I've asked for them to bring us some coffee, so let's wait until it comes, all right?" said Brichter.

"Thanks," said Downey, not looking at Brichter. He drew a deep breath and let it out.

"Are they treating you okay here?"

"Yeah, yeah."

"Is there anything you need?"

"Out, I guess." Downey grinned and flicked a frightened glance at Brichter. Seeing something there, he amended, "Could someone bring me some stuff from the ranch? My shaving gear, and toothbrush and stuff?"

"I'll see to it."

"Oh, and there's money—" Downey stopped short. Theft from arrestees was a cop hobby in Charter.

Brichter paged back through his notebook. "Thirty dollars, inside a Merle Haggard album. You want all of it?"

"Yeah. Thanks." Downey cleared his throat and looked away.

"Kori asked me to ask you about the dogs," began Brichter, bringing Downey's painful attention around again.

"How is she?" asked Downey.

"She's going to be fine."

"I saw her head all bandaged up, but that must've happened before . . ." His voice trailed away.

"She broke her arm and injured her forehead when she fell off Summer Wind," said Brichter.

"I knew that wasn't us," said Downey. "I didn't do that to her. I didn't hurt her at all. You said I didn't." Brichter did not reply and Downey admitted, to show he was being honest and aboveboard, "I might've scared her some, though."

"About the dogs," said Brichter. "She wants to call them in off the track so they can be fed."

"Yeah, they wouldn't touch even a steak outside their cage."

"I understand Shiffler was in charge of the dogs; did you ever watch him call them in?"

"Oh. Sure. There's a silver whistle that no person can hear, but dogs can. It's hanging on the coatrack in the front hall. I seen the way his cheeks move when he blows it." Downey puckered up and blew a long and two shorts in illustration.

"Very observant," smiled Brichter, writing the signal down.

The door opened again and the deputy was back, this time with a plastic tray on which rested two paper cups of coffee, two packets of sugar and two of creamer, and two plastic straws.

Brichter took his coffee black. He saw Downey eyeing his sugar and creamer packets and handed them over. Downey emptied his own along with Brichter's into his cup. The deputy waited until Downey had stirred it to his satisfaction, then gathered up tray, papers, and straws to take them away.

"Got a cig, bro?" asked Downey.

"No, I quit last year, Mr. Downey," said the deputy. Prisoners at the jail were, by strict edict, called Mr., Miss, or Mrs.

"Man," said Downey, after the door had closed, "if even the niggers are scared, maybe I better quit, too." He grinned and picked up his cup, saw Brichter wasn't grinning back and took a noisy slurp, put it down again. He looked again at Brichter, saw business approaching, looked away.

Brichter said, "Mr. Downey, for the record I am Detective Sergeant Otto Peter Brichter of the Organized Crime Unit, Charter Police. I'm here to ask you some questions with regard to the people living at Tretower Ranch, about Mr. Joe Januschka, and about the shooting incident on County General Hospital grounds yesterday. You have the right to remain silent. You have the right to consult with an attorney and to an attorney's presence during questioning. If you want an attorney but can't afford one, we'll get one for you. If you give up the right to silence, anything you say will be taken down and may be used against you in a court of law. Do you understand?"

Downey blinked and nodded. "Yes, sir."

"Are you willing to waive your right to silence and answer my questions at this time?"

"I guess so."

"I'm afraid I have to have a yes or a no on that one."

"Sure. I mean, yes."

"Who lived at Tretower Ranch besides yourself?"

"Mr. Tellios, Shiffler, Riscatto, me, and Kori. Miss Price. And the professor, Dr. Ramsey; only he lived in a little house separate from the big one, and he'd only come up once in a while."

"To give Kori her lessons?"

"No, she'd go down there, like a regular kid would go to school. He'd come up for dinner or a party sometimes. Nick liked to show him off."

"Can you describe the relationship between Kori and Tellios?"

"Nick was crazy about her. Gave her anything she wanted, like fancy horses. And the professor: She said she wanted to go to school, so he went out and found a for-real college professor for

her. And she liked Nick; she was like a little kid with its
gran'daddy around him, sometimes."

"So why did he arrange for her to be kidnapped and murdered?"

Downey looked at his feet. "I don't know. He never said one
thing about it before it happened; he only told us that morning she
was gone and wouldn't be back. My personal opinion is she went
snooping in his desk and found out something she shouldn't.
'Cause it happened so fast."

"Was she in any way involved in Nick Tellios' business of drug
brokering?"

Downey looked scared. "You didn't ask me about that yet."

"About what?"

"Drugs. You didn't ask me if Nick was doing that."

"Are you saying he wasn't?"

"I never seen any drugs."

"What did you see?"

"He had people come in for meetings," said Downey. "There's a
great big room on the top floor, where they used to hold parties and
dances in the olden days. Nick would set up a table in the middle of
it and they'd sit there and talk all day, two, three, or even five, six
of them. Nick would come down and fix lunch and take it up, and
later he'd bring them down to dinner and sometimes they'd go up
again and talk half the night."

"Did you ever hear any of their conversations?"

"Oh, no, no, no. Nick said nobody better come upstairs while a
meeting was going on."

"How about at dinner?"

Downey shrugged. "They never said anything you'd be interested in at dinner," he said.

"What would they say?"

"They'd talk about flying and where to buy expensive clothes
and 'Thank you, Mr. Tellios, for making the arrangements.' But
they never said one word like dope or coke or horse or like that.
Not where I could hear it."

"But you assumed it was dope they were buying and selling."

Downey shrugged. "Shiffler flat out said it was. He'd drive them
to and from the airport. He'd come back full of talk about it. One
time he says the man he just drove to the airport had a suitcase full
of cash money. Says the man gave him a hundred-dollar tip like it
was a dollar bill. Another time a guy got out of the car and his
briefcase had a little bit of plastic bag sticking out of it. Shiffler
said he was gonna just let him go in the terminal like that, 'cause

the man didn't tip him, but changed his mind because the guy might get arrested and turn Nick in—and we didn't want Nick in jail."

"Why not?"

"Because he had it set up that if something happened to him that wasn't natural causes, then everything he had on all of us would be sent to the cops. I said he meant dying, but Shiffler said he meant anything, especially like being arrested."

"Did Riscatto know what was going on?"

"Beats me. He's a lot like Kori; they neither of them say much."

"Did you ever talk about leaving?"

"To Nick? No."

"To the others, then."

Downey sighed and shifted in his chair. His hands had stopped their tremor. "One time I remember we was decorating a Christmas tree in the parlor for Kori, and Nick was being a real pisser over everything. He left for a minute and the professor says, real soft, 'He's three-score and ten this year, you know.' And Guy says that that means seventy and that the Bible says man wasn't meant to live to be older than that. So we all kind of watched him, but a year later we're decorating another tree and nuthin's changed. That's the only time I remember anyone mentioning it."

"Why? I should think you'd think up ways of getting loose all the time."

"*I* thought about it, all the time. And it seems logical everyone else did too. But we never talked together about anything like that. Because if we started talking about it, then we'd have to say where we can't go back to or who we're scared of. Even saying what you're good at could let someone know why you had to come. So all of us kind of watched what we said. It was bad enough having Nick holding something over us, without us holding something over each other."

"What did he have on you?"

Downey hesitated, and his eyes drifted to the file folder under Brichter's notebook. Though Brichter had made no effort to bring Downey's attention to it, Downey's name was featured on the tab in bold black letters. The man's eyes flicked up suddenly at Brichter, who could do a very good poker face. Downey sighed and looked away. "There's a warrant out for me. He said I could hide out at the ranch."

"Who issued the warrant?" asked Brichter.

"Indianapolis PD."

"For what?"

"Burglary."

"You could have turned yourself in, done your time, and been free by now," said Brichter.

"I know. But I didn't know that when I came."

"Where else are you wanted?"

"Nowhere."

"Mr. Downey, if you're going to lie to me, we'll have to stop right now."

There was a silence that went on and on. Downey said suddenly, "All right, Wisconsin, but it's a bum rap; I can beat that one."

"And where else?"

Downey swallowed and stared at the folder. "Minnesota."

"That's the big one, isn't it?"

Downey nodded.

"You wouldn't have to stand trial in Minnesota, would you? Not on the initial charges, anyway."

Downey thumped his fist on the table. "Damn you!" he cried. "I get loose of that bastard and I don't get one hour of freedom! It ain't fair!"

"What about Shiffler?"

"Who gives a shit? He's dead, he don't care anymore!"

"What did Tellios have on him?"

"I told you we never talked about it! Goddammit!" Downey grabbed his cup and took a large swallow of the now tepid coffee and nearly choked. "It ain't fair!" he repeated more feebly, putting the cup down, and coughed into a fist. Brichter again said nothing and at last Downey said, "It was something in Chicago, something real serious, and Shiffler could get real mad if you even hinted you wanted to know more about what it was. He was mad at Nick especially over it, like Nick got him into the jam and then used it to get him to come and stay. Which I wouldn't put past him; he was about the sneakiest bastard I ever run across."

"And Riscatto?"

"For all I know Riscatto came because he liked the work. I told you, he's the kind wouldn't say shit if he had a mouthful." Downey coughed again, harder, cleared his throat and said in a roughened voice, "But you know, I think he thought he'd found a way out. He'd been kind of different the last couple weeks. Snotty to Kori, which it was dangerous to be. Meaner than usual to the horses. Even just a little bit snotty to Nick. And always off into town. I kept waiting for Nick to lower the boom on him, but he didn't. Him getting away with it was starting to give Shiffler ideas, and that made me nervous; because there was no way Nick was gonna let that go on, and I was scared I'd get caught in whatever he did."

"Someone went to the ranch after the shootout and took Nick away. Could it have been Riscatto?"

Downey shook his head. "I doubt it. I wouldn't've, if it'd been me. He'd've taken him off and shot him, maybe, but helped him get away? Not on your life."

Chapter

18 †

"Hello, Rudy?"

"Hi, Pete! How does it feel to be a hero?"

"I'll tell you when I see my next paycheck."

Rudy laughed. "What can I do for you?"

"I want to bring someone over tonight."

"Late in the season for an audition."

"No, just to watch."

"You know I don't allow that."

"I want you to make an exception. It's Katherine Price. I want to take her somewhere special, but I don't want her confronted by a mob. We'll stay out of your hair, I promise."

"I don't know . . ."

"Please? I can't think where else to take her."

"Well . . . all right. Sit in the balcony and don't even clap, okay?"

"Thanks, Rudy." As soon as Brichter put the phone down it rang again. "Organized Crime Unit, Sergeant Brichter. May I help you?"

"Hello, Peter, it's Fran Severance."

"My God, hello!"

"Yes, it's been a while, hasn't it? I know you're terribly busy, but could you possibly come to see me?"

"Something wrong?"

"Well, yes. I need to see you in your official capacity—and mine as your alderwoman."

"I'm sorry, Fran, but you're right about the busy. I'm stuck here the rest of the day. Shall I send someone else?"

"No, don't do that. Could you come this evening?"

"I've got an important engagement—but, if it's really important, how about after? Say ten-thirty? Is that too late?"

"No, that's fine. I'll be at home. Thank you, Peter. Good-bye."

When the relief for the cop on the gate came, he brought three prospective farmhands. They came to knock on the cottage door, looking up and around at the threatening sky. Ramsey answered, and the oldest of them explained, "Some guy named Bricker called the labor pool, said you out here was looking for a worker?"

"Yes. This way; Miss Price is in the barn."

Kori was currying Storm Wind when they came in. She interviewed them one at a time.

The first man was old and frail, looking for a temporary job involving nothing more strenuous than sweeping up.

The second was a graduate student who wanted an afternoon job. He had farmhand experience, but only with crops. He was so patently afraid of the mare she began to shift nervously, rolling her eyes at him.

The third prospect was just eighteen. His mud-colored hair was freshly cut, but he looked as if he were getting over a bad siege of flu. "My name's Danny," he said.

"Have you done farm work before?"

"My aunt and uncle have a dairy farm. I've spent four or five summers working out there. Um, I guess I ought to tell you, I need this job to stay out of jail."

Her heart sank. "What have you done?"

He shrugged, folded his arms across his chest and looked around the barn. "Nothing too serious, really. I was on horse, y'see," he said; and, seeing her uncomprehension, explained. "Heroin. I'm not a dope addict now, and I'll never be one again. I'm out on bail for trying to buy heroin and for hitting this cop just a little bit on his arm. I mean, he laughed when I did it, so I don't think it will count for much. There's this doctor who'll tell you I'm about finished with withdrawal. I'm in counseling; to stay in it I have to find a job. And my dad's a lawyer; he says if I get a job and work hard at it, I'll probably get probation. So you see, I'm what they call highly motivated." He looked at her face and said, "But I guess you don't want to hire me."

That was true, but it had taken Kori all morning just to clean six box stalls. "Do you know anything about real horses?" she asked, and the boy smiled.

"I can ride a little. My aunt and uncle have two work horses. I know how to groom them and muck out their stalls. I can also wash udders and put on the milking machines, but I guess you don't need those skills out here."

"No, I don't."

"Look, I'll work for base wages until I learn the ropes, okay? I know a little carpentry, I can change the oil in your pickup, paint fences and do yard work. Please, give me a chance!"

Kori considered him a moment. "Here," she said, handing him the Dandy brush, "let me see you use this."

The boy took it and began very carefully to brush the mare. "Nice horse," he said after a minute. "Or is she a pony?"

"No, Arabians run small. She's fourteen hands."

"Gee, Uncle Al's pair run over eighteen, I think." He was brushing with more enthusiasm now and the mare was leaning into it with pleasure. "That her filly?"

"Yes. Five weeks old yesterday."

"Looks like a toy, too little to be a real horse."

"Yes."

"Am I doing all right?" he pleaded.

"Yes. I want you to talk to Dr. Ramsey, and if he approves, maybe we can work something out. Would you agree to some strict conditions?"

"Like what?"

"First sign of trouble with drugs, you're out?"

He nodded his head emphatically. "You bet," he said. "Never again!"

A rain squall overtook the Volkswagen and suddenly Tellios could not see. A river of water poured down the windshield and the wipers became stick fish swimming in it. Cursing, he pulled the car off the road and stopped. Rain drew a bright curtain around the car. He cracked his window and felt the coolness of it. He wanted to get out, to stand in it and wash himself. But that, he considered, would only add pneumonia to his problems.

Instead, thinking to find a weather report, he snapped on the radio, turning the volume high against the roar of the storm.

". . . any man who wipes his feet in the blood of Juh-HEE-sus!" bawled a preacher. Tellios twisted the dial.

". . . guest today is a world-class marathon runner . . ."

". . . little green apples . . ."

". . . was kidnapped from her home outside Charter yesterday morning." Tellios snatched his hand away from the dial. "Police are investigating a possible link between the kidnapping and the shootout which followed it. Miss Price, recovering at home today, refused to comment."

Recovering? That goddamn lying punk! She's alive!

He listened for more, but the announcer was trying to sell his audience a systemic bug killer, so he began to hunt along the dial again. If Riscatto had lied about that, had he lied about everything? What really happened?

". . . arrested Mel Downey. Police Captain Frank Ryder says the dead man has been identified as Paul Shiffler, thirty-six, an employee at Tretower Ranch. An intensive manhunt has been mounted for the third gunman, who may have taken Mr. Tellios away with him. Miss Price is reported recovering from her ordeal, but is as yet too shaken to speak with reporters. Now this."

The same bug-killer commercial began again, and Tellios shut off the radio. He felt a fierce joy. *Pretty Koritsimu, alive.* But what had the first one said? Recovering at home. That complicated things.

When Brichter walked back into the squad room, McHugh was waiting for him. He said without preamble, "Riscatto's back."

Brichter halted in surprise. "Where is he?"

"Out at County General Hospital."

"What's wrong with him?"

"Shot. I just talked with the emergency room doctor, who called to report a gunshot wound. A twenty-two in the lower body."

"Tellios turn up?"

"No, and Riscatto's too sick right now to be questioned."

"How bad is he?"

"Perforated intestine, the doc said. They're operating, but they seem sure he'll recover. Some friends are already at the hospital to maintain a round-the-clock watch at his bedside, so us cops don't get too fresh with the poor boy."

"Who are the friends?"

"They're Januschka's friends, actually. It was one of them who brought him in, said Riscatto told him he accidentally shot himself. But the doc says no, there were no powder burns, and anyway, it's a damn queer angle for a self-inflicted wound."

Brichter said, "But no sign of Tellios."

"I didn't say that." McHugh picked up a stack of phone messages. "You know how it is when we ask the general public if they've seen someone." He began to read from the messages. "Tellios went to a movie in Chicago last night. He visited a massage parlor right here in Charter, gassed up a Volkswagen Rabbit and drove off without paying eighty miles north of here, checked into a Rockford motel with a blonde, and bought a roast-beef sandwich in a tavern in Milburn, Iowa. Et cetera, et cetera. This is only half of them; Tonk took the other half and is checking those out."

Brichter went to fill his mug. "So what do you think?"

"I think Riscatto took him away, there was a fight, and Riscatto got shot. What do you think?"

"I think Tellios is dead. If Tellios got away, Riscatto wouldn't come back here. Januschka doesn't like failures."

"You think Kori's right, that Riscatto went to Januschka for help getting free from Tellios?"

"Or Januschka approached him and he grabbed at the offer. Either way, the price was Tellios' head."

"Funny, Riscatto coming in. I'd be nervous about going to a doctor with a wound that would certainly draw me a session with the cops."

"If I were gut-shot, I'd go to hell if I had to for help."

"Does it hurt that much?"

"Your lower gut's a cesspool, Cris. Open it and you die, stinking and in agony, unless you get to a doctor. Actually, put a hole in your body anywhere and you're inviting the grim reaper. We're so used to antibiotics we've forgotten how deadly infection is."

Anxious not to hear more, McHugh said, "My FBI contact says he heard Tellios had been looking for allies in Chicago who'd back him in a war against Januschka; but Tellios never got along with the boys in Chicago, so the answer was 'You're on your own; have fun.' "

"So there *was* a fight brewing! And Riscatto went over to the other side. So Januschka, never looking a gift in the mouth, sicced him on Tellios. But where's the body?"

"Give it a day or two to start stinking. They'll find it then. You getting anything from your interrogations?"

"I got enough from Downey to satisfy me Tellios was the drug broker. I'm going up to see Whitlock. What do you know about him?"

"Meanest son of a bitch in three counties."

"I think he's also a goddamn spook, Cris. I got just a quick look at him last night, and he made the hair on my arms stand up. You never saw anything odd about him?"

"He seemed okay when I was running that scam on him, real friendly and glad to lend me the money. I heard plenty of stories from other people about how glad he was to send them to the hospital—Oh. One of those?"

"Yeah. I wonder why they keep changing the name? Personality defect, sociopath—A psychopath by any other name is still a man without any sense of morality, who'll do whatever he feels like doing, including murder, as easily as we'd eat a Popsicle. We got awful lucky, Cris. When I think of her in that merciless monster's hands . . . I hope that saprogenic little bastard is really dead!"

"Sapro-who?"

"Tellios."

Sammy brought Norman Whitlock along to the interrogation room. The sturdy freckled redhead stood patiently in his rumpled denims while Brichter finished writing in his notebook.

"I'm Detective Sergeant Brichter," he said at last. "Will you sit here, Mr. Whitlock?"

"Sure 'nuff," said Whitlock, sitting down. "But I already told that cop last night what happened, how I saved that purty little girl from those three niggers."

"Yes, I read his report. Is that going to remain your story? That it wasn't you who kidnapped Miss Price?"

"Sure."

"You have a right to remain silent; if you give up your right to silence, you have a right to consult with an attorney before questioning, and to an attorney's presence during questioning."

"And you'll rent me an attorney if I ask you to. I remember. To hell with that; fire away."

"You said you saved Miss Price. How did that come about?"

"Well, sir," said Whitlock, leaning back in his chair, "it just so happened I was at that church when she was brought in. You can just about imagine what them bucks thought when they seen what she looked like under the blood on her face. I tell you, it was all I could do to keep 'em from ripping her clothes off and having at her right there on the floor of the church!"

"And Mr. Tellios would have been grossly offended, of course, if that had happened."

"You said it!"

"Especially as you were his man on the site in charge of taking care of her." Brichter's cold gray eyes raked the man.

Whitlock barely hesitated before flashing his grin. "Your Sergeant Erickson says the old boy's gone missing. I guess that means you can trot out all sorts of stories and not fear him callin' you a liar."

"Would you continue with this particular story?"

Whitlock shrugged. "Mine's the true one," he said. "Y'see, I kinda know those boys. Took a shine to 'em—on a manner o' speakin'—" He winked and grinned. "So I heard they was up to somethin' in that old church, and I went right on over to see what it was, and found 'em just comin' in with this sweet little thing all bloodied up and her poor arm broke about half in two. An' braggin' over how they shot her horse."

"When was this?" Brichter was writing.

"Yesterday mornin', kinda early. I ast 'em what they was about and they said they was holdin' her for ransom. And then they was gonna have their wicked ways with her, and kill her, and send the poor little broken body back to her uncle."

Brichter was taking swift notes. "So what did you do?"

Whitlock raised his eyebrows, looking sincere and serious. "Well, sir, I tried to change their minds. I talked like a daddy to them, told 'em they was wrong, that they should carry her home before they got in more serious trouble. But they said she'd seen all three of 'em, and they didn't dare to send her back to tell on 'em. They invited me to be a partner, but I said I wouldn't be party to such a thing. And then, sir, one of 'em did a purely terrible thing. He went over and told that little lady that I was one of the kidnappers. Yes, he did. Then he came back and told me that I now had an interest in killin' her, seein' as how she'd tell on me as well as on them! I ask you, Sergeant, is that any way to repay an offer of friendly advice?"

"So what did you do then?"

Catching something sardonic in Brichter's voice, Whitlock's small blue eyes shifted, and the accent moderated. "What could I do? I decided to stay with them, to protect the lady. To mess me up further with the law, they held a gun to my head and made me make the first ransom call."

"How many calls were made?"

"Just the one, telling Mr. Tellios we had her and that it would cost fifty thousand in small bills to get her back. They let her talk to him a little bit, to prove they had her and she was alive. There was supposed to be another call later in the day, to find out if he had the money and arranging to deliver it. Since there was to be a wait, they decided to go out and buy some lunch. They said they was gonna kill her with that syringe full of heroin you found on the floor as soon as they got back. But you arrived first, thank God."

"Go on."

"That's it. I'd held 'em off all morning, arguin' this way an' that, but I had lost the fight, and couldn't think what to do when you-all busted in. There's some who'll say I should've gone home an' saved myself, an' others who'll say I should've gone to fetch the police. But I was scared to leave her alone in there. I'm sorry I had to get arrested, but it was worth it to save that purty lady's life."

"Have you ever been out to Tretower Ranch?"

"No, sir, never."

"The evidence and testimony so far seem to indicate that Mr. Tellios was not interested in the safe return of his niece, that he wanted her murdered, and that the so-called ransom would be, in fact, a payoff for her murder. The kidnap was a fake from the start."

Whitlock said slowly, in tones of startled wonder, "An' I foiled it!"

"Well, you see, there's this catch. There are several contradictions between the story I'm hearing from you and the story Miss Price tells."

"Hey, you gonna let a head-injured girl call me a liar?"

"Mr. Whitlock, I'm here to discover the truth. I don't care particularly who tells it to me, or who gets called a liar in the process." He turned back a few pages in his notebook. "Now, in direct contradiction to Miss Price's story that there was no one but you involved in this kidnapping, your story is that the kidnapping was actually done by three black men of your acquaintance and that your role was as rescuer?"

"That's right."

"Can you name them?"

"Pernie Davis, Jack Ford, Leroy Sparkman. Big boys, husky build. Leroy has a beard. Razor carriers, doped up half the time, you be careful how you come up on 'em. Me, I'd have my gun in my hand, all cocked and ready." He watched Brichter write this down with a smile that vanished as soon as Brichter's eyes came off the page.

Brichter reviewed the story so far. "You say someone informed you that these three friends of yours were up to something in an abandoned church and that you went there to recall them to their better selves. Were you at home when this news came to you?"

"Yessir."

"What time was that?"

"I'm not sure. I was in bed, asleep. Maybe six in the morning."

"You live in a fairly distant suburb, nearly as far east of the church as Tretower Ranch is west. You must have broken several traffic laws getting to the church in time to see them arrive."

"Well, sir, I was worried—"

"And your informant," interrupted Brichter, "must have witnessed the kidnapping in order to get the word to you so quickly. Do you know someone who works at Tretower Ranch?"

"No, sir; I don't know how—"

"And if the three kidnappers were willing to kill Miss Price because she'd seen them, why didn't they offer to kill you as well? Cutting you in for a piece of the action seems unnecessarily kind of them. Further"—Brichter held up a hand to forestall Whitlock's explanation—"the syringe under the table has only one set of fingerprints on it, and I suspect I know whose those will prove to be."

"They wore gloves; did I mention that? And I touched the thing, tossed it off the table when I heard you coming in. I thought it was them, y'see."

"We have an eyewitness who can put you on the ranch."

"No, sir, that can't be true. I already said—" Whitlock paused, but Brichter waited. Whitlock grimaced. "I forgot; that was her, wasn't it? The girl on the horse? Cold and wet and far enough away I thought it didn't matter." He laughed. "I guess the joke's on me, all right. If I'd done what the old man wanted, I wouldn't be in this mess."

"So you were out there?"

"Sure. Not long, though. Just a short visit."

"What was the nature of the visit?"

"He wanted me to do him a favor."

"Go on."

Whitlock sat forward in his chair, forearm on the table, and said with disarming frankness. "That little old buzzard has a way of putting things that can purely scare the daylights out of a man. He knew a thing or two about me and he told me that if I didn't help him arrange a kidnapping he'd see to it I was in a whole lot of trouble."

"What things did he know about you?"

Whitlock raised one hand. "Nothin' illegal; just embarrassin'."

"It must be extraordinarily embarrassing information to get you to agree to murder someone."

"Hey, now, I wasn't gonna murder anyone! I just let the old boy think so. I figured I'd agree, kidnap the girl and collect the ransom;

then drop her off on a street corner somewhere on my way out of town. Maybe tip you off from a phone booth."

"Why did Tellios want her dead?"

"He didn't say."

"And you didn't ask?"

"You ever met him?"

"Yes."

"Then you know what he's like. If he'd wanted me to know, he'd've told me. Course I didn't ask!"

"Miss Price seems convinced you seriously intended to kill her."

"Aw, that was just talk, to get her to promise not to snitch when I turned her loose."

"Do you know Joe Januschka?"

"Hearda him." Whitlock looked puzzled in a friendly way.

"I understand you work for him."

"No, sir, I don't."

"Does he know about your involvement with Mr. Tellios?"

"Not one bit."

Brichter raised a sardonic eyebrow. "You sure?"

"So far as I know, he doesn't."

"And he's not involved in this in any way?"

Whitlock appeared to think this over. "Oh, I see what you're getting at. Well, all right, he's a friend. He's hired me a real hot-shot attorney. But Mr. Januschka don't have nothin' to do with any of this, hear? Nothin'!" Whitlock put it strongly, and Brichter suspected Whitlock had the hot-shot attorney only as long as he stuck to his declaration that Januschka was not involved.

"How long have you known him?"

"Five, six years."

"Who introduced you?"

"I don't remember."

Whitlock stuck to that, and finally Brichter called Woody in to take down Whitlock's statement.

While they were waiting for the statement to be typed up, Brichter said, "Funny you didn't try being nice to Miss Price instead of terrorizing her. Why didn't you tell her the sad story of how you were forced into this?"

"She wouldn't listen to any bad-mouthin' of her uncle. In fact, she was like a stone to everything. Why, right at the start, I took her by the arm and told her I was gonna take good care of her, and I just wanted her to behave an' not cause any trouble, but she looked right through me, cold as my ass in January, and give out little one-word answers."

"Kind of made you want to push her, make her react in some way?"

"Yeah. Yeah, you understand that, don't you? It was like she was stuck behind some kind of glass wall. I wanted to help her through, make her really alive. I mean, she should've been scared, right? So why wasn't she crying, or begging? I wanted to make her really react to what I was saying."

When Woody brought the typescript in, Whitlock made a show of cheerfully checking and signing each page, humming the chorus to "Your Cheatin' Heart."

That done, Brichter said to Woody, "Send Sammy along, will you? I think we're done here."

"Be a minute; he's down in booking. But I'll tell him." Woody left.

"Have you talked to your attorney yet?" Brichter asked Whitlock.

"Yeah. He says you're gonna be hard-nosed about bail."

Brichter said, "For whatever reason, you threatened the life of Miss Price. If we let you go free on bail, we'll have to lock her up. Since she's the victim, that hardly seems fair."

"Who says you need to lock her up?" asked Whitlock. He grinned. "Why, if our paths happen to cross, I'd purely enjoy a word with her."

Brichter's icy pale eyes glinted in his tired face. "If, so long as you live, you come within ten feet of Miss Price, I'll kill you."

Whitlock's grin broadened. "It ain't proper for the nice police-man to threaten the poor prisoner."

"All right, then, cards on the table. I bet an intensive investiga-tion into your past would reveal things that would gag a maggot. If, between now and the end of your trial Miss Price sees or hears from you in any way, however remote, or is injured in any way, however accidental, I'm going to spend as long as it takes to find those bodies. I'll testify in court, and if it appears necessary, I'll write annual letters to the Parole Board. You know what consecu-tive sentences means? It means you'll have three hundred and twelve years left to serve when they bury you." He pointed a blunt finger at Whitlock. "You think about that."

Whitlock wiped his mouth. "Hey, lighten up, boy! I didn't mean no harm to Miss Price and I hope she lives long and healthy." He reached out his hand and grasped Brichter's forearm. "Okay?"

Brichter looked down at the hand. "I believe it's in the rules somewhere that a prisoner is not to touch a peace officer."

The door opened and the hand instantly withdrew. "Hi, Obie, sorry to hold you up. All finished?"

"Yeah, and I'm late for an important date. Take him away, Sammy."

Chapter
19 †

It was pouring rain when Brichter left. He drove as fast as he dared to Tretower. "I'm sorry I'm late," he said when he arrived at the cottage. "I hope I haven't spoiled dinner."

"No, no," said Ramsey, taking his raincoat. "It's just a casserole."

"Is she excited about going out with me?"

"Yes, very. Peter . . ."

"Don't worry; I'm not taking her into a crowd scene."

"No, you wouldn't do that. It's nightmares. She won't tell me what they're about, but she woke me up twice with them last night."

Brichter made that sucking sound spelled *tsk*, and followed Ramsey into the kitchen.

Kori was waiting, enveloped in a big white apron, wearing a hot mitt. She did not look the least hag-ridden. "Good, you're here," she said. "The biscuits are getting very brown." She bent to open the oven door and lifted out a tray of biscuits that were indeed very brown. "I helped make them."

She put the tray on top of the stove, pulled off the mitt and untied the apron, revealing a cream knit dress with bell sleeves. "Is this okay?"

"You look wonderful."

"Where are we going?"

"To a rehearsal of Bach's B Minor Mass."

"However did you arrange that?" asked Ramsey, putting two bowls of casserole on the table. "Sit down, both of you, and eat."

Brichter sat. "Rudy Galbraith's a friend of mine—he's the director of St. Gabriel's choir," he explained to Kori. "The college in town."

"I know," she replied. "I've seen him on television. Will there be many people at the rehearsal?"

"Only you and me. Rehearsals are closed. We're under strict orders not to say anything or even applaud, just sit and watch."

"It won't be like a real performance," warned Ramsey. "But I should think it will be interesting all the same."

"I like the recording of the Mass Gordon owns," she said, putting a big dollop of tuna casserole on his plate. "Will there be an orchestra?"

"The chamber orchestra will be there. This is a next-to-final rehearsal; the performance is just a week off."

Ramsey sat down and flipped his napkin open. "I might've known you'd come up with something different," he said approvingly.

"Why were you late?" she asked.

"I was interviewing Whitlock."

"What did he say?"

"I don't think we ought to discuss the case other than officially. There might be legal ramifications if I tell you his story. And I don't want a chink in the case we're building."

She watched him butter and take a bite of his biscuit. "Are they okay?" she asked.

Under its heavy brown crust the biscuit was tough from too much pummeling. But it was her hands that had done the pummeling, so, "Delicious," he said, and meant it.

"When will you be home?" asked Ramsey.

"Lo, the father in you speaks," said Brichter. "About ten. Listen, could you go up to the big house and pack up a paper sack with Downey's razor, toothbrush, underwear, et cetera? Also, there's money in the back of a Merle Haggard album in his room. Include that. I'll take it with me when I bring her home."

A few minutes later Ramsey wrapped Kori in a large rain cape and pulled the hood up over her pinned-up braids. "Have fun, pet," he said.

"I will," she said. Her eyes were glowing with excitement under the white bandage. "Ready?" she asked Brichter.

He buttoned his raincoat up to his neck and said, "Ready."

Ramsey opened the door on a deluge. "Maybe you'd better wait a few minutes," he said.

"No, let's go," she said, already starting out the door. Brichter reached for her arm and they dashed down the curving walk and onto the gravel. It was impossible to discern puddles in such a downpour, and he led her right through one in his haste to get her to his car. She gave a little shriek that instantly dissolved into laughter, and was still giggling when he opened the car door and handed her in.

"Sorry about that," he apologized when he got in on his side.

"I don't mind in the least," she said. Her cheeks were aflame. "Drive fast, like you did last night."

He laughed, because he did like to speed. "Not in this weather." He started the car, and felt a sudden pang about where he was taking her. Rehearsals could be boring. But where do you take someone shy around strangers, someone who knows a lot but has never been much of anywhere? They drove down the narrow lane and turned onto Eerie River Road, headed for town.

Despite the rain she was glued to the window. "The trees lift up their arms to the welcome rain," she said.

"Where's that from?"

"Me." She watched the farms turn to suburbs and leaned forward as they approached the old bridge across Eerie River. The city had recently restored the Gothic lamps along the pedestrian walk of the bridge, and their light made a romantic, mysterious thing of the web of girders. "I *like* this," she said.

"You've crossed it before."

"I know. But it's different this time, somehow."

She grew silent as they drove up the boulevard toward the campus, but it was an eager silence, and again he felt a pang.

They pulled into the parking lot beside the Fine Arts Building on the St. Gabriel campus, and he shut off the engine. The building was a ghostly cube of pale stone, but on the second floor deep-set windows glowed. "This is the place," he said. "And we're right on time. But we'll have to run for it again."

"All right," she said. "Ready? Go." And she was out of the car. He ran behind her to a pair of glass-and-steel doors, they went in, and he took her up some shining pink pebble stairs.

Halfway down the dim passageway on the second floor was an open pair of fire doors, and through them was the balcony section of a small and luxurious auditorium.

They shed rain gear and took seats in the front row. Below, some young people in slacks, jeans, and assorted T-shirts were setting up stepped platforms at the back of the stage.

A man dressed in black slacks and sweater, his thick mat of graying hair combed straight back, bounced energetically on stage. He put a bundle of music on a music stand and looked around the house. "Hi, Peter!" he called, waving. "Everything comfy up there?"

"Fine, thanks," Brichter called back.

"That's him, isn't it?" asked Kori.

"Yes, that's Rudy."

Musicians began to arrive. They unpacked their instruments and made authentic warm-up sounds, but they were in shirt sleeves or shabby sweaters, which diminished their aura considerably.

Kori noticed that the same people who had helped set up the platforms were joining others on them as choir members. "How ordinary everyone looks without choir robes," she said. "And how different from one another."

A lady with a shining helmet of white hair came out and began to play scales on the painted harpsichord. The bearded double-bass player was plucking a simple 1-2-3-4 rhythm over and over. Kori leaned forward, fascinated, and Brichter smiled to himself.

Rudy came out again, rapped with his ring on the edge of the music stand, and the stage quieted. They were not rehearsing the entire Mass, Rudy announced. They would sing no solo parts and would skip the *Credo*.

Rehearsal began with the *Kyrie*. The bass player laid down a rhythm as of a man walking up stairs, the 1-2-3-4 Kori had heard him playing earlier. Rudy stopped the singers in midstride and admonished the altos, "You're too choppy; I want it much more legato."

As they went on, she was surprised at the amount of fine tuning that went on, the time spent correcting flaws she could not detect. Rudy told the English horns at one point, "Phrase more cleanly, please, on measures twenty-four and -five," which she thought amusingly picky.

Then, when they got to the *Sanctus*, they caught fire. The basses and baritones boomed, *"SANC-tus DO-mi-nus DE-us SA-ba-oth"* slowly, ponderously, until the auditorium seemed filled with the tolling of bells. *"SANC-tus DO-mi-nus DE-us SA-ba-oth!"*

Brichter was pulled into the hypnotic repetitions, and when they were over, turned to remark on them to Kori. She was gripping the railing with her good hand, staring stunned at Rudy, who was asking the tenors to sing from ten, please.

"Fy'n galon?" he asked.

She turned to him, her face enraptured. "It's different when you're really here, isn't it?" she whispered.

"Yes," he replied, moved. He would have to be careful of her; in some places she had no carapace at all.

The rehearsal wound up with the *Dona nobis pacem*, a request for peace, and Rudy said, "All right, children, party's over. Let's go home." And the ordinary people who had made such extraordinary music broke into chatter and trailed off the stage.

Outside, Kori and Brichter found the rain had stopped, so they had time to skirt puddles on their way to the car. He opened the door for her, but instead of getting in she turned and threw her arms around him. "Thank you! That was wonderful!"

He let go of the door to hold her close, fiercely happy. "I love you," he said without thinking.

She grew still. "Peter?"

"Yes, *fy'n galon*?"

"Thank you for saving my life. And Gordon's life. And thank you for loving me. I'm sorry I can't love you."

"I haven't asked you to, yet," he said, stepping back from her. "Don't let me rush you, okay?"

In the car on the way home, Brichter said, "I'm really glad you enjoyed that. It's not the usual sort of place to take a girl on a date."

"I'm glad you thought of it. I guess I never realized that human beings perform those choral works, and that there is a lot of labor involved. Are you going to take me other places?"

He grinned. "Where would you like to go?"

"A baseball game. A cathedral. That forest where the trees are outrageously big. Disney World." She was close to laughter. "I could make a list."

"Do," he said. "We'll go down it together, if you like."

She started to reply, then broke off and was silent.

"A penny for that dark thought," he offered.

"No—well, perhaps you should know. This was great fun tonight, and for a while it was as if—as if I were okay. But I'm not, you know. I did a grotesquely wicked thing, so wicked it drove me mad for a while; and I don't suppose I'll ever be free of that."

"I can't believe you did it. You were just a child. Maybe—God knows what sort of provocation—"

"I keep trying to justify it. Self-defense? But nothing I can remember, nothing in the dreams shows I was threatened! I came down and . . . and shot them."

"If you did do it you've served fourteen years in captivity for it. I don't know about your God, but I certainly forgive you."

She blinked, then looked out the window. "You're a very nice man."

He took her to the cottage door, but turned her before she could lead the way in and embraced her. At first wooden, she slowly relaxed, then lifted her arms to return the embrace. When he stepped back and raised her chin, she accepted the kiss he gave her as well. He tried again, this time pressing his mouth against hers hungrily. Her lips were cool under his—then suddenly warm and knowing. His arms tightened, but after a few seconds she began to pull back and immediately he released her. She looked up at him, eyes wide, but saw only Peter, looking as kind and pleased and reassuring as he could.

"Did I just graduate?" she asked.

He laughed. "No, but you're doing very well."

She stepped close again and put head on his shoulder. "It's not what I thought it would be, kissing. But it's nice."

He stroked the side of her head. "What's different about it?"

"It's so—real. There's dreams behind it, but it's real. Like the music tonight."

"You're real; may I kiss you again?"

"Just a little one," she said. "Then we have to go get Downey's paper bag."

Tellios pulled the little car as far as he dared into the copse, hoping he could get it out again in the morning. He had to rest. His chest had never gotten over that pothole. His whole left side was aflame now, and he could barely hold his hands on the wheel. He'd finally gotten straightened around; he was only thirty-five miles from Charter. But he had to rest. He shut the engine off, leaned back and closed his eyes.

He'd hit the pothole while searching for the right road, and driven the next fifteen miles one-handed while waiting for the pain in his chest to subside. He unbuttoned his suit coat, wanted to open his shirt and let the cool night air touch the wound, but the shirt was stuck and the slightest tug brought swift agony.

He wondered how Kori was, and what she was doing. Are they scaring you, little girl? he thought. All those strangers, those cops wanting to drag you out into the wide world, and they won't understand your terror. I'm going to have to do something about Whitlock.

He was thirsty. He'd drunk what seemed like gallons from a not-very-clean stream earlier, but he was still thirsty. Bad sign, he thought. Lost too much blood. Rest will help. Do better tomorrow, in daylight, after rest.

Despite the pain, he began dozing off. I have to have money to get safely away, to pay off a doctor to fix this bullet hole.

That goddamned lying Riscatto. Yelling the cops were on their way—though maybe that part wasn't a lie. It could've been true; everything's come apart for me lately. Even Koritsimu all grown up and turned against me. If only she could have stayed a child . . .

He started a yawn but stifled it when the movement of his ribs hurt. Riscatto thinks I'm dead. Too bad for him when Januschka finds out. I got him once; I hope his hurts him like mine hurts me, that lying, impertinent bastard.

I'll be home tomorrow. Then I can get out of the country, find some hot sun to lie in. Heat cures heat. I wish I could take this stinking shirt off. Heat cures heat . . . I'm tired.

Fran was pacing the floor of her apartment when he rang the doorbell at a quarter to eleven.

"Hello, Fran!" He was alight with joy.

"Come in, Peter." She had seen him in many moods—his black moods had been the eventual cause of their breakup—but this was a new one. He seemed at once excited and at peace, and she watched him curiously as he crossed the plush carpet to stand by the sofa. He looked almost the same, thin and slightly stooped; but the ascetic lines of his face were relaxed, displaying openly what he normally showed to a rare few: a surprising gentleness.

She followed and held out her hand to him, an elegant, beautiful, frightened woman of forty-five, dressed in the russet color she remembered he admired on her. "Would you like some coffee?" she asked, as she took his coat.

"I couldn't drink a drop of anything. But thank you."

"Who is she?"

Brichter smiled. "Does it show that much? I've just come from her."

She was amused and glad of the distraction. "No brighter than a lighthouse beacon." She went to hang his coat in the closet.

"Her name's Katherine McLeod Price," he said, adding, "they call her Kori." She felt a chill. Oh, please, don't let the rumors be true, she thought and turned to face him.

"She's Mr. Tellios' niece, isn't she?"

"Yes. I met her through her tutor, Professor Ramsey."

"Ah, yes, the history professor. He seems a brilliant light to hide under the Tretower bushel." She came to sit in the love seat, at right angles to his sofa. "I can't imagine Tellios approving, though, of Kori making friends with a policeman."

"When he saw how I felt about her, he decided to use her in his plan to suborn me. I let him think he succeeded, and managed to take the bait without getting hooked."

She relaxed. "Oh, I see. Isn't she rather young for you, Peter?"

He sat down and crossed his legs. "She's as much younger than I am as you are older."

He could say things like that to her; the only way their age difference had touched them was to disguise the fact of their affair. She said, "Is she all right? I mean, I've heard—"

"She's fine. Rudy Galbraith let us come watch his rehearsal of the B Minor Mass. She likes Bach." His face changed, remembering.

They're lovers, she thought, dismayed. "Are you sure you know what you're doing?"

"What do you mean?"

"Peter, I met her once, and though I only spoke with her briefly, I came away with the impression of a withdrawn and repressed child. I hope you haven't frightened her, making demands she may find more confusing than pleasurable."

He stared blankly at her, then suddenly laughed out loud. "Easy now, all I've done is kiss her, and that more carefully than you would believe. What made you think otherwise?"

"Your face when you talk about her. And remembering. You are a very sensual man."

He said, "I will have to learn to control my damn face. And I think the rest of me will have to wait until the honeymoon."

"That serious?"

"Yes." He sighed and pulled an ear. "Fran, why did you want me to stop by?"

She started at his abrupt change of subject, then saw he was dead tired. The glow was flagging, and lines around his eyes and mouth were becoming apparent.

She looked at the way her long fingers intertwined in her lap, and into his waiting silence said, "Nick Tellios loaned me some money."

"Fran," he groaned.

"I know. It's been dreadful." She smiled bitterly. "It's put me right off gambling, forever. He made me do some wicked things, malfeasance things. Voting for measures I didn't want passed, against committee members I liked. I've twice asked city officials to promote people I think are incompetent. I can't bear it any longer, waiting for the police to come and get me. Or for whoever succeeds him to call. I want to know what I should do, and—and what will happen to me."

Her terror made her look like a little girl. He went to sit beside her and take her hand. "Nothing is going to happen," he said. "Tellios kept very few records, and the ones he did keep are so cryptic no one will ever decode them."

"But what if he comes back? He may decide to tell what he knows in a plea bargain!"

"He won't be coming back. He's dead."

"Are you sure?"

"For reasons too complicated to relate right now, yes. But with him gone and no other evidence, the police aren't going to arrest you. Tellios trusted no one with the names of his tame public officials, so there's no one to succeed him, either."

"But *you* know! I've just told you I was one of his 'tame public officials'! Aren't you going to arrest me?"

His look was one of such compassion her heart turned over. She had expected kindness from him, but not compassion. "No, I don't think it would serve anyone's interest to arrest you." He sighed wearily. "And anyhow, if I do arrest you, I'll have to take you back to the squad room and get a statement. Then get it transcribed. Then book you. That will take at least three hours, and I don't think I can stay awake another three hours."

"Then I'm free?" She sounded disbelieving.

He smiled. "If you really want to be arrested, come to the Safety Building in the morning and somebody will process you. But I don't recommend that; you've probably been through hell as it is."

"God, yes, I have!" She bowed her head and to keep from crying asked in a shaky voice, "Peter, tell me about what you've been doing."

Seeing her need, he rubbed his eyes and said, "Well, interrogations, mostly. Putting together the pieces of the kidnap and shootout. Everyone involved is either dead, missing, or in jail, except Joe Januschka, and we may never prove his involvement. But with Tellios gone, we can bring big-time drug dealing in Charter under control. Tellios was the linchpin; they can't replace him because no one knows how he operated."

"What about Kori? Will she be pushed off the ranch?"

"The ranch is hers. It's all that's left of her parents' estate. I called the family attorney about the will, and it looks like Tellios, who was her guardian, had access to over a million dollars in assets, which will probably never be found."

She looked startled. "That much? Oh, well, of course! Funny how one forgets, isn't it? Her parents were very wealthy. I vaguely remember them; she was nice and he raised some exotic breed of little horses. I guess I came to think of the ranch as Mr. Tellios', and of her as the penniless orphan he took in. How stupid of me—and poor her."

"Not utterly penniless; there's the ranch, and fifty thousand dollars in cash, which was impounded as evidence in the kidnap scam. She has some valuable horses, but the person who can make horse breeding pay is a rare individual. I think she'll end up selling them and the property. Too bad; that big house is a beautiful thing, and it'll probably be torn down by developers."

"So you're not marrying her for her money," she teased.

He sighed. "I may not marry her at all. I've been an object of fun to everyone since I laid eyes on her, including, I suspect, her. But out of pity, she lets me come and see her."

"Poor Peter."

"She started out terrified of me; I think I'm doing very well." He stood, groaning. "Please, may I have my coat so I can go home? You would not believe how beat I am."

"Of course. Thank you for coming. I was frantic." She brought it for him and helped him into it, her maternal feelings coming to the fore. "Peter, be careful. She can hurt you very badly the way you are now."

He turned and took her by the arms. "I know. But I'd rather thirst and not drink, than not thirst, where she's concerned."

Chapter
20 †

"We're gonna be late," said Danny. "Why didn't you let me drive out by myself?"

"Because I have a little business with your employer," said Phillip Bannister. "Anyway, it's unreasonable to expect an employee being paid what she's paying you to be at work right on the button. Especially when the button's at dawn."

"She expects me to be there." Danny shifted in the passenger seat of the big car. "And I promised I'd be there. We agreed I'd start right at six and it's ten after now."

The senior Bannister glanced at his son with a smile. This reform the kid was into was wonderful. Or was it that the lady had exerted some special authority . . . ? The smile vanished. He was a thin man, not tall, with very keen dark eyes behind square, gold-rimmed glasses worn halfway down his beak of a nose, and a wide mouth with an unlit green cigar he tucked into a corner of it every morning after breakfast and left there all day. His hands on the wheel were not large, but masculine, with widely spaced, big-jointed fingers and broad, beautifully kept nails. Under his unbuttoned overcoat he wore a black pinstripe suit and a loud orange tie. He looked like a very bright and gentle confidence man, which was not far from what he really was: a criminal-defense lawyer.

He was afraid his son might be making a serious mistake in accepting employment at Tretower. Kori Price was, after all, Tellios' niece, and had been raised by him. He remembered her from the few times he'd met her, a shy young thing, very pretty. It now seemed Tellios had lied when he'd hinted her elevator didn't go all the way to the top. What did she know about her uncle's operation—and might she feel herself capable of taking over the business? Phillip did not want his newly redeemed son given an opportunity to go bad again. Nor did he want to find himself back

205

in an ugly trap. Danny insisted Kori was innocent and honest, but Phillip had reason to be wary of the boy's judgment.

"There's the turnoff," said Danny, pointing.

"I see it," said Phillip, slowing, turning on his blinker.

As they came up the narrow lane, Danny groaned. "See?" he said. "Lights on in the barn. I told you! And I'm late, I'm fifteen minutes late! I promised her I'd be on time!"

"Take it easy, son. I'll explain it's my fault." Phillip crossed the racetrack, stopped and asked, "Where do I park?" But he spoke to empty air; his son had opened the door and jumped out.

Phillip swore, turned off the engine and got out.

It was true the sun had not come over the horizon, but the eastern sky was bright and all but a single star had faded from the sky. Phillip crunched across gravel to a small door set into a big one he'd seen his son enter.

Inside was a fenced arena; the gate to it was open, and another gate led from it to a broad passageway; Phillip, alert for things he didn't want to step in, grimaced more tightly around his cigar and started across.

He could see them in the passageway. Kori was standing outside a box stall with a pitchfork in one hand. Danny, who was taller than his father, was looking down at her and, from his hunched shoulders and raised hands, apologizing. He glanced at his father and gestured toward him, then took the pitchfork and went down the row to another box stall marked by a half-filled wheelbarrow. Kori turned to meet Phillip.

She did not look very shy this morning. "Good morning, Mr. Bannister," she said, but did not put out her hand. Which was okay with him; she was wearing a thick, dirty white glove, which went perfectly with the old gray sweater that had straw all over it, mended riding pants, and rubber boots daubed with mud or worse.

"Good morning," he replied. "Or is it morning yet? Kind of early for a guy like me."

"So your son was explaining. He said you had some business with me?"

"Yes, but I also wanted to meet you, maybe find out more about this job you've offered him."

She looked over her shoulder to watch Danny bring a laden pitchfork out to the wheelbarrow. "It's not much of a job. Just stablehand." She turned back. "But Danny can make it into something better, if he proves out. I can't run this place alone; I'll need an assistant, someone to help train and show my horses. I can't afford to hire a professional right now, so Danny has this opportunity to try for the position. He's starting at four dollars an hour; in ninety days we'll renegotiate that. I'm taking out taxes and social security, and he gets a free lunch and three hours off every other afternoon, unless there's a horse show."

"Yeah, he told me all that."

"Then what more do you want to know?"

"What are you really up to out here?"

She looked puzzled, then angry. "I trust I am mistaken in what that appears to mean."

"I hope I'm mistaken too. But this is too important not to ask about. Danny's in enough trouble as it is."

"I am trying to continue building a horse-breeding business. I have not done, nor am I doing, anything dishonest. I will fire Danny if he is caught using drugs or doing anything else against the law. Is that clear enough?" She was looking sincerely angry.

Phillip Bannister was almost as good a judge of character as he thought he was. He nodded curtly, and when he smiled his cigar moved back with it. "Clear enough. This horse business, do you really think you can make a go of it?"

"Yes."

Phillip looked up and down the double row of box stalls. "Say I wanted to buy your most expensive horse. How much would it cost me?"

"Right now that would be Bitter Wind. She's four, had her first foal last year." Kori walked toward one of the box stalls and Phillip followed. The upper half of the wide door was open, and he looked in to see the shining rear end of a black-tailed horse. The front end was engaged in eating and did not look around. "She's by Go to Hell out of Arsenic, who was by Gdansk. Go to Hell, of course, was by The Egyptian Prince."

"Of course," said Phillip. "How much?"

"Forty-seven thousand."

The cigar wobbled dangerously. "Forty—?"

"Seven thousand. I should mention that she was in foal to my late stallion Summer Wind but fell trying to jump a fence in her third month and miscarried. She's a good keeper and very clever."

"At that price she should pass her college-entrance exam any day. Now, will you come out to my car for a minute?"

"Why?"

"Your uncle gave me something to give to you."

She took a step backward, her poise replaced by fright—which can be mistaken for shyness, and he recognized the look on her with a stab of compassion. She said, "My uncle's dead."

"God, I hope so. No, he gave this to me some while back, and said to bring it to you if something happened to him. Praise be, something did, so here I am with it."

"What is it?"

He indicated with his hands a rectangle about two feet wide and eighteen inches long. "A box. He told me not to look inside, so I didn't."

"Organized Crime Unit, Sergeant McHugh."

"Hi, this is Deputy Sheriff Carey in Mickletown, 'bout ninety-seven miles north of you on Highway 49. You the one looking for one Nick Tellios?"

"Sure are! You found him?" McHugh's sharp tone brought Ryder's attention around from the coffeepot.

"No, sir, and the sheriff isn't sure this is the sort of thing you're looking for; but we had some kind of incident in an orchard just outside town. Appears like someone got hurt. Lots of blood, but no body."

"How many people involved?"

"Tracks say one car come in, one person got out or was shoved out, either already hurt or hurt—stabbed or shot—as soon as he or she got out. No sign of a struggle. The car then turned around and drove out, leaving the person behind. He or she—if it was a he, he was on the small side—lay down a good while, to judge by the way the grass is flattened, and bled a pint or three."

"But the injured party left, too?"

"Yeah. Got up and wandered around awhile, then went and stole Mr. Lofton's dark green Volkswagen Rabbit, three-year-old model. Unlocked, but no keys in it. The Loftons own the orchard. They had taken her car to visit her sister. Got home this morning. We put out an all-points on the car just a little bit ago."

"Well, what do you make of it?"

"We thought maybe kids, or some locals settling an old grudge. But all our probables are well and accounted for. That's why we decided to call."

"Find any weapons?"

"No, sir."

"Hmmm. Gimme your phone number, okay?" McHugh scribbled on a pad. "And thanks for calling; this could be what we're looking for. If you get anything more on this, let us know."

"Will do."

"Thanks. Bye." McHugh hung up.

"What was that?" asked Ryder.

"A thin lead," said McHugh, and explained.

"If it's ours, Tellios is alive. He's hurt, but he's alive. Where do you suppose he's headed?"

"Mexico. That's what I'd do. In Mexico you don't need to see a doctor to get antibiotics."

"He may be hurt so bad he needs more than penicillin."

"Maybe he'll have to stop at a hospital," agreed McHugh.

"And they'll call the cops to report a gunshot wound. Tell Obie when he comes in. What's this Peter business with you and him?"

"He says his friends call him Peter."

Ryder said, "I remember the first time I saw him. He was so tight-jawed about his latest transfer he could just about open his mouth enough to speak. He came up to me cold as hell and said, 'Good morning, Captain, I'm Sergeant Otto Peter Brichter. My friends call me Peter; you can call me Obie.' "

"He can be a real smart-ass," said McHugh.

"Yeah, well, I wonder now if he wasn't asking that just one of us would take him up on the offer and ask to call him Peter."

McHugh shook his head. "Probably not. I don't think he was ready back then to be friends with anyone toting a badge."

Ryder shrugged and asked, "Where is he?"

"Dunno. Meeting someone." McHugh's phone rang again and he scooped it up. It was Kori.

"Hey, young lady, how's the world treating you?"

"I'm not so sure. Is Peter there?"

"No, not right now. Is something wrong?"

"I don't know. I got a package from Uncle."

"A package? What kind of package?"

"A box, fairly heavy, fairly large. Uncle left it with someone to bring to me if something happened to him. So it was brought out this morning. I—I'm afraid to open it. Tell Peter, will you? Tell him to come as soon as he can."

Brichter was sitting backward at a picnic table in the park. After the rain of last night, the day had bloomed warm and dry. He was reading with wry pleasure a book he'd found in his mailbox—he was on countless publishers' mailing lists, and spent a lot of his meager discretionary income on books. *The Incomplete Book of Failures*, by Stephen Pile, was a compilation of humanity's inability to plan and carry out tasks ranging from war to a piano recital. He glanced up and saw Jilly Meade walking toward him. He closed the book and got to his feet.

The voluptuous redhead, resplendent in pink trousers and a purple velour top, stopped a few feet from him and said, "Well, here I am."

"Thanks for agreeing to meet me," he said. "Won't you sit down?"

"Here's a change; last time we met, you were damn rude." But she sat.

"Last time we met, it wasn't my idea. Or yours. I hope you reported my feelings about attempts at bribery to the Undertaker." He tossed his book on the table and sat down beside her.

She raised an elegant eyebrow. "He didn't send me to you."

Brichter nodded. "Yes, I thought the order to try that on me came from Mr. Januschka. So how is Joe these days?"

"Not spending any sleepless nights, if that's what you're hoping."

"Doesn't he wonder what the hell happened to Tellios?"

"We all know that one. Nick's dead, Obie."

"I haven't seen the body."

"It'll turn up. Probably today."

"You sound damn sure."

"Joe's got sources."

"It'll be different around here with him gone."

"Not really."

"The town's stirred up about things, Jilly."

"So? It's been stirred up before. You Christer cops are all alike. You never learn: We stay. You know why? Because the johns get stirred up, but they still line up to buy what we sell, and they hate it when you run us out of town!" She smiled a defiant smile. "You'll get sick of it, Obie, and you'll quit, just like the others; but we'll be right here! Nothing's gonna be different; you'll see."

"Yes, we'll see," he said quietly.

She shrugged. "What did you want to talk to me about?"

"I was hoping you'd tell me some things, answer some questions. After all, you're the one who told me Nick was the broker we've been looking for."

"Hey, now!" Her look of surprise was mixed with alarm. "C'mon, Obie, where did you get an idea like that?"

"Because you know how to pronounce my name. I saw you in Chauncey's the other day, and you greeted me by my rank and surname. Not many people can give it the correct German guttural. And the lady on the phone could say it too."

"I'm the only lady in town who can say *Brichter*?"

"But how many women who can say *Brichter* also know Nick was the broker we've been looking for?"

"Who says I know anything about that? I don't have any idea what old man Tellios did or why his being a broker should interest the cops."

"To coin a term, bullshit. You are, I suspect, a very bright and loyal young woman, not content to be just a high-price call girl. How better to demonstrate your loyalty than by striking a blow for your boss's boss, Januschka?"

"What has Joe got to do with Nick Tellios?"

Brichter enjoyed explaining things, no matter who made up his audience. "Joe and Nick were warming up to a fight over who'd be boss in town. Nick started out retired, but within a few months the prickles of boredom were rubbing him raw. So he made a friend here, a friend there, and pretty soon it's safe for him to start up his drug-brokerage business. But that was easy, and didn't ease the itch completely, so he looked around and saw Joe. Joe and Nick are both from Chicago; they probably ran across each other a time or two. And Nick remembers Joe as a mere enforcer up there, a long way from his current position as administrator. But Joe's not as dumb as he likes to pretend, is he, Jilly? He's big, he's tough, he's got a face that's bounced off a few sidewalks in its time and a speaking vocabulary of maybe four hundred words. He has a reputation for savagery that is only a little exaggerated. But so long as he has his way, he's a peace-loving man; and more than once I've suspected there lurks in him a very keen intellect. Nick had this mistaken idea he could move in on Joe, starting like he starts all his other relationships, by making him into a friend, offering him advice or the benefit of his many connections with the regular establishment in Charter. But Joe wasn't having any, once he realized what was happening. And there things stuck, for both of them. Until you."

"What have I got to do with this fairy tale you're telling?"

"I told you, you decided to help Joe in his fight with Tellios. I imagine you thought it would be fun to send that wicked old man to prison."

"But Nick isn't going to prison. He's dead."

"Yes. What happened is, you forgot people like Nick and Joe play for keeps. Or you didn't care."

"None of this is true, you know."

"No? Then why are those people who are sitting at Riscatto's bedside all Joe's men?"

She said, "You're so smart, you tell me."

"Because they're waiting for him to tell them where Nick's body is."

She sat down at the picnic table. "You like fairy tales? Try this one on for size. Once upon a time there was a wicked old man who lived on a horse ranch. Oh, he was so safe out on that ranch! All the rest of the people had to deal with that goddamn Organized Crime Unit, while he worried about planting his sugar snaps too early! So someone decided to give him a taste of real life, to sweat a little, like the rest of us. And when he found out a certain cop knew about him, he got real, all right. The old man was a weird guy in a lot of ways. Like he hated cops—really hated them. Did you know that?"

"No."

"So you didn't know how really strange it was that he let you hold hands with his precious Kori, trying to turn you around. Don't you see? People don't want to get involved in Charter deals any more, because you're breathing down all our necks all the damn time!" She stopped suddenly, pressing a fist to her mouth, coughing a little cough. "I will deny I ever had this conversation with you, you know."

"I know."

"And it was like I said, a fairy tale. If it sounded real it's because I'm an actress. It helps in my profession to be an actress."

"You're very convincing. Would you consider playing Act Two for me some time?"

"Listen, jerk!" she said. "I let my imagination carry me away for a minute and here you go believing it."

He considered that and nodded. "I have a theory about minutes, Jilly. A few days ago, you took a minute to dump on Nick Tellios. A friend took a minute to listen when I needed his magic, and a kidnap victim fought for just one more minute of time before her kidnapper murdered her. And so Tellios is dead, and Miss Price and Dr. Ramsey are alive."

"What are you saying?"

"It's the little minute-to-minute decisions that tell us who we are."

"And what am I?"

"Party to a murder. Oh, not you alone. But you had a significant role in it."

"You're crazier than that milk-faced bitch out at the ranch, you know that? You think accusing me of that is going to turn me into a snitch? Ha!" She stood and sneered. "You'll spend a lot of minutes by a phone that don't ring, waiting for me to call. That's all; I don't have to listen to this." She took two steps away, then turned back. "Say, you aren't going to repeat any of this to anyone, are you?"

"I don't know. I might find myself presenting it as a theory in the squad room some time. We play let's pretend once in a while, too."

She sat down again and took his forearm in a strong grip. "I don't want you to do that, okay? You said my minute killed Nick? Well, your minute could kill me. I could be the deadest lady you ever played let's pretend with."

"We could protect you."

"I've been to funerals of people who believed the cops could protect them. No, no, that's out. What can I do, what can I say to make you understand that you must never, ever tell anyone about this conversation?"

"I never give anyone the names of my informants."

"I already told you I won't do that. It's dumb and dangerous and I'm not cut out that way. Wait a second: I'll trade you. I'll tell you something you'll really be grateful for, if you'll promise to forget we ever met. You have to forget my name and everything. Okay?"

"Tell me first and we'll see."

"No, I can't do that. You won't be sorry, I promise." She was still holding on to his arm, and a sheen of earnest perspiration lay across her forehead and upper lip.

He hesitated. "All right."

"It's Tonk Erickson. He's sleeping with . . . one of the Undertaker's ladies, but he doesn't know who she really is. She spends an hour with Tonk and a minute on the phone with the Undertaker." She smiled wryly. "See, another one of your little minutes. But it was worth the trade, wasn't it?" She tightened her grip. "Wasn't it?"

He studied her a moment. "Yes, all right. Fair exchange."

"Good." She stood. "Now, with your kind permission, Sergeant Brichter, I want to get back to the great indoors. All this grass makes me think of crawly things."

He stood, too. "Thanks again for agreeing to come," he said.

"Well, I can't say it's been nice. I hope it's true what I hear, that you keep your word. I guess you and that kid at the ranch have something going, huh? By the way, she's not the sweet innocent you think she is. Undertaker says her folks weren't just relatives to

Nick, they were friends—that special kind of friend from the way he says it."

And having planted that poisonous seed, she walked away across the bright grass, her heels uncomfortably high, her full round bottom moving a little more than necessary in the loose pink britches. Brichter watched her go and shook his head.

Brichter found Captain Ryder alone in the squad room.

"Can I see you a minute?" he asked. "I've got some information."

"I hope to hell it's good news; I just got off the phone with the mayor. And before him the chief called. Everyone's pissed because we didn't get on to Tellios sooner. And we're under orders to clean up all the corruption in the city attributable to organized crime—right now, this minute."

"Well then, this is good news and bad news. I can tell you about some corruption we can clean up in a hurry, but it's very close to home."

"Oh, shit. All right, what is it?"

"Tonk's sleeping with one of MacNeeley's whores. She gets him to repeat squad-room gossip, which she passes along to her employer, who takes it to Januschka."

"Where'd you get this?"

"I can't tell you." Brichter was pretty sure Jilly herself was the girl who was sleeping with Tonk, but he was holding on to that too, for now, both in payment for her assistance and because he still thought he might turn her around.

"I don't like it when you play that game."

"I know. But I still can't tell you."

"Obie . . ."

"I'm sorry, Captain."

"Yeah, I bet you are."

Brichter turned on his heel and went to the coffee urn.

Ryder sighed. "Okay, I didn't mean that. Maybe it's jealousy; did you see that write-up about yourself in the paper?"

"Some of it," admitted Brichter.

"That used to be me out there, doing brave things. But this time I'm sitting in that goddamn closet faking figures on some report no one will ever read, and everyone else is out there saving beautiful ladies from vicious kidnappers. Oh, the coroner called. It was you who killed Shiffler."

"What? Are they sure?"

"You and Nelsen both hit him; but your bullet killed him."

"Sweet Jesus." Brichter put his mug down; his hands were feeling odd.

Ryder was surprised; he figured Brichter would take the news coldly, maybe even be pleased about it. More than ever he was curious about who it was living behind those walls. "I'm sorry; I guess I shouldn't have sprung it on you like that. He your first?"

"Second. It's all right. I'm just surprised." Brichter resolutely picked up his mug and filled it. "What are we going to do about Tonk?"

"I want to consult with you and Cris about that. Let's have a meeting later today."

"Sure." He went to his desk, found a pink phone message and picked it up. "Kori says I should come out right away and see her. What do you suppose has happened now?"

Ryder said, "You could go out and ask her."

Chapter
21 †

Geoff and Anne would love this place, too, thought Brichter. The beautiful old house stood in brilliant sunshine atop a slope of fresh green strewn with jonquils. A pair of stately silver maples had strewn red bud covers all over the bottom of the walk that led up to the porch.

Brichter was halfway up the walk when the door opened and Kori came out onto the porch and stood waiting. She was wearing a loose-fitting red dress with bag sleeves that hid her cast, and had discarded the sling. Her hair was twisted into knots over her ears, which combined with the dress and the bandage across her forehead to make her look like a Great War poster girl.

"Fy'n galon," Brichter said in his deepest voice.

"Hello, Peter," she replied, smiling back. "Thank you for coming. We're in the library."

Brichter stopped to admire again the big entrance hall, with its black-and-white tile floor, carved staircase, and big stained-glass window splashing color from the landing across the floor. "Is it so very pretty?" Kori asked. "It just looks like things I've seen in magazines and on television."

"Yes, but you know . . ." started Brichter, then he laughed, because she obviously didn't. "Believe me, this is an exceptional place."

Kori led him to the library, a room that appeared to have changed little since electricity was brought to the house. Ramsey was sitting in one of the extremely comfortable tufted leather chairs, waiting for them. He watched as Brichter stood awhile, absorbing the room's peace. Beyond a projecting wall made of bookshelves, two tall, uncurtained windows let in spring sunlight. A faded oriental rug was on the floor, and a small fireplace set in blue tiles crouched under a surround of bookshelves. The bookshelves

216

went to about eight feet, and the walls above were ornamented by old engravings in steel frames. This house is like something out of an old novel, Brichter thought; the library most of all. He imagined himself here on some peaceful evening, reading one of its leather-bound volumes while seated deep in one of these wing chairs, with Kori in another, and a fire, and a bedroom upstairs waiting . . .

Ramsey raised his eyebrows at Kori, who said, "I don't know; he did this in the hall, too."

"I like it here," said Brichter. "I like this whole house, but especially this room. Gordie, I'd think you feel right at home here."

Ramsey smiled. "I do, now Tellios is out of it." He stood and said, "The package is back here, Peter." On the other side of the projecting wall was a tiny black enamel desk, and on it was a package wrapped in brown paper, taped and tied with hairy twine.

"You're sure it's from him?" asked Brichter.

"Oh yes," said Kori.

"How do you know?" asked Brichter, who at the sight of it had reverted to cop.

"That's his pen and his writing," she replied, touching the address label, which had been addressed with a thick nib in a distinctive backhand.

Brichter came and lifted the package, studying the label and the knots of the twine. "Leave us, can you, Gordie?" he said.

"I'll go finish preparing lunch," said Ramsey.

"Who brought this out to you?" Brichter asked when the door had shut.

"Phillip Bannister. He brought Danny out this morning and then took me out to his car. He's pleased and relieved Uncle is dead, and glad to be rid of this last duty." Kori opened the desk's single drawer and found a letter opener, which she handed to Brichter. "I'm not much with only a hand and a half."

Brichter cut carefully along the brown paper wrapping, which was several layers thick and trebly sealed with fiber tape. "Did Bannister wrap this, I wonder?" he asked, aggravated, trying to disturb the wrapping as little as possible.

"No, I'm sure Uncle did it himself," she said. "I've seen him wrap packages; this is very typical of him. I told you, he always did everything very thoroughly."

Inside, the box was lined with heavy waxed paper and filled with Styrofoam peanuts. On top of the Styrofoam was a sheet of note-paper, folded in half. Kori picked it up.

It was a brief note in the distinctive backhand. *Dear Kori*, it began, *If you are reading this, I am dead.* "There," she said, "I told you." She turned a little so Brichter could read over her shoulder.

This package is being left with a friend who will bring it to you if something happens to me.

I want you to know I loved you more than anyone else in the world. I gave up everything I had in Chicago and came down to take care of you when that terrible thing happened to your parents.

Don't believe anything the cops try to tell you about me. I was an honest businessman and when I retired down here, I did a lot of good for my adopted town. I've known a few crooks in my time, and believe me, there is nothing organized about them.

Enclosed are some things you should keep.

The note was signed, *Your Uncle, Nick Tellios.*

"What does he mean about not being organized?" Kori asked.

"He's saying there's no such thing as organized crime."

"Is that true?"

"No. Organized crime takes in more money annually than Mobil Oil."

She put the letter down and carefully swept aside the Styrofoam in the box to reveal a color photograph, a portrait of a man, set in a broad gold frame. Brichter lifted it out for her. The man was square-faced, strong-looking, with brilliant blue eyes and curly black hair. His little collar and narrow tie dated the photograph to the sixties. Smiling, she reached out to touch the man's cheek. "There, I knew it was you," she murmured.

"Is he the man in your dreams?" asked Brichter.

"Yes."

Brichter put the portrait down and she reached into the box for another, this time that of a woman in a dark, sedate chignon. She looked a lot like Kori. Her densely lashed eyes were the same shade of light, clear gray, and she had Kori's shapely mouth, though it was colored with pale lipstick. Kori frowned. "Then this must be . . . well, of course! I remember her now, on the front porch one morning, combing her hair, long and smooth and heavy, not awful stuff like mine; and red where the sun hit it. Then the lady in the dream, all blue and horrible, must be—oh, Mama!" She put a hand over her mouth and turned away. Brichter gave her a moment, then went and put both hands on her shoulders. She turned and leaned against him. "Oh, how could I? All I remember now is loving them!" But she did not cry.

"It's all right," he said lamely. "It's all right."

She stepped away from him and went back to the desk. She dug into the Styrofoam and came up with a little candid photograph in a plain silver frame. "Look, it's Uncle." Her voice creaked a little, but her expression was calm.

A much younger Tellios was squatting in the front yard near the porch steps. He was laughing, his ugly mouth wide open, and holding up a long dark pigtail on a little girl, perhaps four or five, who was laughing back at him.

"Why did he send me this?"

"Maybe that's how he wants you to remember him, to remember a time when you loved him, too."

She put the little photograph down, her face closed, and searched the box again, moving her hand around under the Styrofoam. "Here's something else," she said, coming up with an old book, dog-eared and faded.

"What is it?"

"It's *The Wind in the Willows*. He used to read it to me. Even when I could read it myself, he still read it to me." She opened the book to the frontispiece, a pen-and-ink drawing of a speed-maddened toad driving an old automobile to the public danger. "Papa read this to me too. I *am* remembering."

"It's a very pleasant adventure," said Brichter.

"Then you know it?"

"Sure. My favorite character was Badger."

She smiled. "I should have thought it was Toad, the Terror of the Highway, breaking speed limits right and left." She showed him the drawing.

"Ah yes, 'What dust clouds shall spring up behind me as I speed on my restless way; here today and in next week tomorrow. Poop-poop!' " he said, and she giggled. Brichter picked up the letter and said, "I want to report this right away. May I use a phone?"

"In the living room."

"I'm sorry about your uncle."

"You are? I'm not! Saves you from putting him in jail with the others, where they're treated much too kindly, I'll bet! If Uncle had been out there in that parking lot, I'd have wanted him shot, too! Loved me, he says! Lying, *beastly* coward, sending poor Downey to do his work for him! How dare he write he loved me!"

"Atta girl," said Brichter, and she laughed, and came to hug him.

But she grew serious again, and murmured, "Dear Gordon, he's always known what Uncle really is, hasn't he?"

"Better than any of us, probably," said Brichter.

"What he must have suffered; yet he stayed and didn't let it destroy him. We should name a mountain for him."

Brichter said after a moment, "All right," and she leaned back to look up at him, surprised.

"What do you mean, all right?"

"There are plenty of mountains in the United States that haven't got names. Pick one and we'll send its location to the U.S. Board on Geographic Names. No problem. Well, except one."

"What's that?"

"We'll have to wait until Gordie dies. Okay?"

"Are you serious? We could name a mountain?"

"Sure. But they won't commemorate living persons."

She studied his thin face, his pale eyes intent on her. She asked, "Is there anything you don't know anything about?"

"I don't know," he said, smiling, and after a moment she saw the joke and smiled back at him. She went to talk to Gordon while Brichter called Captain Ryder.

Tellios pulled the car up into the lane. Brush scratched at its fenders as it jounced over the ruts. Every jounce brought a renewal of agony. Was he far enough from the road? Yes, yes, enough. He stopped the car and reached for the wires to shut the engine off. His breath was coming in tearing little gasps. *Rest awhile.* But as he leaned back in the seat, he kept his eyes on the white board fence. Through there, and then across that pasture. He could almost smell the jonquils. He was home.

Kori was waiting impatiently for Brichter when he came out of the parlor. "Look!" she said, showing him page 6.

"At what?" The book had been treated with the disrespect usual among children. An untutored hand had scrawled "Katrin" in pencil in the margin and illustrated the name with what was probably meant to be a portrait, but which more nearly resembled a four-legged insect with long, droopy braids/antennae. He smiled, then noticed other additions. A fat blue-ink line had been drawn under parts of several sentences in the last paragraph, obliterating others. And the character of Mole, at the bottom of the page, had had a cartoon thought balloon added above his head, in which had been printed in a thick backhand, "For you, Kori."

He began to read the underlined fragments aloud. " 'As he sat on the grass and looked across the river, a dark hole in the bank opposite, just above the water's edge, caught his eye . . .' "

"There's a place just like that on the ranch," she said. "It was my secret place, but I showed it to Uncle once, back when I wanted to stay close to him. He'd brought Gordon to me, and I was afraid of Gordon, because he was new and angry and didn't like me. There's a little river that cuts across the back pasture, and a big willow on the bank. I could sit on a flat rock and there—only from there—could I see the cave hidden in the bushes."

"Cave?"

"It's a storm drain, actually, an old one, lined with stones. I used to pretend that fairies lived there, or stranded Martians, depending on what I was reading. Or that it was Ratty's home, like in the book. The viewing rock is under the big willow, and in the summertime the branches come all the way down to the ground, like a big tent, and it was like hiding to sit in there. I took Uncle there, and asked if perhaps Mr. Grahame had visited the ranch and sat there and saw the drain, and written his book because of it. Uncle pretended to consider my idea very seriously and said he thought it was possible. I liked him a lot that day. We promised never to tell anyone about the cave. I think he kept his word, and I know I kept mine; I never told even Gordon."

Brichter said, "Hmmm," and read on. " ' . . . something bright and small seemed to twinkle down in the heart of it . . . like a tiny star.' "

She interrupted, "We agreed that afternoon that pirates might have gotten lost while sailing the Eerie River and buried their treasure in the cave and set a ghost to guard it. He warned me never to go look, and I didn't, in case it might be true—or in case it wasn't." She smiled. "I'd nearly forgotten about it; I haven't gone to sit on the rock for a long time."

Brichter read on, " 'But it could hardly be a star in such an unlikely situation; and it was too glittering and small for a glowworm.' "

He turned the page to read more, but she reached for the book. "That's all," she said. "Don't you see? Uncle left something for me in the secret place. Something small and glittering. A diamond, maybe!"

He made a face and she said, "That's his writing, isn't it? That note to me wasn't in there last time I read it. I remember noticing Christmas before last the book was gone from its shelf; I thought Uncle had thrown it away, because it's a shabby old thing and I hadn't read it in a long time. Don't you see? He took it, marked those lines, and gave it to Mr. Bannister to keep for me, so I would be taken care of if he died suddenly. See, 'For you, Kori.' I'm going to go see what he left; come with me?"

He hesitated—there were other things he should be doing—but her shining eagerness made him decide perhaps he should see if there was something to find. "But I don't think my car would stand the overland trip."

"Who needs a car when I have a barnful of horses? You do ride, don't you?"

"Yes. Well, not for a long time. But if we take it slow . . ."

"Wonderful! You tell Gordon to hold lunch while I change!"

Gordon, a little confused by Brichter's self-serving explanation of the need for the errand she was taking him on, came with them to the barn to see them off.

They detoured to tell the police guard where they were going. He'd been dozing in the warm spring sunshine and grinned in an abashed way when he recognized Brichter. "Yessir," he kept saying, blinking the sleep out of his eyes. "Sure. Fine."

"What's it called, snoozing like that?" asked Gordon as they headed again for the barn.

"Sleeping on duty," said Kori.

"No, there's a police word for it."

"Cooping," said Brichter shortly.

"You're not going to report him for it?" asked Gordon.

"Oh, yes," said Brichter.

"But nothing could have happened," objected Kori. "Uncle is dead."

"Kelly didn't know that when he decided to take a nap," said Brichter. He held the door for them and they stepped into the fragrant dimness of the barn and paused, jostling up against one another, sun-blinded.

Danny was raking the arena. He stopped and waited as they walked along the aisle toward him, his attitude increasingly wary as he recognized Brichter.

Brichter stared. "Roach Bannister!" he exclaimed.

"H'lo, Sergeant Brichter."

"This is your new hired hand?" Brichter demanded of Kori.

"Yes," she said, puzzled at his anger.

"Now, Peter," warned Gordon.

"No way!" he said. "Get your gear, young man; you're riding back into town with me!"

"Hey!" protested Danny.

"Maybe you should—" began Gordon.

"No!" said Kori.

Brichter said, "You're not hiring a goddamn dope addict to work out here! Hasn't this place had enough of that filthy business?"

"He's not an addict!" said Kori. "He's—clean! And anyway, who I hire is my business!"

"Get your gear, Bannister!" ordered Brichter.

"Are you arresting him, Peter?" asked Gordon.

"No, I'm firing him. Did you hear me?" Brichter asked Danny.

"Stay where you are, Danny!" ordered Kori. "You, Sergeant Brichter, have no authority to fire my people!"

He turned angrily on her. "I won't let you keep someone like Roach Bannister around! You're likely to wake up one morning to find he's fired your barn or put the colt onto the racetrack for the dogs to play with!"

"His name is Danny, and he'll do no such thing!" She turned to the boy. "It's all right; you're staying."

"Yes'm," he replied, scared.

"Peter," said Ramsey. "I think you ought not to do this just now. If you give her time to think over what you've said—"

"You mean come away and leave him here? Goddammit, what kind of idiot do you think I am?"

"That's enough!" said Kori.

"No, it isn't!" He turned to confront her again, but was forestalled by her furious retort.

"I *won't* stand here arguing about it," she said. "I'm not firing Danny!"

"Come, Peter," said Gordon, taking him by the arm. "You're not helping matters by shouting at her."

"I'm not shouting!" Brichter shouted. "Now listen a minute," he said, less loudly, shrugging off Gordon's hand. "You don't know anything about people like Roach. How can you? You've never had to deal with anyone like him. Trust me; he's a bad apple. Get rid of him."

Kori, eyes ablaze, said, "Never had to—!" She gestured. "And *trust* you? Why? You—you policeman!"

"You were glad enough I was a policeman two days ago!" he said.

"Enough, Peter," said Gordon firmly, taking hold again and this time starting down the aisle, pulling the angry cop with him. "Don't play that game on her; it isn't fair."

Brichter said, resisting movement, "This isn't a game; I'm serious! Let go of me!"

Kori made a scooping gesture and said, "Keep him going, Gordon; I wouldn't have him near the worst horse I own, now!"

"To hell with the riding; we need to talk about a much more serious matter!"

"Shut up and keep moving!" Gordon kept pulling. He pushed the door open with one hand and pulled Brichter through with the other. Kori followed, saying in a loud voice, "You will *not* speak to me as if I were an underling! This is *my* place; *I* give the orders here!"

Outside, Brichter yanked free and said, "Roach is in serious trouble with the law! He could pull you into whatever he's doing! Get rid of him!"

"You aren't listening to me!" she warned. "How dare you be so stupid and—and imperious?"

"Hush, both of you," warned Gordon, looking over at Kelly, who was standing outside his squad car, drinking in the scene.

But Brichter was beyond warning. "I'm not the one not listening!" he yelled. "And I'm *not* the one being stupid!"

She grabbed his arm and pointed. "There's your car, Sergeant Brichter. Get in it and get off my ranch!"

Ramsey found her in the back bedroom of the cottage. "Is it safe to come in?" he asked around the edge of the door.

"Yes, if you must."

He found her curled into a miserable ball in an overstuffed rocking chair. "That was a remarkable display in the barn a little while ago," he said. "I've never seen you like that before."

"I can do what I like now," she said. "I can even lose my temper if I feel the need for it. Where's Danny?"

"I sent him home," Ramsey said. "He'd finished in the barn. I must agree, pet, that Peter could have handled that better."

"He shouldn't have tried to handle it at all," she muttered. "It's none of his business!"

"We can always use good advice."

"He wasn't giving advice, he was giving orders. And anyway, it was bad advice." She rubbed her temple with one hand. "He gave me a terrible headache."

He caressed the back of her neck. "Being given advice one doesn't want can make one's head ache," he agreed. "Peter can be very pigheaded and stupid about things, I know. It's one of the things about him his friends put up with."

"Perhaps they shouldn't."

"Perhaps not. Ready for lunch?"

"No."

"Maybe after some aspirin have gone to work; I'll bring them to you. Meantime, be thinking about where you want to go. We'll set out right after lunch for a ride."

Her head came up at that. "Yes, we can go anywhere we please, can't we? Glorious, not having Riscatto along. Could we go to a movie? And a restaurant for supper. Then to Chauncey's! I'd love to get into a real poker game!"

"I don't think Chauncey's; gambling is illegal in this state, you know. The way things are moving right now, the police may well decide to commence cleaning up the city by raiding Chauncey's. You could end your first night on the town in jail."

"Well, then, someplace where there's music. Loud music. And cocktails; I've always wanted a cocktail. Maybe someone will ask me to dance."

He was laughing. "You'll meet someone wonderful, elope, and I'll come home alone, brokenhearted."

She was laughing now too. "No, because there can't be anyone anywhere as nice as you. You are my shining star, do you know that? I'd be lost without you."

"You'd manage, I expect."

"No, I'd be desolated." She stopped laughing and asked anxiously, "Will you stay until this is over?"

"Naturally, I'll stay as long as you like."

"No, because then you'd never get away. But we need to talk about it." She stood and a book fell out of her lap, a shabby old children's book. "Oh yes, I nearly forgot. I've still got that old cave to visit."

"Perhaps you should put it off until you feel better."

"My headache's gone, almost. And whatever's there won't mind if I find it angry or happy. And if it is a diamond, that would be one in the eye for Sergeant Brichter."

Tellios woke with a start, surprised he had dozed off. With a soft groan, he opened the door and got out, moving slowly, careful not to jostle anything. He walked up to the fence and grasped the top board with both hands. He felt hot and dizzy. The pain in his chest was a purple flame, and every breath fanned it into white-hot flares. Infection, he thought. I'll have to get some penicillin.

When his attention could be spared, he saw the great heap of earth in the meadow. I don't remember that, he thought. Am I still lost? Is this the wrong place? No, no, it's all right; that's just Summer Wind's grave. This is the right place.

He bent and climbed through the fence, stopping again on the other side to rest awhile, then set off across the meadow. It's across from the big willow, he reminded himself.

Chapter
22 †

Kori rode her gentle gray, Storm Wind, across the meadows of her ranch. The foal Hurricane gamboled alongside, already used to the sight of a human on her mother's back.

But the river was a first for Hurricane, and it was some time before she could be brought to wade the shallow ford. Successful at last, they went downstream a short way, then Kori dismounted.

She loosened Storm Wind's cinch and removed the bridle so the mare could graze. Then she took off her boots and socks and waded, hissing, out into the icy water. She made her way carefully down the slippery rocks to where a mass of brush marked the location of the storm drain. Half hidden by vines and scrub, it was smaller than she remembered. An unsavory mix of mud and water was drooling out.

She bent and crawled into the drain. It stank. Having to crawl on three limbs slowed her progress, and it was a minute or two before she came to a place where the drain forked. It was far enough back that the light was poor, and it was as much by feel as sight that she found the low ledge at the fork, and on it something squarish inside a heavy plastic bag, taped shut.

The drain was too narrow for her to turn around in, so she tucked the package under her bad arm and backed out.

She stepped gratefully back into sunlight, her face streaked with spider webs and winkled in disgust. The package had been slipping downward, and both the plastic and her cast were muddy and wet.

She waded back upstream and tossed the parcel up on the grassy bank, then waded out again to wash the worst of the muck from herself.

Safely back on the bank, she shooed Hurricane away and sat down to tear at the plastic, which was heavy and yielded only after some effort. Inside was a new-looking brown leather attaché case. It was not locked. She held her breath and opened it.

Inside were two black velvet drawstring sacks, an English-Spanish dictionary, and a green passport. Tucked inside the dictionary was a sheet of notepaper.

Kori, it read, *This is my emergency getaway stash. But just in case I don't make it, I'll leave a clue about where it is for you in your favorite book.*

They can't take it away from you; if anyone asks, this is what happened to your parents' estate.

And tell the professor, I burned the letter a couple of years ago when I realized I didn't need it to keep him around. He'll know what I mean.

Your loving uncle, Nick Tellios.

A playful breeze bent the note in half. She folded it again and put it back inside the dictionary. I know what he means, too, she thought. It's that letter from the student Gordon told me about. So he doesn't have to worry about someone else coming up to him with a slimy grin, whispering of favors. Gordon's free.

She picked up the passport; she'd never seen a passport before. It had been stamped by officials in France and Germany, though the dates covered a time when Uncle had been home at the ranch. There was a small, unflattering photograph of her uncle, only he was identified as George Kiriakos of a Chicago address. How peculiar, she thought. She put it back and picked up one of the drawstring sacks.

It was not very large, but heavy, and it clinked intriguingly. She almost laughed out loud. Treasure! She pulled it open and, to her astonishment, there was indeed a treasure inside. Hundreds of small gold coins, all alike, each with a panda stamped on one side. The bag weighed close to five pounds. If these were real gold, how much would so many be worth? Gordon had once told her the price of gold was printed in the newspaper every day; a fact she had never before found interesting.

The other velvet sack, which rustled suggestively, was at first a disappointment. It contained, not currency, but dozens of sheets of faintly blue paper folded into rectangles, with cryptic penciled remarks in their corners. *110 fl d 1.5 ct 27,000/ct 15mm round,* said one. Kori unfolded it. The paper had a crisp, translucent-blue tissue lining—and a glittering diamond that rolled toward the edge of the paper and was barely tipped back in time. She quickly refolded the paper and stared at the cryptic penciling.

Then she began to smile and chose another paper. Inside was an emerald the size of her thumbnail. " 'O bliss! O poop-poop! O my! O my!' " she whispered.

She wanted to look inside all the papers, but not in a breezy meadow with a nosy filly for company. She put the emerald away, put the sacks back inside the attaché case, and snapped it shut.

She had come and taken the case. He had ducked behind the willow when he saw her coming, and she was only fifty yards from him when she dismounted. He had been astonished to watch her wade downstream and crawl right into the drain and come out with it. How had she known it was there?

He had pulled his little gun, and aimed it at her as she waded upstream with the parcel; but his hand was trembling with fever, and in any case it was no good at any distance over four or five yards. He got up painfully and tried to make his distracted brain solve the puzzle: How had she known?

He came down to the river to dip his handkerchief in it, wringing awkwardly with one hand, and wiped his face. He needed a bath; he hated the spoiled smell of himself, the rumpled and dirty suit he wore. He used the handkerchief to brush the front of his coat.

He started along the river and came to the place where she had crossed on her way back to the house. It was a ford used by the horses, the ground was trampled and there was mud; he was ankle-deep before he realized it. Trying too hastily to back out, he slipped and fell. The jolt left him making tiny crowing sounds of pain, and he crawled higher on the bank to lie on the sweet grass and recover. After a while the pounding of his heart slowed and the whistle in his ears subsided.

A boisterous robin chirruped from the willow behind him. Kori could whistle a robin's song authentically enough to fool a real robin. They had all sat on the porch one evening and whooped with laughter at an enraged robin fruitlessly seeking to out-sing her, choking over his own song as she whistled hers at him. She was good with animals. She'd always liked animal stories. Her favorite was that old one about a mole—

The box! That goddamn box with the goddamn STUPID book in it, all marked for her. That goddamn Bannister must have brought it to her right away, as soon as he heard I was gone. Do something nice and you only outsmart yourself, he thought angrily. She's really smart, for a girl; he'd always told himself that without really believing it, but here was proof; she'd figured it out right away.

He sighed shallowly. She was a sweet kid, too, smiling and gentle; she deserved better than what she'd gotten out of life. She should be living in Chicago, married to some doctor. They'd have five or six kids, live in the suburbs. And he'd dress up as a hotdog vendor and sell her kids hot dogs at half price. But the heat from the cooker would begin to hurt his side.

He woke from a fevered doze on the sweet grass. She may be a sweet kid, but she knows. And now she's got my getaway stash.

He rolled over, groaning aloud, and slowly got to his knees. A weight shifted excruciatingly in his chest, making him bend forward, dizzy. Right in front of him he saw one of the black velvet bags, at its mouth a gleam of gold. She must have dropped it. He reached for it, missed somehow, and reached again—and it was gone. He felt a spasm of terror, then saw how a hummock of grass had made a shadow shaped like the bag, a trick that might have fooled anyone. What's wrong with me? Nothing, I'm just tired and a little ill.

He got to his feet. Which way? That way. He'd talk nice to her, and she'd give him the attaché case. And then he'd kill her.

"Pet, you must call Peter about this at once!" said Ramsey, staring at a large ruby glowing in his palm.

"I never want to speak to Peter again."

"Very well, then, to someone else in the police department."

"Why? These are mine, the letter says so. We can take them to a bank and see if they can tell us how much they are worth."

"One does not take gems to a bank to be valued. One takes them to a jeweler, I think."

"Very well, a jeweler then. Can you make out what the writing on the papers means?"

"No. But it doesn't matter; these are stolen, they must be, or if not, they're the proceeds of some drug transaction. You weren't permitted to keep the ransom money, and I can't believe you'll be able to keep these, either."

"Then let's not tell the police. The letter says they're my parents' estate, and so why should the police have them? Don't you see what this means? I'll be able to keep the ranch, all of it, and the house, and perhaps even buy more horses. A diamond is a very expensive thing, and there were eleven diamonds in that bag!"

"And how would you explain your sudden wealth to the police?"

"Bother the police!"

"And the IRS? Pet—"

"Oh, all right, all right!" she shouted. "The police can share them out with the IRS! Only not today, okay? Let me be rich for the rest of the day, at least!"

"I see you had a big fight with Kori," said Tonk as Brichter came back into the squad room.

"How'd you hear that?" asked Brichter, and McHugh also lifted his head.

"Kelly was laughing about it upstairs. He says the professor practically had to pull you off her."

Brichter said, "Kelly should rent that mouth of his. People could store things in it. Snowmobiles. Telephone poles."

"Yeah, well, I guess even a girl who's never been on a date can recognize you as a jerk. And pretty as she is, she'll have her choice of anyone in town in a couple of weeks."

"Tonk, there is nothing you can say I haven't already said to myself, louder, stronger, and more creatively, all right? So just leave it alone."

Tonk yanked open his desk drawer and pulled out a file folder. "Sure," he said carefully. "In fact, how about I leave, period? I just came back for this. Tell Ryder, if he happens to ask, I'm about halfway down his list of chores and I should be back before quitting time." He made his usual door-slamming exit.

Brichter went to get a cup of coffee. It was almost three. Maybe he should call her again. Last time Ramsey, that black-hearted bastard, had said in his coolest British tones that Miss Price was out riding and he did not know when she would be back, but if Sergeant Brichter would reconsider his position and allow him, Ramsey, to tender an apology on Sergeant Brichter's behalf, she might be prepared to speak to him.

"I thought you'd be on my side in this, Gordie!" he'd said.

"Then you thought wrong," Ramsey had replied. "You don't seem to understand, Peter, how little she's been allowed. You must not attempt to take that little away from her."

Brichter had hung up, of course. Because, hell, he was trying to save that little bit, wasn't he? Ass!

Maybe he should go out there after work. It was a stupid quarrel; he'd talk to her, they'd make up and she'd be her sweet, pliant self again.

"Want to talk about it?"

He started, looked up to see McHugh. "Talk about what?"

"Your fight with Kori. Want to tell me what happened?"

"Tonk didn't say enough to satisfy your morbid curiosity?"

McHugh made a gesture of aggravation and turned away.

"No, wait." Brichter sighed and pulled an ear. "Did you hear that Roach Bannister is her new hired hand?"

"He is? How'd that come about?"

"I'm not sure. But he can't be serious. I think he's just trying to see if a job will keep him out of jail."

"I thought he was in detox."

"He was; I took him there myself. But that was three days ago. He wasn't badly hooked; they probably turned him loose."

"So how did he wind up out at the ranch? Why don't you call detox and see what they say?"

"Good idea." While McHugh waited, Brichter dialed the hospital and asked for Dr. Iver.

"Yes, Sergeant, what can I do for you?"

"I brought a young man out there the other night, a Daniel Bannister. In heroin withdrawal."

"Yes, I remember him."

"How'd he do?"

"Very well. He's employed now, at Tretower Ranch."

"Yes, I know. Were you the one who sent him out there?"

"No, he went on his own by way of the labor pool. I found out when he came back to the hospital to sign an agreement on condition of employment to take weekly blood and urine tests for the presence of drugs. Dr. Mellon told me about it. He said Danny seemed almost cheerful about it."

"We're still talking about Roach Bannister, aren't we?"

"He wants to be called Danny now. I'd heard stories about him; I suppose everyone has. But the stories didn't jibe at all with the person I met. I'd say he had some sort of nonreligious born-again experience—did you notice anything before you brought him in?"

"No, when I talked to him he seemed the same potty-mouth I've always known. Sicker of course. Maybe he's snowing you."

"No, I'd say the turnaround is genuine, though only time will tell if it lasts. Funny, isn't it? His parents spent a fortune trying to straighten him out with no luck; and now he's gone and done it by himself. His father came out while Danny was here and they had a long talk. The father appeared quite emotional afterward, but he wouldn't say what they talked about. But he's convinced he has a son he can be proud of now."

"Hmmm," said Brichter. "Well, thanks, Doctor."

"Any time, Sergeant. I wish all our cases were this easy."

Brichter hung up and said to McHugh, "Dr. Iver, who is no fool, says young Bannister did a complete one-eighty in his behavior, though he doesn't know why."

McHugh studied Brichter's face. "But you think you do."

"Maybe. I tried to get Roach—I beg your pardon—I tried to get Danny to open up by pointing out that his addiction may have led to his father being blackmailed. Bannister senior's been doing some damn odd things lately."

"Yeah, I've been noticing. Were you serious about the connection?"

"Oh yes; and I've since found out that attorney Bannister has been out to the ranch a number of times. And he was the one Tellios trusted with a package to be delivered to Kori in case her uncle died."

"That son of a *bitch*!" McHugh, who was a close friend of the Bannister family, slammed his fist onto the top of Brichter's desk. "I hope he's face up in a ditch somewhere, and Mrs. Skunk has brought her family to dine!"

"Very nice," nodded Brichter.

McHugh, nursing his hand, asked, "How did Danny take what you told him about his father?"

"He looked like I'd punched him in the solar plexus. I thought at the time it was just another spasm, but Dr. Iver said father and son had an emotional conversation they prefer not to discuss with anyone, and that the boy appears highly motivated to stay clean."

"So she isn't quite the fool you took her for."

"Who?"

"Kori." McHugh unclenched his hand carefully. "Is that what the fight was about?"

"About her hiring Roach?"

"No, about who's gonna make the decisions out there at the ranch. You say she isn't crazy. Is she retarded or something?"

Brichter turned pale eyes on McHugh. "By God," he said. "Geoff was right; I just don't listen. The ranch is hers; it was her idea, her work, her judgement that built it. And unlike most horse-breeding operations, it makes a profit." He pulled the ear again. "Damn! Thanks, Cris."

"You're welcome, Pete. Anything else I can help you with this afternoon?"

"Yeah. Tell me how to get her back."

McHugh grinned. "Just like all the rest of us proud men retrieve our women: Humbly beg her pardon."

Brichter grimaced. "Yeah, I guess I'll have to try that. But Jesus, she was—" His phone rang and he picked it up. "Organized Crime Unit, Sergeant Brichter."

"Hallo, Peter—"

"Gordon! Boy, am I glad you called! I want to talk to Kori. She was right and I was wrong and I apologize."

"She's upstairs taking a shower, and she doesn't ever want to talk to you again, close quote. Now listen to me, the most extraordinary thing has happened. She came back from her ride with an attaché case Tellios had hidden against a rainy day." He described the contents of the case, concluding, "She says the gold and gems are hers, and she didn't want to tell anyone about them, but I think I've persuaded her to bring it in to the Safety Building tomorrow. Could you arrange to be out and someone else to be in right after lunchtime?"

"If what you've told me is correct, she is absolutely right, the contents of the case are hers."

"You mean you don't want to impound what she found as evidence?"

"Evidence of what?"

"I assume he stole them."

"Why? His note says he stole the money from her to buy them; why admit that rather than that he stole the gems? And the law is clear, if someone steals something and sells or converts it, the proceeds belong to the last legal owner. Tellios stole her estate, converted it to gold and gems, which belong to the last legal owner: Miss Katherine Price. I'd like to take a look at them, and the letter, but they're hers. Oh, the feds will want the passport."

"But Peter, the value—Uh-oh, I can't talk anymore; she's out of the shower. Tell McHugh to be there tomorrow; she likes him." Ramsey hung up.

Brichter put the receiver down and bit his lip. To hell with McHugh; he would be here himself tomorrow when she came in. Maybe he'd better call Geoff tonight, to see if he could help find the right words.

Brichter looked at the notes he had scribbled. Thank God for his notetaking habit; he'd been concentrating on her, not the treasure Ramsey had so carefully described. Brichter was familiar with the code on jewelers' papers, and according to what Ramsey had read to him, one of the gems was a flawless emerald, weighing three and a quarter carats. It had been bought for— He blinked; that one stone cost over $92,600. According to the other figures there were 270 half-ounce Chinese Pandas—which had numismatic as well as intrinsic value—and twenty-six assorted diamonds, rubies, and emeralds. Jesus, maybe the whole inheritance was there. New problem: Could he apologize without making it sound as if he had at least one eye on the contents of that attaché case?

Ryder came out of his office. "Tonk gone? Good. Meeting time." Brichter rose to let Ryder sit down, taking a seat on the edge of his desk. McHugh execu-glided over in his own chair.

"Tell him, Obie," ordered Ryder.

"Tonk's new girlfriend is one of the Undertaker's girls. The poor dumb jerk tells her all about his job, and she repeats everything to her boss, who carries it to Joe Januschka."

"Oh, shit!" said McHugh.

"Yeah," said Ryder. "Something's got to be done, of course."

"Throw him off the force!" said McHugh violently.

Ryder said, "Now, don't be hasty. I was thinking maybe of using this for awhile. Feed him some false information. Screw those bastards around a little."

McHugh thought, then chuckled. "I like it." He laughed. "I really like it! Tell him Tellios named names in that letter he had sent to Kori, and arrests are imminent."

Ryder grinned. "Or that the feds are in town, so they'll run quiet for awhile and give us all a vacation."

Brichter said quietly, "Don't do that to Tonk, Captain."

"No? Why not? The stupid, oversexed bastard set himself up for this!"

"Maybe. Tonk could probably be described as two gonads connected by a single brain cell. But goddamn it, in a few weeks he'll know something's wrong. We'll be laughing at him and he won't know why."

"So what do you suggest?" said Ryder. "Tell him the truth?"

McHugh said, "Hell, we can't do that! The way he feels about whores? He'd pound her to a bloody pulp!"

"And then we'd arrest him, and he'd not only lose his badge, he'd end up with a record. But using him like this isn't much better. Because word will get around, of course. It always does. He'll have to quit, and without ever knowing just what the hell happened. Is that what you want?"

"Shit, Pete," growled McHugh, "he's no good to us!"

"Who's 'us'?" argued Brichter. "The Organized Crime Unit?

Agreed, he's about as piss-poor a detective as I've run across. But he's not a bad cop. He just should never have taken off the uniform. He didn't ask to come to the OCU; I suspect he's a victim of political influence."

"Victim?" asked Ryder.

"Sure. Okay, we were the target. Tonk is taking up a desk and collecting a salary that could go to someone who knows what he's doing. But I don't think Tonk likes us any more than we like him."

McHugh asked, "You think someone got Tonk assigned here as a way of hurting us?"

"That's an interesting idea," said Ryder, remembering a certain phone call. "I kept wondering who Tonk's friend was, getting him promoted. Some favor, the poor bastard. And I never turned it around to see him as a stick hitting us. Interesting." He looked at Brichter. "All right, what do you suggest?"

Brichter, who had a feeling the whore in question would be moving out on her own fairly soon, didn't want to say so, because then he'd have to say why he knew. And he felt he owed Tonk a favor for the way he'd been treating him. He said, "What Tonk wants, and where he belongs, is back in the squad car, on patrol. Captain, don't you know someone upstairs who can arrange that? He's still on probation, right? So he didn't make it as a detective; that's no dishonor. If you could arrange a quick, quiet transfer for him, after a week of hearing about stickups and domestic disputes, his new girl would pack her bags, and everyone's happy but Januschka."

Ryder considered this. Finally he said, "You take all the fun out of things, you know that?"

"I'm sorry, sir."

"And after the way you've been bad-mouthing him," grumbled McHugh. "I thought you could carry a grudge better than that."

"When it's your turn in the barrel, I'll do better," promised Brichter.

"Now don't start in, you two," said Ryder. But he was smiling.

Chapter

23 †

"Demetrius Christoforus. Yanis Philistos. Tsakis Alenikos," McHugh murmured at his notebook.

"What are you doing over there, conjuring demons?" asked Brichter. They were alone in the squad room.

"Picking a name."

"Another sting already?"

"What do you mean, already? I've been researching this one for weeks."

"Oh yeah? Who are you this time?"

"First mate off a Greek freighter. Got a kilo of raw Turkish opium in my seabag. Feeling friendly, looking for a buyer. *Yasoo, ti kanis!* That means, 'Hi, how are you?' Got my tavern talk in gear: *Ella!* That means 'c' mere.' *Tee thelis?* 'What do you want?' *Poteri krazi,* 'a glass of wine.' " McHugh raised his imaginary glass in a salute.

Brichter dug for his own notebook, turned over leaves in a hasty search. "*Ella,* did you say? What does *see agga poe* mean?"

McHugh rolled his eyes and sighed, "I love you." Then he waggled his eyebrows at Brichter. "What dark and lovely Mediterranean lady haunts your past?"

"I got it from Kori. Her uncle taught it to her."

"Huh? Oh, of course, Tellios is a Greek surname. Come to think of it, Kori means 'girl' in Greek. I thought you said she was Scottish and Welsh."

"She is. Her real name's Katherine."

The phone rang on McHugh's desk and he scooped it up. "Organized Crime Unit, Sergeant McHugh."

Brichter was staring at his notebook. Tellios hadn't taught her a secret language, just a few words and phrases of modern Greek. So

237

Koritsimu was probably 'my little girl,' since that was his favorite description of her.

Of course, she wasn't a little girl, but a grown and lovely woman—funny how blind some people can be. She was a good businesswoman, too, judging by the way the ranch was being run. A risk-taker, as witnessed by the buying of the aged mare and the poker games. Gentle and competent, by the way she'd handled that foaling. Scared and guilt-ridden, too, poor kid.

But her most salient characteristic? Courage. Years of it, facing Tellios every day, bravely living down a past she hardly remembered, one day at a time. And hanging cool and tough with Whitlock. It was that old-fashioned author Albert Payson Terhune who had written, "Courage consists of hanging on just one more minute."

Courage consists of telling a police officer who saved your life to get the hell off your land.

Why should he think he'd won her by accidentally saving her life? Why did he think of her at all as a prize to be won in a contest? She was the one who deserved to have a mountain named after her, while he—

We'll talk about you later, calf-brain, stick to the current subject, a summation of this woman he loved. What else about her? Come out, come out, Kori.

A light bulb went on over his head, just like in the comic strips. *I am fourteen kinds of an ass; no wonder he had wanted her dead.*

McHugh tossed his phone back into its cradle and said, "Riscatto's dead."

It took a moment. "*What?* What happened?"

"Murdered. Suffocated with a pillow while asleep in his hospital bed."

"Who? Why?"

"No one knows. That was Graybill, calling from the hospital. He says the two men who were supposed to be in the room with Riscatto went down the hall for a smoke, and when they got back, he was dead. But there's no witness to their little trek, and no witness to a third person coming into or going out of the room, which, being only negative evidence, means no one's been arrested."

Silence, while both thought. Brichter spoke first. "Tellios. Tellios is alive."

"And went to take revenge on Riscatto? Come on!"

"No, Riscatto was killed because Tellios is alive. Riscatto got well enough to tell them what happened, but the body wasn't where he said he left it. That orchard was the spot, Cris. Riscatto thought he'd killed him there, but that little old man got up, stole a car and drove away. Jesus, I wonder where he is."

Ramsey was with Kori in the middle of the arena with Bitter Wind and her foal Copper Wind, the latter on his hind legs in an argument over being led away from his mother.

"Hold him, Gordon!" Kori said, amused and annoyed, tugging at the strap around the colt's hindquarters. "If he wins this one, he'll be twice as bad next time."

"This will teach me to send your hired hand home without checking with you first," grunted Ramsey, holding the other end of the strap and a thin rope attached to the colt's halter. Copper Wind was twisting and leaping, but every time he came down he was a few inches farther from Bitter Wind, who was watching but not objecting. They were not really fighting with the colt, just not letting him have it any other way.

Very abruptly the colt decided he'd had enough and began to follow Gordon across the arena as if it had been his idea from the start to do so. As instructed, Gordon led him to the fence on the other end, then brought him back to his mother, where he was nuzzled by one and stroked by the other, to his obvious delight.

"He'll do," said Kori. "That's enough for today, I guess." She unsnapped the lead rope from the foal's halter.

"I wonder why it was I thought it came naturally to a horse to be led by his halter," said Gordon, dusting his hands against one another. "I'll be glad it's Danny helping you next time. I thought it was brave of you to stand up to Peter for Danny."

"Courage had nothing to do with it. I need Danny."

"I hope you're over being angry with Peter."

"Only until he tries something like that again," said Kori. "Which I've no doubt he will," she added.

"Are you sure Danny's right for this job?" asked Ramsey, making shooing motions at the foal as Kori led the mare toward the box stalls.

"Yes, he's a hard worker, and a lot easier to manage than Riscatto." She continued moodily. "Why does Peter have to be such an ass?"

"I have it on good authority that he's asking himself that question this very moment. What would he have to do to make it right with you?"

"Nothing. There are other men out there, a great many of them nicer and better-looking than he is. I don't need him." She tossed her head in a feminine way unlike her, her mouth set in an unhappy line. Bitter Wind snorted and Ramsey wished he dared follow suit.

The mare and foal were put into their loose box and Ramsey and Kori walked back across the arena. "Pet, I know you're unhappy—"

"I'm not unhappy, and I don't want to talk about it anymore."

He opened the gate to the arena for her. She went through and stopped so abruptly he almost bumped into her. In front of them, coming out of the shadows, was a small apparition, pale and dirty. Ramsey felt that bright terror that comes from seeing a ghost.

"Uncle!" said Kori.

"Koritsimu," the apparition said in a thin rasp, and then they saw the gun in its hand.

"What do you want?" asked Ramsey.

"Let's go in the cottage and talk," Tellios said.

The squad-room door opened, and Tonk came in grinning in an embarrassed way, followed by Ryder looking chipper.

"Hello, guys," said Tonk. "Guess what? I'm going back to Patrol!"

"Captain Felska says he'll be glad to have him," said Ryder complacently. He gave Tonk a warning, encouraging look, and the big man ducked his head and walked to Brichter's desk.

"I think maybe I was wrong about you," said Tonk.

Brichter replied, "No, you weren't. I'm a jerk when it comes to people, always have been. Maybe if I'd done a little less sneering and a little more helping, you'd have enjoyed your stint as a detective."

Tonk considered this. "Maybe. But I'd still be glad to be out of it." He stuck his hand out, and Brichter took it.

Ryder said, "You two were looking pretty unhappy when we came in. Something wrong?"

"Riscatto's been murdered," said McHugh, "smothered in his hospital bed. Pete makes a pretty good case that Tellios is alive and loose, that we were right about that orchard thing."

"Well, he can just unmake it again," said Ryder. "If Tellios stole a car, it'd be halfway to Mexico by now, right? Or parked in Winnipeg somewhere. He's got no reason to come back here. And Captain Felska got a report from some farmer that the stolen VW was spotted a little northeast of here, on County W. A drunk driving it."

Brichter leapt for his phone and dialed. He listened for an answer. And listened. He threw the receiver down. "I'm going to Tretower, now, to bring them in. How long ago and how far away was that sighting?"

"This morning, probably thirty-five miles from here. Why? What the hell, Obie?" said Ryder.

"Tellios. He's alive, and he's in the neighborhood."

"How do you figure that?" asked Tonk.

"Dr. Ramsey called here a little bit ago to say Kori found an attaché case with a large fortune in gold and gems in it, along with a fake passport featuring Tellios' picture. That's his ticket out of the country. That's what he's doing back here, he's come for it. And when it isn't in its hiding place, he'll go ask her if she's got it. And he'll kill her; Kori can finger Tellios for the murder of her parents."

"Wait a minute; I thought she said she did it," said McHugh.

"She thinks she did it, but what she saw was him doing it. Send me a backup, will you? I'll call from out there."

"Hold it!" barked Ryder. "Take thirty seconds and make sure we understand. If you're saying what I think you're saying, you shouldn't be heading out there alone."

Brichter gritted his teeth, but obediently turned back. "What she remembers is seeing them dying or dead, then hiding in a cupboard and hearing someone call, 'Come out, Kori.' She says it was a policeman, but at that time, *Kori* was a word in a 'secret language' Tellios had taught her. Don't you see? The only person in the world who called her Kori when she was six years old is Tellios."

"I get it," said McHugh. "She thought it was that she was remembering *fy'n galon*, but it was remembering the voice in the nightmare saying, 'Come out, Kori.' "

"Shut up, Cris," said Ryder. "Go on, Obie."

"In a storm drain on the ranch, across a creek from a big willow tree, Tellios hid an attaché case with something over a million dollars in unset gems and Krugerrands, his emergency getaway stash. But being the thorough, careful person he is, he arranged that Kori would get a clue to its existence and location if something happened to him. Well, something did. And as instructed, Phillip Bannister brought her a package. In it, among other things, was a children's book, and in the book some sentences were underlined, sentences about something shining in a hole in a riverbank. I was going to go with her to look in the drain, but we had a fight. So she went out alone and found it, just where he told her he put it. Now, Riscatto reported Tellios dead, but he didn't die. He's wounded, and without money. He'll come looking for his stash, and when it isn't there, he'll come ask her for it. And, provided that opportunity to finish a botched job, he'll kill her."

"All right," said Ryder. "Cris, get out the transceivers. Take one and go with Obie to the ranch. Tonk, you come with me. We'll come in the back way; maybe we can cut him off at the storm drain."

McHugh, driving, asked, "Why would Tellios kill her parents?"

"MacNeeley told someone, who told me, that Mr. and Mrs. Price weren't just relatives of Tellios', they were friends, with the special Tellios twist on that word. That may or may not be true, If it was, maybe they were trying to get loose. If not, maybe they stumbled across something incriminating by accident. In either case, I figure they were threatening to go to the police. He came down for a confrontation, there was a fight, and he shot them. Kori walked in on it, was warned to run by her father and did. So Tellios went after her, calling in a friendly voice that was to become a background for nightmares. Meanwhile Mr. Price, wounded, pulled the telephone table over and called for help. The noise brought Tellios back to finish him off, but he had to leave before the cops came. Instead of continuing up the road, he stopped, waited for the squad car to go by, then came back, pretending he was just arriving. It took a lot of nerve, but it was a chance he had to take, to get to little Katherine before she told on him. The cop found her first, but fortunately for Tellios, Nelsen was as good at handling hysterical children as he was at noticing such anomalies as the arrival at ten in the evening of a visitor without an overnight bag. I wonder what Tellios said to her, what tone he used, that drove her mad out on that porch? Drive faster, can't you?"

Tellios followed them across the barnyard and up the walk to the cottage. Ramsey fumbled with the door and she turned to look at her uncle, grotesque and horrible in the afternoon sunshine. He was damp in places—and dirty; mud was smeared all up and down him. He was thin and gray and shrunken, except for his eyes, which were unnaturally brilliant. The hand that held the gun had a fine tremor.

Inside, in the hallway, she became aware of a new horror. He stank, not merely of dirt but of corruption. If he had clawed his way out of a grave, he would look and smell like this, and she began to wonder if this wasn't another nightmare, from which, please God, she would soon awaken to Ramsey's anxious words of comfort.

"I will go and sit down," rasped Tellios, "and you will come and stand in front of me."

"Very well," said Ramsey, taking Kori by the hand and obeying. "Why have you come back, may I ask?"

"Kori has something of mine," said Tellios, "from the storm drain." He looked at her, and she shrank under that brilliant stare. "Where is it?"

"Upstairs."

"Go get it. Come right back, don't stop to do anything else. If you aren't back in fifteen seconds, I'll shoot the professor."

She ran from the room. The case was under her bed; she pulled it out and tumbled back down the stairs.

"Put it on the floor beside me."

"I should think you'd want to take it and be quickly on your way," said Ramsey.

"I have a few other matters to take care of," said Tellios.

Kori put the case on the floor beside Tellios and asked, "How did you get past the dogs?" They were out; she left them out except to feed them.

He smiled at her. "Do an arithmetic problem for me," he said. "How many feet in a mile?"

Such non sequiturs happened in dreams. She wrenched the answer out of her scared and puzzled mind. "Five thousand, two hundred and eighty."

"And there are five dogs on a one-mile racetrack, spaced evenly—did you know they did that?"

"I did," said Ramsey, and the bright eyes shifted to him. "I walk round it for exercise, and discovered they've divided it into territories. One escorts you to the limit of his territory, and hands you to another."

"So tell me, Koritsimu, how big is each dog's territory?"

Again she thought. "Something over a thousand and fifty feet long," she said, unable to divide with him watching her that way, "and the track is about thirty feet across, I think." She began trying to multiply a thousand and fifty by thirty in her head.

"Plenty of room," said Tellios, not waiting for her answer. "I simply shot one dog and got across before another could catch up with me. The gun makes very little noise. Then I went into the barn to rest, and heard you there talking about the policeman and the Bannister boy."

"You know Danny?" she asked.

"He hasn't told you about me?"

"No."

"You're lying. Just as you lied when you said naming the colt Copper Wind meant no tribute to Sergeant Brichter, and that all you discussed that evening in the cottage was an English king."

"Danny and I have never discussed you," she said. He was going to shoot her; she could see he was working himself up to it, but she would not endanger Danny to gain another minute of life.

"Liar."

"She would never betray you," said Ramsey boldly.

"Bullshit." She blinked; Uncle had never used strong language in her presence. "She has lied to me for years, pretending to love me, pretending she never wanted to leave me, pretending you meant nothing to her. Her parents were lying traitors, both of them, no sense of family loyalty; and she is their daughter."

"My parents were good people," she said.

"Your parents were scum!" She could see his finger tighten on the trigger.

Suddenly there was loud thumping. Someone was banging on the door, hard. Someone began shouting, "Gordie! Open the door!" She turned, delighted. *Peter!*

There was a confusion of movement. Ramsey had rushed Tellios, crashing into him, grabbing for the gun. Kori ran for the door. She yanked it open and a gun went *crack!* in the living room. "Quick!" she said.

Brichter brushed by her in a large hurry, and a larger man followed him. McHugh. She followed them, and with them stopped just short of the entrance to the living room.

"Give it up, Tellios!" Brichter said loudly, and the little gun went *crack!* again, shattering part of the doorway frame, sending splinters flying. He ducked back. She stepped over their legs to look into the room. Ramsey was on the floor, clutching his side. "Gordon!" she screamed, or perhaps whispered, and started for him.

He came partly up, braced on the elbow of the hand holding his side. "No, pet! Get out of this! Run, run away!"

She froze, staring at him, at the blood seeping through his fingers. Her eyes moved in little steps to the right. Uncle was there, just like before. Uncle-with-a-gun. "You!" she said. "It was you! It wasn't—" The little gun cracked at her just as someone grabbed her by her broken arm and yanked her back into the hallway. Peter.

"It wasn't me," she told him. "It was Uncle who killed Mama and Papa."

"Yes, I know." Of course. Peter knew everything. She was shaking; she noticed that before she realized the reason: Uncle had shot at her.

McHugh spoke into a walkie-talkie. "Frank, he's here, in the cottage. Kori's with us, but Ramsey's in the living room with him. Ramsey's injured. Get us some help, fast." He put the device down and inched closer to Brichter. "How many shots was that?" he murmured.

"Three," said Brichter softly. "Plus one to shoot Riscatto. That's four."

"Kori," said McHugh, "what kind of gun does he have? A revolver? A semi-automatic?"

"I don't know. I don't know anything about guns."

"Does he have more bullets with him?" asked Brichter.

"I don't know that either."

What they wanted to know was how many bullets Uncle had left. If she could have told them what kind of gun, then they'd know with how many he'd started out in the gun—eight? a dozen? "He shot a dog," she said. "So that makes five."

In the living room someone groaned, "Sweet Jesus, have mercy upon my soul. *In manus tuas, domine, commendum spiritum meum.*"

Gordon, reciting in Latin the words recommended to a dying Christian: Into Thy hands, O Lord, I commend my spirit.

"Nooooooo!" She was making that sound; it was coming out like retching. Wake me, someone; get me out of this. Don't die, Gordon; don't leave me here all alone in this nightmare. Brichter grabbed her with one arm, wrapping it around her shoulders, pulling her close. She pressed her face against his chest, and when he spoke, she felt the vibration of his voice as much as heard it.

"Last chance, Tellios! Throw down that gun!"

The little gun spoke again, sending a shower of plaster into the hall.

There was a sound of furniture being shoved aside, then a scramble of feet, then the sound of one of the windows banging back. "He's going, get him!" shouted McHugh, and Brichter pulled away from her. There was more scrambling, then feet running off outside. A gun went off, a big, loud gun, not Uncle's little one.

She got up and hurried into the living room. Ramsey lay on his side, eyes closed. "Gordon?" she said. He did not reply. He had stopped clutching himself, and was bleeding freely all over the beige carpet.

She ran upstairs to snatch two towels out of the linen closet and the puffy comforter off the foot of Ramsey's bed. She stumbled back down to the living room. She made a fat pad of the towels and put it over the wound, holding it in place firmly. Then she dragged the comforter over both of them. "Help is coming, Gordon," she said. "Please hold on, help is coming." He didn't answer.

Chapter
24 †

They found the place on the riverbank where someone had fallen. "Kinda little," said Tonk, pointing, "but those look like a man's footprints."

"Damn," said Ryder; "we're too late; he's been and gone."

The transceiver in Tonk's hand spat and said, "Frank, he's here, in the cottage. Kori's with us, but Ramsey's in the living room with him. Ramsey's injured. Get us some help, fast."

"Oh, hell!" said Ryder. "Gimme that," he said to Tonk, taking the transceiver. "Your legs are younger than mine; you go ahead, see if you can back them up somehow—but be careful!"

Tonk said, "Right!" and set off as if running from the long shadow that loped after him.

Ryder clicked the knob over to change channels and said, "Four-eleven, Mobile."

"Four-eleven," responded a crisp female voice.

"We have an emergency at Tretower Ranch. We need some backup and an ambulance, over."

Tellios had gone out the window and around the corner of the cottage, then changed direction. There was a row of lilac bushes off to his left, and he ducked along them into a cluster of fragrant evergreens, where he stopped to rest. There was an agonizing pressure in his left lung; that pervert Ramsey had landed on him hard enough to break something loose inside.

He should have left as soon as he realized Price had called the police.

No, that was the other time.

So where the hell did the cops come from this time? That goddamn Brichter, spoiling everything he tried to do. As soon as he got away, he'd arrange for Brichter to be taken care of. Joseph had

247

been right; there was something uncanny about Brichter. Not that
Joseph wouldn't pay, too. And her, that lying bitch. "No, Uncle,"
she'd said. "Yes, Uncle." And all the while lying to him. She knew,
she'd always known. He'd heard her tell Brichter: Uncle did
it. Goddamn right, Uncle did it, and Uncle would finish the job,
soon, soon.

He reached for the briefcase. It was gone. Someone had come
and gotten it. No, he'd left it behind. But that was fine, fine, fine, he
told the familiar rising panic. Everything was fine. He had his little
pistol, he could get more gold and gems. And with them buy another passport.

Meanwhile, there were people out there looking for him, he
could hear them. One of them was Brichter. If I make a noise,
Brichter will come, and I can shoot him.

No, if he shot Brichter, the others would hear and they'd all
come. He couldn't shoot everyone. The thing to do was get back to
the car and get into town. He had friends there; one of them could
bring a doctor to him. Time to get moving again. Which way? That
way. His left arm was no longer obeying his wishes. Why hadn't he
asked for a glass of iced tea? His thirst was almost as bad as the
pain.

But he could still move like a ghost, like a shadow.

Brichter heard someone pushing his way through a cluster of
young pine trees and evergreen brush. He weaved back and forth,
trying to see. Then whoever it was broke loose, heading for the
fence. Too small to be McHugh, the figure stumbled the few yards
as if in great pain.

"Tellios! Hold it right there!"

But the figure ignored him, and on reaching the fence bent
slowly and more fell than climbed through onto the racetrack.
Brichter began to run. "Tellios!" he shouted. "No! The dogs!
Watch out!" Tellios turned and aimed a gun at him. Brichter fell
and rolled, braced for a bullet, still calling, "Come back!"

How many feet in a mile? And there were only four dogs now. He
was very good at arithmetic, and so knew he had lots of time. Look
both ways before crossing the street, he told himself. All clear? Go.

"Tellios! No! Come back!" someone shouted. He knew that
voice. He turned, gun up, looking for Brichter. "Watch out!" the
man shouted, from over there. "The dogs!" Tellios didn't think
he'd pulled the trigger, but Brichter fell. Good. Now for the dogs.

He knew about the dogs; he had planned for the dogs. He straightened and looked around. Here came a dog. Watch this, Sergeant Brichter. He aimed and squeezed the trigger, but there was no answering *crack!* That was wrong. He had time to squeeze again before the animal was on him, knocking him down, biting past his protesting hand with rude and tearing teeth, searching for his throat. His last thought, only half-formed, had to do with arithmetic and bullets.

Brichter wrenched himself to his feet as Tellios turned toward a pale shepherd hurtling toward him, aiming the little gun. Shoot, thought Brichter, running for the fence. Now, *shoot.* But Tellios didn't fire. Then the dog was on him, knocking him down, ripping.

"NO!!" yelled Brichter, running. "Oh my God! Cris!" he shouted. "Over here!"

The buff-colored dog was standing on Tellios, pulling fiercely and silently at his throat, its own neck and face spattered with darkness. Brichter dropped to one knee and aimed carefully through the boards. He shot the dog in its head, knocking it off its victim. It thrashed clumsily, making muffled yipping sounds.

Another dog came trotting up and Brichter prepared to shoot again. But it hesitated, sniffing, and then began a careful, cadenced bark, a trained, summoning bark. The shot dog subsided into stillness.

Brichter rose stiffly.

Tellios lay in that relaxed, uncomfortable-looking pose corpses sometimes assume. One hand was badly chewed, the fingers broken and laced with blood. His throat was torn completely open, the shattered larynx showing. His face was unmarked and oddly serene above the mangled throat. Brichter felt no desire to go confirm what the second dog knew, that Tellios was beyond any recall. Sirens, which he'd been half aware of, were suddenly loud and even more suddenly cut off. Help had arrived.

"Judas Priest!" McHugh ran right into the fence and stood there, staring at the wreck of Tellios. "What happened to him?"

"That dog. Tellios went out there, I couldn't stop him. I shouted to watch out for the dog, and he turned and pointed his gun at it, but didn't fire."

McHugh shook his head, then said, "Yes, he did. But he was carrying a revolver; see it there beside him? He was out of bullets. You'd think someone as smart as him could count as high as six."

Brichter said, "I'm going back to the cottage. You stay here and wait for Ryder and whoever."

"How do I shut that damn dog up?"

"Shoot him."

He hurried back to the cottage and walked into a rescue scene. Ramsey was being given heart massage and mouth-to-mouth resuscitation by two paramedics. A uniformed policeman was holding a plastic bag half full of a clear liquid like a talisman over Ramsey, and a plastic line ran down from it to Ramsey's arm. Kori, pale and disheveled, stood with two more uniformed policemen, watching from near the fireplace.

Brichter went to take a closer look at Ramsey, who was a very ugly gray, shrunken except for his belly, which was grotesquely swollen under a thick bandage. A wad of blood-soaked towels was on the floor beside him. As Brichter approached, Ramsey jerked and gagged and began to breathe on his own. The sweating medic who'd been doing mouth-to-mouth sat back. He glanced up and saw Brichter.

"Hi, Obie," he said breathlessly. "This's the second time he's quit on us; he's about bled out. C'mon, Brian, let's transport him." Brichter and the policeman holding the plastic bag steadied the wheeled stretcher while the paramedics hefted Ramsey onto it and threw a blanket over him. Then they hustled him out.

Kori looked as calm as she had in the church. Brichter went to her. The two cops, catching something in his face, stepped aside.

"Did you shoot Uncle?" she demanded.

"No, we—"

"I heard a shot."

"McHugh shot at him, but missed."

"Did he get away?" She was speaking in a normal tone, but a bit too fast, and she had taken his hand in a painfully tight grip. Her hands were covered with drying blood.

"No, he went out on the racetrack before I could stop him, and a dog got him."

"Is he dead?"

"Yes."

"Gordon's dead, too, isn't he?"

"No."

"But he's dying. He's that terrible color and he keeps stopping breathing."

"Come with me; you need to sit down awhile." Without giving

her a chance to say no, he led her down the hallway to the kitchen and sat her on a stool. "Listen to me," he said, sitting down across from her. "He's been bleeding into his belly, which is why it's swollen like that and why he's that color. But he's alive, and he's on his way to an excellent trauma-care room. He'll go from there to surgery, where a surgeon will operate to repair the damage. And some time later this evening he'll wake up and ask for you." *And God, don't make a liar out of me.*

"I want to go to the hospital, to be with him."

"They won't allow you into the emergency treatment area, or into surgery. But they have a place you can wait, if you like. I'll take you."

"No." She got up, went to the wall phone near the door. "I'll call Danny."

"There's no need to call Danny." He got there in time to hold the receiver in place by putting his hand over hers. It was icy under the dried blood, and he chafed it between his two barely warmer ones.

"Please let go."

He obeyed, and she seemed to see the condition of her hands for the first time. She went to the sink and turned on the water. "I suppose you want to know what happened."

"If you feel up to telling me."

She squeezed dishwashing liquid into her palm. "He was in the barn, I don't know how he managed that. I put the horses away, and Gordon and I were coming out, and he was there, like something that had escaped from a grave. He made me go get the briefcase, and then I could see he was going to shoot me, but I was too scared to move. Then you knocked on the door and Gordon jumped on him."

"And saved your life."

"I wish he hadn't." She rinsed and reached for more dishwashing lotion. "I don't know how I'll live without him; he made life bearable for me. And he was an important man; he could look into the past and make it live for others."

"Will you stop talking about him like he's dead!" he said, so roughly she winced. "I'm sorry, I'm sorry. Let's just not bury him before he's really dead, okay? He may be fine. Look, *fy'n galon*—"

She winced again. "Okay. Look, Katherine. I always seem to pick strange times to say things to you, but will you listen a minute, to an apology? I was wrong to go sticking my big fat oar into those parts of your life that are none of my business. I could kick myself for not knowing better. That argument over Danny, for instance; I had no right to inflict that on you."

"You promised you'd cut off your right hand before you hurt me."

"I know, but that was a stupid promise to make. Socially inept people like me hurt the people they love—they like—all the time. But I'm getting better. Since I met you I'm easier to get along with. Ask Cris. Or Captain Ryder. So I really would appreciate it if you'd let me hang around. Maybe if we could start over, I'd get it right this time."

She pulled four or five sections of paper towels off the roll. "I don't think I can start over with you."

"Sure you can. How do you do, Miss Price? I'm Otto Peter Brichter. My friends call me Peter, but you can call me Obie for now, if you like."

She finished drying her hands and stuffed the towels into a tall wastebasket beside the sink. "Where's Sergeant McHugh?"

"Waiting outside for Captain Ryder and the Mobile Crime Lab to arrive—Jesus, there are still dogs on the track!" Brichter turned toward the door, then back. "I don't want to shoot them; come and blow that magic whistle and bring them in."

"All right."

The whistle was hanging by its thong on a nail inside the front door.

Outside, the light was fading. They walked in silence to the kennels. He was careful to maintain a small distance between them.

She stopped by the kennels, blew a silent long and two shorts on the whistle, and in a minute a dog came running into the kennel, to paw in disappointment at his bowl. Two more came, and Brichter said, "That's all there are left," and she raised the lever that lowered the kennel doors.

"Where's Uncle?" she asked, and when he looked in that direction, she set off.

He called after her, "Don't, okay? It's not pretty."

"I don't expect it will be," she said, and kept going.

Tonk was standing beside McHugh as they came up, and Brichter stayed behind her to wave a warning at them not to interfere. She stood at the fence a long minute. "He doesn't look so different," she said at last. "He's still Uncle. Except he hasn't breathed once since I've been looking."

Brichter said to McHugh, "We called the dogs in," and to Tonk, "Where's Captain Ryder?"

"He'll be along. I came across the field, but I guess he went back to get his car."

"Look," said McHugh, "here's the lab van."

"Yeah," said Tonk, "and there's Ryder's car right behind it."

Pat Mahan, the county medical examiner, a little man with a leprechaun's nose and graying crew cut, judged it was dark enough and had the area flooded with lights powered by a noisy generator in the van. Under his curt direction, pictures were taken of Tellios, the dog Brichter had shot, and the dog up the way Tellios had shot on his way in. The little pistol, empty, was tagged and put into a plastic bag.

Sergeants Larson and Graybill turned up. They said they were from Homicide, that Dr. Ramsey was in bad shape and in emergency surgery; that they wanted to talk to Kori about what had happened. She was taken back to the cottage with them. That's torn it, thought Brichter; now she's sure Gordie's dying.

The investigation progressed to the point where Tellios' body could be searched. Dr. Mahan found a bunch of keys and seventy cents in change in one pocket and a wallet and comb in another. The wallet contained two ten-dollar bills, an expired driver's license, a Quick Cash card, and a dry-cleaning ticket.

The ME opened Tellios' suit coat and poked at the blood-stiffened shirt. "I thought you said you didn't shoot him," he said, glancing up at McHugh and Brichter, who were leaning on the fence with Tonk and Ryder, watching.

"I shot at him, but I missed," said McHugh.

"Yeah? Then how come there's a hole punched in this?" The ME unbuttoned the shirt and pried it open. "Holy Mother of God," he breathed. "Come take a look, one of you."

McHugh waved Brichter on; he didn't like looking at things that startled a medical examiner. Brichter stepped through the fence and walked into the pool of light cast by the floods to squat and look at the exposed chest. Just under the collar bone there was a suppurating hole surrounded by a large, swollen red area with rays in all directions. "Get a whiff?" asked the ME.

Brichter bent over the wound and immediately jerked back. "Whuff! What the hell?"

"Massive infection. He was starting to rot inside. Probably out of his mind with fever."

"He did act a little odd."

"I'm surprised he was able to act at all. By the look of this, he was in agony. Much as I'd hate to have my throat torn out by a dog, if I had a chest like this, I might find it a relief."

"Jesus. Bullet wound?"

"Looks like it. I'll do him tonight and have the report on your desk first thing tomorrow."

"Thanks, Pat."

Dr. Mahan signaled for a stretcher, and Brichter went to confer with Tonk, Ryder, and McHugh. "Looks like he was shot a couple of days ago and infection set in. He was almost, but unfortunately not quite, dead on his feet when this happened."

Ryder asked, "What happened?"

"He had both of them in the cottage. He was about to shoot her, and Ramsey, trying to stop him, took the bullet himself. Cris and I had just arrived, and she ran to let us in. Tellios escaped through a front-room window, Cris and I followed, but lost him on the grounds. Then he tried to cross the racetrack and a dog got to him. I shot the dog, but it was too late."

"Those goddamn dogs!" said McHugh.

Brichter, severely stressed, lapsed into his lecture mode. "They aren't regulation guard dogs, you know. The real thing thinks it's a game, knocks you down and stands on you grinning until his trainer comes and calls him off. These have been systematically brutalized; that's the only way to turn them into killers."

"Then it serves him right," said Tonk.

"Well," said Ryder, "Wilbur's got his pictures; the remaining dogs can be destroyed. Call Animal Control in the morning."

"I will make that recommendation to Miss Price." Brichter did not need to learn some lessons twice.

"We 'bout done here?" asked Tonk.

"Yeah," said Ryder. "Let's go home. I'll see you all at eight in the morning for a wrap-up. Obie, you'll keep in touch with the hospital about Ramsey?"

"Yes, sir. Uh, Captain? My friends call me Peter."

Ryder grinned broadly. "Mine call me Frank."

Brichter went back to the cottage to find Larson and Graybill nearly finished with Kori. "Since I have to go to the hospital anyway," he said to her, "may I offer you a ride? Unless, of course, one of these people has already offered."

Larson, who was single, lifted weights, and had thick, dark, subtly permed hair, said, "I was about to offer her a lift."

She said to the floor, "Since Sergeant Brichter is going anyway, I'll ride with him."

Chapter
25 †

Brichter stopped at the information desk on their way in and identified himself and Kori. "Can you tell us anything about Gordon Ramsey?" he asked.

The lady checked, then made a phone call. She came back to say, "He's still in surgery. That's third floor; there's a waiting room at the east end."

"Thank you," said Brichter, and took her to the elevators.

The waiting room was a little area at the end of the hall, carpeted in blue and furnished with two yellow-green plastic couches, an old color television, and an end table. Brichter sat Kori down and went to elicit a promise from the charge nurse that she would keep them advised. He came back and sat down across from her.

The television was on, tuned to a cable station featuring rock videos. She was watching a group of painted, ragged performers display their inflamed libidos and said, "No wonder Uncle wouldn't let me watch this stuff."

He shut it off and came to sit on the other couch, facing her.

She asked, "How long will we have to wait?"

"It depends on how much damage was done."

"How does one go about arranging a burial?"

"I wish you wouldn't—" he began without some exasperation.

"I mean for Uncle."

"Oh. Well, the autopsy is being done tonight, so some time tomorrow the body will be released and you'll get a call from the medical examiner's office saying so. Call a funeral home, and they'll pick up the body and prepare it for burial. Or do you want it cremated?"

"Which is cheaper?"

"Cremation. Then you have to decide what you want done with the ashes."

255

"Can I just throw them away?"

"No. They can be buried in a cemetery, stored in a vault, put on a mantel or attic, or scattered over a lake or piece of land."

"I remember a television show about cremation, and they showed what's left after. It didn't look at all like ashes, but like bone meal."

"Yes, that's right."

"So I could put them on his roses, I suppose."

He smiled. "I appreciate the sentiment, but I'm not sure it's legal. I'll check if you like. What may happen is you'll get a call from someone in Chicago who will offer to take him up there directly from the funeral home."

"Should I agree?"

"Why not? Now that he's dead, all will be forgiven, and they'll throw a big funeral for him and invite you to come."

"Must I go?"

"No."

A silence fell, a heavy one, and to lift it he brought out his notebook. "May I ask you some questions about what happened today?"

"All right."

He drew a detailed account of events from her, beginning with the surprise arrival of Tellios in the barn.

"You've already asked that question," she said at last. "Twice."

"That's the way it's done," he replied. "We have to go over a story again and again to be sure we've got it right. You'd be surprised how much I miss the first time I'm told something. But if you've had enough, we can stop." He closed the notebook.

After another minute of the heavy silence, he said, "I was going to ask him to stay on. I was thinking he might want to teach at St. Gabriel's, do you think they'd take him? He's not very young."

"They'll fall all over themselves offering him a position. He was once very well-known in academic circles."

"Maybe he would even agree to go on living in the cottage, so I could see him often." She looked at her hands, clenched in her lap. "I want to pray for him, but I can't think of the words."

"When I'm really scared, I just say please."

"Are you ever really scared?"

"Often."

"Then why do you do it? Why don't you quit?"

"Because it's something I do well. And when I take another piece of garbage off the street, it makes me feel good."

"You seem to take criminal behavior as a personal affront."

He nodded. "It's my authoritarian attitude. Most cops acquire it, but I come by it naturally."

"Excuse me." They looked around and saw a woman in stained green scrubs. "Are you the ones waiting to hear about Dr. Ramsey? I'm Dr. Rice, his surgeon."

Brichter said, rising, "How is he?"

"Still critical, but we've got him stabilized. He's in the recovery room right now."

Kori had also risen. "He's not going to die?"

She smiled. "His chances of recovery are increasing every minute he stays stable, and he looks very stable right now. Because of the damage done by the bullet, we had to remove his spleen and do a partial gastrectomy—" Kori gestured alarm, and she explained, "Remove a small part of his stomach. The bullet lodged near a rib and has been recovered. We're giving him blood to replace what he lost."

"When may I see him?" she asked.

"He'll be moved to intensive care sometime in the next few hours. If you care to wait, you can see him briefly then."

"Yes, please." She was looking at Dr. Rice as if she were a heavenly vision. "I—I don't know how to say thank you."

"You're welcome. I'm afraid I can't stay and talk. I have another patient waiting."

"Thank you for coming to tell us, Doctor," said Brichter, but it was to her back; she was striding swiftly away. He said to Kori, "There, see? As soon as Gordie wakes up, we'll tell him to start drawing up his lesson plans." He was grinning, trying not to look as relieved as he felt.

"You were worried too!"

"Yes, I guess I was."

She swayed and went chalky, her lips became bloodless. "I feel—odd."

"Here, sit down. Put your head between your knees." He took her by the shoulders and bent her forward. "Better?"

"Yes, thank you! Please let go!"

He did, and moved to sit across from her again, his joy fading rapidly into something big and clumsy and lost.

Head still down, she said, "Sorry. It's just that I don't like people to touch me without warning." She straightened, eyes closed. "See, I can be even more socially inept than you are. And with Gordon—I was so sure he was going to die, and I couldn't bear it."

She brushed impatiently at a loose strand of hair. Her eyes were still closed. "When I was younger, I used to pretend he was my father, and that because he was a homosexual he could never admit it, and so I must never mention it to him. But the way he looked at me when he thought I wasn't aware of it—" She stopped short, confused, and her eyes opened. "I didn't mean to speak of that. I never speak of that. I don't know what's the matter with me."

"Nothing's the matter with you."

"Then why am I telling you what a fool I am, full of silly fantasies?"

"Is it silly? My mother left me and my drunken, abusive father when I was seven, and I used to fantasize that she was on a secret mission and would come home covered with medals in a car driven by the President of the United States. Gordon told me you are as precious as a daughter to him, so it was very perceptive of you to choose that particular fantasy."

She half reached for him, but pulled her hand back. "Sometimes you say exactly the right thing."

"Not often enough."

"You were wrong to yell at me and Danny."

"That's true."

She smiled; she was in control again. "You've changed your mind about him?"

"I didn't say that. I think he's a punk kid who got into something nastier than he dreamed existed, and the scare straightened him out. Whether it will last or not, I can't say. But it's your ranch, and your decision."

"I hope it lasts; he's got a knack with the mares. And a good head—you know, he pointed out that there is far more land than we need with only seven horses. We can rent out half of it, he says, to farmers who will plant oats and hay in return for a percentage of their crop, and never buy feed again."

"You're rich, you don't need to worry about that."

"Nobody's so rich she should spend money when she doesn't have to." She frowned. "And how do you know I'm rich?"

"Gordon called and told me about you finding the attaché case. And a good thing, too," he said to the rising indignation on her face; "it was knowing about the case that made me figure out Tellios was on his way back to get it."

"Oh."

"I told Gordie to apologize to you *before* he told me about the gems and gold."

She said, puzzled, "Yes?"

"So it isn't your being rich that made me decide to apologize."

The puzzled look deepened—then cleared and she laughed. "No, it wouldn't be, not with you. You were worried about that? How interesting."

He felt his face get hot. "Well, it's going to be bad enough with people thinking I'm after you for your money, and I wouldn't want you thinking so too. I want to go all the way down that list of places."

"What places?"

He got out his notebook. "A baseball game, a cathedral, Sequoia National Park, Disney World, the Catskills to look for a mountain we won't ask them to name after Gordie just yet."

Again the truncated reaching gesture. "How incredibly nice of you to actually write them down."

He shrugged. "I write everything down; my memory isn't always reliable."

"Will you apologize to Danny?"

"If you like."

"It may help. He needs to talk to a policeman about what happened to him. He may be able to tell you things of value. How often must I shout at you to get you to behave like this?"

"Not very often, I hope."

"Me, too. I don't like shouting. I don't like days like this, or hospitals, or—" The control was slipping again. "Could I have a hug, please?"

"Sure." He stood and lifted her to her feet, and took her into his arms; and she put her head on his shoulder. Her cast felt strange against his back, and she smelled of horses. But the arm would heal, and he had never thought the smell of horses a bad smell. And her head fit right against his neck, right where it belonged. That wouldn't change.

She said into his collar, "He's not going to die."

"No."

"You came just in time, you know."

"Yes."

"Thank you."

"Anytime."

"I feel strange," she said. "My throat hurts, my head aches, I hur—hur—" And she was crying, great huge sobs that were the outward sign of a resurrection in her soul.

"There," he said. "There, there." And he stroked the back of her head. But he didn't try very hard to get her to stop; he lacked the words, and, anyway, she'd needed to do this for a long, long time. What a funny kid she was. He'd marry her, of course.

Here's a preview of the third book
in the exciting Peter Brichter mystery series
by Mary Monica Pulver . . .

Ashes to Ashes

Coming soon from Diamond Books!

The phone burred softly, just as the cattle stampede was really getting out of hand. It burred again and Zak reached for it without taking his eyes off the TV screen. John Wayne was galloping frantically after the lead animals, trying to turn the herd. "Yeah," Zak said into the receiver.

"We've got a request for a ten-fifty at 901 East Baron," said a woman's brisk voice.

Zak straightened and glanced at his watch. Quarter to midnight; another fifteen minutes and they'd've called Ron. "Okay," he said. "I'm on my way."

His wife looked up from her needlepoint as he hung up the phone. "Where is it?" she asked, knowing what.

"Over on East Baron. Warehouse district."

She nodded, relaxing a little. No bodies piled up in a hallway this time. "Better put on a sweater; it's cool out tonight."

He went upstairs, a short, broad man in his late fifties with graying brown hair, a droopy mustache, and dark, tame eyes behind gold-rimmed spectacles. He changed his house shoes for steel-toed lace-ups, then pulled a thick gray sweater over his flannel shirt. He took a metal box out of the back of a dresser drawer, unlocked it, lifted out a clip-on holster and an aluminum-frame Colt Agent revolver. He fitted the holster to the back of his belt and tucked the gun into it. He was zipping up a hip-length jacket as he came back down the stairs.

She waited at the bottom with his big Thermos. "Be careful, dear," she said.

"I will," he said, offering his cheek for a kiss before going out the door to his little Datsun.

Zak skirted the small downtown area, turned onto Baron and east toward a cluster of warehouses. As he approached, he noted a

263

haze of smoke in the air and then the characteristic stink of burning building. He slowed, pulled to the curb to look. Ahead was a single-story building with smoke boiling up and outward from the roof, window openings glowing at one end. The building was old, half a block long, divided into four stores. The biggest store, Crazy Dave's TV and Appliance, on the end, was well alight. It looked as if two alarms had been called, and the place was busy with pumper and ladder companies: red lights flickering, spots illuminating the building's face, pumper engines roaring. There was virtually no wind, but the fire appeared to have gotten a running start on the fire fighters.

Zak leaned over sideways to punch the glove box open. He reached in for a pad of graph paper and a soft pencil. When he straightened he saw a pair of firemen smashing the window of the Tell the World T-Shirts store next to the appliance store. As the window broke, a large gout of brown smoke was released. A team swinging axes was on the roof of the Bear Foot sporting shoe store. As Zak watched, orange flames leapt up between them. So probably Say It Again Used Books on the end only appeared untouched. Zak grunted, tucked the pencil away in a pocket. He got out of his car, went around to the back and put the tablet on the roof. He opened the rear hatch and fumbled out the big boots and yellow rubber coat of a fireman.

Zak buckled himself into the coat and reached back into the trunk for his red fireman's helmet. A multi-layered scream of approaching sirens told him a third alarm had been called in. He rolled the tablet and put it into his coat pocket as he walked slowly toward the burning building, noting that the windows in the appliance store had broken outward. The smoke roiling out and up was dark in color; pale hoses tumescent with water led into it. He pulled the strap of his helmet under his chin, looked for and found the white hat that marked the Battalion Chief, counted the number of citizens—nine—who had braved the hour and November chill to stand and watch. A police officer was standing in front of them, and they were all watching a ladder-pipe being cranked up. The firemen on the roof were climbing down.

Zak angled across Baron Avenue and continued up Ninth. There was a pumper near the alley, and another behind it; fat five-inch hoses linked them to a hydrant at the curb and pale snakes of smaller hoses wound up the block and into the alley. He'd heard four-alarm trucks arriving, not three.

A squad car blocked the street near the corner, lights blinking—

not that there was any traffic to divert. A fierce dance of reflected flame lit the windows of a big old warehouse across the alley from the burning building; the fire was leaping through a double doorway and a small window in the burning building, scattering light up the face of the warehouse.

He retraced his steps to Baron, angled across again, and stopped on the corner to watch. The ladder-pipe spat once, hugely, then began pouring its thick master stream of five hundred gallons per minute onto the roof. The spectators made appreciative noises.

The policeman turned, saw Zak and gestured at him to cross, but Zak shook his head. One of a pair of women in bowling jackets said, "This is a serious fire, isn't it?" The fire engines' roar enveloped her voice, making it flat.

"Yes, ma'am; I'm afraid it is. Was it already burning when you got here?"

"Yeah, but not as bad as it is now."

"Were you the first spectators to arrive?"

"Uh-uh, but we were next. We were on our way home from the League Night banquet, but decided to stop awhile. I didn't know you went right into a place that's on fire. I thought you stood outside to spray water."

"And they broke the door down to get into that shoe store," said the other woman. "Is that legal?"

"Yes, ma'm. Who was already here when you arrived?"

The second woman pointed at the trio of businessmen next to her. "They were."

The trio glanced up and came around the bowlers. They stood in the gutter facing Zak, engulfing him in an aura of alcohol. One said, "Yah, we seen the whole thing, right, guys?" and they all agreed they'd seen the whole thing.

"Were you the first to arrive?"

"You bet," said the man proudly. "We followed the fire trucks. Saw them barrelin' along an' followed. Very interesting to see how fast they set up."

"Would you mind telling me your name?" asked Zak.

"Me? Why?" asked the nodder, abruptly suspicious.

"Because I'll be investigating this fire, and you may be able to tell me something of value. But I won't know until I can go in for a look; so rather than ask you to wait around, perhaps for hours, I'll take your names and phone numbers and call you if I need to talk to you."

"Oh. Sure, why not?"

Zak reached for his paper and pencil. The men gave their names and said they were computer-marketing reps, in town for a regional seminar. They all agreed Zak could call and leave a message at their motel if he had any questions.

Zak also took the names of the lady bowlers and four college sophomores, one of whom was finding the scene totally awesome.

Zak put the notepad back in his pocket and crossed the street, bound for a pair of firemen in white helmets. Here the engine noise was louder, and the two were leaning in turn toward one another's shoulder, shouting an exchange of information. As Zak stepped up on the sidewalk near them, one nodded in comprehension, clapped the other on the shoulder and climbed into the back of a big van, a mobile command post that was the department's newest acquisition.

The other, preferring to supervise out in the open, stepped back into the street for a look at the master stream drenching the roof.

Zak followed. "You sent for me, sir?" he shouted politely.

The man, much bigger and taller than Zak, started. "Oh, hi, Zak! When did you get here?"

"A couple of minutes ago! Is it a bad as it looks?"

"Worse!" Battalion Chief Tellerman said gloomily. "I think we're going to lose the whole building! Here, let's get back where we can talk!" He led the way up the street, away from the burning building, then turned to listen.

"Where was the fire when you arrived?" asked Zak.

"Just in the appliance store. Two fires, back and front, much bigger in the back."

"Completely separate?"

"I guess not, but linked by a thin line. It was the smoke made me call you. It was dark enough to be from a refinery fire. And when the first team broke in, they reported a smell of gasoline."

"Damn. Are you close to knocking it down?"

"In the appliance store, maybe. In another twenty minutes." Tellerman smiled down at Zak. "How about you lend a hand while you're waiting? I've got a spare air bottle."

Zak grinned back up, his droopy mustache lifting to display small square teeth. Tellerman was teasing, of course. Years of eating smoke had damaged Zak's lungs. When his heart had begun complaining of the extra work, they'd offered him the job of arson investigator to hold him until he could retire, which would be next year. But it was kindly teasing, a way of saying, I know you're still a fireman, that you remember how. "No, thanks. I'll check in with the Deputy Chief. Then can I come back and talk to you some more?"

"Sure. I'll wait in my car."

Zak found the Deputy Chief busy and distracted in the command post, so he merely announced his presence on the scene. The man waved over his shoulder in acknowledgment; Zak closed the door and climbed back down.

Tellerman's official red sedan was parked kitty-corner from the burning building, engine running, heater on. Zak climbed into the passenger side of the front seat and produced his pad of graph paper. "You must have put in a call for me as soon as you arrived," he said.

Tellerman had removed his white helmet and unbuckled his coat, but was still a massive presence in the car. He consulted his watch. "Yep, I'd make that about forty minutes ago."

Zak noted the estimation of time. "How did you get into the building?" he asked.

"Front and back doors of the appliance store," said Tellerman. "Both locked."

"Any sign of forced entry?"

"One small windowpane broken in back. Snap lock, you can reach it from the window. Talk to Breck; he led the handline in back there and reported the window."

"But it's a double door, isn't it?"

"Double width, but just the one door. I went back for a look myself."

"Other windows intact when you arrived?"

"The front windows blew outward just as we arrived. Apart from the window in back, that's all there is."

"What about the other stores?"

"You'll ask, of course, but I didn't see any sign of a break-in, and no one else has said anything. They broke into the appliance store, Zak, must have. You can't get from one store to the other from inside, and the fire started in the appliance store. But once the fire got up into the cockloft, it just ran along and fell into the other stores through the ceiling. Not a thing anyone could do to stop it. There's not a wall in the place that'd slow a fire down for more than fifteen minutes. No firewalls, no sprinklers, and a common cockloft—my favorite recipe for losing a building."

"Anyone inside?"

"No, thank God."

"Was there anyone around outside when you arrived?"

"Uh-uh. There was a carload that must've followed us. But no-body already here having multiple orgasms over the flames, if that's what you're hoping. And no guilty-looking car speeding off, either. No traffic at all, in fact."

"Who cut the utilities?"

"Breck, I think. He found the boxes."

"Who turned in the alarm?"

"It came in on the 911 number. We got a report of flames in the warehouse, but it turned out it was the store. Reflection of flames in the windows." Zak nodded, remembering how real the reflected flames had looked when he'd walked down Ninth. "You're sure the fire started in the appliance store?"

"It was going very well in there with no sign of it anywhere else when we arrived."

"You said black smoke?"

"And your characteristic dark-red flames. Also, this fire was a real boomer."

The big walkie-talkie on top of the dash said, "Tellerman?"

Tellerman picked it up. "Yes, Chief?"

"The owner of the building, one David Wagner, has arrived. He's asking to speak to someone in charge."

"Ten-four," said Tellerman with a sigh. He turned to Zak. "You've heard of him, no doubt."

Zak frowned. "Have I?"

"He's Crazy Dave, remember? The guy who did those crazy ra-dio commercials a few years ago. He sold stereo equipment for weird prices, like ninety-seven dollars and twenty-two cents for a turntable."

Zak nodded. "That's right, I remember now." His son and daughter had listened to the rock station playing those commer-cials, which, for a while, were almost as popular as the terrible mu-sic they sponsored. Funny how something as pervasive as that could almost vanish from the memory once the repetitions of it stopped. "I'll come with you and talk to him."

"Be my guest."

Dave Wagner was a handsome man with a strident voice, so well proportioned that they had come quite close before Zak realized how small he was. Wagner stood in the street in front of the specta-tors, arguing loudly with the policeman that he should be allowed to cross. His dark sweatshirt had a white motto on it, and his pale jeans ended in clean white sneakers. "That's my place! All my stuff is in there!" he was yelling. "Get outta my way, dammit!"

"Mr. Wagner?" said Tellerman when they were close enough to be heard.

"Yeah! Can you tell this turkey to get outta my way?" The motto on his sweatshirt said "Hell I'm Better."

"I don't think that's a good idea, sir. I'm Battalion Chief Tellerman. I understand you wanted to talk to me?"

"I got a lot of money tied up in this building, you know! You gonna let me try to rescue some of my stuff, or would you prefer we stand around and watch it burn up?"

"It's like this, Mr. Wagner. I can stand here and argue with you over the merits of going into a building full of superheated air without so much as a hat for protection—or you can promise to behave like an intelligent person, and I can go back to my job." Tellerman's voice was perforce loud, but his tone was gentle.

"So how about in the meantime some of you firemen try saving some of the merchandise? That building's gone, right? I mean, look at it! But I got some big-screen TV sets in there, VCRs, and high-quality microwave ovens. We got plenty of sidewalk over there; can't you bring some of my stuff out before it all burns up?"

"No, sir. Our task is to get the fire out before it spreads to the rest of the block." He raised a forestalling hand. "Wait, just wait, and think a minute. The kind of fire we've got going here won't leave anything to rescue even if we started now."

"Are you telling me just to stand here and watch my whole life go up in smoke?" yelled Wagner.

"Surely you carry insurance," offered Zak mildly.

Wagner scowled at him. "Who the hell are you?"

"Captain Isaac Kader."

"Well, that's terrific! Now there's two of you not doing your job! Shouldn't you be squirting water or something?"

"No, sir, I'm from the Arson Squad."

". . . Arson?" It was as if someone had unscrewed a leg and drained all the fury out of Wagner. Suddenly he was hard to hear. "You think someone set this fire?"

"I'm here to determine the cause, that's all."

"Oh."

"Can I assume from what you just said that you own the entire building, not just the appliance store?"

". . . So what?"

"Nothing, except that the owner should be notified of the fire."

Belligerence crept back into Wagner's voice. "So I'm notified, okay?" He turned his shoulder to Zak to ask Tellerman, "You think it's gonna burn out all the stores?"

"I take it you are refusing to answer any more of my questions, Mr. Wagner?" said Zak.

Wagner glanced at Zak. "What are you, a cop?"

"No, sir; I'm a fireman."

"So what does that mean? You don't have to tell me I've got a right to remain silent?"

"Do you think you need to be warned? I was thinking I ought to find out what happened before I arrest anyone."

Wagner shifted to confront Zak, frowning. Tellerman stepped back out of range, and when no one objected, he turned and hurried away. The uniformed patrolman, still recovering from Wagner's fury of two minutes ago, remained watchful. Wagner asked, "If you're only a fireman, how can you arrest anyone?"

"I get a warrant from the county prosecutor," said Zak, with an air of stating the obvious. "But first I have to find out if anyone needs to be arrested, and I do that by finding out what happened. Do you have any objection to that?"

Wagner glanced at the burning building. Smoke was still choking the broken windows, despite the broad stream of water pouring across the threshold of the appliance store. He grimaced, disgusted. "Hell, there's probably nothing worth saving in there anyhow. What do you want to know?"

"How about we get out of the way of the fire fighters here? My car's parked just up the way, and there's a Thermos of coffee in it. We might as well get comfortable while we wait."

"Sure, okay."

Zak's glove box held a bag with half a dozen Styrofoam cups in it. He removed two, filled one and handed it to Wagner. "It's decaffeinated, I'm afraid," he said. "And there's no sugar or creamer."

"I like it black," said Wagner, taking the cup. "Thanks." He sipped gingerly; the coffee was very hot.

Zak filled the other cup for himself and leaned back in the seat to look at the fire. The entire building was now involved, despite the aerial ladder's efforts. "Do you have a list somewhere of just what was in your store?"

"Sure, only it's in a hanging file in a drawer of my desk in my office, in my store."

"Does that file come before or after the one with your insurance policies in it?"

Wagner laughed. "Just after." He sipped again. "My policies are at home, actually. My insurance agent has an appointment with me Monday evening to discuss increasing my coverage. How's that for locking the barn door after the horse has been cremated?"

"Do you know if there are any code violations in the building? Wiring or heating, like that?"

"No, the building inspector was in early this summer. We had to replace a light bulb in an exit light, and a couple other little things, as I recall. All taken care of months ago." Wagner snorted. "A freakin' light bulb, as if that makes any difference now!"

"You were very prompt on the scene, if I may say so. How did you find out the building was on fire?"

"Hell, we were the ones who called you!" Wagner grinned at Zak. "Sounds crazy, right? Just like the old Crazy Davey—but it's the truth! I was engaged in a friendly game of cards with four buddies and we saw it out a window. Counted the streets over and—by God, it's right behind me—we thought it was the warehouse, y'see. We called 911 and then I got to thinking how narrow that alley is between the warehouse and my place, so I figured I better come on over, and son of a bitch, it's my place all the time!"

"You saw it out a window?"

"Yeah." Wagner looked over his right shoulder and pointed. "See those three high rises over there? Summerside Condos. I was in the middle one, twelfth floor, place belongs to Ron Tollefson." He looked back, saw Zak writing, and added, "The other three were Toby Modreski, Murray Jones, and Dennis Baer." He spelled the names. He didn't know Dennis' street number, but gave his phone number and the addresses of the two others.

"You'd all been there some while before you noticed the fire?" asked Zak.

"Oh, hell, yes. Been there all evening. Toby and I had supper there with Ron, then Dennis and Mur came over and we started playing." He looked out the window at his building and sighed. "Should I call my tenants tonight or try to catch them in the morning?"

"That's up to you, Mr. Wagner."

"Is there going to be anything worth saving when this is over?"

"Not much, I'd guess."

"Then what the hell, let them get some sleep. It's the least I can do."

† † †

The fire was still burning in the bookstore when Zak sent Wagner home. He consulted with Tellerman, who agreed he could begin looking around.

Burdened with his heavy metal kit, prepared to drop it and run at a shouted warning of collapsing roof or flashback, he picked his way around puddles and over water hoses to the entrance of the appliance store.

There, he stood and let his nose confirm what Tellerman had reported. Sure enough, there was, faintly, a raw stink of gasoline under the greasy stench of burned building. He put the heavy steel box down, pulled the graph-paper tablet from his pocket, twisting it between his hands to remove its curve, and fished for his pencil.

The ceiling was partly intact, though firemen from the ladder companies were using long pikes to pull down what was left of it. Above the ceiling Kader could see giant holes in the roof, acting as chimneys for the smoke still in the air. Several large, heavy floor lights had been brought in. Their beams cast eerie shadows, piercing the gloom like lighthouse beacons on a smoggy night.

The wrecks of appliances were everywhere—except the center of the floor, which had a hole about nine feet in diameter in it.

Partially burned console TV sets formed an uneven row along the front wall under the broken windows, their imploded screens like eyeless sockets. A ruin of refrigerators lay on their backs near the rear of the store, doors open; beside them, a sextet of stoves looked—in the smoky light and at this distance—as if nothing more than a good scrubbing would restore them. Filthy water stood in pools over what had once been carpeting.

A half dozen fire fighters were sifting debris in a search for remaining crumbs of fire, walking gingerly on the weakened floor and staying well away from the hole.

The face masks fire fighters wear distort vision, and the air tanks are cumbersome, so they are removed as soon as possible. A man working near Zak was snuffling loudly, his blackened face was tear-streaked, but his face mask hung loose around his neck.

Zak began a swift sketch of the store's layout, confirming what Wagner had told him. Television sets in front; VCRs, stereo tape decks, record turntables in what remained of the middle; stoves, microwave ovens, refrigerators toward the back. Small appliances over there, floor and table lamps on this side—he bent and picked up a flap of metal, rubbing it with a gloved thumb to disclose a tarnished, partly melted brass leaf. The floor lamp it had come from was leaning against what had been a big window fan, and Zak noted its location on his diagram before going back to the kit for a small, empty, unused paint can and a Sharpie pen. He put the fragment into the can, marked the can with the pen.

The appliance store had once been two stores, and the wall between them had not been completely removed; a ruined partition thrust out from the back. Zak went cautiously to the front of the partition, squatted to note the depth of the charring at its base and looked up to trace the burn pattern where the flames had climbed to eat into the ceiling. He marked the place on his sketch, then squatted to press his fingers into the guck on the floor. He sniffed at the sample thus gathered; then went back for another, larger, paint can and a spatula and collected a few ounces of the guck.

Paint cans are relatively cheap, chemically inert, and airtight. They're harder to break than glass bottles, and they don't tear like plastic bags. Zak marked and initialed the can, then looked for other significant evidence. He wasn't being thorough at this point; he was merely gathering sights and samples that might evaporate or get moved out of place.

Shelves on the partition had held telephones. Wilted metal parts stood up around the plastic puddles that had been their shells. Beyond them more melted plastic—radios? tape recorders?—made surrealistic shapes on the shelves. This had been a quick, very hot fire.

A line of char formed a narrow border along the base of the partition. He followed it to the rear wall and through a set of doors to a room where appliances were delivered or sent out. At one end of the room was a big old freight elevator, its interior blackened, and beside it a stairway to the basement. The shattered door hung open, and the steps were badly spalled. Zak went down.

Appliances from the first floor had fallen through the hole into a jumbled heap in the middle of the basement, and water pattered from a dozen places around the edge of the opening, forming an unholy fountain. Otherwise the basement was mostly empty. Three refrigerators loomed blackly above and beyond the shattered jumble in the center, and near the back two stoves huddled together like frightened orphans.

Keeping an ear cocked for warning shouts or the creak of disengaging timbers, Zak moved slowly away from the foot of the stairs. A fireman was on the other side of the basement, pulling crumbling boards from the brick wall.

Nearby was a waist-high heap of mushy stuff that might once have been flattened refrigerator boxes. Zak stooped and used his pencil to probe the mush, measuring its depth. It became solid a few inches down, and he used his gloved left hand to lift the mush aside. It was cardboard, all right, and in the middle intact, barely even wet. He lifted an edge; farther down it became charred again. He looked around. The boxes had probably been leaning against that wall, falling over after the fire had reached them, to burn again on top, sandwiching the unburned section.

The heaped shape of the cardboard made it appear to be draped over something. Zak lifted it further to look—and dropped it, backing off, swallowing. The fireman pulling down the plaster saw his hasty move and called, "Whatcha got? More fire?" Without waiting for a reply, he came at a trot and used his pike to lift aside the burned cardboard—then backed off himself, sucking air through his teeth. A new smell wafted into the room, a sweet smell mixed with the stench of burned meat. "Oh, Jeez!" whispered the fireman. "Oh, Jeez!"